Montana
MAVERICKS

A HOT COWBOY COLLECTION

Montana
MAVERICKS

A HOT COWBOY COLLECTION

NEW YORK TIMES BESTSELLING AUTHOR

REBECCA
ZANETTI

Montana Mavericks © 2020 by Rebecca Zanetti.
Against the Wall © 2013 by Rebecca Zanetti.
Under the Covers © 2013 by Rebecca Zanetti.
Rising Assets © 2014 by Rebecca Zanetti.

Entangled Publishing, LLC
10940 S Parker Road
Suite 327
Parker, CO 80134
Visit our website at www.entangledpublishing.com.

Amara is an imprint of Entangled Publishing, LLC.

Edited by Liz Pelletier
Cover design by LJ Anderson, Mayhem Cover Creations
Cover art photography by Paul Henry Serres
and AdobeStock/Atmosphere
Interior design by Toni Kerr

Print ISBN 978-1-68281-565-6
ebook ISBN 978-1-68281-587-8

Manufactured in the United States of America

First Edition April 2021

AMARA

ALSO BY REBECCA ZANETTI

Against the Wall

a Maverick Montana novel

NEW YORK TIMES Bestselling Author

Rebecca Zanetti

*This book is dedicated to my friend Tina Jacobson,
who has supported my writing from the beginning...
and who also came up with the name for this book.*

CHAPTER ONE

The silence bordered on bizarre.

Shouldn't there be crickets chirping? Birds squawking? Even the howl of a hungry wolf in the muted forest? Of course, such sounds would send a city girl like Sophie Smith barreling back through the trees to her rented Jeep Cherokee. The quiet peace had relaxed her into wandering far into the forested depths, but now the trees huddled closer together, looming in warning.

Enough of this crap. Time to head back to the car.

Her only warning was the crack of a stick under a powerful hoof, a thumping, and a shouted, "Look out!" A broad arm lifted her through the air. The arm banded solidly around her waist, and her rear slammed onto the back of a rushing horse. She yelped, straddling the animal and digging her hands into its mane. The image of the man attached to the arm flashed through her brain, while his rock-hard body warmed her from behind.

A cowboy.

Not a wannabe cowboy from a bar in the city. A real cowboy.

The image of thick black hair, hard-cut jaw, and Stetson hat burst through her shocked mind as muscled thighs gripped both the back of a massive stallion and her hips. The beast ran full bore over rough ground.

Only the sinewed forearm around her waist kept

her from flying through the air.

This wasn't happening. Sophie shut her mouth on a scream as the powerful animal gracefully leaped over a fallen log and her captor pulled her into his solid body. He moved as one with the animal. Her hands fisted the silky mane like it was a lifeline to reality.

Maybe it was.

Screw this. She threw back an elbow and twisted to the side, fear and anger finally galvanizing her into action.

"Stop." A deep voice issued the command as warm breath brushed her cheekbone.

With a mere tightening of his thighs on the great animal, they skidded to a stop. The arm trapping her shifted so she slid easily to the ground and stayed around her waist until she regained her footing. With a sound that was more growl than gasp, she backed away from man and mount until she collapsed against the bark of a towering tree. The horse tossed his head and snorted at her retreat.

The man sat straight and tall on the animal, dark and curious eyes considering her.

The smell of wet moss surrounded her. She gulped in air and studied him. He was huge—and packed hard. Scuffed cowboy boots pressed down on the stirrups while a dark T-shirt outlined impressive muscles. Long lashes framed incredible eyes, and she could swear a dark eyebrow lifted in amusement.

Two more horses charged suddenly through the meadow, sliding to a swift stop behind her captor. One animal was a pretty white, the other a spotted paint, and both held powerful cowboys complete with boots, jeans, and Stetsons. All wore black hats—like the villains in every Western movie ever filmed.

"Unbelievable," she muttered under her breath.

At her voice, her captor jumped gracefully off his mount and stepped toward her.

"What should we do with her?" the man on the white horse asked. His gravelly voice contrasted oddly with the glint of humor in his tawny eyes. Filtered sunlight illuminated the gold, brown, and even black hair flowing unchecked around his shoulders. He was a symphony of twilight, whereas the other men wore the ominous tone of midnight.

"I caught her. I get to keep her," her captor said, his eyes intent as he took another step toward her, firm muscles bunching in his upper arms.

"Another step, and you get to land on your ass." Sophie readied herself to target his knees as fear uncoiled in her stomach. He stood at least a foot taller than her own five foot four.

His grin was quick and unexpected. It also added to the nerves still jumping in her belly. He might be a psychotic throwback to the pioneer days, but he belonged on a Calvin Klein underwear billboard.

The forest pressed in, and a smattering of pine-cones hit the earth. Their soft, fragrant *thunk*s shot adrenaline through her veins. Something high in the tree twittered a soft screech, reminding her she was far from home.

From safety.

She centered her breath and decided on a groin shot.

Just then, a happy feminine shout yanked her attention toward a petite young woman rushing toward the horses. The female whirlwind all but collided with Sophie's tormentor. "Jake, you're the best! I got the best picture ever. The action shots are amazing."

The woman released Jake and jumped at Sophie to grab both hands. "Didn't you hear them coming? They nearly mowed you down. But Jake has great reflexes—he saved you. The picture is phenomenal. Your eyes were huge, and you looked so scared! I am going to nail this project."

Sophie wrinkled her brow at the stunning woman. She had long black hair, straight features, and aquamarine eyes, which were alight with happiness as she pumped Sophie's hands in her own.

"You're welcome?" Sophie pressed her backside against the tree trunk.

The woman threw back her head and laughed. "I'm Dawn, and you already met my brother Jake." She gestured behind her to the motionless cowboy. "Those are my brothers, Quinn and Colton."

"Ma'am," both men said, tugging on hat brims while remaining perched comfortably on their stallions. Colton had the colorful array of hair, while Quinn's hair and eyes were as dark as Jake's.

Dawn stomped wet grass off her boots. "We're from the Kooskia Tribe. I was trying to capture an action shot, but you stepped right into their path. This was perfect." She patted Sophie's hand. "Don't worry. You weren't in any danger. Jake's an excellent rider."

Wait a freakin' minute. Sophie glared at Jake. What an asshole. "Why didn't you put me down sooner?"

"Sorry if we scared you," he said softly, his eyes anything but apologetic as his generous lips tipped in humor. "Dawn needed a picture for her college project while she and Colton are home for spring break, and I didn't want to stop until I was sure she'd gotten what she needed. It was a long setup—or so she told us."

Temper stirred at the base of Sophie's neck. *"I caught her? I get to keep her?"*

Colton chortled. "You should've seen your face."

"Yeah, you looked ready to faint," Quinn said as his horse tossed its head and sidestepped in a graceful prance.

"Actually," Jake said, his eyes narrowing, "she had shifted her stance to kick me in the knees." He cocked his head, almost seeming wishful she had tried it.

She wondered if she could've taken him down and ignored the annoying voice in the back of her head laughing hysterically.

"Really?" Colton grinned. "I would've liked to see that."

"Me, too." Sophie returned his grin, and her temper dissipated. She bet she had looked terrified. She had been.

"I'm a junior at the University of Montana, and for my photography project, I need to capture a series of action shots. There's nothing like horses rushing through shadowed trees to show action." Dawn smiled even white teeth. "You're probably lucky Jake was able to pick you up before running you over."

Sophie cleared her throat, her gaze lifting again to Jake. Warmth spread through her abdomen. The man standing so solidly next to wild beasts and surrounded by untamed land was something new and definitely out of her experience. He was all male, and something feminine in her, deep down, stretched awake. Her heart kicked back into gear. Fighting her suddenly alive libido, she smoothed her face into curious lines. "Why didn't you just shout for me to get out of the way?"

He cocked his head to the side, those dark eyes softening. "I did, but you didn't move fast enough. One second the trail was clear, the next you were about to get trampled. I turned my horse and grabbed you before one of my brothers could run you over."

So he had actually saved her. Sure, he'd had some fun at her expense, but at least if she needed to kick him later for it, she still had legs. She lifted her chin. "Thanks for the rescue."

His cheek creased with a dimple before he turned and remounted his horse. "Any time, Sunshine."

"What were you doing in our forest, anyway?" Dawn asked.

Sophie's heart dropped to her stomach. This was where the niceties stopped. "I'm Sophie Smith from Green Par Designs."

"Oh, the golf course lady." Dawn nodded.

That was an easy, accepting tone. Sophie frowned. "Yes. I'm here to design the golf course next to the lake, so I was checking out the land." Now the pretty woman would get angry, considering the Kooskia Tribe opposed the project. The pine-filled canopy blocked the sun's warmth, and Sophie shivered.

"Oh. Well, that explains it, then." Dawn tossed ebony hair out of her face.

Sophie gaped and quickly closed her mouth. "Aren't you opposed to the golf course?"

"Of course. For one thing, it's bad placement because the fertilizers will pollute the lake." Dawn softened her rebuke with a smile.

"And the other thing?" Sophie asked.

Dawn shrugged. "A golf course just doesn't fit the land right there."

"Doesn't fit?"

"Nope." Dawn tugged her toward the clearing. "Come on, I'll show you my shot before Jake takes you back to your car. Thanks again for the picture—it was perfect."

"You're welcome." Sophie shook her head and let the woman lead her from the forest while three muscled cowboys followed tamely behind them.

• • •

Jake drew in air, his gut tightening as if Guardian had kicked him. Sophie's vanilla scent still wrapped around him. His hands itched with the desire to haul her back on the horse, but he contented himself with studying her head to toe. Sunlight turned her mass of shoulder length curls to shiny wheat, the color both sweet and sassy. She was beautiful. Maybe not in the conventional movie-star way, more like a fierce "I'm going to knock you on your ass" way. He'd fought in combat, and he'd seen courage. The woman had shown bravery and brains when she'd faced him and settled her stance to fight. An irresistible combination.

At only an inch taller than Dawnie, Sophie was small. Faded jean capris cradled her sweet heart-shaped ass. An ass he'd love to dig his hands into. Her waist was tiny enough his arm had easily wrapped around it, and he couldn't forget the feeling of the full breasts resting just out of reach.

But those eyes.

They were the color of the deep blue irises his mama carefully tended each spring. And Sophie was a scrapper. She had been more than willing to try and knock him on his butt.

Quinn caught his eye, amusement lifting his lips.

Jake half shrugged. Yeah, he was checking out the city lady. The fierce look in Sophie's pretty eyes had contrasted nicely with her pale skin and classic features when she had prepared to take him down. As a lawyer, he enjoyed a good contrast. His gut heated as he steered Guardian through the meadow. He'd love to wrestle with her.

She made the appropriate noises while looking through the viewfinder of Dawn's digital camera before his sister removed it and folded the tripod.

"I guess Jake will take you back to your car," Dawn said absently, handing the equipment up to Colton. Then she reached an arm to Quinn, who tugged her to sit behind him on his pawing horse.

Jake fought a grin at the panic that rushed across Sophie's face.

"No, er, I'll just walk." She peered uncertainly around the clearing into the nearby trees, her pretty pink lips pursing.

"We came a lot farther than you think." Jake tried to sound reassuring. "I promise I'll go slow."

Sophie shook her head, sending blond curls flying. "Not a chance, sport. I'm walking." She turned and headed toward a trail barely visible between two bulky bull pines.

Quinn shrugged. "You're on your own. I have to get to work." Jake's brother clicked his mount into a gallop, and he and Dawn took off, leaving him with Colton.

Sophie escaped between two trees.

"Do you think you can handle the pint-sized city girl, or do you need help?" Colton grinned as his horse danced impatiently to the side.

"The day I need help from you, shoot me, little brother." Jake tightened his knees on Guardian who was ready to run again. His brother would have to return to graduate school in just a few days, and it didn't make sense to smack him around right now.

"With pleasure." Colton nodded toward the tree line. "You'd better get going. She just turned the wrong way."

Jake grinned before pressing in with one thigh, turning the mount. Guardian plodded impatiently into the forest. Sophie came into view, picking her way carefully along scattered pinecones and exposed tree roots. Her spine straightened, and her shoulders firmed as he narrowed the gap between them, but she didn't acknowledge him otherwise.

Why did he like that about her? The woman was lost as a person could be, yet she marched forward into darkness. The trees soon thickened with prickly brushes and slash piles.

"You're going the wrong way," he said.

She came to an abrupt stop at his soft words. Jake reined in Guardian, waiting for Sophie to turn around and face him. It took longer than he would have thought—stubborn was an understatement with the woman.

As she slowly turned, he could have kicked himself at the intelligent wariness in her gaze. She was alone in the middle of the forest with a strange man. He had a daughter, a little sister… He should've known better.

They stared at each other, forest sounds surrounding them. Jake searched for the right words. "I won't hurt you. I just want to get you to your car."

Sophie lifted her chin but otherwise didn't move.

"I'll let you drive," Jake cajoled.

The smile that lit her pretty face warmed him. "There's no way I can drive that beast." She took a small step toward him.

"Sure you can." Jake reached down to offer an arm. He didn't question why it mattered that she trust him. It just did.

Vulnerability glimmered in her eyes. "Maybe we should walk instead."

He forced himself to relax, to appear as unthreatening as a guy twice her size could look.

Thunder rolled in the distance. Storm season had definitely arrived early.

He slid his most earnest, trust-me, closing-argument grin into place. If the storm brought lightning, they'd need to dive for a ditch. The last thing he wanted to do was scare her. "Believe me, this is faster, and there's a heck of a storm coming."

Sophie eyed the darkening sky. With a deep breath, she stepped up to the quiet horse. "Okay, but we go slow. I mean, unless lightning starts to strike. Then we go fast. How do I get back on?"

The woman's bravery tempted him to haul her close, but he gave them both a moment as he shifted his weight. The thunder bellowed louder.

They only had minutes until the rain hit. He balanced himself with his thighs, reached down, and lifted her by the waist to perch in front of him. She fit nicely into his hold, and something clicked into place.

"Relax," he whispered in her ear, placing her hands securely on the silky black mane. "If you're relaxed, the horse will relax."

"Right." Sophie coughed, and her muscles eased into something slightly less than rigor mortis.

"Okay, now grip the horse with your thighs, and tug him the way you want to go." Jake forced his libido into submission. The act was difficult, considering how tight his jeans had just become.

Sophie tugged, and Guardian shifted around to retrace his steps. "He's going," she whispered, her voice lowering in delight.

"Yep." Her voice was sexy as hell. The soft tenor shivered across his nerves. He hardened. *Basketball scores. Baseball stats. National holidays.* His mind reeled facts around in a futile effort to control his reaction.

Sharp pangs of light shot through the awning of pine needles and the clouds rolling in. The horse meandered through the trees and past rambling huckleberry bushes. Jake let Sophie set the pace, and her muscles soon relaxed against him. Finally, they emerged out of the forest to the narrow dirt road where her Jeep waited.

Jake helped her to the ground.

She self-consciously stepped away and tossed curls out of her face. "Thanks for the lift," she said, backing up even more.

"Any time," he said.

"It was, ah, nice to have met you." She pivoted and all but bolted for her Jeep.

The woman wanted to be rid of him. He fought another grin. Too bad she wasn't going to get what she wanted—this time. Boy, was she in for a surprise.

He waited until she jumped into the vehicle and watched until it was out of sight, his heart lighter than usual as Guardian waited for the command to run.

CHAPTER TWO

Several hours after her unexpected horseback ride, Sophie pored over papers scattered across the bedspread as hazy light glinted off the brass bedrail in her room. She loved the bed-and-breakfast with the burnished antique furnishings and lemon-oil smell. The milk-glass lamp added to the moonlight from the open window as she lay back in her warm T-shirt and boxers. The needles from the massive bull pine outside her window scraped against the glass.

Get out of town before you get hurt. The peaceful surroundings washed away her unease as she perused the hastily scrawled note that had been stuck on her windshield. She rolled her eyes. If they thought that would scare her, they were crazy. She shifted her attention to the legal documents her staff had faxed to her, and her head started to pound as she prepared for the early meeting with the Kooskia Tribe.

Her cell phone chattered a nameless tune, and she stretched to reach it.

"Hi, Sophia. How's life in the middle of nowhere?" The deep voice elicited a familiar fluttering in her lower stomach.

"Hi, Preston. I'm in Montana. I think it's somewhere." She settled more comfortably against the flowered pillows. "Why are you calling so late? Don't tell me your date had an early math test tomorrow." She grinned at her own joke as she imagined his blue eyes sparkling with humor.

"Funny. The blonde you met before leaving town works at Shinnies and isn't a college freshman. Do they even have running water where you are?"

"Running water, paved roads, and even electricity." Sophie lost her grin at the image of the too-perfect waitress. "When are you going to stop dating bubble-headed Barbies?"

"When the right girl comes along, I guess."

The words hurt more than they should have. She reminded herself they were just friends. One freakin' kiss didn't make a relationship. She cringed as she thought of how distant he'd been afterward—at least until she reassured him they were just friends and the kiss had been a mistake.

"In fact," Preston's cultured voice reached across the miles, "I've been thinking quite a bit about that kiss at the Christmas party."

Sophie focused all her attention on the little phone against her ear and struggled to keep her voice calm. "What kiss?"

Preston chuckled. "You know exactly what kiss."

Of course she did. She'd only relived the whole evening in her mind for months afterward. "I know. But Preston—"

"I can change, Sophia."

"I doubt that." She snorted even though her heart warmed. She'd had a crush on her debonair coworker for so long. She again wondered, *What if?*

"Well, I've done something…" Preston's voice lowered.

What in the world could he have done? "What?" she asked, keeping her voice level.

"I booked us on a Caribbean cruise next fall to

celebrate your successful design."

She coughed. "That's a bit premature, isn't it? We don't even have the permit yet."

"You'll get it."

She wasn't so sure. "Wait a minute. What do you mean by 'us'?"

"I mean *us*. You and me. I'm tired of dancing around this. Your uncle is going to retire soon and wants the business taken care of. You and I have a comfortable relationship, and it could be even better." Something clinked against the phone as he swallowed—probably his usual scotch in a crystal tumbler.

Her heart sank. She may have had a crush on the man, but her brain still worked. "Wow. Sounds like a successful merger."

"It would be. Add in the fact that we want each other, coupled with similar tastes and interests, I think we have it made."

"What about love?" she asked.

"Seriously? What are you, twelve?" he asked.

Sophie laughed. "Yeah, seriously. Shouldn't love, fire, passion…and all that be the goal?"

"Whose goal? Plus, we have the fire and passion, so love's probably just around the corner."

Sophie was quiet for a moment. Preston was exactly who she'd always wanted. Young, ambitious, already successful. He had even designed his own home overlooking the Bay in San Francisco, and he resembled a tall, blond, Nordic god. Plus, she genuinely liked him.

She sighed. "I don't know."

"Come on, Sophia. Be realistic and stop daydreaming—puppy love is for naive morons." Self-ridicule and an odd loneliness wrapped around his tone.

Her head jerked up. "Who hurt you so badly, Pres?" Her question surprised her even as she asked it.

Quiet reigned over the line. "I don't know what you mean." But he did. She could tell.

"Sorry. It just slipped out." So much for a routine phone call. For the first time, doubt filled her about the successful architect.

"It's all right." His voice hinted at sensual promise. "Also, I want to thank you for taking this project on so I could concentrate on the Seattle proposal."

She relaxed as they returned to business. "No problem. I've been waiting for Uncle Nathan to let me take the lead on a golf course design, and this is finally it." Of course, they'd only use her design if the county approved the construction plan. Hope inflated her chest.

"Yeah, I know. It's a big job. The Charleton Group stands to lose a boatload of money if this project doesn't come to fruition." The sound of paper shuffling came over the line. "More importantly, we have five more projects lined up with them. Our bottom line for the next three years depends on the Group."

"No pressure there," she muttered.

"Sorry. But you need to understand. We're in trouble," he said.

The breath caught in her throat. "How much trouble?"

Silence echoed from a world away. Finally, Preston cleared his throat. "Your uncle met with financial restructuring specialists yesterday."

Holy crap. Sophie sat straight up. "We're going bankrupt?"

"That's one option." Preston sighed. "The economy has hurt us pretty badly. I think we can crawl our way out of this mess with your current project and mine in Seattle. They both need to work."

Her mind spun. Uncle Nathan couldn't lose the company. "Don't worry. I'll get the job here."

"Your uncle mentioned the local tribe is opposing the course," Preston said.

She picked at a thread on the bedspread, her shoulders hunching. "Yeah. That's why I decided to stay at the B and B on the reservation instead of in Maverick. I meet with the tribe tomorrow. They own the lake just below the proposal site and they're worried about pollution from fertilizer and people."

Preston sighed. "Our science is just as good as theirs, and the lake will be fine. But you still have to get the conditional-use permit with the county, and the tribe may have the influence to sway them."

Her skin prickled. "Yeah, I know. That hearing isn't until a week from next Monday, so I thought I'd see what headway I could make with the tribal elders tomorrow." She leaned against the pillows and forced her muscles to relax.

She loved to design land but the legal issues involved in land-use planning caused a drumming in her temples. An ache between her eyes. A rolling in her stomach that forced her to take deep, measured breaths. "I don't understand why we need a permit from the county, since this is privately owned land."

"Well, the land is zoned rural, meaning you can put a house on every five acres. One of the possible uses is a golf course, but you have to get a conditional-use permit to build it as well as the houses surrounding it."

Preston took another deep swallow. "You need a public hearing in front of the county commissioners before they can make their decision. Sometimes those hearings get a bit, well, energetic."

"Great." Sophie sighed. "I meet with the Maverick Chamber of Commerce early next week as well as with a citizens' group concerned with development. Maybe having their support will help at the hearing."

"Sounds like a good plan. I'll let you get some rest before your big day tomorrow." What sounded like ice clinking in a glass chattered across the line. "Give some thought to my idea about our, er, personal merger. We'd be a good match."

Sophie started to reply when a loud beep came across the line.

"Oops, that's my second line. I'll talk to you later, Sophia." The line went dead.

Sophie powered down her phone and switched off the light. She stared at the muted ceiling. Moonlight glinted off the brass rail from the open window and lent a coziness to the room. Who would be calling Preston so late at night? Why would either of them be content to just have a good match in life? Was that what she wanted? Probably not. She wanted passion and desire and comfort. All feelings, no planning.

Her mother would be disgusted.

Sophie's thoughts flew again to the mad dash through the forest in the hard arms of a modern warrior. She had felt safe and protected in those arms even before she knew who he was or why he'd grabbed her. Even before she knew that she was, in fact, safe. His eyes had shown interest — and promise. A fluttering winged around her abdomen that had nothing to do with her fear of horses and everything to do with the man who controlled wild beasts. Would she see Jake again?

Surprise filled her at how badly she wanted that to happen.

• • •

Jake put the truck in park, slipped the manila files into his briefcase, and tried to focus on tomorrow's hearing. It was a big one, and if he won the motion for his client, the other side would settle. As a lawyer, he liked a good trial, but it was always better for a client to settle before all the stress started. Unlike him—he thrived on stress and the unexpected.

As a working single dad to a six-year-old, it was a good thing he enjoyed a challenge.

As he stepped onto the gravel drive, his mind kept flashing to the pretty blonde who'd so bravely tried to steer his horse the previous day. Guts and beauty in such a small package was a temptation he'd never resist.

He glanced down at his watch. Damn it. He was late.

Why had he agreed to meet at the tribe's main lodge instead of in his office? He grimaced. He hadn't wanted Sophie to be uncomfortable, and the lodge was a thing of beauty. Next he was going to agree to her terms.

Which he couldn't do.

So he marched into the lodge and headed toward the main conference room, sliding inside the door.

The woman sat at the far end of the table, looking

spring-fresh in a flimsy blouse and pencil skirt.

He loved a woman in a pencil skirt. She looked like every hot-librarian he'd ever dreamed about. "Miss Smith," he said smoothly.

Her eyes opened wide, her gaze sweeping from his boots to his suit. "What the heck?"

Amusement filled him, and he fought the insane urge to tug her from the chair for a kiss. "Not who you were expecting?"

Her eyes narrowed. "No. I was expecting a lawyer."

"I'm the tribe's lawyer." He couldn't help reaching for her hand to shake. His palm enclosed hers, and he made sure not to squeeze the delicate bones.

"You're kidding me." She tugged her hand free, a pink flush wandering across her high cheekbones.

"Afraid not." He slid into the nearest chair, inhaling her fresh scent of strawberries and vanilla. "I've read over your proposal, and while I think the golf course is magnificent, it doesn't belong on the site you've chosen." Much better to get the business out of the way before he asked her out.

Sophie smiled then, and he felt his first sense of unease. Maybe this wouldn't be as easy as he thought.

• • •

An hour after meeting him, Sophie wondered if she'd be arrested if she cold-cocked Jake Lodge across his arrogant face. "Mr. Lodge—"

"Jake," he reminded her. Again.

Sophie growled low in her throat. "*Jake*, you are not being reasonable."

"Yes, I am." Strong arms crossed over a hard chest

as he sat back in the dark leather chair.

"Are not," Sophie spouted before she could stop herself. A raised eyebrow and glint of amusement met her frustration head-on. She took a deep breath. "You. Do. Not. Own. The. Land."

"I. Know. That." The amusement turned to a full-out grin. "I hate clichés."

"Excuse me?" she whispered.

"Clichés. They're boring." He placed two broad hands on the oak table between them and leaned forward, into her space. "But you are absolutely stunning when angry."

Her heart gave a nasty *thud*. Sophie shook her head. Even indoors the man was as primitive and dangerous looking as he'd been controlling a powerful stallion. His presence overwhelmed the small conference room with its tan leather chairs and burnished wooden table. Light filtered softly through several open windows, and the breeze carried the scent of wildflowers through the small room.

The scent of man tempted her much more than the flowers.

A long-sleeved black T-shirt emphasized strength and muscle, while faded jeans hung low on tight hips over his long legs. Black cowboy boots crossed negligently at the ankle, and he'd tied his dark hair back at the nape, throwing the sharp angles of his face into stark relief. Black eyes reflected humor and determination in equal parts as he held firm. The panoramic window behind him framed rugged mountains and a placid lake in gentle stillness.

The wildness outside only enhanced his.

His watchful intelligence made the floor beneath

her pumps shift like quicksand. She smoothed curls back from her face and blinked to keep from glaring. "I thought I was meeting with a tribal elder today."

"You are, but the chief wanted me to explain our legal position to you first."

"You don't look like a lawyer." She said what she'd been thinking for the last hour.

"Good." Jake grinned an even row of white teeth. "I'd rather you didn't see me as a lawyer."

"What do you want me to see you as?" Good Lord, she was flirting with the man.

The grin narrowed, and his dark gaze roamed across her rapidly warming face. "Hopefully someone you'd like to get to know better while you're in town, City Girl." His eyes hardened to deep coal.

"What?" She would've taken a step back had she been standing. As it was, her body tensed as she focused on the large man seated across the table from her.

The oak door behind Jake swung open, which prevented him from responding. An elderly man with long, shockingly white hair strolled into the room and crossed over to Sophie.

She rose to her feet. His hands clasped hers warmly, and two dark brown eyes twinkled at her. "Miss Smith, I'm Chief Lodge of the Kooskia Tribe."

"It's nice to meet you, Chief Lodge." Sophie smiled up at a face similar to Jake's. Strong features set into a bronze face with lines created by laughter, although the sculpted jaw hinted at a stubbornness she'd already encountered in Jake, who had to be related. Charisma and charm surrounded the elder. If the chief was anything to go by, her new nemesis would age well.

"Please call me Sophie."

"Ah, Sophie. Such a pretty name." The chief gestured for her to retake her seat as he turned and sat at the head of the table. He wore faded jeans over scuffed brown cowboy boots with a deep red button-down shirt. "I see you've met my grandson and lawyer, Jake."

"Yes." The warmth deserted her as she eyed Jake. His grin in return made her want to throw something. At his head.

"So." The chief's upper lip quirked. "What can I do for you, Sophie?"

Sophie focused on the elder's calm facade. Those deep lines sat comfortably on a smooth face—he could be anywhere between fifty and a thousand years old.

"I'm here to explain the golf course proposal and earn the support of the Kooskia Tribe." She hoped to have better luck with the elder than his grandson.

Wisdom flowed through the chief's eyes along with amusement. "Is that why you're here?"

"Um, well, yes." Sophie tossed a quick look to Jake. Did the chief know anything about her proposal or not?

"Oh, I've studied your design," the chief reassured her. "Sometimes what we think we know isn't what we really know."

"I don't understand," she said.

The chief shrugged. "You don't need to." He reclined in his chair. "I have to tell you that your design is magnificent."

Sophie's eyes widened. "Really?"

"Yes. Wonderful—looks like a great course to play. I love to golf, you know," the chief said.

Sophie slanted a glance toward Jake, but his implacable face revealed nothing. She turned back to the chief. "The development will bring money to the tribe and casino."

"Yes, I believe that it would." He clasped broad hands together on the hard table. Hands that reminded her of Jake's. The breeze tossed the sweet scent of berries through the room as the chief breathed deep in appreciation. "Huckleberries. Should be quite the crop this year." He focused on Sophie's face. "They grow wild all over your client's property."

Sophie maintained her smile. "I understand huckleberries grow wild across all the nearby mountains, even by the roadside."

The chief flashed an amused grin. "That they do. You're a spunky one, Sophie Smith."

"Thank you." Sophie ignored Jake's sudden grin.

"The course really does look like a fun one. I especially like the water hazards." The chief nodded.

"So you'll support the project?" Her heart leaped into full gallop.

"Oh, no," the chief said sadly, still with a twinkle in his deep eyes. "I can't do that."

Even though she'd expected his rejection, a ball of dread slammed into her gut. "Could I ask why?"

"The golf course doesn't fit with the aesthetics of the land there," the chief said.

Not this again. "Of course it fits." Sophie tried not to sigh in exasperation.

"Nope." The chief grinned. "Have you surveyed the land in person?"

Sophie's spine straightened at Jake's quiet snort. "Um, no, not really."

"Well then, it's all settled." The chief rose.

"What's settled?" Sophie lurched to stand.

"Jake will take you tomorrow to inspect the land. You two can ride over the northern ridge and maybe have a picnic overlooking the lake."

"Grandpa," Jake started to protest as he took to his feet. His chair echoed his annoyance as it slid back with a creak.

"That's an order from both the chief and your grandpa, boy," the chief said with a hard glint in his eye.

Jake turned to Sophie, his broad form blocking the sunlight. Humor creased his cheek, adding charm to the lethal angles of his face. "I'll pick you up at ten tomorrow morning."

"Wow." Sophie smiled at the chief. "Can you order him to stop being obnoxious and arrogant, too?"

Jake shot her a warning glance.

The chief roared out a deep laugh. "Sorry, Sophie. Those traits are from his grandma's side." The elder chuckled as he ambled out the door.

"I am not going horseback riding with you." Sophie rounded on Jake and threw her hands in the air before leaving the conference room for the exit. Sure, she needed to see the area to get a better idea for her design—just to make sure she'd covered all her bases. But she'd drive there.

"It appears you are, darlin'. Where we're going is only accessible via horseback. No vehicles." He moved silently, his scent of man and musk swimming over her as he reached the door and opened it.

Just wonderful. Now she needed to ride another horse.

Jake turned her, and a broad hand at her lower back propelled her into sunshine. Natural pine scent filled the air, and gravel crunched underneath their feet. He walked her to the Jeep and opened the driver's door, his hands sliding around her waist.

The gentle touch slid right under her skin, zinged around, and throbbed between her legs. She coughed. "I can get into the Jeep."

He grinned and lifted her inside. "I know, but my mama taught me to be a gentleman."

Sophie swallowed. "That wasn't gentlemanly."

His chuckle caressed her skin as if his tongue traced each inch. "I didn't say I was good at the lessons." His hands lingered on her waist, and his midnight dark eyes caressed her heated features.

Sophie tried to ignore the strength in the hands at her hips. He had lifted her into the Jeep like she weighed nothing. His broad chest blocked out the sun. In fact, all she could see were those onyx eyes devouring her. Interest and something even darker lurked there. Flutters cascaded through her belly.

The man wanted to kiss her.

Why wait? Against all logic, she leaned up and pressed her mouth to his.

CHAPTER THREE

Jake took her invitation and captured her lips, the jolt of instant lust shocking him.

So he forced himself to slow down and explore softly, gently, at his leisure. He wasn't a man who lost control. Ever.

One hand cupped her head, holding her where he wanted her. Her eyes closed, and he took the kiss deeper, his cells exploding as heat shot through his blood. His gentle hold kept her firmly in place as he controlled them both.

Desire and a shocking intimacy careened through him. Under his touch, the woman stilled, no doubt fighting to keep sane. It was too late for sanity. Way too late. With the hint of a growl, his tongue invaded her mouth. He took his time learning her texture, memorizing her taste. The hand at her nape threaded into her hair, and he pressed her against the seat.

She clenched his shirt and slid her tongue against his.

Fire boiled through him, and his groan of approval filled her mouth. His hand slid from her waist and relaxed against her thigh, her toned muscle tempting him to yank the material away. Then he pulled her closer, and her breasts flattened against his chest, her nipples pebbling.

Lava cascaded down his spine to spark his balls. He wanted her naked. Now.

Obviously, the woman had no clue how close to the

edge he'd slipped. She burrowed farther into his body, returning his kiss. They both panted when he finally lifted his head.

Her eyes had darkened to dangerous blue depths, wide and unseeing on his.

He released her curls before stroking along her jaw to cup her chin. He watched the path of his thumb as it ran along her swollen bottom lip. Tempting. Too damn tempting. Her tongue slipped out and grazed his thumb.

He bit back a growl and forced himself to relax. They were fully clothed, in a parking area next to headquarters, and he'd never wanted a woman more. But this was neither the time nor the place. *Definitely* not the place.

At that second, seeing the promise in her pretty eyes, he knew he'd have her –without question. But he wanted all night from dawn to dusk to explore whatever this was.

Awareness slid across her face, and she yanked her hands away. "I, ah, have to go."

He'd grant her a brief reprieve. Jake leaned in and pulled the seat belt between her breasts before clicking it firmly in place. "Go ahead and run, Sunshine. I caught you once before." The door closed, but he made sure she could still hear him. "I will again."

• • •

After a sleepless night where he couldn't stop thinking about kissing Sophie, the morning sun poked through a light gauze of clouds while Jake maneuvered his truck across town.

"Why can't I come on the picnic and meet the golf course lady?" The litany of questions continued from the backseat.

Jake drove the Dodge pickup around a pothole, then glanced in the rearview mirror and met piqued feminine eyes. Eyes so much like his own. "Because you have plans to bead necklaces with your grandmother, pumpkin."

"I don't wanna bead necklaces. I wanna go on the picnic." Irritation turned to sweetness. "Please, Daddy? I want to meet the city lady."

"Nice try, Leila." His grin matched hers.

His daughter's expression turned dreamy. "I bet she has Manolo Blahniks."

"Manolo what?" He turned down a narrow dirt driveway lined with lodge pole pines.

"Ah, Dad," Leila huffed in pity. "Blahniks. Shoes. Really pretty shoes."

"You're six years old. Since when do you care about shoes?"

Midnight black eyes widened on his before Leila gave a delicate shrug and stared intently out the window.

"Leila?" He used his best no-nonsense tone. The one that promised a lack of ice cream in the future if she didn't answer.

Leila sighed before turning back to meet his eyes. "Since me and Grets and Sally watched *Sex and the City*."

Jake gaped at his daughter. His baby with her long dark hair pulled into two pigtails and her pert little nose. "*Sex and the City*?"

"Yep." The grin showed a gap from a missing tooth.

Jake's lips tightened. "Where?"

Leila plucked at a string on her shirt. "At Sally's house after school last week."

"Her mother let you?"

"Well, not zactly."

"Meaning?" He stopped the truck before a two-story log home surrounded by wild purple, yellow, and red flowers. He shifted in his seat to face his daughter. She looked innocent and pretty in her blouse and light jeans with tiny tennis shoes.

"Um, well, her mom thought we were watching a cartoon about kittens in her room, but we kind of put in the other movie instead." A guilty flush stole across Leila's olive skin.

"Well, I will call Madeline later today so she knows what you three were up to," Jake said sternly before jumping from the truck and opening the back door. He released the seat belt and helped his daughter out of her car seat before shaking his head. "You get no television for a week."

"A week?" Leila wailed just as Jake's mother opened the door and gracefully crossed the faded deck.

"Want to make it two?" he asked.

"No." Leila took off at a run toward her grandma the second Jake put her on her feet.

Jake turned in exasperation as the two women in his life embraced.

"Daddy's being mean," Leila whined.

"Men," his mother agreed, a twinkle in her dark eyes.

Jake gave her a warning glance before stalking over and kissing her weathered cheek. His mother was truly a beautiful woman. Nearly a foot shorter than him, petite, and slender, she had passed on her black eyes as well as her straight, patrician bone structure, whereas he had inherited his broad frame from his father.

The braid through her gray hair deserved a tug, and Jake complied.

"Why are you picking on my granddaughter?" She smacked his arm.

"Because your granddaughter watched *Sex and the City* last week."

"Oh my." Loni Freeze grinned before turning to her urchin. "Why did you watch that?"

"To see the pretty clothes. And shoes. And the big city with the big stores and buildings." Leila sighed.

Jake's gut rolled at her words. "The city isn't everything it's cracked up to be, Leila."

"Jake, all girls dream of big stores in pretty cities," his mother chided.

"I'm well aware of that," he replied grimly. And he was. He and Leila had lost too much due to the lure of the big city life.

His thoughts flashed to Sophie. Even her name screamed city girl. He couldn't believe that he'd kissed her. What had he been thinking? A slow grin ripped across his face. He wanted to do it again.

"You have that look." His mother's eyes narrowed thoughtfully.

"What look?" he asked, all innocence.

"That look. The one you had right before riding that untamable stallion, Satan. Incidentally, does your arm still ache before a storm?"

Jake didn't answer.

"The look you had when your brother dared you to

jump off Smitty's cliff into the lake." His mother continued with a huff. "The look you had when—"

"All right. I know the look." The grin deserted his face. "I don't have it right now."

His mother opened her mouth to speak, only to have Leila interrupt. "Where's Grandpa Tom?"

"He's mending fences in the south pasture. He'll be back in time for lunch with you," Loni assured her granddaughter.

"Jake frowned. "Mending fences? Why didn't he call?"

"Because"—Loni reached up to peck him on a cheek—"your stepfather is just like you. He doesn't ask for help."

"I ask for help." Jake nodded toward his daughter.

"Humph," Loni replied with a twinkle. "Shouldn't you get going on your date?"

"It's not a date," he said.

She shrugged. "I heard it's a date."

"Your father had better not be matchmaking, Mom."

"I have no control over *your grandfather*." A smile lit her pretty face. "Have you noticed that we never quite claim him?"

Jake glanced at his watch. "No. I have to get going—for my *business meeting*." He emphasized the last two words before swooping down to kiss his daughter on the head.

His mother's voice stopped him just as he reached the truck. "Maybe it's time to date again."

"Maybe," he allowed with a cautious look at his suddenly curious daughter. "But not some city girl with Manolos. Whatever the heck those are." His gaze narrowed at his mother, who had an arm around his child. The homestead sat strong and solid behind them. Happy whinnies cascaded out of the deep green paddocks to the south, while the scents from steers to pasture wafted around.

Dust, dirt, and nature commingled into a combination of *home*.

With a shake of his head, he tossed his black Stetson across the front seat and jumped into the truck to meet the woman he'd kissed. A woman who belonged on his dusty ranch as much as a stallion belonged on Park Avenue. But first, he had a stop to make.

He drove through town to the general store, dodging inside to make his purchase. Within fifteen minutes he was back in the truck heading toward the edge of town, wondering when his daughter had stopped watching cartoons. His thoughts still whirled when he wiped his black boots on the mat adorning Shiller's B&B's large porch, removed his hat, and knocked on the door.

Sophie opened it immediately, fresh and pretty in dark jeans, frilly white blouse, and a braid looking too similar to his mother's.

"These are for you." Jake handed her a large white box. Roses came in big white boxes, and he wondered belatedly if she'd be disappointed. They weren't flowers.

Sophie stuttered in surprise as she accepted the box. She flipped open the lid and sighed out loud. "You brought me boots?" Her face wrinkled in confusion.

"Yeah. They're not Manolos." Jake shuffled his boots. "Plain old cowboy boots, and you'll need them for your ride today."

"They're beautiful," Sophie breathed out. Soft calfskin leather colored a creamy beige with a pointed toe. She hurried over to the wide porch swing covering one side of the wraparound porch and slipped off her tennis shoes.

"Dawnie picked them out. She had to guess at the size." Thank goodness his sister had time between classes to help him out.

"They're perfect," Sophie said after yanking both boots up under her jeans. She stood, the boots giving her a couple inches in height. "But I can't accept them." Regret colored her words to reflect in her blue eyes.

Jake grinned. He couldn't help it. What was it with women and shoes? Sophie looked like she was about to cry at giving up the boots. "Montana law, ma'am," he said.

"Huh?" Her brow wrinkled more.

"Montana law. A representative of the bar association, *me*, gives an associate boots, *you*, then state law dictates you have to keep them," he said.

"Really?" Sophie laughed and shook her head.

"Really," Jake affirmed solemnly.

"No, Jake—"

"Please, Sophie? You're probably used to more lavish gifts, but I really want you to have them," he said.

She looked in wonder at her pretty new boots. "I'm not used to gifts at all. Thank you. These are perfect." She balanced up on her toes and back down like a graceful ballerina.

"You're welcome," he said thoughtfully. How odd.

Why wasn't she used to gifts? "I don't suppose you know how to ride a horse?"

Sophie's gaze flew to his face. Her partial lesson the other day on his horse probably didn't count. "Um, not exactly…"

CHAPTER FOUR

Too soon, Sophie was giving it a try. "All right Mertyl, that's right, slow and easy," she crooned to the painted mare, her entire body tense and expecting to hit the ground. Eyes forward, Mertyl plodded ahead with a bored whinny. At least, it sounded like boredom.

Thick pine trees unfolded lush branches on either side of the dirt trail as a woodpecker beat a sharp staccato tune somewhere high up. Orange honeysuckle and thick huckleberry bushes fought for dominance throughout the trees, their sweet scents mixing with sharp pine. A cool breeze wafted through the sharp sunlight angling through branches and brought peace to the area.

They truly were alone.

Sophie fought to relax her muscles, butt, and thighs as she balanced. She couldn't help but remember Jake's hard thighs bracketing hers on the big black horse he rode again today. She studied his broad back as he maneuvered two tons of near-wild animal along the old trail easily, naturally.

Today he was all cowboy in faded jeans, black Stetson, and boots, his hair tied back at the nape. He was even bigger than she'd remembered. A dark gray shirt emphasized the breadth of a muscular chest that her body remembered well.

She grinned, and then her gaze softened as one of her new boots caught her eye. He'd bought her boots. Then she shook her head. He was a cowboy. A lawyer, no less. If that wasn't bad enough, his main job was to prevent her from doing hers. She needed to remember they were opponents in a battle about to begin. A battle that could determine the rest of her career and save her uncle's company. Boots or not.

As the trail angled upward, Sophie had to admit Jake was right about her horse. Slow and steady. Pretty safe. Mertyl had looked almost grateful when Jake led her from the deep rust-colored paddock on his ranch. Sophie had admired the color of the building, and Jake told her it was the trim color of his parents' paddocks, since he'd wanted consistency throughout all the ranches. His warm tone illustrated a closeness with his parents.

She had looked around for his home, but several mature blue spruce trees down the private driveway hid it.

Suddenly, the lake sparkled as the trail broke into a clearing of trampled wheat and sagebrush holding large rocks baking in the sun. Thick trees surrounded the vista on three sides while a steep incline led down to the water far below.

Jake jumped lithely off his stallion near the edge of the trees, turned, and reached to lift Sophie from Mertyl. His hands remained warm and strong around her waist as she regained her balance and stretched already protesting muscles. He waited until she met his gaze.

"That wasn't so bad, was it?" Amusement wove through his tone.

Her heart accelerated as his midnight eyes ran over her face in an almost physical caress. Sophie shook her head. She'd agreed to the trip so she could see her client's land from a different perspective, not to flirt with the sexy lawyer. So she stepped back, and he released her.

Sophie turned toward the lake, letting its placidness calm her nerves while Jake tied reins to trees before grabbing two backpacks slung over his horse. He deftly shook out a tightly woven blanket with white, red, and brown-stitched patterns and spread it on the ground before adding plates, containers of food, and a bottle of wine.

"You really come prepared." Sophie sat gingerly on the beautiful blanket.

A dimple flirted in his left cheek as Jake opened the containers. "My daughter helped pack the essentials."

She blinked. "You have a daughter?"

"Yeah." Pride shone in his deep eyes. "Leila. She just turned six."

"Pretty name," Sophie murmured. Caution stiffened her spine. "You're not, I mean, you're not married, are you?" The heated kiss from the previous afternoon flashed through her mind.

Pain stamped down hard on the sharp angles of his face. "No. My wife died when Leila was only two."

"I'm sorry." It wasn't enough.

"Me, too." He handed her a plate before opening the wine.

An orange-breasted robin hopped closer to the blanket, its beady eyes on the feast. "How did she die, Jake?" Sophie asked.

He handed her a glass of chardonnay. "She died running away from me." He effectively ended the conversation by passing her a container filled with fried chicken.

They ate in silence. Sophie wondered about his deceased wife but didn't want to spoil the afternoon with sadness. She'd ask later.

"It's so peaceful here," Sophie mused as two more robins joined the first.

"Yes. Without a golf course," Jake said dryly.

"Golf courses are peaceful places." Sophie tossed her empty plate into a garbage sack. "At least if they're designed correctly."

"Not the same, Soph." Jake gestured at the deep green lake below them. "The risk isn't worth it."

Irritation jangled her nerves. "The golf course won't pollute your lake."

"The science doesn't confirm that. Again, it's not worth the risk. Besides, you don't own any of the land, do you?" he asked.

She exhaled slowly, holding on to her temper. "No. A private company owns the land. They just hired us to design the golf course." The sun beat down, and she inhaled the crisp air.

"Well then, maybe we're on the same side here," he said.

Sophie rolled her eyes. "Is this when I notice a golf course doesn't belong here?"

Jake reached out one broad arm and yanked Sophie down beside him to face the clouds. "The land has been whispering since you arrived. You just need to listen."

Sophie quieted with her head on Jake's muscled shoulder, her face turned to the sky, her back comfortable against the blanket. She really should get up. Or move away. But he was so warm, so solid. She ignored her inner voice and shut her eyes to listen.

A breeze scattered pine needles to the hard earth. Honeysuckle layered the wind with sweetness. Birds twittered to each other in song, and Jake breathed deep and sure next to her. She opened her eyes.

Clouds drifted lazily across a beach-warm sky as a sense of peace slid through her bones into her deepest marrow. "I think a golf course would still be peaceful here."

"Why aren't you used to presents, Sophia?" he asked.

"Ugh. Please don't call me that." The wind brought a chill, and Sophie snuggled closer into Jake's side. Just a bit.

"What's wrong with Sophia?" Laziness coated his deep voice as he stared upward.

Embarrassment heated her cheeks. "It's pretentious. I mean, seriously. 'Sophia Smith'? What was she thinking?"

"Your mother?" he asked.

"Yeah." Unease settled in her stomach.

"Is she French?" he asked.

"No, she wasn't French. She just wanted to be somebody." And she'd reached her goal.

"*Wasn't* French?" he asked.

Remembered pain slithered down Sophie's chest. "Wasn't. She and my stepfather died in a car accident when I was eighteen."

"I'm sorry. But she was somebody."

Sophie pushed old hurts out of her mind. "How do you figure?"

"She was your mother," he said.

"That wasn't enough, believe me." Sophie's shoulders tensed.

"I still don't understand." He tucked her closer.

Sophie let out a deep breath. "I'm not sure she knew who my father was. If she did, she never said. We were poor. Trailer-park poor. She always wanted more."

"Did she get it?"

"Yeah. She married my stepfather, Roger Riverton, when I was fourteen. Then she got to travel everywhere."

"What about you?" he asked.

Sometimes loneliness snuck up and chilled her skin, like now. "Boarding school. It was all right, I guess."

"Did you like him? Your stepfather?" Jake's deep voice wound nicely through the silence.

"Not so much. He was quite a bit older and had already raised his family. In business, well, he was ruthless," she murmured.

Jake ran a hand down her arm, as if to offer warmth and reassurance. "How did you know he was ruthless?"

Memories flashed, bringing a dull pain to her temples. "A girl at school told me. I guess Roger raided her dad's company and then tore it apart. It's what he did." She watched the clouds drift. "Once a man came to visit when I was home for school break. He was almost crying, practically begging Roger not to destroy his family's construction business. I shouldn't have listened at the door, but…"

Jake tightened his hold. "What happened?"

"Roger didn't care. He was so cold, so *mean*. Like a shark. He told the man to forget it, that he deserved to lose his company. That he was weak." She shivered. "That's how Roger made so much money."

"Some of the money went to something good,

right? I mean, to your schooling?" Jake asked.

Sophie tightened her jaw. "No. When they died, everything went to his kids. I had a scholarship to school and took out some loans, so it all worked out." She had never wanted Roger's money.

Jake was quiet for a moment. "How did you choose golf course design?"

Sophie laughed, her heart lightening. "I loved art. Drawing and creating. When I met Uncle Nathan, Roger's brother, he helped me to channel that into design. He's my boss now."

"Ahh. You love him," Jake said.

"Yes. When I was younger, I used to wish he was my dad. That Mom had married him instead." Sophie rolled onto her stomach to face Jake. His muscles were relaxed, and he had one hand behind his head. "What about you? Are your parents still living?"

"My mother is. My father died in a snowmobile accident when I was eight and Quinn was six." Jake's eyes darkened with pain.

Sophie reached out to pat Jake's chest. "I wondered about Colton and Dawn. They look so different from you and Quinn."

Jake's eyes crinkled. "Yeah. Mom married Tom a couple of years later and then they had Colt and Dawnie."

"Were you upset she remarried?" Sophie asked.

"Not really. I mean, he isn't Kooskia, so I wasn't so sure for a while. But Tom's great, and he makes Mom happy. Though Dawn…" Jake grinned. "She has been a handful. For all of us."

"Three older brothers? Poor Dawn." Sophie grinned back. "Is it important to you? I mean, was

Leila's mother a member of the tribe?"

"Yes. She was full Kooskia," Jake said.

For some unknown reason, his admission deflated her.

Then he frowned. "I thought being a tribe member was important—that we'd want the same things."

"But you didn't?"

"No." The color of Jake's eyes deepened, and his hand slid to the back of Sophie's head.

"No," she said as she placed both hands against his chest and pushed to a seated position. "No way. No more kissing."

"Why not?" Jake sat up, his eyes intent on her mouth.

Despite her resolve, heat flared in her abdomen. "Because this is business. We're on opposite sides."

"We don't have to be." His voice deepened to a husky tone.

"Yeah, we do." Her brain told her body to get a grip. "Unless you're going to support my design?"

"No." Regret colored his words.

They were on opposite sides, no matter how sexy he was or how much she wanted to kiss him again. "We should get back." She shivered as the wind caught a chill.

His gaze ran over her face. Then he nodded and rolled to his feet, holding out a broad hand to help her up. "Yeah, we should. The spring storm season should be arriving any day, and while impressive, you don't want to be caught outside."

"Spring storm season?" She moved to help him repack.

"Yes. Probably not until next week, though the

breeze coming off the lake has more of a chill than it should." He turned and lifted her onto the mare, helping her insert her new boots in the worn stirrups.

Sophie felt slightly more at home on the pretty horse, but while her body relaxed, her thoughts spun. What had he meant that his wife had run away from him? How had she died? What would it be like to kiss Jake again? Maybe the first time was just a fluke. It didn't matter that she wasn't Kooskia—one silly kiss didn't mean anything.

What she needed to concentrate on was how she could convince Jake to change his mind and help her get the tribe to support her proposal.

They arrived back at the paddock before she knew it. Jake's indulgent sigh as they drew closer should have provided warning to whom obviously awaited them.

"Hello, Sophie." Chief Lodge strolled out the big double door.

"Afternoon, Chief Lodge." Sophie gratefully took his offered hand and swung down from the horse. Her leg muscles protested in a spasm, and she stumbled.

"Did you see the land?" The chief steadied her until she could stand on her own.

She put both hands on her hips and stretched her back, ignoring the loud pop from her spine. "Yes, I did survey the land."

"And?" the chief asked.

"I think a golf course would fit perfectly in that spot." She grinned at the elder.

The chief threw back his head and guffawed. "Oh, Sophie, you're a pip." He wiped his eyes with one gnarled hand. "That settles it, then."

"Settles what?" She shrugged tense shoulder muscles. Her entire body revolted from her earlier ride.

"You have to come to the branding picnic tomorrow, out at Rain's," the chief said.

"Grandpa…" Jake swung from his horse to stand at her side.

She threw a disgruntled look his way. *His* muscles seemed fine.

"There now, Jake agrees. We have to be there early, but I can give you directions." The chief patted her on the back. "Besides, the entire tribal council will be there, so you can talk to all of them about your proposal."

"Well…" She chewed her bottom lip while flicking another glance toward Jake. It would be nice to talk to the entire council, so maybe she should go. Though the frown on his sexy face didn't warm her heart any.

"Good. Saturdays are meant for fun." The chief offered her an arm. "Now, why don't we let Jake take care of the horses, and I'll give you a ride back to Shiller's B&B."

"Oh, er, okay." She'd grab any opportunity to sell him on her plan. Taking his proffered arm, she gave Jake a small smile over her shoulder. "Thanks for the picnic."

"No problem, Sophie. I'll see you tomorrow," Jake said.

Why did that sound like a threat?

CHAPTER FIVE

After a quick ride to the general store, Sophie spent the rest of the day fine-tuning her proposal. She ignored the new note on her Jeep. This time the note had been more explicit: *Your development will destroy the land—please rethink your plan.*

At least the anonymous person had asked nicely this time. She placed the note with the first one, wondering if she should file a police report. The last thing she wanted was to appear like a hysterical female—and the notes weren't exactly threats. They were more like pleas. Nice, polite pleas. She could handle this. The tribe was certainly against the development, but she couldn't imagine Jake leaving a cowardly note for her. He was more likely to beat down her door to challenge the proposal.

She ate a quiet dinner with Mrs. Shiller, the sole proprietor of the B&B. After helping clear the dishes, she escaped to her room and the purchases she'd been thrilled to find in the general store. She pulled out the sketchpad and new charcoals from the brown bag. They were beautiful, untouched, and ready to be used. The charcoal felt warm and solid in her hand as it vibrated with possibilities. The blank sheet before her called for something. Sighing happily, she reached out to create.

Her first drawing captured the clearing with its amazing view of Mineral Lake, tall pine trees, and bouncing robins. Flecks in the rocks sparkled light back to the hazy sun as clouds dropped toward the ground. The movement of charcoal against paper calmed her; even the smell of charcoal dust inspired her to continue.

Her second drawing took hours as she lost herself in every line and shadow. About midnight, she stretched her aching neck and scrutinized her work while spraying a light coat of fixative over the paper. Her nerves hummed as Jake stared unapologetically back at her from the paper, his eyes warm and serious, his cheekbones sharp angles over dark hollows, and his mouth full and slightly tipped. Black hair cascaded away from a broad forehead—strength and power flowed through every line across his face.

He was perfect.

And he wasn't hers to draw.

Her cell phone shattered the peace and she jumped, dropping the sketchpad and checking the number. Preston. She thought about it. With a sigh, she turned the phone on mute and went to bed.

The hours spent drawing had calmed her to the point that she fell asleep easily. She dreamed a dark, dreamless sleep until the early morning hours, waking up with some decent energy. It must be the mountain air.

She pushed snarled curls off her forehead and swung her feet over the bed. The cold wood floor forced a chill up her legs, and she darted to her suitcase for socks and a comfortable cardigan. Her eye caught the soft light filtering through the silk curtains—and the clock. She gasped as she noted the time—she'd better hurry. What did one wear to a branding party?

With a shrug, she donned dark jeans and a light

purple blouse, fetching a sweater in case the weather turned. A quick swipe of mascara and a clip to contain her curls finished the look. After pulling on her new boots, she secured the chief's directions in one hand and darted out the door.

Once in the Jeep, she sat for a moment. With an irritated sigh, she jumped out of the car and back inside to grab her sketchbook. She was going to be late.

The directions were simple. Sophie drove through town and turned left at Rain's Crossing. Soon enough, freshly painted white fences lined both sides of the road where horses ranging from light tan to colorful paints frolicked to the right, while steers and cows dotted the field to the left. She'd have to return when she had more time to sketch the placid scene of contrasting colors.

She pulled in behind a green Ford pickup beside a trio of large brown cows chewing grass in their large mouths, only separated from her by a wooden fence. Sophie gave the three an uneasy smile before following the line of trucks up a slight hill. She stopped at the rise and surveyed the ranch below. To the left of a large two-story log-planked house, colorful picnic tables perched among the trees near a large bunkhouse. Several barns, paddocks, and fenced areas stood to the right, as did most of the crowd.

Her boots clomped a rhythmic tune down the hill, toward the sounds of hooting and hollering. Several people stood on or by a three-slatted white fence, shouting encouragement. She spotted Dawn standing on the bottom rail of the sturdy fence and made a beeline for her new friend. She had just placed one foot on the bottom rung when a cheer rose from the spectators.

"This way, Colt!" a man called from inside the square corral.

She knew that voice. Awareness fluttered in her stomach at hearing Jake's deep baritone. She shifted up to see over the top rung.

Good God. The man was wearing chaps.

Actual chaps.

Jake's worn cowboy hat perched atop a grimy forehead as sweat ran in rivulets down his dirty face. Mud and dust caked his black shirt, and light jeans poked through the deep brown chaps protecting his legs. He dug scuffed cowboy boots into the earth while twisting two large horns in his leather-gloved hands, rolling a massive steer to the ground. Jake's face set into hard lines of determination as he battled the beast.

The steer bellowed when Jake shifted to press one firm knee into its neck, his hands pressing the horns to the ground, effectively immobilizing the animal's body. Colton rushed in with a needle and inoculated the animal just before another man pressed a hot iron to its flank.

The stench of burning fur filled the air in tune with the steer's protest. Jake released him and jumped back. The steer leaped to its feet and ran out a narrow side exit into another pasture. The beast had to weigh at least a ton, maybe two. Fortunately, the pen safely kept the spectators from danger.

Jake grinned at Colton across the dusty pen, his dimple winking through the grime. "It's your turn to roll 'em to the ground." He yanked off his hat and wiped his forehead with one muscled arm.

"But you're so good at it," his brother returned, his

face caked with mud.

Sophie stood in shock as warmth pooled deep in her belly. She was so completely out of her element. Yet what a display. She had never seen such masculinity before.

Man against beast.

And man won.

Jake was filthy. Covered in dirt and who knew what else. The urge to kiss him again tempted her. Her mother would be shocked.

His dark gaze found her, and she forgot all about her mother. She may have forgotten how to breathe. Then he smiled and she forgot how to think.

"Well hello, Sunshine." He pounded his cowboy hat on his chaps and dust flew as he stalked toward her. "You look pretty today." Then his dimple winked again. "I like your boots." He stopped just on the other side, eye-to-eye with her as she stood, riveted, on the fence rung.

"Me, too." Warmth flushed her face. "They're my favorites."

"You wear them well." Something unidentifiable flashed through his eyes. For some reason, his look streaked heat through the rest of her. "Are you going to eat lunch with me?" The dimple returned.

Her eyes fixed on his mouth. "I didn't bring any food."

"I brought enough for both of us." The sound of another steer prodding toward the pen echoed behind him. "I have about ten more to do before lunch." He turned back just as the beast rushed into view. "Dawnie, tell Sophie the rules for watching," he called over his shoulder, his attention on the animal.

Dawn tipped back her cream-colored cowboy hat and gave Sophie a big smile.

"Rules?" Sophie muttered.

"Oh yeah, there are always rules, trust me," Dawn said with a practiced eye roll. "Basically, if a steer comes your way, take three steps back."

Sophie rubbed dust off her wrist. "Why?"

"Well, we haven't had one bust through the fence in a while, but it has happened," Dawn said.

Three steps? Man, she'd run for the car. "Okay."

"So how was your date?" Dawn asked.

Now Sophie rolled her eyes. "It wasn't a date. It was business."

"Right." Dawn straightened. "Colton, watch your left," she yelled just as the steer turned its head.

Sophie gasped as Colton shifted to the left, narrowly missing being gouged. "Good thing you're here to watch your brothers," she said quietly.

Dawn nodded toward the third man in the pen. "I'm here to watch Hawk."

"Hawk?" The name fit. Thick black hair was cut short above a face too sharp to be rugged. Deep green eyes watched the steer as he waited with the branding iron, his chiseled face fierce in concentration. He stood well over six feet and filled out his black shirt hard. "Can't say I blame you. Though he looks older than you."

"Yeah. This is actually his spread. He's been Colton's best friend since they were in diapers, and they're only three and a half years older than me. Though it might as well be a million," Dawn murmured.

"Oh. Sorry." In love with her brother's best friend?

That did suck.

Dawn shrugged. "I'm of age. I'll graduate from college in a year, and maybe I'll go to graduate school. Someday, he'll be on leave, and he'll see me as an adult. Finally."

"On leave?"

"Hawk's in the navy, a SEAL. He's on leave for a week and then he goes back. But," she said, sadness creeping into the young woman's words, "it seems like every time he returns home, he's even further away." She was quiet for a moment before perking up. "Though Jake was like that, too, and then he got over it."

"Jake was a SEAL?" Sophie asked.

Dawn shook her head. "No. Army Ranger. I don't know what he did, but I think it took a toll." A wry grin lit her face. "Though he's all better now." A thoughtfulness entered her pretty features. "Not so sure about Quinn."

"Quinn?" Sophie asked.

"Yeah. He was Special Forces—and he doesn't like to talk about it much. He came back and is the sheriff now."

"Your brother's the sheriff?" Sophie asked.

"Yep. Believe me, if it wasn't bad enough trying to find a date with three older brothers, having one of them become the law in town really makes it tough," Dawn said.

Sophie shook her head. "I can imagine." What would it be like to have family actually care about you, actually be involved in your life? The Lodge-Freeze family intrigued her. "What about Colton? Is he in the service?"

"Nope. He's on spring break. He'll graduate next month in with a doctorate in finance. He runs all our family businesses now, but we won't give him the title or salary until he finishes school and then studies international finance abroad for a year or so." Dawn grinned. "It's a family joke."

Probably had to be family to understand it. "The family business is the ranch?" Sophie asked.

Dawn shrugged. "The ranches are included in the family holdings. We've diversified over the years."

Sounded impressive. Sophie eyed the cowboys. There was a lot more to the Lodge men than she'd thought. "What about you, Dawn? Are you studying finance as well?"

"I'm double majoring in business and photography." The woman teetered on her boots. "The photography is just a hobby, but I do have fun with it."

A hush came over the crowd, and several more people moved toward the fence.

"Buttercup's next," Dawn whispered.

"Buttercup?" Sophie asked, her eyes riveted on Jake.

"Yeah," Dawn confirmed, amusement echoing in her voice. "Jake named him a few years back after he connected with a horn."

"Was Jake hurt?" Sophie asked.

Dawn shrugged. "He needed stitches, but it didn't slow him down any." Her gaze stayed on the opened gate to Hawk's left as cowboys prodded the steer inside the pen. The gate slammed shut, and the beast sauntered into the pen.

Sophie lost her breath.

CHAPTER SIX

Two sharp, massive horns perched ominously on the largest animal head Sophie had ever seen. Gray fur covered a gigantic body that had to be at least double the size of the last animal, and its black eyes shone with a devil's light. It pawed the ground and huffed, its enormous head swiveling to challenge Jake.

Jake leaned casually against the side fence. "Hi, Buttercup," he said to the amusement of the watching crowd.

Buttercup flicked its tail and muscles bunched as it snorted again.

"Ready for the timer, Jake?" an older man, his face hidden by the brim of a brown cowboy hat, shouted from the far side of the pen.

Jake looked to Colton and Hawk, who both nodded. "Start the timer."

Fast as a whip and just as unforgiving, Jake struck. His gloves latched onto those deadly horns. Buttercup blew out a snort and tossed his head. Jake slid to the side, his face set in brutal concentration, his hands holding tight. A roar rose from the crowd as the steer bucked both feet toward Colton while frantically trying to shake off Jake.

Jake's head jerked back.

With a burst of speed, he pivoted and thrust a muscled thigh into the steer's side. His foot swept the animal's hind legs before he threw all of his weight back, his arms twisting.

Dust swirled around the two.

Buttercup bellowed, legs pawing the ground, before throwing his enormous bulk toward Jake. With a fierce grin, Jake dodged to the side, barely avoided being crushed, and let the steer's momentum propel them to *thud* against the hard earth.

Smooth as silk, quick as lightning, Jake rolled to his side and wedged one knee against the steer's neck, his hands pressing the horns to the ground. The beast fought to regain its feet. Both man and beast panted furiously as dirt drifted around them.

"Sorry, Buttercup, I win today," Jake said softly to the animal.

A round of laughter rose around the pen.

"Whose steer is he?" Sophie released the breath she had been holding, ignoring a sudden buzzing in her ears and a tightening in her belly.

"He's ours," Dawn said.

"So are the rest of the steers owned by the tribe?" Sophie asked.

Dawn shook her head. "Some are owned by tribal members, some by other ranchers in the area. The entire Maverick County gets together once or twice a year to inoculate the animals. Plus"—she jumped down from her perch and sent dust flying—"it's a good reason for a party." She peered up at Sophie. "I'm going to meet some friends by the picnic tables. Do you want to come?"

"No thanks." Sophie smiled down at her. "I'll stay here."

"Don't blame you. There's nothing like a man in chaps, is there?" Dawn headed off.

Sophie turned back to the pen where sharp green

eyes followed Dawn's movements. Hmm. Maybe Hawk wasn't as oblivious as Dawn thought. And the woman was right. There was nothing like a man in chaps.

A tall figure took Dawn's place at Sophie's side. "How are my boys doing?" A deep voice rumbled the question as one scuffed brown boot perched on the bottom railing and two broad arms rested on the top fence slat.

"Your boys?" Sophie glanced into eyes the exact shade of Dawn's.

"Yes. Those two…" He nodded to Jake and Colton. "And that one's close enough—his mama died way too young." He inclined his head toward Hawk. "I'm Tom."

"Sophie." She appreciated the gentle touch in the large calloused hand enclosing hers. "They're doing well." She met him eye-to-eye from her position on the higher rung. Thick gray hair was cut short under a brown Stetson, a prominent jaw claimed a rugged stubbornness, and dark Wrangler jeans showed a man still fit and ready to ride. Competency and kindness swirled around him like leaves around a massive tree trunk. Her chest tightened at Tom's words. He considered Jake his son. Roger had always referred to her as "June's daughter, Sophia."

"Oh man, did I miss Buttercup?" Tom glanced toward the far field.

Sophie shook off old memories and laughed. "Yeah, a few minutes ago."

"Darn it. Who won the bet?" Tom asked.

"What bet?"

Tom looked around as if for answers. "On how long it took Jake to take him down."

"I don't know," Sophie admitted.

Tom shrugged. "I would've heard if I won. How was your date with my son?"

"It wasn't a date," Sophie protested as Colton wrestled with the newest steer while Jake remained ready on the sidelines.

"Pity," Tom murmured. "It's about time that boy had some fun."

Sophie nodded toward a grinning Jake. White teeth were illuminated against trails of dirt and sweat. "He's having fun now."

"He sure is," Tom agreed. "I meant the other kind. I thought he might finally be moving on."

"Moving on?" It wasn't any of her business, but…

Tom sighed before answering. "After Emily died, well, we wondered if he'd ever smile again. But he had Leila to worry about."

"He mentioned his wife died young," Sophie said.

"Too young. Way too young to learn what matters in this life." Soberness mellowed Tom's words as Colton jumped back from a newly released steer.

"Which is?" Sophie asked.

"Hawk, to your left," Tom called out, tensing until the young man shifted away from kicking hoofs. He returned to their conversation. "You know, learned what's important. People. Memories. Family." Tom focused over the fence and acknowledged Jake's nod with a nod of his own. He turned toward Sophie and extended an arm. "That was the high sign from Jake. Why don't I escort you over to the picnic tables? He'll be along shortly." All around them people stepped back from the fence, though most kept their attention on the pen.

"High sign?" She took his proffered arm and jumped from her perch.

Tom chortled. "The next three steers are known kickers. Tulip always goes for the crowd."

"Tulip?" Sophie chuckled.

"Yep. Tulip, Snuggles, and Lola. The boys have a sense of humor." Tom grinned.

Sophie shook her head as she allowed Tom to escort her across the road to the picnic tables. The walk took some time, since they stopped to chat with people along the way. Most had heard of her, some asked about her date, and all seemed to like Tom.

Bright red, yellow, and blue-checked cloths covered massive tables where people dug in to delicious-smelling chicken, steak, and sweet fruit salad. Children ran around gleefully while elderly women patted babies and people chatted. Several were obviously of native descent, but just as many people were blond with blue eyes. The whole county must have been in attendance.

"Here we are," Tom said as they arrived at a table where a petite Native American woman uncovered plastic containers. "This is my wife, Loni." Pride filled his words.

"Hi." Sophie released Tom's arm to extend a hand to the pretty woman. Jake's eyes gleamed from a tanned oval face with delicate features and a genuine smile.

"It's nice to meet you, Sophie." Loni smiled and shook her hand. "Please sit. The boys should be along shortly."

Sophie sat and studied Jake's mother. Intelligence that matched Jake's glimmered in her eyes. Sophie took a sip of the sweet, tart lemonade she offered, realizing how thirsty she'd become. "Thank you."

"Sure. So what did you think of the branding? Did you see Buttercup?" Loni asked.

"Yes. Very impressive," Sophie said.

"I heard Quinn won the bet," Loni informed her husband.

"Again?" Tom rubbed his chin. "Man, that boy has a second sense about that stuff. Unless…"

Loni shook her head. "He and Jake are not in cahoots, Tom. Give it up."

"I don't know." Tom tugged his wife's braid before pecking her cheek with a kiss.

Sophie marveled at the couple's closeness. Her mother and Roger had never seemed to actually like each other. Well, the few times she saw them together, anyway.

"Hey, Mom." Quinn moved into sight, carrying a little girl snuggling her face into his neck. "We have crocodile tears here."

"Tears?" Loni reached up as Quinn transferred a small girl into her waiting arms. "What's wrong, Leila?"

A feminine sniff came from the small child. She lifted her head. "Tommy McAlister pulled my braids and the sheriff won't shoot him."

"Oh." Loni stifled a laugh. "I'm pretty sure the sheriff isn't supposed to shoot people, even if he is your uncle. So, your braids, huh?"

"Yeah." Sniff.

"Did it hurt?" Loni snuggled her closer.

"Well, no…" the girl said.

"But it hurt your feelers?" Loni asked.

"Kind of." Another sniff.

Loni patted Leila's braids. "Now honey, remember when we talked about boys not being quite as smart as girls?"

Twin *hey*s of protest came from Tom and Quinn, as Jake's brother slid onto the bench next to Sophie.

Leila giggled and nodded.

"Okay. Well, they don't know how to talk about important stuff like feelings, so they do stupid stuff instead." Loni winked at Sophie. "Tommy probably just wanted your attention, and that was the only way he could think of to get it."

"Boys are stupid." Leila turned twin dark eyes on Sophie. "Hi."

Sophie smiled at the little girl. She was going to be an incredible beauty one day.

"You're the golf course lady. You went on a date with Daddy," the girl said.

"Ah, no, it, ah, wasn't a date," Sophie sputtered. Quinn coughed back a laugh, and if she had known him better, she'd have elbowed him in the ribs. She settled for giving him a small glare.

"Did you go on a picnic?" Shrewd black eyes met hers across the table.

"Well, yes." Sophie fought to keep from fidgeting under the scrutiny.

"Did you have a pretty view?" Leila asked.

"Definitely." Where was the child going with this?

"And you ate lunch with some wine?" Leila continued.

Sophie's face heated. "Well, yes."

"Sounds like a date to me." Leila grinned in triumph.

Quinn didn't even try to mask his laugh this time.

Loni bit back a grin. "Here, Leila, why don't you color for a while?" She pushed crayons and a coloring book in front of her granddaughter, causing a blue pencil to roll to the ground.

"I can reach it." Leila leaned down and grabbed the pencil before emitting a soft gasp. "I like your boots." She peeked her little face above the table and stared at Sophie.

"Thank you." There was no way she'd admit they were a gift from the girl's father.

"Do you have Manolos?" Leila sked.

Unease pricked Sophie's skin. "I do actually have a pair. They were a gift from my mother for my eighteenth birthday." She had wanted an art easel.

"Oh, are they pretty?" Leila breathed out in longing.

"Um, yeah. Pink and sparkly." Sophie smiled.

A frown marred Leila's pretty face. "I wish I could see them."

"Well." Sophie reached for a blank piece of paper and the pink pencil. "Let's see what we can do about that." Her hand moved with sure strokes as she drew the shoes. Leila watched intently. Sophie handed over the paper.

"Wow, they are pretty." Leila sighed at the delicate sandals dangling from a pine tree. "Is this for me?" She held the paper as if it were infinitely precious.

"It's all yours," Sophie confirmed.

"Sophie, you are so talented," Loni noted in admiration just as a shadow crossed the table.

Pleasure slid through Sophie. Although these people were all strangers, she felt comfortable.

Accepted. She marveled at the little girl surrounded by such warmth and affection.

"What's that?" Jake asked from behind her. Sophie's heartbeat increased.

"My Manolos, Daddy." Leila's excitement made the effort seem much more than it was. "See?" She held out the paper to her father, who took it over Sophie's shoulder.

"Wow. They are pretty." Jake handed the drawing back to his daughter. "My mother's right—you are very talented." He slid onto the bench next to her, effectively trapping her between two hard male bodies. Talk about immovable objects.

His compliment had her feeling like she'd just aced a difficult test. Gaining control over her emotions, she glanced at the lawyer. "You showered."

Jake nodded. "In the bunkhouse. Believe me, it was necessary." Clean jeans hung low on tight hips over black boots while a light black shirt emphasized the corded strength in his upper body. His dark hair curled over his collar. For once, it wasn't tied back, and the mass lent him a dangerous air.

Almost primitive.

• • •

Jake settled onto the picnic bench, his attention on the woman who had fit so nicely into his family gathering. Though her pretty picture of city shoes should be a dose of cold water.

Except cold wasn't something he equated with Sophie.

Pure heat. Full sunshine. Raging fire. He wanted

nothing more than to jump into the flames and get burned. His cock flared to life behind his zipper, and he fought a groan. Now wasn't the time.

Quinn sent him a smart-assed grin over Sophie's head.

Damn younger brother had always been a mind reader. Jake scowled back.

Colton loped up and slid into the seat across the table. He'd showered and stolen one of Jake's shirts to wear. The guy was a genius with money, but he couldn't remember to bring a complete change of clothing.

"Let's eat. I'm starving," he muttered. He flipped open a lid covering freshly prepared fried chicken as Loni passed plates all around. Different salads and cookies completed the meal.

Sophie nibbled on a drumstick, and Jake fought another groan. Those pretty lips were much too talented to be wasted on chicken.

Colton glanced around. "Where's Dawnie?"

"She went to eat down by the pond with a bunch of friends." Tom scooped more pieces of watermelon onto Leila's plate.

"What friends?" Colton handed Leila the napkin she'd dropped.

Loni shrugged. "I just saw her with Adam." She handed the bowl of chicken over to Colt.

"Adam?" Quinn shook his head. "I don't like her being in that band with him."

"Me, neither." Jake bit his lip. Maybe it was time to intervene and pull Dawn from the band. She didn't belong in a bar.

"Dawn's in a band?" Sophie put her napkin on her empty plate.

"Yes. The gal sings like an angel," Tom said with a proud grin.

"She should be singing in church, not with Adam," Quinn muttered.

Loni rolled her eyes. "Adam is Hawk's best friend, Quinn. He's as safe as they get."

"Adam is anything but safe, Mom," Quinn said.

Loni shook her head. "Leave Dawn alone, all of you. She has to find her own way, and you three"—she peered at her husband—"I mean, you *four*, are going to do nothing but push her in the wrong direction. Trust me."

Colton opened his mouth to respond and then jumped as a small hand slapped him on the back.

"Nice job with the steers, Colt," a curvy brunette said, smiling. "Hi Loni, Tom."

"Hi, Melanie." Loni grinned and introduced the young woman to Sophie. "Have you eaten?"

"Yes, ma'am." Melanie nodded to Sophie and smiled. "I'm just heading down to watch Jonsie ride a bronc in the left pasture."

"Count me in." Colton jumped to his feet and slung an arm around Melanie. "See you later, Mom." He pulled the woman away.

"They make a nice couple," Sophie noted with a pretty smile.

Loni sighed. "They've been the best of buddies since preschool. Though," she said, her eyes twinkling with mischief, "I can't wait until he looks up one day and realizes she's all grown up."

"Boys are stupid," Leila muttered, and her grandmother nodded.

CHAPTER SEVEN

Monday morning, Sophie found herself in the middle of her pretty room with the golf course design calling from the desk and her sketchbook beckoning from her bed. She had work to do. But she wanted to draw the scene of Colton chasing a steer. She had spent half the night capturing Jake wrestling Buttercup to the ground. It was her best work.

The shrill of an antique pink phone saved her from having to make a decision, and she jumped across the bed to answer it. She stretched out on her belly before saying hello.

"Hi there, Sophie, I hope I'm not calling too early." A country ballad wafted through the line.

"Hi, Loni, no, I'm just getting to work." Well, she'd been thinking about getting to work, anyway.

"Oh, good. That's why I wanted to call you. I'd like to hire you. Well, I mean, that we would like to hire you. The tribal council, that is," Loni said.

Sophie sat up. "Hire me? For what?"

"We finally have enough funds to build a garden in memory of a good friend of mine. We want it near the base of headquarters, right before Spades Mountain, you know, the one that leads to all the hiking and horse trails?" Loni asked.

No, Sophie really didn't know. "What do you need from me?" she asked.

"We need you to design it. You have a landscape design degree, right?" Loni asked.

A garden? Sophie's breath caught. "Well, yes. But I specialize in golf courses." Though it would be interesting to design a garden—and probably be good for her résumé. Just in case.

"But your public hearing isn't for another week and your designs are all finished, aren't they?" Loni asked.

"Yes." Sophie's heartbeat quickened as her mind spun with creative ideas.

"Then this might be fun. Plus, you'd be working with the council, so you'd have time to sell everyone on the golf course." Loni's voice turned even more chipper.

"You dangle quite the carrot, Loni," Sophie said, laughing.

"Yeah, it's a gift. We'd pay you for the garden design," Loni said.

The project sounded interesting, and branching out to another type of design appealed to the artist inside Sophie. "I don't know…"

"Tell you what. The council is meeting for lunch today. Why don't I schedule the first fifteen minutes for you to present your golf course design, and then you can stay and listen to our plans. Plus, Mrs. Shiller has bridge today, so you'd be eating all alone. What fun is that?" Loni asked.

"All right." Sophie needed to take every opportunity to convince people her designs worked. "I'll be there. Tribal Headquarters at eleven?"

"Yes. See you then." Loni ended the call. Probably before Sophie could change her mind.

• • •

A couple of hours after the phonecall with Loni, Sophie climbed the hill toward headquarters, her new boots working the pedals of the Jeep. She told herself that she'd taken extra care with her makeup to prepare for a business meeting and not because Jake may be at headquarters.

Then she told herself to stop lying, that it wasn't healthy.

Loni met her at the door and took one of the large mounted designs from her hands. They headed into the familiar conference room and placed the designs on easels. Loni then introduced Sophie to three men, ranging in age from sixty to ninety, named Earl, Jacob, and Freddie, along with two silver-haired women, June and Phyllis, whom she'd already met at the picnic.

"The chief may pop in, and Jake should be here sometime." Loni gestured for Sophie to grab a plate and sandwich from the table.

Sophie sat beside Freddie, whose smile took up his entire face. "Jake is on the council?" she asked.

"No. But we act much like a Board of Directors, and every board needs a lawyer." Loni sat on Sophie's other side and selected a turkey sandwich.

"I hear the sheriff won the pot again this year." Freddie pushed his plate away. His long jowls swung as he spoke, and his deep brown eyes surveyed a platter of cookies with interest.

"Quinn has a knack for that kind of thing." Loni grinned. "Those boys are not in cahoots."

"Humph," Freddie replied around the cookie.

Sophie dropped her napkin on her empty plate. "What was the pot, anyway?"

"About two grand this year." Freddy rubbed his chin.

Sophie swung her gaze to him. "Two thousand dollars?"

Loni shrugged. "It's an event. Every year." She sat back. "All right, Sophie, show us your plan." She nodded toward the colorful renderings.

Drawing in a breath, Sophie stood and passed out packets detailing the project that had residences scattered every two acres. "The group is proposing a golf course community, most likely for retirement folks, with a clubhouse and restaurant. It's close enough to Maverick that the public could come golf for the day, maybe on the way to the tribe's casino, three miles down the road." She paused and walked to the renderings. "The Charleton Group has developed similar properties all over the world with great success."

"Didn't the Group buy this property with a development in mind?" Phyllis asked, her face buried in the papers.

"I believe so, yes." Sophie tightened her knees so she didn't tremble.

"That was gutsy since the county commissioners could refuse their permit," Freddie chimed in.

Sophie nodded. "The Group seems confident the law will allow the development. Their lawyers are more up to date with the legal aspects of the proposal than I am. My area of focus is just the golf course."

"This does look like a fun course," June mused. Her deep eyes looked large and round behind thick glasses. "Check out those sand traps around the fifth green."

Jacob nodded. "And the water hazard on the sixteenth hole. Man, that'd be fun."

Loni grinned. "This is a wonderful design, Sophie. I

like how the residential lots are two entire acres while keeping the feel of the country. The council meets again tomorrow, and we'll discuss an official position on your proposal."

The council had been more receptive than Sophie had hoped. Pleasure lifted her lips in a smile and her shoulders relaxed. "Thank you." She retook her seat.

"Our next item on the agenda is Willa's Garden at the base of the road." Loni perched narrow glasses on her nose.

The group peppered Sophie with suggestions— everything from a gazebo to flowerbeds and ponds.

Loni turned toward Sophie. "Willa served on the council until she became too ill and passed away. She taught school for thirty years before that and never married. The tribe was her family."

"So was the entire community, tribal or not," June spoke up.

The loving way the board spoke about Willa touched Sophie. Ideas shot through her head. A community garden? "How much land are we talking? Do you want fields for sports?"

Loni shook her head. "No. In fact, we're going to build an entire sports complex on the other side of the high school. That could be your next project. For Willa's Garden, we just want peace and tranquility."

Sophie's hands itched to get ahold of her charcoals and start designing, but she'd never designed a garden. "Well, I can draft up a design for you and then see what you think."

"By Wednesday?" June's eyes lit up.

Sophie nodded, trying to contain her own excitement. "I can have a rough design by then."

"Excellent." Earl leaped to his feet. "Come on guys, bingo starts in an hour at the casino." The other two men tossed their empty plates into the trash and followed him out the door.

"Thanks again, Sophie," Freddie called over his shoulder.

Sophie smiled. They'd drawn her in as if she were one of them. Being included shouldn't matter to her. Yet she couldn't lose the smile. She stood and expected handshakes, but both ladies gave her gentle hugs on their way out the door. Clearing her throat, she moved to help Loni clear the rest of the table.

A deep voice from the doorway startled her. "Drop those sandwiches, Mom." Jake strode into the room, his eyes focused on the food as his mother handed over the plate.

Sophie had thought the man was devastating in chaps. That was nothing compared to his look in full charcoal-gray Armani. The strength of his upper torso was evident through the dark silk, and his red tie breathed of power. The subtle stripe in his pants emphasized the impressive length of his legs. Butterflies danced in her stomach.

She lived in a big city. Muscles were earned in gyms and exercise rooms. Jake earned his the hard way — outdoors battling nature, lending a wildness to a man she should resist. Men like him didn't exist in her world, and she didn't fit in with theirs. But those butterflies beat with furious wings and didn't give a hoot about logic. Or safety.

She needed to shut her mouth before she drooled.

His dimple winked and his gaze slid over her face like a kid eyeing licorice in a candy store.

Her gaze dropped to his lips. She remembered how his mouth felt against hers, his tongue tangling with hers, and she flushed. His lips curved in response.

"How was court, dear?" Loni pushed the plate of cookies toward her son.

Jake released Sophie's gaze and dropped into a vacated chair. "Idiot EPA," he mumbled between bites.

"Jake, are you done for the day?" Loni asked.

"Definitely," he said.

Loni edged toward the door. "Good. Sophie needs to see the five acres for Willa's Garden, and I have an appointment in town. Would you show it to her?"

"Subtle, Mom. Yes, I'd love to show Sophie around," Jake said.

The double meaning wasn't lost on Sophie. Probably wasn't lost on any of them.

"Good. 'Bye." Loni made her escape.

Sophie clasped her suddenly trembling hands. She had the oddest urge to tackle the lawyer to the ground and steal a kiss but busied herself gathering the extra copies of her presentation. What was wrong with her?

"So they suckered you in, huh?" Jake turned amused eyes on her.

Oh yeah. Her job. The one she loved. Man, she lost all sense of reality when Jake was around. She ran a quick hand over her face. "Completely. Easily and without much of an effort." Of course it helped that she wanted to design the garden.

"They do that." Jake grabbed another cookie. "But—" He paused, obviously to choose the right words. "The tribe isn't going to support the Charleton Group's proposal on that land no matter how much we like your design."

Sophie stilled. "Are you sure?" Maybe he was wrong about the council. They'd seemed to like her golf course design.

Jake rubbed his chin. "They may seem like a sweet, old, bingo-playing group, but they're ruthless. Before you know it, ten years will have passed and you'll have designed everything from memorials to summer gardens. We both know you're meant to be in the city."

She frowned. "We both know I belong in the city?" The man had just met her. At his nod, she raked her gaze over his now relaxed form. "Look who's talking. Armani looks good on you, Jake." She'd bet anything he was a force to watch in a courtroom.

One eyebrow lifted. "I was in court today."

"Obviously. What wrong are you and the EPA trying to right?" she asked.

"Ah, stereotyping, are we?" His narrowed eyes belied his lazy drawl.

Heat roared through her ears. "Excuse me?"

"I sat on the opposite side from the EPA today, sweetheart." He explained why the tribes often sat across the fence from the government.

She tilted her head. Every time she thought she had a handle on Jake Lodge, he surprised her again. His analytical mind complemented his sexy grin in a way that would intrigue any woman, but she had to fight her attraction in order to save her uncle's company.

"Come on, we can load these, and then I'll take you to the memorial site." Jake stood and tossed his trash into the can before grabbing both foam boards with the golf course designs and holding out a hand.

She relaxed and placed her hand in Jake's much larger one. Warmth shot heat to her lower stomach. Warmth she didn't want to feel.

Because he was right: she was a city girl.

Wasn't she?

CHAPTER EIGHT

Sophie sketched a quick design for a garden including natural stone paths, a koi pond, and picnic areas. The site had been perfect for the memorial, and she'd enjoyed tromping through the brush with Jake after he'd thrown on cowboy boots. Even in a suit, the man looked natural surrounded by wild nature. He hadn't tried to kiss her again, and she told herself she was glad. There was no future for them.

Although that hadn't stopped her from agreeing to dinner with his family. She glanced at the clock. He'd return for her in less than an hour.

The cell phone jarred her out of her musings.

"Hi, Sophia." Preston's voice came smooth and sure over the line. "Miss me?"

Not so much, actually. *Interesting.* "I've been working. How's the Seattle job going?" she asked, instead of answering his question.

"Don't ask. We've run into some interesting competition. How's it going with the tribe?" Preston asked.

Her shoulders hunched. "I'm not sure. They all like the design but don't want it on the Charleton Group's land."

"Still?" He rustled papers over the line.

"We may not have tribal support when we face the county commissioners next week." Dread chilled her gut.

"The Group's lawyers are pretty good. You'll just

describe your design, and they'll do the proposal for the permit," Preston said.

Thank goodness she had backup at the hearing.

Preston cleared his throat before speaking again. "I've done a bit of research. You haven't run across Jake Lodge, have you?"

The air caught in her lungs. She took several deep breaths. "I've met Lodge. He's the tribe's lawyer." And the man who had kissed her into oblivion. "Why?"

"He's good. Really good. Took on the state twice, won both times in the U.S. Supreme Court. Tell me he's not involved in opposing the project," Preston said.

Sophie coughed. "I'd say he is involved. Very. Though he hasn't seemed too fired up about opposing us."

"Probably the calm before he strikes. I've heard he's the shark of all sharks. Plus, there are rumors that the tribe wants to build its own golf course over by the casino and are out to prevent any competition," Preston said.

"No, you've got it wrong. Jake's not like that," Sophie said.

Quiet slid across the line. "Just how well do you know him?" Preston asked.

"I've met with him regarding the proposal." Heat slid into her face.

Preston cleared his throat. "Of course. Well, I guess I'd just tell you to watch your back."

She needed to get off the phone. Now. "No problem."

"Have given any thought to taking the cruise with me?" Preston asked.

No. Not at all. She'd been too busy mooning over a

dangerous, country badass of a lawyer who might just torpedo her proposal. "The cruise? I, ah, don't know. I should probably concentrate on work right now. We need to save Uncle Nathan's company." She didn't want to hurt Preston's feelings. He was a good man. On paper, they so worked. In reality? Maybe not.

"I'm not taking no for an answer. Keep thinking about it. 'Bye." He ended the call.

Sophie set her phone down and stared sightlessly at the drawings before her. Just a week ago she would've jumped at the chance for a cruise with Preston. Now she balked. Why? She reached for her sketchbook and flipped it open to the second page. The answer stared back at her with Jake's eyes.

What was she thinking, agreeing to a dinner at the Lodge house? Jake stirred feelings in her that all but guaranteed a broken heart when she left—when she returned home.

Why did home seem so far away?

Hurriedly, she changed and then headed downstairs. She waited for Jake on the wooden porch swing, her nervous motions swaying it back and forth.

Thick boots thudding on the wide steps announced his arrival.

"No Armani tonight, Jake?" Sophie raised an eyebrow at his dark graphic button-up shirt, low-slung jeans, and polished cowboy boots. Combined with the deep black eyes, rugged face, and jet hair curling over his collar, he all but screamed bad-boy handsome. A true temptation for some girl to try and tame.

Some *country girl* to try and tame.

"You look spring pretty." His grin was pure sin.

Electricity zinged through her when she took his

proffered hand and walked to the truck with him. "I think your family is matchmaking." It wasn't what she'd meant to say.

"They like you." He stopped her at the black Chevy truck, pressing her against the hard metal. "So do I." He lowered his head, giving her all the time in the world to resist or shift away.

She didn't move. Her breath caught with anticipation.

Warm and soft, his lips wandered over hers before he deepened the kiss to something intimate, something demanding. Sophie sighed deep in her throat. One broad hand molded itself to her lower back and pulled her against him. Sheer masculine strength met her softness.

Her heart pounded, and need thrummed between her legs. Her nipples peaked to sharp points. Fire lashed through her nerves—fire for him.

Jake raised his head, his face an inch from hers, his eyes the dark clouds of a summer storm. "You have a decision to make."

"What?" Confusion battled with the desire ripping through her veins.

"There's something here." He dropped a gentle kiss to her lips. "I want to explore it."

"Jake—"

Broad, warm hands slid down her arms. "I'm not asking for forever. We both know our lives exist in different worlds. But we're here now. For a brief time," he said.

She fought a shiver. It was tempting. To lose herself in all that strength. The pure maleness of the man. "I'll think about it."

His triumphant grin made her question her sanity. She barely knew the man, for goodness sake. He released her and opened his door. She scrambled over the seat and secured her seat belt. He gracefully sat and ignited the engine, driving away from the B&B. "How's the garden design going?" he asked once they were on the way.

She shook her head to concentrate. A dangerous ache pounded through her body, blooming at the apex of her legs. "The garden? Great. Mrs. Shiller helped with the placement of flowers and shrubs."

"It's very nice of you to include her," Jake said, speeding out of town toward the surrounding mountains. "Are you seeing anyone?"

Sophie jumped at the unexpected question. "No." An invitation to a cruise didn't count.

"Me neither."

"I said I'd think about it," she said. Jake Lodge was becoming too much of a temptation. Her body pressed her to say yes. Her mind reeled to keep sane. She turned and admired the changing landscape, searching for a safe topic of conversation. "Rumor has it Quinn won the Buttercup pot the last couple of years." She sent a sly glance Jake's way.

Jake grinned. "Yeah, Quinn has a knack for it, I guess."

"You're not in cahoots?" she asked.

"No." It was Jake's turn to glance sideways. "But… you won't tell anyone?"

"I promise." For once, she'd be in on the joke.

Jake lifted one shoulder in a tough-guy shrug. "Quinn has a formula."

"Your brother has a formula?" she asked.

Jake nodded. "Quinn takes last year's time, subtracts two seconds for Buttercup's aging a year, and then multiplies it by a factor of how many injuries I'd sustained the past year."

"Really?" Sophie asked.

"Yep. He's won the last four years in a row." Jake's deep chuckle sent a skittering along her nerve endings.

Injuries? Wait a minute. "Do you get injured a lot in court?" She couldn't help teasing him.

He chuckled. "Not usually in court. I work my ranch, and injuries are common. But my brothers and I have the routine down, so we're fairly safe."

"You and your brothers seem really close." Longing flowed through her as she realized she'd missed out on something important by being an only child.

"We are. If for no other reason than to keep Dawnie safe. That woman's a menace. The second she started noticing boys, one in particular, life changed for all of us," Jake shook his head and took a sharp right around a country road.

"Hawk seems like a decent guy." A group of horses caught her attention, their manes spraying a myriad of colors through the wind as they galloped over hills.

Jake flashed her a surprised glance. "He's way too old for her. And a dead man if he goes near her. Besides, his job's screwing him up as bad as—" Jake's jaw snapped shut.

"Screwing him up as bad as the Rangers did you?" Would he let her in? Actually let her know him? The desire for his trust caught Sophie unaware.

"Who've you been talking to?" His attention was riveted completely on her.

Man, he probably nailed witnesses on cross-examination. "Nobody." Sophie struggled not to squirm.

Jake turned his focus to the road. "I've made my peace with the things we did in the service. And no," he noted as she leaned forward to speak, "I won't tell you about it right now."

"Oh." She sat back, way too much pleasure coursing through her at the idea that they had more than "right now." "Were you married while in the army?"

"No. I married Em one month after my discharge." He frowned. "She was too young. Wanted a big life in the big city. I just wanted a normal life. After the service." He turned the truck through the massive logs standing vigil at the foot of a spectacular ranch. "We had dated in high school and ran into each other my first night back. I hadn't even seen my parents yet. Tequila led to bourbon, and one thing led to another. We found out she was pregnant three weeks later." He shook his head. "Leila is the biggest blessing of my life, but I wish things had been different for Emily."

"How did she die?" Sophie kept her voice low. He was trusting in her, whether he knew it or not.

Jake sighed. "I'm not sure what happened. I knew she was unhappy here, but it could've been postpartum. It was the dead of winter and I was back east arguing a case. She asked my mom to watch the baby. Then Emily packed her bags into a little two-seater sports car I'd bought her during the summer and headed out. In a blizzard. In a summer car." His voice turned hoarse. "She slid off the road and down an incline. Doc said she was dead on impact—that she didn't suffer."

Sophie's heart clenched. "I'm so sorry, Jake." She ran a hand along his tense arm, and the muscles rippled at her touch.

Jake nodded. Then he stopped the truck in a circular drive of a two-story log home and turned toward her. "Enough bad memories. We're supposed to have fun tonight." His knuckle brushed her cheekbone. "And you're supposed to be deciding to sleep with me."

CHAPTER NINE

Tom saved Sophie from having to reply when he hurried out a massive double-wooden door and opened her truck door. She accepted his hand, and he helped her to the ground. Sophie smiled at her savior and turned to admire the large, custom log home. A wide, gleaming wood porch ran the length of the front and invited people to sit on swings or comfortable-looking chairs.

"Sophie, we're so glad you could make it." Tom gently took her elbow and led her up the porch and into the warm interior of a stoned entryway. The smell of apple pie filled the air while soft country music floated throughout.

Directly ahead, floor-to-ceiling windows showcased Mineral Lake and the surrounding mountains. A massive stone fireplace took up one wall while beautiful Western oils filled the other. Sophie took a moment to admire the deep colors of a Gollings painting of barely tamed horses stamping the snow near a jagged mountain, and then she swept her gaze around the rest of the room.

Leather couches and hand-carved wooden tables sat comfortably on a thick Native American rug. Several coloring books and a smattering of crayons scattered across the largest table, and the smell of leather and pine mixed with the apple pie scent.

An excited feminine shriek made Sophie jump when Leila flew into her with Colton on her heels.

"Help, Sophie, help me." Leila shielded herself behind Sophie's body, her tiny hands tight on Sophie's waist.

"She can't protect you," Colton growled out in a low, monster-like voice.

"Yes, she can." Leila poked her head around to stick her tongue out at her uncle. "I'll tell the sheriff on you, Uncle Colt."

Colton grabbed for her just as she dodged to the other side of Sophie, who struggled to keep her balance. "Then I'll have to tickle both the sheriff and you, squirt."

"Don't let him get me." Leila giggled from behind her.

"I'm pretty sure we can take him, Leila," Sophie said solemnly, trying not to laugh.

The game ended when Jake yanked his daughter into the air to smack noisy kisses along her face. "Is Colton picking on you, precious?" He shut the front door with a *click*.

"Yes, Daddy." Leila giggled again. "Beat him up."

"Ah, Leila, it's just too easy. A man my age needs a challenge." Jake swung her onto his back.

"A man your age needs a walker," his brother retorted. Then he turned vibrant blue eyes on her, reaching in. "Hi, Soph."

His easy hug brought a lump to her throat. They were just like the families she used to watch on television.

"Oh, hello, Sophie." Loni walked in from the left, wiping her hands on a dishtowel. "Come give me a hand in the kitchen, would you?" She nodded to the men. "The salmon isn't going to barbecue itself, boys."

Sophie grinned as the men headed through the kitchen and gathered around a humungous silver barbecue on the outside deck with Leila still perched on her father's shoulders.

"What can I do?" Sophie glanced around. Chopped vegetables sat on a large cutting board near a deep red bowl.

"Sit at the bar and keep me company." Loni nodded toward thick brown barstools on the other side of the spotless silver granite countertop. Sophie took a seat while Loni poured them both a glass of wine.

"How are the designs coming?" Loni asked while resuming her chopping.

"Great. I should have something concrete for you by tomorrow's meeting." The buttery chardonnay tasted of smooth sweetness.

Loni looked up with serious eyes. "I'm so glad. Also, the council met, and we all really like your golf course design."

"But?" Sophie steeled herself for the news.

Loni sighed. "We don't like it in that location. We've put out some feelers for alternate places. Sorry."

They were rejecting Sophie's design and not her, but her stomach rolled. "I was afraid of that. Jake already warned me the council wouldn't support the project."

"Really?" Loni raised an eyebrow.

"That's the only property the Charleton Group owns, and they're pretty determined to develop it." There *had* to be a way to convince the tribe to back the design. What if her uncle lost his business? Failure tasted like ashes.

"Well, the county commissioner meeting should be interesting, then." Loni scraped the veggies into the bowl. "Let's head out to the deck."

Sophie took a deep breath. She'd enjoy dinner with a nice family, and then go back to her room and figure out another angle. Her design could still win without the tribe's backing.

She grabbed the other salad sitting on the counter, followed Loni to the deck, and settled into a cushioned chair between Jake and Leila at the round glass patio table. The sun set to the west, spreading fingers of pink and orange across the sky. Colton sat across from her, and the disappearing sun highlighted the myriad of colors in his hair. She should've brought her oil paints.

They all dug into the fish and salad, and Loni passed homemade rolls around that smelled better than anything found in the city. After a short time, Sophie relaxed and started to enjoy the excellent meal.

The casual teasing between Jake and Colton made her laugh. Their easy camaraderie was something she'd missed, being an only child. Both brothers stilled when she asked about Dawn's absence. Apparently the girl was on a date. Maybe having older brothers had its drawbacks.

"Who is she out with?" Sophie took another sip of wine after Tom topped off her glass.

"Some college senior." Colton said the word *college* like an expletive.

Tom nodded. "She's just out with Frankston to make Hawk jealous."

"Hawk's too old for her." Jake reached over to tug his daughter's ear. She squealed and slapped him playfully before digging back into her apple pie.

Loni slid another piece of pie onto Colton's plate. "He's only a few years older."

"I wasn't talking birthdates, Mom." Jake's eyes hardened as he stared at something only he could see.

"He's a good kid." Tom pushed his plate away from himself and groaned. "But Jake's right. He's too old for our girl."

Loni grinned as Jake yanked on his daughter's braid again. "Our girl knows her own heart, boys."

"Knock it off, Daddy." Leila grinned around a mouth full of apples. "Or I'll tell the sheriff on you."

Colton frowned. "What's up with all this *telling the sheriff* talk, kid? I'm the cool uncle."

"Yeah, but Uncle Quinn has a badge. And a gun." Leila's eyes lit up as Colton sat forward.

"I'm way tougher than the sheriff," Colton said.

"Yeah, but he really loves me, Uncle Colt," Leila said.

Sophie didn't miss the sly grin Jake gave his mother.

"I love you more, baby doll," Colton said.

"Enough to give me that new pony Merriment foaled last month?" The little girl pursed her lips.

Tom guffawed in laughter. "Boy did you walk into that one, son."

"I was thinking the new foal would make a good Christmas present for a really good little girl." Colton raised an eyebrow at Jake, who gave an imperceptible nod.

"I'm really good." Leila widened her eyes to pure adorable innocence.

Colton shook his head. "Hm. I don't know."

"You'd be my favoritest uncle, Colton." The little

girl flung herself onto his lap and wrapped tiny arms around a strong neck.

Colton's eyes softened as he gazed at the little minx. "You are going to be one very dangerous woman someday, baby doll."

"Then it'd be good to be my favoritest uncle, wouldn't it?" Leila smacked his cheek with a wet kiss.

"Without question." Colton pecked her on the nose before Leila jumped down, a successful grin on her face as she returned to her seat.

So this was what families could be. Should be. A pang hit Sophie in the solar plexus.

"Speaking of the unfavoritest uncle, where is Quinn?" Colton finished off his pie.

Tom shrugged. "I heard that maybe he was dating someone from Maverick." Tom rolled his eyes at Loni.

"Her name's Juliet, and she tolt Uncle Quinn to take a flying leap," Leila piped up. All eyes swung to her and she grinned.

"I knew it!" Loni exclaimed, leaning forward. "How do you know that, sweetheart?"

"I axed him." The little girl pushed her plate away. "When me and Uncle Quinn got smoothies at the ice-cream place, Juliet was just leaving. I tolt Uncle that she was pretty and he should take her to the movies, and he said he'd already axed, but she said to take a flying leap." Leila screwed her face into a frown. "He didn't say where he was 'posed to leap to."

"The plot thickens," Colton murmured with a pointed look at his brother.

"Nah, she somehow got the gist of his sparkling personality." Jake exhaled and grinned.

Sophie shook her head. The family was so involved

with one another, whether they all liked it or not.

In too short a time, she sat in Jake's truck next to Leila as they drove her back to the B&B. They both walked her to her door, and she was grateful Jake couldn't press her for an answer to his invitation for wild sex.

She wasn't sure she would say no.

• • •

Morning arrived all too soon. Sophie drove the twenty minutes toward Mineral Lake and followed the directions to the headquarters of Concerned Citizens for Rural Development, located about halfway between town and the Kooskia Reservation. The headquarters was housed in a large metal shop with a hard-packed dirt floor lined with wooden benches. A rectangular metal table perched on a one-foot dais in the front of the room, and three matching chairs faced the crowd. A narrow podium stood over to one side, and a hand-sewn emblem of the planet adorned the wall. The smell of dirt and sweat assaulted her nose.

Her cell rang just as she walked inside the cool interior, and she quickly said hello.

"Hi, Sophie. There's a two-hour break in my trial today. Want to do lunch?" Jake asked.

She fought an involuntary smile. "Um, maybe. It depends if I'm done by then."

"Where are you?" he asked.

A woman up front waved, and Sophie started up the aisle toward the tall blonde in tan capris and a high-collared blouse. "Meeting with Concerned Citizens."

"In Mineral Lake?" he asked.

"No. About fifteen miles outside of the town," she said.

Silence filled the air for a couple of beats. "Not the Concerned Citizens for Rural Development Group."

"One and the same," she said, looking at the rows of seats.

"By yourself?" Jake's voice dropped to a low tone.

Her steps faltered. "Um, yeah."

"Soph." Exasperation lived on his exhale. "Wait to go inside."

"Too late. Have to go, 'bye." She shut the phone and dropped it into her bag before extending her hand to the woman. "I'm Sophie Smith."

"Judy Rockefeller." Classically straight features in a pale, makeup-free face frowned as they shook hands. Her mood was cool and her shake stiff.

Maybe Sophie shouldn't have come alone. "So, where do you want me?" She shook off unease while people filed into the room and took their places on the benches. If the tribe refused to back her design, she needed support from county citizens. She stepped back from Judy.

Judy pointed to the closest metal chair behind the table. "You can sit there. Reverend Moseby will sit next to you, and my husband, Billy, will sit next to him. Billy is our president."

"Okay." Sophie dropped her bag next to the seat. "Do you want me to do a presentation or just answer questions?"

Judy waved at newcomers before turning back to Sophie. "Billy will talk for a bit, and then people will ask you questions. You don't need to describe the proposal. Everyone has already studied the golf course plan from the county's records."

"The records? You mean the application for the conditional-use permit?" Sophie's stomach danced uncomfortably as several people watched her from the audience.

"Yes," Judy said.

A side door opened and two men entered, walking close. The first wore all black with a priest's collar, his belly stretching the dark fabric until streaks of white showed through. Sharp blue eyes rested on Sophie. "Miss Smith, I'm Reverend Moseby." He extended a beefy hand for her to shake, his ruddy face contrasting with his sparse white hair.

Sophie shook his hand and tried not to grimace at his dampened flesh. She unobtrusively wiped her palm on her flowered skirt upon being released.

"I'm Billy Rockefeller." The second man held out a hand and gave Sophie a firm shake. Judy's husband wore his blue jacket with a presidential pin like a Masters champion. His perfect posture hinted at an unyielding spine.

"Hi," Sophie released him to go take her assigned seat.

Billy sat as the reverend approached the podium and opened the meeting with a recap of the previous month's meeting before everyone bowed their heads to pray.

"Please bless this wondrous gathering of these wondrous people out to protect the earth itself." The reverend's voice rose in pitch and volume. "And bless our guest today. Let her see the folly of destroying the God-given earth and all its bounty. Let Christ guide us, his hand firm and deadly if need be. May the might of the Lord fill us, guide us, and pummel those who oppose us."

The group gave a collective amen as Sophie searched for the closest exit, her heart in her throat. Did he say "deadly"? The twangy song from *Deliverance* danced through her head. The reverend turned the podium over to Billy Rockefeller.

Billy stood and crossed to the podium, his black flack boots ringing loud and strong across the stage. Flack boots with a fancy jacket? Weird.

He rested both hands on the hard wood and waited with a dramatic pause before speaking. "Thanks for coming out today, folks. The first item on the agenda involves the protection of the wolves in the area."

Sophie felt the blood drain from her face when she noticed a handgun tucked casually into Billy's waistband.

He continued. "At this point, the wolves are threatening our livestock—our very livelihood. What do we do to threats like that?"

"Eliminate them," came the collective response.

Surely this wasn't a veiled threat directed toward her.

Billy nodded. "There's a court trial going on regarding the wolves near tribal lands right now. I'll let you know the outcome as soon as I can."

Sophie frowned. She felt safe disagreeing with the tribe; she felt anything but safe sitting like easy prey behind the metal table. What had she gotten herself into? She mentally shook her head. Boy, was her imagination going crazy.

Billy cleared his throat. "The second item on the

agenda involves the new development proposal in front of the county commissioners. It includes a golf course. The designer, Sophie Smith, is here today to answer any questions." He inclined his head toward Sophie.

She stood, her legs shaky. Was she supposed to go to the podium or just turn around? Not wanting to be too near Billy, she just partially turned with her back to the wall so she could see everybody.

A sandy blond–haired man with a thick goatee raised a hand, and Billy nodded at him. "I'm Fred Gregton. I'm wondering how much human life is worth to your development group?"

Sophie frowned. "I don't understand your question, Mr. Gregton."

"Of course you don't. More traffic on the road from Maverick is going to kill somebody, Miss Smith. I'm just wondering if your development group gives a shit about that," Gregton said.

A couple of people nodded.

"Well…" Sophie leaned forward, her heart beating rapidly. "It's my understanding the traffic study conducted by the developer shows that the road is fine."

"Bullshit." Gregton spat on the floor.

Sophie's temper began to stir among the fear.

Another hand went up, this one belonging to a middle-age woman in a denim jumper. "I'd like to know why you're the only one here today. Where is the developer?"

Sophie floundered for an answer. "Their headquarters is in southern California."

"Will more people go to the hearing in front of the

county commissioners?" the woman asked.

Sophie nodded. "I know one of the Group's attorneys will be there, but I haven't heard who else will attend."

"So," Gregton spoke up again as the crowd seemed to get restless, "we're not important enough for them to meet with."

"They sent me, Mr. Gregton." Just how out-of-hand would this crazy group get? It was apparent most of them were armed. Why were so many guns needed just for an informational meeting? Sophie's gaze flew to the door at the sound of hoofbeats outside. Great. More people to contend with.

Two imposing forms soon filled the doorway.

CHAPTER TEN

Sophie's stomach stopped churning as Quinn and Colton strode inside and sat on the farthest bench from the dais. They'd both dressed in dusty jeans, denim shirts, scuffed boots, and cowboy hats, obviously having been working on the ranch.

"Are you a ranch hand or the sheriff today, Lodge?" Billy asked from his podium.

Quinn tipped back his gray Stetson and slowly pulled off his leather gloves, his dark gaze meeting Billy's across the room. "I'm always the sheriff to you."

Billy flushed a deep red and glared. "I find it interesting you'd attend today."

"Why?" Colton settled back against the hard wood. "We're concerned citizens."

"Isn't the tribe opposing the development?" Reverend Mosby asked.

Quinn shrugged. "Our attorney can describe our official position when he arrives."

"Your attorney is coming?" Judy said from her seat in the front row.

"Yes. He was a bit farther away and asked us to come and save him a seat," Colton said, his eyes warm on Sophie.

Sophie's heartbeat slowed to a dull gallop. She was safe. At least for now. "Are there any more questions about the development?"

A young woman in faded calico raised her hand.

"Have you done any studies about what the development will do to the local tax base? I mean, will our property taxes increase?"

Billy answered before Sophie could. "Of course they'll go up, Jeanine. A high-end country club development with mansions right next door? We'll all pay more just so out-of-towners have a place to golf for a couple of months in the summer."

"What about the lake?" A twenty-something man with long blond hair, faded jeans, and a green flannel shirt hissed out. "Does anybody care that a golf course will do nothing but pollute Mineral Lake with fertilizers, sewer problems, and such? And what about water supply? Our wells go dry now. Add watering a golf course in, and we're screwed."

Sophie sat up and placed her hands on the table. "The plan calls for a type-one irrigation system, which basically recycles water, cleans it, and then reuses it to irrigate the golf course. Your wells won't be affected." A rumbling of disbelief filled the room as several people shook their heads. It didn't matter what she said. The crowd didn't want to hear it. Her heart sank. "Are there any more questions?"

Gregton raised his hand again, his eyes lasers through the dim light. "Yeah. How much did you pay to bribe the county commissioners this time?"

A shadow fell across the aisle as Jake asked from the doorway, "What was that?" Danger coated his voice with a softness that slammed silence into the room.

Gregton shifted in his seat, and Sophie fought the urge to cheer.

"Don't tell me you represent the commissioners

and are going to sue me for slander," Gregton sneered.

"Yes, I do. And I will sue, if need be." Jake took three steps into the room—all male animal in a deep navy suit with tan silk tie.

Gregton dipped his head toward Sophie. "You gonna sue me on her behalf, too?"

Jake's eyes darkened to coal as he ran his gaze over her from head to toe. He turned back to Gregton and slowly shook his head, his jaw tightening to iron. "No. You insult her, and we're stepping outside."

"Is that a fact?" A thick man next to Gregton clomped to his feet while two others followed suit.

"It is," Jake affirmed.

Quinn and Colton moved behind him. The three brothers formed a powerful wall that gave Sophie the first peace of mind she'd felt all day.

• • •

Jake eyed the crazy son-of-a-bitch and shoved all anger into a box to be dealt with later. It took the combination of his military training and his legal education to keep him from going for Gregton's throat. Even with a strong hold on his temper, chances were blood was going to fly.

The fanatical group used intimidation to get their way, and he doubted bloodshed would bother them much. When he'd heard Sophie had headed there alone, he'd panicked for the first time in years.

Truly panicked.

Thank goodness for his brothers. Quinn would back him in an instant, even if it meant losing his sheriff's position. Colton would fight to the end for him, too. As Sophie stood so defiantly up front, he wondered who'd fought for her in the past. Suddenly, his chest hurt.

So he smiled to reassure her that he was there for her. "This is over. Come on, Sophie."

She faltered, her blue eyes too big in her pale face. Then she pushed away from the table.

"Now there, boys," Billy said from the podium, his eyes on the crowd. "I believe we're finished with our questions for Miss Smith." He nodded her way. "Thank you for coming today." His gaze beseeched her to make a quick exit.

"Thank you for inviting me," she murmured while walking into the aisle.

Jake moved slightly to the right so she'd keep her focus on him and not on the angry people.

Relief filtered across her face, and she made it to his side without mishap. When he took her arm and ushered her toward the door, his muscles finally unwound. Several pairs of eyes bored holes into their backs as they left.

She released a pent-up breath as they walked into the sun. "I can't thank you enough."

"We're not hitting anybody?" Colton grimaced and stomped toward the chestnut stallion tied to a nearby tree.

"Guess not," Quinn rumbled as he stalked toward his own mount and lifted himself into the saddle. He smiled. "It's always interesting, Sophie."

Jake cleared his throat and tightened his grip around Sophie's bicep. "Thank you."

Both of his brothers nodded.

Sophie gave a halfhearted wave as Quinn and

Colton rode into the nearby trees. "Thanks for the support."

For now, they needed to get out of there. "Get in your car, and I'll follow you to Shiller's." Jake gave her a gentle push toward her Jeep.

Sophie escaped into the green vehicle and drove toward the main road and Jake followed, keeping a close eye until they reached Shiller's.

He was out of his truck before she'd even closed the door of her rental car. "What in the hell were you doing meeting with that crazy group all by yourself?" He knew he towered over her, and maybe frightened her, but something in him didn't give a shit. How dare she put herself in such danger?

She shifted so her back rested against the hard metal of the vehicle and shrugged. "They wanted to meet. I didn't know they were nuts."

"They're nuts," Jake confirmed. He had no right to be so angry with her—she wasn't his. Yet tension still squeezed up his throat. "*The Rockefellers* changed their name three years ago. They used to be *the Johnsons*."

"No." Sophie laughed.

Jake nodded, forcing his shoulders to relax. He had no right to yell at her.

Sophie grabbed his suit lapels with both hands. "I wasn't in any real danger, was I?"

Lust clawed through Jake's gut. If this was her way of appeasing him, it was definitely working. "Probably not. But they're a bit off."

"Yeah, I got that." She lifted smiling eyes to his. "I guess I owe you a thank-you, huh?"

Oh yeah. A thank-you sounded nice. "I guess you do."

She tugged. He complied by dipping his head. Sophie stretched to her tiptoes and pressed her lips gently against his. "Thank you." Her voice was husky as she dropped back to her feet.

"You're welcome," Jake murmured. If she thought that was the end of it, then she'd misjudged him. He lowered his head and kissed her, going deep. The woman tasted like strawberries and vanilla, and he wanted to feast for days. Maybe weeks. His hands encircled her waist to pull her against him. Finally, he let her go. "You make up your mind?"

Sophie smoothed out the wrinkles she'd caused. She kept her eyes chest level. "Still mulling it over."

Jake stepped back and released her waist before placing one knuckle under her chin and lifting it until her gaze met his. "Take your time, Soph." He'd learned patience as a lawyer and knew when to back off— which is why he always won. Sophie's acquiescence was much more important than any case he'd ever taken, and finesse was necessary. "I need to get to court. I'll call you later."

He jumped into his truck, not looking back. If he looked back, no way would he leave. The woman had to make up her own mind to come to him. When she did—then he'd take over.

•••

Saturday night arrived, and again, Sophie had once again agreed to dinner with Jake. It was as if she *wanted* to get her heart smashed.

She'd spent Friday alternating between designing the garden, playing in her sketchbook, and pondering

Jake's proposal. The time would soon come for her to make a decision. She wanted him, without question, but the last thing she needed was a broken heart.

She wore a light pink skirt with deep blue blouse for dinner, and she waited for him on the porch swing. Her new boots finished the outfit perfectly.

Tall, broad, yet somehow graceful, he approached from his truck, a sexy predator in civilized clothing.

She smiled from her perch on the swing. "I have something for you."

"What's that?" His boots made dull *thud*s as he crossed the painted wood.

She handed him the charcoal of Leila with her pretty hair in ribboned braids, her eyes sparking with spirit and intelligence as she won a new foal from her uncle. Softly rounded cheeks and delicate features hinted at the lovely woman who would one day emerge from the impish body.

The scents of natural pine and wild berries lifted the air around them as Jake accepted her gift.

"Sophie," Jake breathed, holding the thick paper at arm's length. "It's beautiful. She's beautiful. Thank you." His eyes warmed her.

He really liked her work. Delight flashed through her as she accepted his hand and walked to the truck. They drove for a while, both lost in their own thoughts, and Sophie stilled in surprise when he pulled into his long driveway.

"I'm cooking you dinner." Intimacy and something deeper wove through his words. Sophie took a deep breath. "I won't push you. Just dinner." He enfolded her hand with his larger one.

She nodded. The need to see where he lived, where

he slept, propelled her from the truck. Thick logs made a three-story home with large wraparound porch and deep green door. A massive three-car garage sat apart from the house to the right.

"That's a big house," she murmured.

Jake nodded. "It was my family's. Mom moved to Tom's when they married. I bought out my siblings when I married Emily."

"Where do your siblings live?" Sophie climbed the burnished oak steps.

"Colton plans to build a house over behind the east ridge with a great view of the lake, and Quinn already built his over on the south side next to the river. It's closer to town so he can get there in a hurry if they need the sheriff. Dawn still lives at home and hopefully will until she's forty." He opened the heavy door and gestured her inside. "We own the ranch equally, so whoever's working it takes a salary, and then we split the profits or losses."

"Wow. That's great that you guys split it so fairly." Renewed longing for a family washed through her.

"How else would we have done it?" he asked.

Sophie turned and gasped at the amazing view. While Loni's house overlooked the valley and Mineral Lake on the north side, Jake's home overlooked it from the west side. The mountains extended well into Canada in the distance.

"It's beautiful," she breathed. "I'd love to paint it."

"You should." Jake closed the door behind them. "I've seen your work. You should paint all the time."

There he went again, making her feel strong and talented. A girl could get used to such security.

She smiled at the comfortable room laid out

similarly to Loni's. Big stone fireplaces must be required during the cold Montana winters. Thick green couches, Western oils, and floor-to-ceiling windows made the house a home. She followed Jake into a pale yellow and tan kitchen and out a slider onto a huge cherry-wood deck. The glass table was set for two with the candles flickering in the twilight hour. The smell of barbecued steaks filled the air.

"Sit." Jake pulled a chair out for her, and she sat, her gaze still on the amazing view. The lake and mountains looked too still to be real. Too beautiful with the vibrant pink and orange sunset to exist naturally.

Jake brought side dishes out from the kitchen and then flipped open the barbeque lid and speared a steak for her plate. He filled his own and took a seat across from her, pouring the wine.

"This looks great, Jake," she murmured.

"So do you." His gaze roamed her face over his wineglass. Heat and interest combined into an irresistible invitation in his fathomless eyes.

Desire skipped past humming to raging within her in no time. How did he do that?

They ate in silence, comfortable in the warm night. The food was delicious.

"Are you ready for the hearing Monday night?" Jake refilled their wineglasses.

"I think so. My part is just describing the golf course and maybe the clubhouse." She took a sip of the red wine. "Are you going to be there?"

"Yes."

Her hand stilled. "Opposing me?"

"No. Opposing the location of the Charleton Group's development," he said.

"That's me." She set down her wineglass.

"No, it isn't. I want to make you happy, Sophie. But a golf course does not belong so close to Mineral Lake." His tone was firm.

Her heart hitched. "I don't like being on opposing sides from you."

Jake grinned. "Worked for Hepburn and Tracy."

She reclaimed her wineglass. The thought of sparring with him thrummed awareness through her veins. "Where's Leila?"

He leaned back in his chair. "Girls' night at Mom's." He continued at her inquisitive look. "Don't ask me. Mom, Leila, and Dawn all paint nails, do hair, eat popcorn, and who knows what else. Girl stuff."

"Sounds like fun." Wistfulness filled her tone, unbidden.

"I'm sure you could join them sometime. Though if you talk about boys, I'd trick a rundown from my daughter. Maybe my mother, too." Jake grinned.

Sophie rolled her eyes.

"Why don't you paint more? You're an amazing artist." He smoothly switched topics.

Pleasure flushed her at the compliment, but then quickly died. "Artists don't make any money, Jake. I need security, and my job provides that."

Coal-dark eyes surveyed her. "Those words don't sound like you. They're not yours, are they?"

"Of course they are." Sophie tossed her napkin on her plate and pushed back from the table. "I'll clear these for you."

One strong hand around her wrist stopped her. Then he tugged, and she lost her balance. Straight into his lap.

"I'm sorry if I upset you." His mouth was an inch from her ear. Heat and hard masculinity surrounded her, and she repressed a groan. She perched on granite-hard thighs against a too-warm chest as firm arms held her tightly. As if he'd never let go. She turned her face to meet his.

"I'm not upset." Breathiness quieted her voice.

"Whose words were they, Sophie?" His eyes held hers captive while he shifted her into a more comfortable position.

The need to confide in him swelled. "My mother's."

"Do you still believe them?" he asked.

Right now, she was finding it difficult to believe anything. To concentrate on anything but the talented lips of the man before her. She had known what would happen when she accepted his dinner invitation. She leaned forward and pressed her mouth against his, her hands splaying against firm pectoral muscles earned on the ranch.

Jake stiffened, one hand moving to cup her head and ease her back enough for their gazes to meet. "Are you sure?"

"Yes." It came out a breathless dare.

He didn't ask again.

CHAPTER ELEVEN

She met him halfway as his mouth plundered, as his tongue explored. He smoothly shifted her so she faced him, her thighs on either side of his, her core to his. One hand went to her hips and pulled her even tighter into his hardness.

They both groaned at the contact.

Strong hands deftly released the buttons of her blouse. He pressed hard kisses along her jawline and down her neck. Each touch of his lips sizzled against her skin. A wildness filled her—a sense of power she hadn't expected. He flicked her bra open with a quick movement, and her breasts spilled into the cooling night.

"So pretty," Jake murmured.

His heated mouth enclosed one nipple in heat. She gasped and gyrated against him. She was already wetter than she'd ever been.

He ran his tongue around her nipple, his teeth scraping.

Her breath caught. Reaching out, she shot both hands through his thick hair. "Let's go inside."

Releasing her, he leaned back. "No."

She opened her mouth, but no sound emerged. So much want filled her it was hard to concentrate.

He gripped her waist. Then he easily lifted her until her butt hit the table. His strength sent butterflies winging through her.

He grinned, nimble fingers reaching for her nipples.

"We need to get you out of your head, Sunshine."

She shook her head, her mind spinning, her body on fire. "No, we don't." She gasped more than said the words. The chilled glass cooling her thighs contrasted with his heated hands on her breasts.

His smile gleamed with predatory charm. "Spread your legs."

Her eyes widened. Half naked, exposed on his table, her mind rebelled. They were outside, and while his deck seemed secluded, his family or ranch hands could walk into the backyard at any time. "No."

He rolled her nipples. Pain and pleasure melded together, shooting electricity straight to her pounding clit. She gasped, her lids lowering to half-mast. Her hands lifted.

"Hands down." His order held bite, and her hands slapped the glass.

Then he tugged her breasts just enough to show he was serious. "I said, spread your legs."

Like prey in a trap, she stilled. He'd let her leave if she wanted — heck, he'd drive her home. The next moment was hers to control. If she stayed, she'd give up control to the force of nature that was Jake Lodge. His sensual gaze promised dark pleasure, but at what cost?

Need trembled through her. The man could quench the fire he'd already stoked in her. Her body leaped to life with want for his sexy promise, while her brain bellowed caution.

Screw her brain.

She panted, lifting her breasts even as he kept his hold. Licking her lips, she hesitantly, sensually, widened her knees.

He blinked. Slowly.

Her skirt rose up her thighs. Her ankles dangled on either side of his chair. Lowering her chin, she met his gaze with as much challenge as she could throw from her eyes. He wanted control? The man had better earn it.

He shot to his feet. Fast. The man was fast. Keeping her gaze, he leaned over her and shoved plates off the table. They crashed to the wooden deck, shattering. Surprised, she dropped back on her elbows and gasped.

Heat cascaded off him and onto her bare skin. Sliding his palms along her arms, he removed her shirt and bra.

She trembled.

He leaned closer, trapping her. Crimson spiraled across his high cheekbones, enhancing the dangerous hollows in his chiseled face. His calloused hands manacled her thighs.

She jerked. Desire uncoiled inside her abdomen with the force of nature. Thunder rolled in the distance, in tandem with the slamming of her heart.

Pinning her with a look, he ran his abrasive palms up the flesh of her thighs. His hips kept her open, his gaze kept her captive.

She bit back a whimper.

Pure instinct tilted her pelvis toward him.

"Hold still, Sophie," he commanded softly.

Her breath hitched. Hold still? No way. She shook her head.

"Yes." He ran a thumb along the outside of her panties.

Nerves fired to life. Her body trembled with the

urge to move. "Please—"

"No." He leaned over her and kissed from her collarbone to her jugular. "The begging comes later," he whispered in her ear.

His heated breath shivered along every nerve she owned. "W-who do you think will be begging?" she forced out.

He moved her panties and plunged one strong finger inside her.

She cried out, sparks flashing behind her eyes. Her orgasm was so close. Needing to move against him, she nearly growled in frustration as he held her still.

His finger rotated. "I believe you'll be begging." Low, guttural, his voice rasped with hunger.

A strangled moan slipped from her mouth.

"Now that's a pretty sound." He released her to tug off her panties and skirt, leaving her completely nude. Lust glimmered in his eyes as he looked his fill in the waning light. "You're stunning."

For the first time in her life, she felt stunning. Beautiful and somehow…safe.

His hand curled around her nape, gripping just hard enough to show his strength. Then he slid his rough palm down between her breasts, over her tightening abdominal muscles, to stop at her mound, his heated gaze following his touch.

She started to shake with a need that bordered on painful.

The lingering daylight faded, leaving his face shrouded in darkness. The moon lit him from behind, a strong, dangerous figure who held her captive in his spell. He was as wild as the land that had created him.

So much for safety.

He dropped back to his chair, his hand sliding under her butt.

Panic seized her. She struggled to sit up, even with her legs dangling over the table. "No—"

His thumb pressed on her clit just as his mouth found her.

She arched her back with a garbled cry. Mini-explosions rippled through her—not enough. Not even close to enough.

He licked her again. "Lay back down."

It was too much. "No—"

His hard hand slapped her clit.

The world sheeted white and went silent. She dropped on her back, lost in the erotic sensations he'd created.

His mouth found her again. A low hum against her vibrated through her entire body. She teetered on an edge, a fine, dangerous edge. More than anything in the world, she wanted to go over.

But that pinnacle lay within Jake's control. At the thought, her need spiraled even higher.

His finger entered her. Easily. Another finger—stretching her. Pain and pleasure spasmed through her. Then his rough tongue flicked and caressed her clit. Circling. Tempting and teasing. Her muscles tightened, her abdomen rolled.

He sucked.

The universe detonated. She arched her back, screaming his name. Explosions of electrical fire roared through her, sparking every nerve, shaking every muscle. Hot pleasure rippled through her and crested into waves.

He worked her, prolonging the orgasm until she

really did want to beg.

Finally, the waves settled. Her body relaxed on the table, her muscles turned to mush.

Wetness slid along her face. Her eyes fluttered open. Was she crying? No. Then she frowned. "When did it start raining?"

He chuckled, finally releasing her to stand. "The rain started a minute ago." Drawing her toward him, he lifted her against him. Her thighs settled against his hips, and she clasped her ankles behind his back as he kissed her again.

Aftershocks of pleasure rippled through her sex. More. She needed more.

He lifted his head, his grin pure sin. "Hold on."

She nodded before lowering her mouth to his neck. He tasted of salt and man—earthy and sensual. The corded muscle along his neck and jaw tempted her to nibble and nip, uncaring of their movements.

Or where he was taking her.

The scrape of a door failed to stop her exploration until the world shifted and she found herself on her back, spread out on a comfortable bedspread.

Rain glistened in Jake's darkened hair, while hunger flared in his eyes. He stood by the bed and ripped his shirt over his head.

Such raw strength hitched her breath.

She couldn't match him. A tornado couldn't match him. "Um—"

"I'll keep you safe."

He slowly drew his belt free of his pant loops, the leather whipping through with a whisper that caressed down her body. After unsnapping his jeans, he kicked free of his clothing.

She swallowed. His cock was solid and huge. He reached into a side table for protection and rolled on a condom. Settling on his knees on the bed, he lowered himself so they were flesh to flesh.

She moaned in pleasure at his heavy weight, her nipples scraping against his hard chest.

Finally, she could explore him. Hard ridges of muscle filled her palms when she ran them across his chest. He vibrated, barely civilized, barely contained.

Then, his muscles bunching, his forehead sweating, he slowly, purposefully entered her, inch by swollen inch.

"Jake, hurry up," Sophie groaned, digging her fingers into his shoulders.

"Patience." He dropped his forehead to hers. "I don't want to hurt you."

"You won't." Her words emerged garbled and breathy.

He chuckled against her lips and then kissed her deep and sure. With a hard push, he embedded himself fully in her. Man, he was big. Almost too much. "Are you all right?"

Concern from the strong, controlled man above her shot emotion straight to her heart. Right where she didn't want it to go. "If you don't move, I really am going to hurt you," she hissed.

His dimple dared her to try it. She nipped his bottom lip. His eyes darkened to liquid midnight. One hand held her hip in place. The other tangled in her hair. "You were being so good. Now you don't get to move." His hand slid around and clasped her butt.

"Not a chance." She tried to move against him.

He kept her in place.

Fire rushed down her torso.

His weight pinned her, the hand in her curls tethered her, and the hand at her butt kept her still. He was in complete control. He waited, his gaze determined, his focus absolutely on her.

At least a minute passed.

Finally, she relaxed beneath him. Obeyed his silent demand to submit. She could trust him—and she did.

He moved her against him. Then moved faster. Then started to pound. As he took over her body, he breached her last emotional shield. Heat coiled inside her, rolling outward, powerful waves lighting her nerves. She exploded. Tears filled her eyes as the intense ripples devastated her.

He thrust harder, prolonging her orgasm, filling the world with Jake Lodge. Finally, with a low growl of her name against her skin, he leaped into pleasure with her.

Exhaustion shuttered her eyes closed before he'd removed the condom and tucked her close. He smoothed a kiss against her damp forehead. "Go to sleep, sweetheart."

This was too much, but she was too tired to deal with any emotion. In the morning, she'd figure everything out, and right now, she was just going to enjoy the hard-bodied cowboy. With a sigh, she turned boneless. Warm and safe, she stretched into oblivion.

• • •

Sophie awoke to a large hand idly caressing her hair on the pillow. Her back was pressed against his broad chest, and warmth flowed around her, through her. She slowly stretched sore muscles that hadn't been used in much too long. And never like that. Jake had awoken her three other times during the wonderfully long night, and it was well worth it each time.

"Good morning." His voice rumbled with sleep.

"Morning." She snuggled into his warmth and stilled as parts of him hardened instantly. "What are you, a machine?"

He chuckled. "No. All of me just likes all of you. A lot."

"Ditto." She stretched like a lazy cat with a big yawn.

"We have to talk," he said.

Uh oh. Not exactly what a girl wanted to hear after an incredible night of sweaty sex. "'Bout what?" She masked her yawn this time.

"The condom broke," Jake said.

"Which condom?" Her brain was too fuzzy to capture his meaning.

Strong arms tightened around her. "The third one."

"Oh." Reality slammed with a *thud* as her eyes focused on the painting of a desert landscape on the opposite wall. Thick rust and orange cascaded in firm swipes illustrating hard rock. "The condom broke."

"Yes," he said.

"Inside me."

"Yes."

"Oh," she murmured.

His hand resumed playing in her curls. "How's the timing on that? You know, cycle wise?"

Her heart pretty much stopped beating. "Ah, the timing." She calculated in her head. Once and then again. "Um, the timing would be ideal if we were planning to procreate."

He stiffened behind her. Not in the good way. "Ideal, huh?"

"Yes." Dread made her limbs heavy. "But, hey. No worries to you. Really. I've got this." Could this be any more awkward?

One smooth motion had her under him. All of him. Amusement warred with intent in his eyes. "You've got this?"

"Uh, yeah." She nodded vigorously against the pillow, her face aching as embarrassment spiraled heat into her cheeks. She bravely met his gaze even as her breasts pebbled in response to his welcome weight. Condoms broke—it was possible, even in this day and age. Nothing was a hundred percent, even though people acted like condoms were. The warning was on the box, for goodness sakes.

"Sophie?" He lowered his face. His muscled body pressed her into the mattress. "Do you think you've gotten to know me during the time we've spent together?"

She groaned. Even with the recent revelation of a broken condom, her body reacted to the feeling of him against her. She fought to keep from moving against him. From stretching up into his heat. "Yes?"

Jake's jaw firmed. "If you had to guess, how do you think I'd react to your statement?"

"My statement saying that I got this?" Her voice whooshed out in a breathy whisper. She tried to concentrate on the subject at hand. Instead of the hardness caressing her flesh.

"That statement," he said.

"Um. Not so good?" she whispered.

His eyes glittered in the morning light. "Not so good," Jake affirmed.

"Ah. Sorry."

"If you are pregnant," Jake said, enunciating each word, "we will deal with it together." He pressed a hard kiss against her lips. "Got it?"

"Yes." She gave up the fight and moved against his hard erection.

His gaze was intent. "Sophie?"

"Yes?" She moved again.

"Are you trying to distract me?" he asked.

"No. I'm trying to motivate you. Is it working?" She flashed a grin.

His eyes flared, hot and bright. "Yes."

"Thank God. Use a good condom this time," she said.

CHAPTER TWELVE

Monday morning, she found a third note on her windshield. This one was even more threatening. *Last chance. You don't wanna ruin the land.* Should she tell Jake? Or the sheriff?

She stuffed the note in her purse and spent the day preparing for the hearing. She'd call Quinn the day after.

The doorbell chimed as night approached, and she flew down the stairs to keep from disturbing Mrs. Shiller, who'd gotten sick.

"Preston." Seeing Aquaman on her doorstep wouldn't have shocked her as much.

"I flew in with the Charleton Group's attorneys, grabbed a car, and came to surprise you. Surprise." Sunlight glinted off his silver watch as he leaned forward to peck her on the cheek. His beautiful suit with a Burberry tie complemented his deep eyes and wavy blond hair, and he looked as out of place on Mrs. Shiller's country porch as a scarecrow by the Eiffel Tower.

Relief filled her that she wouldn't be alone. "I'm surprised."

"I thought you could use moral support tonight." He lifted foam boards she'd stacked by the door and led her to a silver Jaguar.

Sophie handed over the remaining exhibits, sank into the front seat, and squirmed. Her uncle's company must really need the job if Preston had left a city for the country.

"You rented a Jag in Maverick, Montana?" she asked.

"There was only one, pretty lady." Preston shut her door then placed the colorful boards into the trunk of his car and climbing into the driver's seat. "We can celebrate later tonight

Her mind reeled. She had enough to worry about without hurting Preston's feelings about the cruise. No way could she go with him now, considering she'd had crazy monkey sex with Jake Lodge last night. "I'm sure I can catch a ride home. I think my friend Loni will be there."

Thunder rumbled in the distance as Preston maneuvered the sleek vehicle through the windy road past town. "How have you managed this last week? I thought I was kidding when I asked how it was being in the middle of nowhere." A hard rain began pelting the car, and he flipped on the wipers.

"It's peaceful here." How could he not see how quaint and safe the town was?

A jagged arc of lightning lit the forest on either side of the narrow road and belied her words. "So is the moon, but I don't want to live there," Preston said tersely. "The casino is on the other side of the reservation?"

"Another twenty miles on the way to North Dakota." Sophie shivered in her white summer suit as the night grew even darker outside the purring vehicle.

"I did some checking and the tribe wants to build its own golf course on the other side of the land, away from the lake. They're supposed to break ground in the next few months," Preston said.

Her saliva dried up in her mouth. "Are you sure?"

"Yes," he said.

If Jake was fighting her for monetary reasons and not "for the land," she'd kick his butt.

"Why don't you fly home with me tomorrow? The commissioners might not make a decision for another week." Preston wrenched the wheel to the left as a branch crashed into the road, scattering green pine needles all around.

"Actually, I thought I'd stay. I was hired to design a memorial garden and should be able to finish it this week." She'd come up with a great plan and couldn't wait to share it.

"Hired? By whom?" Preston asked.

"My friend Loni."

Preston stiffened. "Is she from Maverick?"

"No. She's on the tribal council," Sophie admitted.

"Sophia. They're on the opposite side of us on this," Preston drawled.

Just because the tribe opposed one of her clients didn't mean the tribe couldn't also be her client. Plus, she wanted to create that garden. "They're not involved in the golf course design. The tribe is a separate entity, just like any other citizen, and it happens to oppose the proposal. It's not us against the tribe…"

"Are you sure about that? I heard their lawyer is ruthless." Preston's knuckles whitened on the steering wheel.

"Jake Lodge." Just saying his name skittered heat across her lower belly.

"Yes. Jake Lodge."

City lights came into view, and Sophie shook her head. "Jake isn't like that." He couldn't be. He was a good guy.

"You sound like you know him, Sophia." Preston's voice lowered to a timbre she'd never heard before.

She shifted uncomfortably in her plush seat. "For the love of Pete. Would you please stop calling me Sophia?"

"That's your name," Preston said.

"I go by Sophie." She hunched her shoulders, feeling like an idiot for not complaining sooner.

"Why didn't you ever say something?" he asked.

"I don't know. Sophia sounded right coming from you." Until Jake Lodge came into her life.

"What is going on with you, Soph…ie?" Preston parked in front of the brick County Justice Building. Fat raindrops plopped onto the windshield, and the wind rattled against the glass.

Sophie could only shrug as she jumped out of the car and looked up at the five-story stately brick building presiding over Main Street. Preston retrieved the exhibits from the trunk, and they dashed inside the double doors.

She smoothed her white pencil skirt as her tan pumps clacked on the wood floor while she followed signs to the public meeting room. Her stomach dropped at the sheer number of utilitarian blue chairs lined up in rows.

Preston waved to two men seated at a long table and nudged Sophie in their direction. She skirted the rows of chairs and strode toward them.

"Miss Smith." Oliver Winston stood and smiled. Sophie shook his hand, having met the Charleton Group's managing partner several times while creating her design. Stateliness defined him in his burnished brown suit with D&G loafers, and his Rolex shot prisms of light around the room. His red tie appeared to be hand-sewn silk.

"This is Niles Jansten, our attorney." Jansten took her hand in a firm grip—almost too firm. His shrewd brown eyes were set in an aristocratic face, and he smiled perfectly bleached white teeth. His silk tie screamed luxury. His eyes roamed from her eyes to her breasts and Sophie removed her hand. She gave a silent prayer of thanks she was seated between Preston and Oliver.

Niles said, "First I'll introduce the development, and then Miss Smith will show her design to the commissioners. They may or may not ask questions at that time. Then the public will testify. Most will babble on about how development, any development, is bad. The commissioners have heard it all before." He gave Sophie a quick once-over and she fought an irritated shiver. "Then I'll have a few minutes to rebut all of that and we're off."

"What about the tribe?" Oliver murmured.

Niles tapped his watch. "Either they'll all testify with the public, or just one representative will testify on behalf of the entire tribe. It could go either way."

"I think their attorney will be testifying." Preston turned to watch the public file in and take seats.

"Oh good. A country lawyer to deal with. Can't wait," Niles sneered under his breath.

Preston raised an eyebrow at Sophie. "Not so sure Jake Lodge is an ordinary country lawyer, Niles."

"We'll see. Please tell me he'll be wearing cowboy boots," Niles muttered.

"Actually, I've seen him in slate gray Armani."

Sophie kept a smile plastered on her face. "Though I doubt we'll see that tonight."

"Why not?" Niles asked.

She crossed her sandaled feet under the table. "The crowd is small town. The commissioners will be as well, I assume."

Preston nodded next to her. "Good point. We're overdressed, aren't we?"

"I'm not." She nodded toward a group of newcomers. "There's Jake Lodge." Chocolate Dockers over buffed brown cowboy boots showed long and lean legs. His crisp white dress shirt with red tie emphasized his tanned face and strong jawline, while his navy sports coat accentuated his muscled torso. His jet-black hair was tied back at the nape, giving him a primitive appearance. His brothers, Hawk, the chief, and his parents filed in behind him, along with several other members of the tribe.

"He certainly has presence." Preston settled back in his chair and laid a casual arm along the back of hers.

Coal-black eyes instantly shot their way. Sophie straightened in her seat and her heart dropped to her stomach. Jake said something to his family, his gaze holding hers across the room. The others began to take their seats.

Jake started forward, forging a path directly toward them.

CHAPTER THIRTEEN

Several people nodded to Jake, but nobody attempted to stop his forward movement. Sophie couldn't blame them. The look in his eyes warned of determination, and she had the oddest urge to ask Preston to remove his arm from her chair.

"So that's how it is," Preston murmured. "I had a feeling…"

Energy emanated around Jake when he reached her table. "Did you drive here in that storm, Sunshine?"

"No, I drove her." Preston stood and extended a hand. "Preston Jacoby."

"Jake Lodge." The men shook hands. There was no question they were sizing each other up. "I played the Mintwell Island course you designed outside of D.C. It was a great challenge," Jake said.

"Thanks. You like a challenge, Lodge?" Preston smiled.

Jake showed his teeth. "Haven't lost one yet."

"There's always a first time." The men released each other.

Jake nodded. "Not now. Stakes are too high, sport."

Sophie's stomach dropped. They weren't talking about the golf course anymore. If they ever had been.

Jake turned to the other men. "You must be Oliver Winston and Niles Jacoby."

Surprise flashed across Niles's face. "You do your research, Mr. Lodge."

"Of course." Jake dismissed the men with a quick grin at Sophie. "Good luck with your presentation." He moved away after saying to Preston, "I'll make sure she gets home tonight." He returned to his family and took his seat.

Loni waved at Sophie and mouthed, *Good luck*. Colton gave her a wide grin, Quinn nodded, and the chief winked. Several other people she had met at the branding picnic filed into the room. Ignoring the knotting in her stomach as people filled the room to capacity, Sophie waved back.

Three county commissioners entered through a side door. First came Madge Milston, a pretty white-haired ex-librarian, then Jem McNast, a silver-haired farmer from outside Maverick, and finally Jonny Phillips, the retired high school football coach.

Madge introduced the board and set forth the rules for the hearing. Then she called Niles to the podium.

"He's good, isn't he?" Preston whispered about halfway through the presentation. Sophie nodded. Niles's lengthy PowerPoint presentation illustrated the Group's other developments as well as the economic advantages it had brought to other areas. He showed beautiful homes, golf courses, and views. Finally, he turned the podium over to Sophie.

Her knees wobbled. Taking a deep breath, she stood and maneuvered around chairs to the front of the room. Squaring her shoulders, she placed exhibits that showed the layout of the golf course, the club-house, and some possible home sites on the easels behind the podium. She gave a quick speech, recapping what Niles had said.

She answered the board's questions regarding

setback requirements, golf course maintenance, and preservation of indigenous trees.

"Did you draw those, young lady?" Commissioner Phillips asked, pushing his spectacles up on his nose while pointing to the detailed drawings of the eighteenth hole and clubhouse.

"Yes, I did, Commissioner," she said.

"They're just beautiful, dear." Commissioner Milston smiled. "I heard you're designing the garden for Willa."

Sophie's spine prickled with awareness. "Yes, Commissioner," she said slowly.

"You know, we should have a nice garden on the other side of Maverick, don't you think?" Madge Milston asked the other two members of the board, both of whom nodded instantly.

"Well," Sophie said, scrambling to stay on topic, "both the golf course development and a community garden would draw tourists to the area, not only for day trips but for longer periods of time."

"That is so true," Commissioner Phillips agreed. "We'll have to get together and see what kind of funds we can obtain." He coughed. "Do you plan on having those pretty fish ponds at Willa's Garden?"

"Um, yes." She disliked losing control of the meeting, although being treated like one of the community tickled her. She cleared her throat. "Commissioners, if there are no more questions about this design, I'll turn the podium over to the public."

The board nodded, and Sophie escaped back to her seat. She didn't need to look to know Jake's amused eyes tracked her progress.

Several members of the public asked for a halt to

all development. Some complained the golf course was too far from town, while others argued it was too close and would cause traffic problems. The Concerned Citizens Group sat toward the back, and only Billy Rockefeller testified about the perils of government control and why Montana needed a citizens' militia. The board looked as if it had heard it all before.

Finally, Jake's name was called.

He strolled like a lazy panther to the podium, all grace and confidence. An unwelcome hum whispered through Sophie's blood. The hum pooled in a very private area as memories from her time in his bed flashed through her mind.

"Commissioners, I'm Jake Lodge, and I represent the Kooskia Tribe tonight." He placed a stack of papers on the podium, but his earnest gaze stayed on the commissioners. "The tribe opposes the development. First, as you know, we own Mineral Lake just below the proposed site." Several tribal members nodded their heads in the audience. "Now, the last thing we would ever want would be to sue the county for allowing a development to pollute the lake."

Sophie tensed. Jake's threats chilled her desire.

"Damn," Preston breathed next to her. "He did not just threaten to sue the entire county if the development is approved."

The commissioners straightened to focus on his testimony. "Jake, are you really saying you'd sue the county?" Commissioner Milston looked down her librarian nose at him, and Sophie fought a smile. Retirement hadn't diminished that look at all.

"You know we take preservation of Mineral Lake very seriously, Commissioner. You bet we'd sue the county, as well as the developer and every applicable land owner, should the lake be threatened."

"Young man, I don't appreciate being threatened," Commissioner Phillips noted.

Jake smiled. "I understand, Commissioner, but I had an excellent football coach who once taught me that hiding your game plan wasted time. It was better to lay it out there, show your strengths, and you'd know right off where you stood in battle. It's a lesson I took straight to the Supreme Court."

Commissioner Phillips's eyes warmed, and his lips twitched into a grin.

Jake turned toward Commissioner Milston. "A savvy librarian once chastised me for tricking a girl into the back stacks. She told me that if I wanted to kiss a girl, I should just say so and not create a story. That way the girl could make up her mind and I'd know the attraction was mutual."

He turned then, his gaze warming on Sophie for a heartbeat. She swallowed, unable to move.

Then he focused back on the county commissioners. "I'm just saying what's what so the county isn't surprised by future repercussions."

He turned to Commissioner McNast while Milston smiled at him in exasperation. "Also, I spent more than one very hot, very tiring summer moving watering pipes to irrigate fields of hay and wheat while learning to respect the land around us." Jake grinned, all charm. "Those pipes didn't have wheels like they do today. It was unhook, lift, move, and hook again."

A couple of knowing laughs came from the audience.

"But," Jake said, turning serious, "I learned that if

you pay attention, the land will show you what's right. Geography will show you where to place the pipe, where the water needs to spray. In this case, we need to look at the land and preserve it for future generations. I know Mineral Lake is as important to Maverick County as it is to the tribe." Several heads nodded. "Besides the lake, the tribe has serious concerns with this particular developer."

Sophie's stomach dropped. Thank goodness she was sitting.

"What do you mean, Jake?" Commissioner Milston pulled papers closer to her face.

"I mean that the Charleton Group is known for pitching one design and then building another once a permit has been granted." He punched in a couple of keys on the computer next to him and a golf course design came up on the big screen in the corner. "This design shows a golf course with homes set every acre apart and was approved in Michigan three years ago." He hit a couple of buttons. "This is the actual development." It was still a golf course, but four-story condominiums lined the sides. Jake showed three more examples, all with the same result. "All of these were developed by the Charleton Group." A muted gasp arose from the crowd.

Then Jake turned to Sophie. "Miss Smith's golf course is beautiful and is designed for homes to be scattered every two acres, right?"

Sophie nodded, fighting the urge to push back from the table. To put distance between herself and the man commanding the podium. Sharp hurt angled through her chest.

"Now, Miss Smith, would your design work if

condominiums replaced the homes?" he asked.

All eyes turned to Sophie, but she only saw the black ones pinning her. He was hard and cold. Determined. A slow anger started to build between her shoulder blades and pushed the hurt aside. For now.

"Miss Smith?" he asked again.

How dare he put her on the spot like this? Every muscle tightened in her body, her eyes shooting sparks at his. They'd shared a bed. The things she'd let him do to her! "My design includes homes every two acres."

"I understand that." His voice gentled. "That wasn't my question. I asked you whether or not your design would work with condominiums."

Sophie was silent for a moment as she struggled for the right answer. His look told her he'd wait all night. Her chin lifted. They were so freaking done. "No. My design would not work with condos."

"Why not?" he asked.

The bastard. He was going to get her fired. But the truth was the truth, and she wouldn't lie to the county. "The setbacks would be off. The golf course is designed to complement the lake, which would be blocked by condominiums." Strength infused her voice as she met his challenge. No way would she let him see the pain he'd just caused. She'd trusted him.

"Did you know?" His voice lowered even more. They could've been the only two people in the entire room.

"Know what?" She didn't like this Jake. The same mouth that had explored her the other night was set in a firm, uncompromising line. He looked big. And dangerous. Exuding a threatening undertone of anger if she answered wrong.

"Did you know that Charleton usually altered designs?" he asked.

"Of course not." How could he think that? Hurt made her sway in her chair. She'd looked over many of their finished projects, and that had never happened. But they'd commissioned tons of designs, and she surely hadn't studied them all.

Niles jumped to his feet. "We've had enough of this slander. I can assure you, Mr. Lodge, you can expect a lawsuit from this."

Jake's eyes didn't leave Sophie's face as he replied, "Truth is an absolute defense to slander. In other words, bring it on." Then he gathered his papers, nodded at the commissioners, and retook his seat.

Niles turned toward the commissioners. "The tribe opposes our development because it wants to build a golf course over by the casino."

Commissioner Milston turned toward Jake. "Is that true, Jake?"

Jake stood. His voice easily reached around the room, even without the microphone at the podium. "I stated why the tribe opposes the project, Commissioner. It's bad for the land, and a shady developer is bad for the county."

Preston hissed out breath as Jake continued. "However, as you are well aware, the tribe has made no secret of its plans for the casino, hotel, and golf course. We do plan to put in a golf course." He flicked a glance their way. "I'm sure you are also aware that two, even three, golf courses in close proximity actually benefit them all. We'd like to be a golf course haven. People could stay at the hotel for several days and play several different courses."

"Bullshit," Niles muttered under his breath as he sat.

Sophie clasped her hands together under the table to keep them from shaking. To keep anyone else from seeing them shake.

"Still think he's a nice guy?" Preston whispered dryly.

"Is he right about the condominiums?" she asked under her breath.

"Not to my knowledge, but we'll definitely have to follow up on this," Preston said.

Madge banged a gavel and said they would issue a decision within a week. They stood, and the crowd began to mill around Jake, everyone talking at once.

"You have to get me out of here," Sophie whispered to Preston.

"Of course," he said.

Loni suddenly appeared across the table. "Oh, there you are, Sophie. I drove myself in today. Would you mind driving home with me? I came in earlier to do some shopping and didn't know the storm was coming. I'll drive, but I really can't see very well at night and the boys all brought their own cars. I just don't want to go alone." Guileless brown eyes beseeched her.

When Preston started to speak, Sophie held up a hand. "Of course I'll drive with you, Loni. Let me grab my exhibits and we'll go." Loni was safe. Sophie needed time to think. Time away from Preston—and Jake.

"I'll help." Loni hurried over to the easels.

Sophie turned to Preston. "It's okay. I'll call you tomorrow."

"Are you sure?" he asked.

"Yes." She had to get out of there before Jake escaped from his admirers.

"If you're certain. Don't worry, Sophie. It'll all work out." Preston dropped a light kiss on her forehead.

The fury leaping into Jake's dark eyes across the room snared Sophie's gaze. She instinctively moved away from Preston and toward the exhibits. "Let's go," she whispered to the older woman. With a concerned look at her son, Loni let Sophie tug her out a side exit while Jake was stuck in the crowd.

Sophie breathed a sigh of relief when they were finally alone on the road home.

As Loni maneuvered the car onto the freeway, Sophie watched the flicker of lights across her friend's face.

"I'm not sure what I should say," Loni said softly, her eyes intent on the wet asphalt.

"There isn't anything to say," Sophie returned.

Loni's hands tightened on the wheel. "He was just doing his job," she said.

"It was more than that," Sophie muttered.

"It *was* more than that." Loni sighed. "Jake, his heritage, it's so important to him. Mineral Lake and the land, plus the future of the tribe. He's a fighter, my Jake is."

Sophie's nerves jerked until she wanted to puke. "The tribe is everything to him."

"Not everything. Family is right up there. Of course, the two usually combine," Loni said.

Sophie stared miserably out the window as drops of rain began to fall again. His heritage was everything to him, and he'd really turned into a shark at that meeting.

She didn't know the real Jake Lodge at all. One day he was a gentle cowboy who cooked her dinner and made love to her. The next he became the cold, methodical lawyer, taking the Charleton Group apart piece by piece. Or was he the powerful cowboy controlling a wild stallion with his thighs? Whoever he was, the man would win. Would do anything to win.

She just couldn't be pregnant. She couldn't have a man like that in her life controlling her. Controlling her baby. What was she even worrying about? It was one broken condom. The idea that she'd be pregnant was crazy, and she needed to just relax and forget about it. She needed to forget about Jake, too.

She didn't notice as Loni stopped at the B&B.

"Will you be okay tonight?" Loni asked.

"I'll be fine. Thanks for the ride," Sophie said woodenly as she grabbed her exhibits from the backseat and ducked into the rain. She kept her head down against the deluge as she crossed the walk and climbed the steps to the front door. After she turned to wave, Loni flashed her lights and headed down the road. She put her boards on the porch, shifted to unlock the door, and jumped when a voice interrupted her thoughts.

"Running, are we, Sunshine?" Jake asked from the darkness.

CHAPTER FOURTEEN

Sophie pivoted, safe from the rain beneath the porch overhang. The shadows sat comfortably across the hard planes of Jake's face, his back against the porch swing, his long legs extended to cross at booted ankles. He was relaxed, a predator surveying its prey. "I think we should talk, don't you?

"No, I really don't think so." She turned back toward the door and stiffened as the swing moved. Hurt and fury commingled until she wasn't sure what she'd do. "How did you beat us here?"

"Back roads. My mom drives slowly… I don't."

She'd kick him in the groin. Yeah. Good plan. "Whatever. Go away," she said.

"It was business." He stood right behind her, his breath warming the top of her wet head.

"Baloney." She didn't turn around.

"Maybe not completely," he admitted.

Her breath fogged the square pane of window. A part of her wanted his reassurance that their night together mattered. "You didn't have to put me on the spot."

"No, but I knew you'd tell the truth and that most of the crowd already liked and trusted you," he said.

An unwelcome warmth spiraled through her. She was such a dope. "Sounds like a calculating, strategic move, Jake."

"Maybe." His hand latched on her elbow and swung her around. "But it was the truth."

"Was it? How about the tribe's golf course? Afraid of a little competition?" Fury heated her face and cascaded down her spine.

"Not in the slightest." His calm demeanor was going to get him punched. "I meant what I said. An additional golf course would only draw more tourists to the area. Look at Coeur d'Alene, Idaho. There are at least nine golf courses within fifteen miles of one another; some you can see across the lake from others. I told you our reasons for opposing your project."

"Why didn't you tell me the tribe planned a golf course?" she asked.

His chin lowered. "I am a lawyer, darlin'."

"Yeah, well, I must have forgotten that." Sophie jumped as thunder rumbled directly overhead and gusts of wind sprayed rain at them. It matched the fury screaming through her blood. She gestured toward the rainy night while jerking her hand from his grip and stomping a safe distance away. "Even the weather worked to your advantage—I saw your mother home."

"Thank you. I believe she was trying to help you." Rain dripped from the rapidly curling hair across his forehead. The scent of man and musk filled the space. "You think I control the weather now?"

"No." Sophie squeezed the water out of her wet curls. "I'm sure you'd like to control even the weather, but that seems to be out of your reach."

"*You're* not," he said in a low timbre.

"Not what?" she asked.

A swift arm grasped her and yanked her into his hard body. "Out of my reach."

Sophie put both hands on his chest and pushed. Hard.

His only reaction was a slow, dangerous smile that set her heart sputtering. "Brute strength isn't how you'll get what you want."

"Oh, but it is for you?" Her hands clenched with the need to belt him.

A nonchalant shrug and raised eyebrow belied the seriousness of his gaze. "If need be."

"Meaning what?" His hands burned through her linen jacket and matched the heat flowing through her blood. Her body thrummed to life, her nipples peaking in contrast to the anger rippling through her. What was wrong with her?

"Meaning…" His hands tightened imperceptivity on her upper arms as his face dipped to within an inch of hers. "If Preston puts his mouth on you again, he'll be gumming his food for the immediate future."

"Y-you wouldn't."

"Wouldn't I?" His gaze hardened ever further as one hand lifted to tangle in her wet curls.

Erotic tingles cascaded along her scalp. The man was beyond male. Primitive and powerful.

A satisfied glint lit his dark eyes as he gave one short nod. "I don't share. You would do well to remember that."

She couldn't help it. He'd done nothing but push her all night, and she was just done thinking. Done trying to do the right thing. Just done. Going on instinct, she grabbed his shirt and leaned up, kissing him as hard as she could.

He paused for one second. Then his mouth took over. He wasn't gentle. And he wasn't sweet.

The kiss was all fire, depth, and strength. Desire speared directly south through her as one broad hand went to the front of her blouse and snapped the buttons free. She groaned as his mouth abandoned hers to trail hard, sharp kisses along her jawline and down her neck before both hands ripped her shirt apart. He roughly cupped her bra-covered breasts.

Then he paused. "Are you sure?"

"Yes." She pushed into his hands, groaning at the contact. "I'm sure."

One quick flick of a finger and the front clasp opened, spilling her flesh into waiting hands. Into warm hands that instantly, expertly, molded her to him.

This was crazy. The road may be quiet this time of night, but anybody could drive by. Oh, she could stop him, but nothing in her wanted to do so.

His head dipped. Liquid heat engulfed her nipple, and she cried out. How was his mouth so hot? His tongue flicked her even as his hands manacled her hips to hold her in place. Jake was all fire.

Suddenly, she was lifted into the air. Her shoulders smacked against the wall. She wrapped her legs around his hips as the rough wooden planks of the old house scratched her back.

She should be yelling at him. But need—a dangerous, dark, primal need—had her in its grasp. Or maybe she'd jumped headfirst into desire. Either way, she was tired of thinking. Tired of being alone. Tired of taking the safe route.

She yanked his shirt over his head. Dark smoothness filled her aching palms. She ran them urgently over the tight muscles of his chest. He was hard. And strong. Everywhere she was soft. Even with her head spinning, she marveled at the differences between them. Wanted more. Wanted everything.

He'd hurt her at the hearing. A feminine part of her needed reassurance…needed to know she mattered. But even deeper, a hunger uncoiled inside her that only Jake Lodge could appease.

So he damn well would.

She stiffened when he snapped her thong in two. His hand found her, and she bit her lip. He cupped her, his index finger sliding easily into her heat. Mini-explosions rippled through her sex.

A soft gasp escaped her lips to echo in the night. She leaned her head against the ridges of the wall, her eyes fluttering shut. Her hairclip dropped to the floor, and her hair tumbled free. "Don't stop," she breathed.

"Didn't plan on it," he said, rough and amused.

She almost swore as his hand left her aching, needing more. Then she helped him make short work of his pants and boxers before he shifted and impaled her against the wall.

"Oh God," Sophie whimpered.

He more than filled her. The vein in his shaft pulsed deep inside her. One hand seized her ass, holding her in place. The other hand threaded through her hair and twisted.

Her neck elongated, while she clawed his rock-hard shoulders.

His broad chest lifted as he inhaled slowly. Nearly nose-to-nose, he caged her in place, his body warming hers. A small scar near his ear gave him an even more dangerous edge. Even his ridiculously long eyelashes only served to enhance the hard angles of his face. The firm set of his jaw matched the determined glint in his midnight eyes.

"Now we talk," he said very softly.

A shiver wound down her spine. Her sex gripped his cock, and her thighs undulated with the need to move. Fast and hard. "No. No talking." Not while he was inside her, slowly killing her.

His absolute focus landed on her, gaze piercing hers. "I'm sorry if I upset you at the hearing."

No way. He did not get to slam inside her, until all she wanted was him to move, and then apologize. "Fuck you, Lodge," she gasped out.

Amusement creased his cheek. "In a minute."

She coughed out a laugh. "Don't be cute."

"I can't help it." He pulled out and then slid back in. Sparks of intense pleasure lit her from inside. "I'm sorry I hurt your feelings."

"If you truly hurt me, I'll destroy you." The man had just been doing his job—and he hadn't really come after her, just the Charleton Group. She squeezed her internal walls around his shaft.

His nostrils flared. "I think that's fair, sweetheart." He started to move.

She tightened her hold, lifting her pelvis. Sensation after sensation rammed against her clit. Her eyes closed. Sparks flashed behind her lids.

He increased his speed, easily holding her in place. His strength impressed her. His hands entranced her. But the tension spiraling deep inside stole every thought from her mind. She wanted what he promised. It was the light at the end of a railroad tunnel—the final plunge of a roller coaster—the slash of yellow through deep gray clouds.

It was so close.

Plunging even harder into her heated core, Jake

gave her what she sought when his mouth took her nipple. With a sharp nip of his teeth, Sophie's world spun away from her. From reality.

She cried out his name as the orgasm beat through her with merciless intensity, as she saw stars. Jake followed her into oblivion with a groan that sounded like her name. His head dropped to the curve of her neck, dripping cool rain down her back in contrast to the heated lips claiming the area between her neck and shoulder.

Sophie came down from bliss to the smell of rain, pine, and man. She lifted heavy eyelids and masculine satisfaction met her gaze without apology.

She shivered as the cold wall along her back and buttocks permeated her fog. Jake lowered her to the floor, then pulled her skirt back into place. Sophie stood motionless as big, gentle hands fixed her bra and straightened her shirt. The sweet kiss he placed on her swollen lips shot tears to her eyes.

"I'm not letting you go, Sophie," he murmured.

"Yes, you are." There was no half loving Jake Lodge. He was an all-or-nothing type of guy. She couldn't take the risk. She pushed back with both hands.

This time, he moved. "Meaning?"

"This is over," she said, aftermaths of her orgasm still rocketing through her.

A raised eyebrow met her declaration.

"I mean it." Her mind spun as her heart ached. "I am leaving. We just had sex on a porch, without protection. Again."

Jake straightened. "We did."

"At this rate, there's no way I won't get pregnant.

We're done. You said it yourself—we'd have some fun until I left."

"You're not leaving yet," he said slowly.

"I don't care. It's wild and exciting but…I don't want to get hurt. I'm not made for this." It was way past time to protect her heart. Though something told her that it was too late. Way too late.

Jake's eyes softened in the dim light. "You might be pregnant."

"Please. Stastically, it's improbable. Even so, we'll deal with that if and when." She felt small and vulnerable in the dark night.

"It'll be all right." Promise whispered through his deep voice as he turned her toward the door, shielding her from the storm. "I promise."

CHAPTER FIFTEEN

Preston's phone call woke Sophie from a dead sleep the next morning. She blinked at the early morning light as it hazed through gauzy curtains. She reached for the cell, her mumbled "Hello" nearly a hiss.

"Hi, Sophie." The sounds of traffic and people filled the background. Preston raised his voice. "We're at the airport on the way back to San Francisco, and I just wanted to call and let you know."

"What's the plan?" She sat up and placed her back against the brass bedrail. Curls tumbled forward and she swatted them out of her eyes.

"We have a late afternoon meeting with the rest of the Charleton Group. Niles wants to discredit Jake Lodge before the commissioners make up their minds."

Unease folded Sophie's hand into a fist. "Do you think he'll be able to do it?"

"No," Preston said flatly. "I researched the guy. Lodge is solid." He paused for a couple of beats. "He seems like one of the good guys."

"I'm not so sure about that," she murmured.

"If you need anything, and I mean anything, promise you'll call. Until you give me a definitive answer, I'm keeping the booking on the cruise. Things will look better once you're home where you belong," Preston said.

"I will, thanks." She disengaged the call and got out of bed. The sooner she finished with Willa's Garden, the sooner she could get home. She grabbed her toiletries and headed for the shower.

An hour later, Sophie crept quietly down the hall, not wanting to wake Mrs. Shiller.

"Hello there, dear." Mrs. Shiller poked her bespectacled face out of the kitchen at the bottom of the stairs. "I have huckleberry pancakes and fresh coffee coming up."

Sophie inhaled the sweet aroma of the purplish fruit filling the air as she descended the steps. She walked into the kitchen and took a seat at the large wooden table. Five places with delicate Prince Edward floral china perched atop linen placemats.

"Are we getting more guests?" she asked while pouring herself a cup of coffee from the old blue cast-iron pot.

"I have some friends coming for breakfast." Mrs. Shiller bustled around the kitchen. "I hope that's okay? I'm known for my hotcakes." A pretty pink blush filled her papery face as she placed butter and syrup on the table.

"The more the merrier," Sophie said. Nothing like coffee and pancakes to brighten a girl's day.

Voices filled the entryway in the other room. "Oh good, here they are." Mrs. Shiller smiled as Commissioner Milston and a tall, slender woman entered the room. "Sophie, you know Commissioner Milston, and this is our friend Juliet Montgomery."

"Call me Madge," the commissioner said with a soft smile as she took a seat at the table.

"Okay, Madge," Sophie agreed slowly. "I'm not sure we can really talk until you render a decision."

"Oh, of course we can talk. Just not about your golf

course proposal." Madge helped herself to some coffee. A black silk tank top sat comfortably over black silk shorts and red sandals. She looked more like the sexy type of retired librarian than the stodgy one.

"Well, that makes sense." As much as anything else did these days.

"It's nice to meet you," Juliet murmured as she took a seat. She looked to be in her twenties with red hair and deep blue eyes. She wore a long flowered skirt, blue peasant blouse, and dangly silver earrings. A silver Celtic knotted pendant hung from a thick silver chain around her neck.

"Here we go." Mrs. Shiller set an overflowing platter of pancakes in the middle of the table. "Dig in, ladies. Loni is running late this morning."

"Loni is coming?" Sophie accepted the platter from Juliet. She dropped three cakes onto her plate before passing it to Madge. "Why do I have the feeling this is more than friends gathering for breakfast?" Had she and Jake been seen last night? Making love against the house?

"Well, it isn't," Mrs. Shiller twittered as she sat next to Madge. "There's really no reason to turn bright red, Sophie. My goodness. Are you all right?"

"Fine," Sophie choked out while grabbing her coffee cup for a deep swallow. She was saved from scrutiny by the front door banging shut. Though it wasn't Loni who strolled in.

"Why, Sheriff, what a pleasant surprise." Madge smiled.

"Yes, would you like to join us for pancakes?" Mrs. Shiller moved to rise from the table.

"No thank you, Mrs. Shiller." Quinn gestured for

the older woman to sit. "I have a meeting with Fish and Game in five minutes but wanted to give Miss Montgomery these papers." He extended a stack of official-looking papers to the young woman sitting as if frozen at the table.

Crimson covered Juliet's pretty face as she accepted the stack. "Thank you, Sheriff."

Sophie felt for the woman but was relieved to be out of the limelight. Today Quinn looked like a tough country sheriff should. Long and lean with faded jeans, gray cowboy boots, and a thick blue button-down shirt open at the collar that emphasized his deep black eyes. A mean-looking gun rode his hip, appearing for all the world like it belonged just there.

"Are those the reports on the break-in?" Mrs. Shiller leaned forward.

"Yes." Juliet glanced at the papers. "Have you arrested anybody?"

Quinn shook his head. "Not yet, but we have two suspects in custody. A couple of kids from Billings looking for quick money to buy drugs. We're waiting for one to crack." He ran a hand through his hair. "Read those over, sign your statement if it's correct, and we'll meet up later today to talk about it." He turned toward the door.

"Actually, I'll just give them to Loni after our meeting today," Juliet said, her eyes still on the paper.

Quinn stopped at the kitchen doorway and turned, one dark eyebrow raised, his square jaw set hard. In that moment, Sophie could see the resemblance between the brothers. "No. Be at my office at noon, Juliet." Then, he was gone.

Sophie broke the uncomfortable silence hanging in

Quinn's wake. "He reminds me of his brother."

"Pain in the butt," Juliet said with an eye roll.

"Exactly." Sophie shared a grin with the redhead. Odd as it seemed, in that moment, she made a friend.

"Well, I wouldn't mind having that kind of a problem." Mrs. Shilling tittered, her eyes on her pancakes.

"Amen, sister," Madge agreed with a grin as she dug in. "Though I'm sorry about the break-in at the gallery, Juliet. Were many paintings taken?"

Sophie swallowed a bit of huckleberry flavored heaven. "What gallery?"

"Yes. I own the Maverick Art Gallery." Juliet wiped her mouth on a frilly napkin. "I lost one painting and one statue. Hopefully they'll be recovered."

"You were at the gallery during the break-in?" Sophie asked, her eyes wide.

"Well, not really. I have a small apartment above it, so I was at home. Didn't hear a thing, either." Juliet returned to her breakfast, her shoulders hunched.

The discussion concluded as the front door closed quietly, and Loni rushed into the room. "You started without me." She took the final seat at the table and reached for the platter of pancakes.

"The hotcakes were ready." Mrs. Shiller passed butter and syrup toward her friend.

"Have you asked Sophie?" Loni asked before taking a bite and closing her eyes in bliss.

"Asked Sophie what?" Sophie narrowed her gaze.

Loni's eyes popped open in surprise. "Oh. Hmm. Guess not."

"We were waiting for you." Madge nudged Loni with an elbow. "Plus, we watched Quinn try to boss Juliet around first."

"Those boys, I don't know where they get it." Loni shook her braided head.

Twin humphs of disbelief came from Mrs. Shiller and Madge.

Loni rolled her eyes. "Here's the deal, Sophie. Juliet owns an art gallery and has promised us a showing of art depicting Maverick County, the Kooskia Tribe, and the Montana wilderness."

"That's a great idea." Sophie hoped she'd get a chance to see the artwork before leaving town.

Loni turned back to her breakfast. "It's all settled, then."

"Ah, wait there, Loni." Juliet sat forward. "I haven't seen Sophie's work yet."

Sophie took a drink of coffee. "My work? Why would you see my work?"

"Of course." Loni nodded. "Sophie, would you go grab your sketchbooks for Juliet? Then we should probably come up with some sort of timetable."

"Wait a minute. My work? Timetable? What exactly is going on here?" Sophie set her cup down with a dull *thud*.

Juliet tilted her head to the side. "You said she was onboard for the project, Madge."

Madge shrugged and concentrated on the bite remaining on her plate.

"Why, you're our artist. I thought that was obvious." Loni gestured to Mrs. Shiller, who rose from the table and exited the room.

Sophie shook her head in disbelief. "I'm not an artist. I'm a landscape architect. Specializing in golf course design."

"You're an artist working as a landscape architect.

Your heart and soul belong to your craft. Anybody can see that," Loni said.

"Loni—" Sophie began.

"Sophie left her pad in the parlor last night. Here we are." Mrs. Shiller returned with Sophie's large sketchbook and handed it to Juliet, who peered over the top at Sophie.

"It is okay?" Juliet asked quietly.

Sophie blinked several times, overwhelmed by the compelling force of the women around her. "S-sure, I guess." Her stomach dropped as Juliet flipped open the cover. Juliet was a real gallery owner. What if she thought Sophie sucked?

"That's him. That captures him so perfectly." Loni breathed out at the charcoal of Colton grinning. She made similar comments as Juliet flipped the pages one by one.

"It's me!" Mrs. Shiller exclaimed at the sketch with soft sunlight sparkling over her face as she kneaded bread.

"Look at Tom." Loni's eyes softened at the portrait of her husband perched on a paddocked white fence. "And me." She turned smiling eyes on Sophie. She had captured Loni watching her sons at the picnic with a mixture of love and resignation.

"Oh my," Madge murmured at the charcoal of Jake staring out of the page. Determination lit his eyes while strength ruled his face—all male, all warrior. "Look at that man."

Juliet closed the book. "These are incredible. Do you also work in oils?"

Hope flared to life in Sophie's chest. She didn't even try to quash it. "Yes. Watercolors, too."

"You have the showing if you want it." Juliet gave her a slightly apologetic grin.

"She wants it," Loni chimed in as both Madge and Mrs. Shiller clapped.

"Now wait a minute." Sophie rose from the table. "A project like that would take a year, maybe two. I'm only here for another week, ladies." She carried her empty plate to the sink to rinse off and felt the silent communication going on behind her.

"Will you at least think about it?" Loni asked.

"I'll think about it." Sophie wouldn't be able to think about anything else. She kinked her neck to the side before turning around. A real art showing—of her work. The thought was beyond anything she'd dared to dream about.

If she wasn't careful, however, Maverick Montana would become too wonderful to leave. She had to leave. Right?

• • •

Jake found Sophie sketching in an alcove in Shiller's backyard. She sat on a stone platform surrounded by rose bushes, climbing flowers, and greenery, looking like a sexy forest sprite. "I decline your offer," he said softly, tucking his hands in his jeans.

She started and glanced up, her eyes refocusing. "What offer?"

"When you said we're over last night. I decline." He'd spent a restless night trying to figure out how to change her mind, and finally decided the direct approach would be best.

Her grin flashed a flirty dimple. "It wasn't an

offer—it was a statement."

That dimple roared a hunger through him that weakened his knees and hardened his cock. "Then I reject your statement."

She closed the sketchbook, her gaze dropping to the bulge in his jeans. "Doesn't look like rejection to me."

Was she being coy? "Don't underestimate me, Soph." It was only fair to give her warning, even while claws of need ripped through him.

She blinked back at him, her eyes darkening to cobalt. "Look who's talking." Desire washed her delicate cheekbones with pink, matching the cute skirt that only went to her knees. Those cowboy boots made her legs look impossibly long.

He could find happiness with this woman. The thought flew out of nowhere, and he batted it away. For now, he just wanted a taste. So he knelt between her legs, his palms sliding up her thighs.

Her eyes widened, and she grabbed his hands. "We're outside."

Ah. He liked her off-balance. "I know."

"Jake." Her lips parted, lush now with the arousal he could see running through her.

"I do like how you say my name." He shook off her hands and continued his journey, his shoulders forcing her knees farther apart.

"I, ah, don't know." Her eyes flicked around the peaceful backyard, even as her nipples hardened beneath his gaze.

"I do." Her scent was driving him crazy. "All you have to do is say yes." If she pushed him away, he'd need to go jump in the lake go cool off.

She gingerly touched his chin, her gaze blazing.

"Every moment with you is something. Yes."

Ah, she was a sweetheart. He leaned in and captured one nub in his mouth, sucking through her shirt. No bra. His head might just explode. Her fingers tangled in his hair, and she gasped.

His other hand found her, hot and wet. He groaned around her nipple, and her thighs trembled against his arms. She was about as perfect as a woman could be. He abruptly released her, then lifted her shirt over her head.

"Well, okay. I guess we can see each other just until I leave town," she said breathlessly. She fell back onto her elbows, her smile a siren's song. Apparently, for this stolen moment in time, she was willing to forget her vow to leave him.

Keeping her gaze, allowing her to see the hunger raging through him, he slowly unbuckled his belt. He wanted to bury himself in her so deep she'd never consider leaving him. He kicked the jeans and briefs to the rosebushes and slid on a condom.

Feminine awareness, feminine strength, glowed hot and bright in her dangerous eyes. Teasing him, she slowly reached under her skirt and slid her black panties off her legs. Then she smiled.

It was the smile that did it.

Moving so quickly she yelped, he grabbed her up, turned to sit, and slowly, so slowly, lowered her onto his raging dick. She breathed out and yanked his shirt over his head. He rumbled with pleasure when her palms met his pecs.

No way would he go for easy and gentle right now. Later. Much later. Right now, he was burning for her. Her tight body wrapped around him, so much heat, so much grip. Grasping her hips, he lifted her, and then plunged her back down.

Pleasure sparked along his entire shaft. He dropped his head to her neck, nipping.

Nothing felt as good as this moment—as this woman taking him, milking him. His balls drew tight against the base of his cock. She gave a hungry moan and arched.

He yanked her up and back down, snarling at the dark pleasure he felt being so deep inside her. For two heartbeats, he forced himself to stop, to remain still. To just feel.

Her sex clenched him, vibrating around his shaft, rippling over him. "I'd give anything to stay inside you forever—just you and me, feeling you come over and over again," he murmured against her skin.

A long, winding shiver moved up her spine. She whispered his name against his neck as she lifted up and shoved back down.

His hands tightened on her hips, and he set a furious rhythm. Harder, faster, blinding strokes slammed her against him, his thrusts deep and sure. A roaring filled his ears. Heat clawed down his spine to flare in his balls.

She stiffened, crying his name, her internal walls gripping him like a vise. He exploded, lightening flashing through him. Deep, violent spurts tore from him as he held her close.

Finally he relaxed, his knees going weak. His face dropped to the haven where her neck met her shoulder. She panted and huddled against him, her heart beating so rapidly he could feel it in his chest.

There was no way he could let her go.

CHAPTER SIXTEEN

The week sped by as Sophie finished the design for Willa's Garden to the council's satisfaction. Jake won his local trial and was asked to consult on a trial in D.C. He'd called on his way to the airport to let her know.

Pleasure had filled her that he'd checked in with her before leaving. Just like they were a couple. During that week, it had seemed as if they were. Quick lunches, a few dinners around his hectic schedule, with a hot, hungry cowboy taking her to new heights in his bed afterward. Man, she was lost.

Without Jake around, Sophie used the time to think instead of sleep. She was sketching the porch from the swing one morning when her phone rang.

"How's my favorite girl?" Her uncle's gruff voice charmed through the line.

"Uncle Nathan! How are you?" she asked.

"I'm fine. Just got word—your commissioners denied the development and golf course," he said.

Defeat slumped her shoulders. "I'm so sorry." Would they go bankrupt now? Tears filled her eyes. She wanted to be furious with Jake, but if what he said was true, she couldn't blame him for exposing the group. Though he certainly hadn't needed to use her to do it.

"Not your problem, sweetheart. Had an interesting phone call from a Jake Lodge, however," Nathan said.

"Really?" Suspicion laced her tone.

"Offered to buy your design for a fifty-acre parcel next to some casino," Nathan affirmed

Sophie kicked the wooden floor so the swing started to move. "You're joking."

"Nope. Of course it'll have to be reconfigured for a different space. He also said that you staying on was a condition of the sale, however." Curiosity filled her uncle's tone now.

"Son of a bitch." Her temper ignited until her throat closed. Sure, she had feelings for the lawyer, but nobody manipulated her.

Her uncle chuckled. "I thought you'd be pleased."

"What? Pleased that he's trying to run my life? Trying to keep me here? It isn't bad enough that his mother has given me an art showing, now he's going to buy my services? I don't think so." She kicked the floor harder. It was only because she might be pregnant. He had been more than happy with a short fling before the stupid condom broke.

"What art showing?" Nathan asked.

Sophie told her uncle in great detail about the showing, pausing once and again to kick the floor. The swing complained with a soft squeal.

"Wow, Soph. Isn't that what you've always wanted?" he asked.

"What are you talking about? I want to design golf courses." Her protest sounded weak, even to her own ears.

"You like rendering the designs for golf courses. Your favorite part begins when you pull out the colored pencils," he said

She bit her lip. "So?"

"So, why not give the art a shot?" he asked.

Dread filled her. "Are you firing me?"

"Of course not, but I want you to be happy. I'll adore you no matter what you do for a living," Nathan said.

Warmth for her uncle filled her chest. He'd always been there for her. He knew how much she wanted to paint—to be a real artist. But she wouldn't be bullied into it by Jake Lodge, who only wanted to keep his possible kid close. "It's my decision on what I do for a living, and nobody is going to railroad me into a career. Any career." The term *so there* echoed in the silence.

"Like your mother?" Nathan asked.

She jolted. "Uncle Nathan—"

"Say the word and you'll have a plane ticket waiting for you at the airline counter. I'll bring you home immediately if you want," Nathan said.

Sophie stopped swinging. If staying in town would save her uncle's company, she'd suck it up and do it. "Are we going bankrupt?"

He sighed. "No. Well, I don't think so. That's not something for you to worry about, sweetheart. I'll take care of it."

"I love you," she whispered.

"I love you, too. Want me to send you a ticket home?" he asked.

"Thanks, but I have some business to take care of here first." Then she would make her own decisions— without any interference.

"Call me if you need me." He ended the call.

Sophie pushed back from the porch swing just as a blue Toyota Sequoia rumbled to a stop behind her Jeep.

Leila waved from the backseat's open window. "We came to take you to lunch. And to see your surprise."

"Hop in." Loni reached across the front seat and pushed open the passenger door.

Sophie wavered at the top of the porch stairs.

"Come on. You get a *surprise*," Leila called out impatiently.

Grinning, Sophie bounded down the wide steps and hopped into the large SUV.

"We should've called," Loni said as she drove away. "Sorry about the commissioners."

"It wasn't much of a surprise after the hearing, anyway," Sophie admitted.

"Now you can design the tribe's course, right?" Loni asked.

Sophie stiffened. "I don't think so."

"I guess that'll be between you and Jake. " Loni focused intently on her driving. "Should we do lunch first or go see the surprise?"

"The surprise!" Leila chirped from the backseat. "You are going to love it, Sophie."

Sophie turned smiling eyes on the little girl. "I do love surprises."

"Are you and Daddy getting married?" Wise charcoal eyes twinkled.

Loni gasped out a cough. "Uh, Leila, that's private." She shot a curious sideways glance at Sophie.

"No, it isn't. If Sophie marries Daddy, then I get a mama." Wistfulness filled the girl's tone.

Sophie's heart splintered. "You and I are friends, no matter what."

"Oh. So you won't be my mama." The girl sniffed.

"I'll be your friend," Sophie said softly.

Leila shrugged, crossing her arms. "That'd be good, too. Though Daddy's a catch. Somebody else will marry him and be my mama if you don't."

Loni smothered a laugh with her hand. "How do you know your daddy's a catch?"

Leila clapped her hands together. "Grets's mom said so last week."

"Grets's mom shouldn't say things like that," Loni said.

"Well, Grandma? Is Daddy a catch or not?" Leila asked.

"Of course he's a catch." Loni rolled her eyes.

"Told you, Sophie." Leila giggled.

Sophie turned a surprised glance toward Loni when they entered the drive leading to Jake's house. Loni smiled.

"You could live here. It's pretty great." Leila continued her campaign.

The vehicle rolled to a stop before Jake's expansive home, and Sophie was saved from answering as the little girl jumped out of the Toyota.

"This way." Loni's eyes sparkled as she got out of the car and turned toward the stand-alone garage with triple brown doors.

"My surprise is in the garage?" Sophie asked. Leila placed a small hand in hers, and Sophie's heart swelled.

"No, upstairs." The little girl tugged her toward the stairway to the left of the doors then released her to run up and push open the door. Sophie followed at a slower pace with Loni on her heels and gasped as she entered the empty room.

A high-pitched roof and exposed beams gave the shadows angles to play while light filtered in wide windows scattered across all four walls and illuminated the oak floor. Sophie focused on the lone easel set on a drop cloth in the middle of the room.

"Jake always planned to make this into an exercise room, but he uses the gym in town instead. It looks perfect for a studio." Loni's voice echoed around them.

"It is perfect," Sophie breathed, the possibilities entrancing her. "But I don't understand."

"Don't you like it?" Leila asked, her eyes gleaming.

"I love it." Rolling pastures dotted with horses spread out the back window, mountains rose high and proud out the side, and Mineral Lake stretched out to the left. "But Loni—"

Loni opened her arms. "Looks like a nice place to work on the exhibit for Juliet. The girl really could use a successful launch."

"She could?" Sophie asked.

"She just moved here a few months ago. An exhibit would surely put her in good form. But we hadn't found the right artist. Until now," Loni said.

"I don't know…" Sophie's gaze softened on the easel and empty canvas. "I'm shocked Jake would create this for me at his house. I mean, we're not really dating or anything." Why would he create something like that for her at his home? She hadn't decided to do the gallery showing and hadn't agreed to the tribe's golf course—as far as he knew, she was returning to San Francisco soon.

"It's just a great place where you can capture the surrounding area easily, and it wasn't being used. We help each other here, and you needed a place to paint. Although, whether you're dating or not, take that up with Jake. I believe my boy can be extremely persuasive." Loni turned for the door and beckoned Leila forward. "Where should we take Sophie for lunch?"

• • •

Sophie wasn't surprised when her cell phone rang. Jake's deep voice slid over the line like warm honey. "How are things?"

"I'm not sure what to say." She leaned against the wall in her room.

Silence pounded across the line for a minute. "Say about what?"

"The art studio," she said quietly.

"What art studio?" he asked.

She jerked. "Um, the art studio in the top of your garage?"

He cleared his throat. "There's an art studio in my garage?"

"Oh, no." She sank on the bed and yanked a pillow over her face. Jake had no clue. "Your mother and Leila—"

Jake swore. "Aw, shit, Sunshine. I'm sorry. I didn't know."

"I figured that out," she mumbled. For a brief time, she'd thought maybe he was considering something permanent. Heat filled her face until her cheeks ached. What in the world had she been thinking? She hadn't wanted that anyway—the man was too controlling.

"The town, my mother, they love you." Jake sighed. "They interfere, but they mean well."

Could the world just open up and swallow her? Please? "I like them, too," she said.

"Maybe it's a good thing. The studio at my place… In case you're pregnant," he said slowly.

Oh, for goodness sakes. There was no way she was pregnant. "I'm not, and even so, I could be pregnant in San Francisco," she ground out. She threw the pillow across the room.

"A baby needs a father," he said.

"We're way ahead of the issue, here. I am not pregnant. Seriously, Jake. It was one. Well, two, times." Her embarrassment turned to irritation. "Besides, I won't let you manipulate me—trying to buy my design and everything."

There was a shuffling and then, "Damn it. I have to go. But I'm not trying to manipulate you."

"Are, too," she retorted.

"You're impossible. We'll discuss it as soon as I can call back." With that, he disengaged the call.

"Jerk," Sophie muttered into the empty room.

• • •

Sophie finished the designs for Willa's Garden but neglected to redesign the golf course for the tribe. Jake didn't call, and she told herself she was happy about that. The last thing she wanted was to fight with him. Loni and Leila found an excuse each day to drop by and take her to lunch, and one day the three of them even rode horseback to a picnic spot overlooking Loni and Tom's ranch. Loni patiently related tribal history, probably to nudge her into doing the paintings, while Leila blatantly brought Jake into every conversation along with not so subtle reminders that if Sophie didn't snatch him up, somebody would.

Sophie found herself wishing the little girl were hers. To love and protect.

Finally, she just couldn't deal with her thoughts alone any longer. The voices in her head were starting to argue with one another. She called the one person in town who might understand. "Juliet? How about we meet for lunch?"

CHAPTER SEVENTEEN

The Dirt Spoon diner smelled of grease, burgers, and home-cooked food. Sophie settled into the worn booth, careful to avoid the rip in the vinyl. "Thanks for meeting me," she said after they'd ordered.

"I figured you'd want to discuss the art showing." Juliet smiled and unfolded the paper napkin to place on her lap. Her loose dress and Celtic jewelry made her look like an Irish princess.

Sophie almost agreed—almost took the easy out. But it was time to grow a pair, as her uncle always said. "Actually, I, ah, just wanted to talk… I mean, you're new to town, so am I, and I don't really have, I mean, even at home, I don't have—"

"A lot of friends?" Juliet asked, an understanding smile curving her lips.

Sophie sighed. Yeah, she sounded like a loser. But she'd never connected with people. Her mother had seen to that. "I don't have many friends at all."

"Me neither." Juliet shrugged. "I'm glad you called me." Her blue eyes lit up. "That took courage."

More than she knew. "Everyone knows everyone in this town, and it seems like they all know what's best for everyone else," Sophie said.

"When somebody gives you directions, they always start with, 'Turn left by the field where Sam Boseby's horse died, and then right by the oak tree where Bobby Johnson fell and broke his leg two years ago…'" Juliet said.

Sophie laughed, her shoulders relaxing. "Exactly."

A couple of men in the far booth argued loudly.

Sophie glanced around but couldn't see them. Then they went quiet. Good.

Juliet sipped from a sweating plastic glass. "Jake is out of town?"

"Yes. He's consulting on a trial in D.C." Sophie traced her fingers over the scarred table. "His mom and daughter created a very cool art studio above his garage for me to paint."

"That's wonderful," Juliet said.

"Without telling him," Sophie finished.

Juliet's eyes widened. She covered her mouth, mirth filling her face.

"I know." Heat spiraled into Sophie's cheeks. "I thanked him on the phone."

Juliet snorted and dropped her hand. "You didn't."

"I did." Sophie shook her head. "The poor guy had no clue what I was talking about."

Juliet laughed harder. Finally, she took a deep breath. "This town, I'm telling you. They embrace you and dictate your life. That means they like you. It's nice to belong."

"I know. Even Jake is trying to push me into staying—and it's not like he's made any big declaration of love or anything." As she said the words, the truth of her hurt slammed home..

Juliet sat back as the waitress delivered their club sandwiches and waited until the girl left. "Have *you* declared anything?"

Sophie stilled in bringing her drink to her mouth. "Um, well—"

"That's what I thought." Juliet took a bite and then

swallowed. "Those Lodge men."

"Speaking of whom. What's up with you and the sheriff?" Sophie asked.

Juliet flushed a pretty pink. "Nothing. I mean, he's overbearing, bossy, and always around."

"I think you're protesting too much." Sophie chuckled.

"No kidding." Juliet quirked her lip. "He's my landlord, so I have to get along with him."

Sophie took a sip of water. "Your landlord?"

"Yes. The Lodge-Freeze families own more real estate than you'd believe." Juliet sighed.

That must've been what Dawn meant by family holdings. "Must be nice." Sophie grinned. "Who knows, maybe I'll sell a painting someday and then, ah, diversify."

"Speaking of which, I saw how your eyes lit up about the art showing," Julie said.

Sophie blew out a breath. "I'd love to have a real art showing. To paint Montana and have people come and actually want to buy my work. It'd be a dream I hadn't ever thought I'd get the chance to explore."

"You're saying yes." Delight danced in Juliet's eyes.

"I'm saying yes. I'll do it on my terms, and some of that may mean I take pictures and then paint in San Francisco." At home. Even though it no longer felt like home.

"Fair enough." Juliet glanced back as the men in the far booth got louder. "What's going on behind us?"

Sophie glanced up as Billy Rockefeller and Fred Gregton slid out of the far booth. "The guys from the Concerned Citizens for Rural Development Group seem to be having a disagreement." Frowns lined both men's faces. "And they're dressed for, ah, war."

The two men wore camo outfits and flak boots. Billy Rockefeller looked a lot more dangerous in the army outfit than he had in the fancy jacket.

He stopped at their table. "Ladies."

Sophie made the introductions, and he shook Juliet's hand. Fred hovered near the counter and didn't approach.

Billy cleared his throat, his eyes piercing. "I heard the county commissioners were smart enough to deny your plan."

Sophie cut her eyes to Juliet. "Good news travels fast."

Billy shifted to reveal a gun in his waistband. "I also heard the tribe is trying to buy your plan. I'd appreciate it if you refused to sell. We don't need a golf course."

"I'll keep that in mind." Sophie's breath scraped her throat as she eyed the gun.

His lip curled, and he lowered his flushed face to hers. "I'll do anything to save the environment, lady. Anything."

Sophie saw red at his obvious intimidation tactic. Enough with people pushing her around. Her temper exploded. After grabbing a bottle on the table, she squeezed it in his face. Ketchup squirted out and spread over his forehead.

She gasped.

He hissed and moved to grab her.

Juliet swung with her purse, smashing him in the nose. He stumbled back toward the counter, where Fred caught him before he tripped.

Billy started to lunge forward when a sharp voice

in the doorway snapped his name.

Everyone froze.

Quinn Lodge stalked up the aisle, his gaze taking everything in. "What's going on, folks?"

Sophie gulped air and pointed to Billy. "He has a gun in his waistband."

Billy snarled and stepped far enough away from her that Quinn's shoulders relaxed. "I also have a permit, a fact the sheriff is well aware of."

Quinn eyed Juliet and then Sophie. "Are you ladies all right?"

"Fine." Juliet crossed her arms. "This was a little misunderstanding about ketchup. Right?"

Sophie swallowed several times. "Um, right." Actually, she was the one who had committed battery, considering she'd doused the asshole. But he had tried to scare her, so it was probably all right. She glanced at Quinn. "Let's not tell Jake."

Quinn grinned. "Not a chance, Soph. Not a chance in hell." He took in Juliet's ketchup-covered purse with a raised eyebrow but didn't say a word. Then he waited until the two men left before giving Juliet a hard glance and then sauntering out the door.

After lunch, Sophie drove into the city to make a purchase. It had been enough time, and she just needed confirmation that the broken condom hadn't led to anything. Or the second time against the wall when they'd forgotten protection. There was no way she would buy a pregnancy test in town—the news would be all over within minutes.

The feeling of leaving home grew stronger as she pulled away from Mineral Lake and headed outside of Maverick County, the sharp peaks of mountains providing a shield from rushing winds.

After driving for an hour, she shivered as dark clouds gathered across the sky and figured she'd get back in time for a good storm. Lightning cracked across the sky, and a hard rain began to pelt the vehicle. She flipped on the wipers and lights. Her phone rang just as she pulled into Billings, and she accepted the call. "Hello."

"Where are you?" Jake's deep voice stirred something inside her she struggled to suppress.

"Running an errand. Are you back in town?" She was *not* miffed that he hadn't called. Really. Though fury still rode her at his attempted interference in her life. With her job. With her emotions.

"Just got home," he said.

She peered through the rain-soaked windshield for a drugstore. "Great."

"Do you want to meet for dinner?" The low timbre of his voice caused a fluttering in her lower belly that irritated her, pure and simple.

The lights of a store shone through the darkened night. "No. I may be a while."

"I'm sorry I didn't call, Sophie. We worked twenty-hour days to finish the case up in a week." His frustration came clear and sure through the line.

"No problem, Jake," she said, keeping her voice casual.

"Sounds like a problem." Silence sprawled across the line. "Where are you?"

If she could take on crazy Billy Rockefeller, she could handle Jake. "None of your business."

"Excuse me?" Heat colored his words, even through the static. The wind lashed against her windows.

"You heard me. Nice offer you made my uncle. You're not running my life," she said.

"Not trying to." His voice dropped an octave.

That tone was a mite too sexy for her to keep angry, darn it. "Good. Well, since we fired the Charleton Group, I'm sure that Uncle Nathan will sell you the design," she said.

"I assumed as much," he admitted.

"Preston will be here working on it, not me," she said.

Several seconds of silence filled the line as Sophie turned into the fully illuminated parking lot.

"No," Jake said calmly.

"What?" She switched off the ignition.

"I said, no. The deal is for you to redesign the course. Not Preston. You designed the original course, the one that fits in well here. We want you to work with your design. Plus, I understand your uncle stands to lose quite a bit of money if that design isn't used," Jake said.

Sophie's temper stirred. "That's blackmail."

"No, it isn't. It just makes sense to have the original designer alter the same course. Now, where are you?" he asked.

"Bite me, Jake." She ended the call powered down the phone. Not the most mature response, but he deserved it. She squared her shoulders for courage and jumped into the rain to dash for the drugstore.

• • •

The small bag sat like a stone in her purse during a quiet dinner at a small diner just outside of Maverick

County. When she finished eating and paid the check, she figured she'd stalled enough. She needed to find out now, because there was a fairly good chance Jake would be waiting for her at Mrs. Shiller's.

She marched slowly into the small bathroom and dug into the bag. She opened the box and read the instructions. Not too difficult. With a sigh, she peed on the stick. Then she placed it on the back of the sink, turned around, and thrummed her fingers against her arm. She waited a minute. Then another minute, her eyes sightless on the pale yellow walls.

Someone tried to open the door and the lock jiggled.

She'd have to come back.

Finally, three minutes were up. Sophie took a deep breath and turned around.

Through the control window, a plus sign glowed in bright pink.

She was pregnant.

CHAPTER EIGHTEEN

Fifteen stunned minutes later, she found herself in the Jeep headed toward Mineral Lake. "I'll have to schedule a doctor's appointment." She had been talking to herself for several moments but didn't think it mattered much at that point. Statistically, the pregnancy was just unreal, but it happened. She couldn't believe it. Rain slashed the car while thunder rumbled overhead, but neither pierced her calm. "A good doctor. One with experience. Lots of it."

The windshield wipers made a comforting swishing sound against the glass. "I wonder if it's a girl or a boy."

The car crawled through the deluge as she crossed into Maverick County and then finally the town of Mineral Lake, an odd sense of relief filling her.

"You'll be a member of a tribe, baby, and," she mused idly, "I think that means extra scholarships for college. Among other things." She turned onto her street and parked by the B&B. "Look. There's Daddy waiting on the porch. Wow. Daddy's pissed." She felt drunk. Why should she feel drunk? She only drank lemonade at dinner.

Jake opened her door before she could. One strong hand around her arm helped her to the protected porch. "Where in the hell have you been?"

Sophie stared up into his furious face, her eyes blinking as if in a dream. "The city."

"You drove from town in that?" He gestured

toward the driving rain.

"Yes."

"Why?" He put both hands on her arms, obviously fighting the urge to shake her.

"I'm pregnant, Jake." Then she pitched forward and darkness overtook her.

• • •

Jake dodged forward and caught Sophie before she hit the hard wood porch. Pregnant. The woman said she was pregnant. The odds were so against it, he truly hadn't thought she'd be pregnant. Condoms broke all the time. Jesus. She was really pregnant?

He cradled her easily, fumbled for the doorknob, and shoved inside. She felt too small—too fragile in his arms.

A baby. Another baby.

He shook his head. Warmth flushed through him along with unease. As he looked down at her pale face, something in his chest tightened. He wanted this baby. He wanted this woman.

Setting her down on the sofa, he reached for his phone to call the doctor. She shouldn't have fainted like that, should she? His gut clenched hard. Everything had to be okay. Sophie was just surprised by the pregnancy. And tired. He needed to make sure she got more rest.

The nurse answered, and he made his request. Thank goodness for small towns and good friends. The doctor would arrive soon.

Jake dropped to his knees and smoothed Sophie's hair off her forehead. They should get married.

He closed his eyes and took a deep breath. His one marriage had begun the same way and ended in disaster. What mattered was Sophie, this baby, and Leila. He'd do what was best for all of them.

What was best?

"Sophie, wake up," he murmured.

She didn't move, and fear caught him by the throat. He took another deep breath. Sometimes faints took a while to awaken from. She was fine. She had to be fine.

They'd have the doctor examine her, and then they'd come up with a plan. He was born to strategize, and this was no different than a trial. Okay. Considering it was his entire life, it was a little different. But he could make it work.

They'd come up with a plan, and it'd be a good one. Deep down at his core, he knew he'd never let her go. Now all he had to do was convince her.

• • •

Sophie awoke some time later laid out on Mrs. Shiller's flowered couch with a cold cloth pressed against her eyes. She flopped a hand on the cloth and tugged it across her face to drop on the floor. Her eyes met Jake's as he knelt by the couch.

"Feeling better?" His voice was soft—his eyes hot.

"Yes." She pushed to a seated position and dropped her head into her hands. Then she struggled to reach her feet.

"No, wait a minute." One gentle hand pressed down on her shoulder. "Give it a minute. You were out for some time."

She shrugged off his hand and the pleasure of

seeing him again in the flesh. "I'm fine." As much as she hated to admit it, she had missed his solid presence, his reassuring strength.

"We'll see." Lights cascaded through the window, and a car pulled through the puddles. The splash of the tires echoed even through the storm. Jake ran a rough hand through his thick hair. "Doc Mooncaller just arrived."

Sophie brushed wet curls off her face. "You called the doctor?"

"Of course I called the doctor," Jake growled. "You just passed out."

"I'm fine. Tell him to go away." Panic spiraled through her. She had never quite gotten over the fear of doctors and needles.

Jake stood and strode to open the door, letting rain blow in from outside. "No."

"Hey, Jake." A portly man with a long gray braid moved gracefully into the room, black bag in hand. Kind brown eyes shifted to Sophie. "You must be Sophie."

"Yes." Sophie eyed the stairs. Maybe she could escape to her room.

"This is Doc Mooncaller." Jake closed the door with a muted *click*.

The doctor crossed and bent down to one knee in front of her. "Rumor has it you fainted, young lady."

"She's pregnant." Jake leaned against the door, broad arms across a muscular chest.

Sophie gave him a baleful glare. Weren't lawyers supposed to be good at keeping secrets? "He's guarding the way out," Sophie whispered to the doctor, rolling her eyes.

The doctor chuckled. "Why, you going to run?"

"I might," she muttered.

Twinkling eyes met hers. "Good luck with that. How far along are you?"

"A couple of weeks." She swallowed, her stomach churning.

"Just found out?" He pressed a steady hand against her forehead.

"Yes." She fought to keep her voice normal.

"Tired?" He reached into his bag for a stethoscope, which he pressed to her chest.

"Yes." Yes, but that might be from fighting her attraction to the pissed-off lawyer.

"Overwhelmed?" the doctor asked.

"Yes." Her voice thickened this time.

The doctor reached out gentle hands and pressed lightly along her neck and glands. "Feeling dizzy now?"

"No," she said.

He left the stethoscope hanging from his neck. "It's time for you to get some rest, dear. Things will be better tomorrow." He stood, his knees popping. "I'd like to see you for a full examination tomorrow—say, after breakfast?"

"She'll be there." Jake moved away from the door.

"She needs peace, Jake." The doctor placed a hand on Jake's arm while opening the door. "Don't upset her." With that, the doctor escaped into the stormy night.

Silence ticked across the room before Jake moved toward her, bent, and lifted her.

"I can walk." Why did it have to feel so good to be in his arms? Solid and warm, the man provided a comfort she could become addicted to.

"I know." He climbed the stairs to her bedroom and laid her gently on the bed. "We can talk about this tomorrow."

"You're not sleeping here." Alarm flared in her as he shrugged out of his shirt. Jake didn't answer as his hands went to his belt. She sat up. "I mean it. Mrs. Shiller would be shocked."

His jeans hit the floor. "Mrs. Shiller and her friend, Lily Roundbird, left this morning."

"Oh. I forgot about their week-long trip to Yellowstone." Sophie relaxed. Though the man still didn't need to stay.

"They spend more time in the various casinos on the way down, and probably just a day at Yellowstone." He kicked his pants to the side.

"I'm not living in Montana." Sophie sat still as stone while Jake gently pulled her shirt off and tugged his much bigger one over her head and threaded her arms through. Once again, her body won over her mind. She wanted to be held. Heck, she needed it.

"We'll figure that out, too." He dragged the covers over them. Then he tucked her into his large body and warmth enfolded her. She couldn't have remained awake if her life depended on it. "Where's Leila?"

"At mom's," Jake said.

Okay, then. She slid into sleep as smoothly as warm cream from a pitcher, toasty and safe in Jake's arms.

Her sleep was a dreamless one.

Orange blossoms and spice swirled around her as she struggled to awaken. She slid one eyelid open to see a thick mug.

"Wake up, sweetheart. We have a doctor's appointment," Jake said, his voice deep and strong.

Sophie groaned and rolled over before yanking the pillow atop her head. It was instantly removed. "I am not getting up." She curled into a ball and leaped for dreamland.

"Yes, you are." After placing the cup on the nightstand, he lifted her from the bed.

"No." She snuggled her face into a warm chest.

"Yes." He lowered her until her feet rested on the smooth floor.

She groaned as her feet cooled, and she pushed away from Jake. "I'm pregnant, and I need sleep." It was a last-ditch effort that resulted in a deep male chuckle.

"Nice try. Drink your tea, and I'll make my famous scrambled eggs while you shower."

"Your scrambled eggs are famous?" She opened blurry eyes on a freshly showered man, and her libido picked up. Just a bit.

"Extremely," Jake said solemnly with a twinkle in his eyes. "If I leave, do you promise not to go back to bed?"

Sophie looked longingly at the bed and then at Jake's determined face. "Fine," she huffed and turned to grab her toiletry bag, "but those eggs better be worth it." She stomped out of the room and headed for a warm shower.

An hour later found her refreshed and dressed. She sat at the table, her stomach growling in response to the aromatic concoction on the stove.

"You're a bit of a grouch in the morning." Jake failed to hide his grin as he dumped scrambled eggs with ham, onions, and cheese onto a plate before her.

"Am not," Sophie said before taking a healthy bite

of eggs and closing her eyes in appreciation. "I'm tired. And pregnant." She glared at him before taking another big bite.

"So this morning attitude is new?" he asked.

"Not exactly."

Jake wisely sat and ate his eggs in silence, pausing from time to time to make sure she ate hers.

"So you've been to the Supreme Court?" Sophie leaned back in her chair, her stomach all but bursting.

"Twice." Jake took the empty plates to the sink. His faded jeans curved over a rock-hard ass, and Sophie couldn't help but lick her lips. Then her gaze trailed over the crisp black shirt and the muscles shifting beneath it when he moved.

"You could probably get a job anywhere," she said.

His back stiffened as he ran water into the sink. "Probably."

"And make a lot of money." Her mind spun with the possibilities.

"More than likely." He placed the plates in the dishwasher before turning to face her, his back against the counter, his arms across his chest. "I'm not leaving Montana."

"Why not?" she asked.

"It's my heritage. I want Leila to grow up here and know it. And know her grandparents and uncles. Maybe cousins someday." His face hardened.

"You've had this discussion before," Sophie said softly.

Jake nodded.

"I like my life." She rose to her feet.

"Your life just changed. Both of ours did." Jake folded the dishtowel on the counter and put a hand to the small of her back. "Let's go to Doc's and make sure you're all right."

Sophie nodded. There really wasn't anything else to say. She followed him out of the house and climbed into his truck. They didn't speak on the way to the town center. All too soon Jake pulled to a stop near the spraying fountain, and Sophie turned toward a deep blue door set into a log-cabin-type building with Doc Moon written in yellow letters.

"There wasn't enough room for his whole name." Jake grinned and helped her from the Jeep.

Sophie sighed in relief at the mostly empty sidewalk before darting through the blue door into a comfortable mauve waiting room. The last thing she needed was the entire town knowing she was pregnant with Jake's baby.

"Well, hello, Jake." A fiftyish woman fluffed her poufed white hair and smiled capped teeth from behind the receptionist counter. "This must be Sophie. I'm Gladys, and I need you to fill these out." Gladys handed her a clipboard with several papers attached and a pen. Sophie took them and dropped into a wooden chair. She had finished about half of the forms when a door to the right of the receptionist's desk opened. Doc Mooncaller poked his gray head out. He was wearing an official-looking lab coat with a stethoscope draped over his neck.

"Sophie, come on in. Just bring those papers." He moved back down the hall.

Sophie stood and wasn't surprised as Jake bounded up. She lifted an eyebrow at him.

"Can I come in?" His hopeful expression was too much to deny.

"Okay," she whispered, "but you have to leave if I need to get naked."

"I've seen you naked, Sunshine," he whispered back as they headed down the hall to the open examination room.

Sophie raised her arms in exasperation as she walked inside and plopped on one of the two brown guest chairs.

"Aren't you supposed to be on the table?" Jake sat next to her.

Sophie frowned. Suddenly, this was all too personal. "Maybe you should return to the waiting area."

"Too late," Jake whispered as Doc walked into the room.

"Well, Sophie. I guess you didn't make a run for it, huh?" Doc settled onto a rolling doctor's chair. "I'd like to do a full examination and medical history." He nodded toward the table. "My nurse will be in to give you a gown and take your blood pressure in just a minute. Jake, you go back to the waiting room."

Jake straightened. "But Doc—"

"I mean it. You can come next time. Right now you're just in the way," the doctor said.

"Fine. But if you need me, call me." Jake dropped a light kiss on Sophie's head before grudgingly leaving the room.

CHAPTER NINETEEN

Sophie walked down Doc's hall, relieved he'd given her a clean bill of health. And prenatal vitamins. She took a deep breath and opened the door to face Jake. Then she stopped cold at the sight of Loni, Tom, Dawn, Colton, Quinn, and Hawk all sitting in the waiting room.

Jake held his head in his hands but looked up at her gasp. "Melanie Johnson saw us come into the office earlier and called Mrs. West, who called Jeanie Dixon, who called my mother."

Loni jumped to her feet and rushed to take Sophie's hands. "Are you okay?" Loni wore a light blue blouse with the buttons lined incorrectly, jeans, and mismatched flip-flops. Her hair perched in a lopsided ponytail, and she'd applied mascara to only one eye.

Sophie nodded numbly.

"Good." Loni patted her hands as the rest of the group rose. "We hurried down here so quickly we missed breakfast. Why don't we all—"

"No." Jake reached around Loni to take Sophie's hand and pull her toward the door. "We're going somewhere else. To talk."

He led her to the truck, and she sat inside without a protest, her mind whirling. She was pregnant. Everyone knew it. She didn't notice when he started the ignition or pulled onto the road, and she paid no attention to their trip. The truck stopped.

"You brought me to your house," she said wood-enly.

Jake faced her across the middle console. "Are you all right?"

"Doc says I'm perfectly healthy. You had a huge head when you were born," she mused.

"He told you that?" Jake laughed.

"Everybody knows I'm pregnant." She would've liked a chance to come to grips with the idea on her own.

He rubbed a large hand over his eyes. "I know." He turned and unfolded from the truck before crossing and opening her door to help her out.

"Are you going to sue me for custody?" Sophie regained her footing on the smooth drive, then lifted her eyes to meet his, which narrowed. She fought a shiver as the pine-scented breeze rippled through her hair, and thunder sounded in the distance.

"No," he said.

"What about the Federal Indian Act?" Her knees trembled.

"You mean the Indian Child Welfare Act?" Jake rubbed warmth into her suddenly freezing arms.

"Yeah, that." Sophie eased back from his too-appealing touch. "Don't tribes get a leg-up in custody battles?"

Jake studied her for a moment, realization dawning over his rugged face. "No. That is not what the Act does."

"Really?" Sarcasm laced her tone.

"The Act's purpose is to protect Indian children taken out of a home, so they are put in a foster home or adopted by another Indian couple. It does not give a leg-up to anyone in a normal custody proceeding." Jake propelled her toward the house. "I cannot believe you've actually been worrying about this." He opened the door and ushered her inside. "That you think I'd fight you in court for our child."

Sophie turned to face him as he shut the door with a soft *thud*. "What are you going to do?"

"Negotiate." The smile he gave her should have provided a warning. Instead, it warmed her from the toes up.

"Negotiate? What exactly do you mean?" Sophie sat on the leather couch and stretched her legs over the matching ottoman. The view of Mineral Lake and sharp peaked mountains relaxed her, bone by bone.

"Well, what would it take for you to live in Montana?" The matching leather chair creaked as he sat and faced her.

Sophie stiffened. "Live here?"

"Yes. In what circumstances can you see yourself based out of here?" he asked.

"What about you,? What circumstances can you see yourself living in San Francisco?" she asked.

"I don't." Jake's jaw set. "It's not only me. I can't take Leila away from the rest of my family. Even if I wanted to."

Sophie could understand that. "I'm surprised you're not spouting that we need to get married before the baby is born."

Jake sat back in his chair, his voice softening. "Already made that mistake."

Sophie clamped down on the sudden pang through her heart. She reminded herself she didn't want to get married just because she was pregnant, either. "I don't know where we stand."

"Me neither. I think we should look at it in steps," he said.

"In steps?" she asked.

Determination and an odd vulnerability lit his eyes. "The pregnancy as the first step. Sophie, I would not like to miss any of it." "You'll come to San Francisco?" she asked.

"I thought you'd stay here. You know, work on the tribe's golf course and the art showing for Juliet. You'd still be working at what you want, and I'd pay to fly you to California any time you wished. So long as Doc okays it," Jake said.

"I'm not sure." The idea did sound appealing.

"Just think about it. Then we could figure out a schedule that works for both of us after the baby is born, if you decide to live in the city." His smile was too charming.

Sophie frowned, her mind reeling with static.

A slam of a truck door saved her from having to answer, and Leila rushed into the room. "Daddy, look what Aunt Dawn made me." The little girl jumped into her father's arms and handed him a blue knitted hat.

Jake raised his eyebrows. "Dawn learned to knit?"

"Uncle Hawk bet her that she couldn't do it." Leila turned curious eyes on Sophie. "What's 'knocked up' mean?"

Sophie's breath caught in her throat. She dropped her legs off the ottoman.

Jake shot her a concerned glance. "Where did you hear that, sweetheart?"

Dawn answered from the doorway. "That cow Betsy Phillips said it to Mary Whitmore at the grocery

store when we dropped by for some flour for Mom."
She turned wide eyes on Sophie. "Oh. Hi, Sophie."

"Hi, Dawn." Sophie leaned back again and crossed
her arms over her face.

"Well, 'bye." Dawn made a quick exit.

"What's knocked up?" Leila asked again. "That
cow Betsy Phillips said that you're knocked up, Sophie.
Does it hurt?"

Sophie huffed out a laugh, and she peeked between
her arms.

"You shouldn't call Mrs. Phillips a cow. Even if it is
true," Jake admonished his daughter.

"Sorry." Inquisitive eyes met Sophie's. "Well?"

"Um, well." Sophie panicked as she stared at Jake.

Jake took a deep breath before cuddling his daughter close. "It means Sophie has a baby in her tummy."

"Like old Bula?" Leila's eyes dropped to Sophie's
stomach.

Jake sputtered. "Uh, kind of."

"Who's Bula?" Sophie asked warily.

"A milk cow over at my mom's." Jake stifled a grin.

"How did you get a baby in your tummy?" Leila
asked.

• • •

That night found Sophie struggling to find sleep, even
though her body was exhausted after Jake and Leila
dropped her at home. She giggled at the thought of
Jake quickly changing the subject to shoes with his
daughter to avoid explaining the birds and the bees.
Though they'd have to tell her about her future sibling
sometime.

As much as she didn't want to admit it, Jake's offer made a certain kind of sense. Designing the tribe's course would help Uncle Nathan, and she'd get a chance to put together a real art exhibit. A dream she hadn't dared given any hope.

A tiny voice in her head whispered that she wouldn't be alone during the pregnancy, either. But instead of reassuring her, that made her want to run. Fast and hard in the other direction. The phone rang, and she reached for it like a lifeline.

"Hey, Sophie, I hope I'm not waking you," Preston said.

"No, Preston, I can't sleep," she admitted.

The sound of Preston settling back against leather, probably his desk chair, filled the line. "I just wanted to let you know Charleton has dropped their threats of a lawsuit."

Sophie's stomach heaved. "How? Why?"

"Apparently our new attorney talked to theirs and they backed off. Fast," Preston said.

Sophie groaned. "We have a new attorney?"

"Yeah. You might know him."

"Son of a bitch." Sophie took a calming breath. At this rate there wouldn't be a place in her life Jake hadn't infiltrated.

Preston laughed. "Well, I figured I'd give you a friendly warning. Your uncle thinks Lodge walks on water."

"Great. But what about the other four developments? We needed those," she said, her head hurting.

"Nah, we'll be all right. I'm flying to New York tomorrow to meet with Luxem Hotel Executives. They're building seven more hotels next year, all with golf courses. I think we'll get the job," Preston said.

"That'd be great." Hope filled her with warmth.

"It'd be even better if you were here to help design some of those," he cajoled.

Sophie stared at muted moonlight playing across the ceiling and searched for the right words. The scraping of pine needles against the window was the only sound through the room.

"Or…" Preston sighed. "I'm sure you could help design them from anywhere in the world."

She breathed in. "Really?"

"All you need is the Internet and a cell phone," he said.

"I have those," Sophie said softly.

"You have me, too. You're a good friend. If you need me for anything, I'll be there," he said.

"Thanks." She kept her condition to herself for now. She wasn't ready to share.

"Night." Preston ended the call, and Sophie stretched to place the cell phone on the antique nightstand. It sounded like her old friend was saying good-bye. Sadness at what might have been slid through her before she rolled over to count sheep.

She reached the two hundredth white fluffy animal before an odd smell tickled her nose. She lifted her head to survey the air. Hazy beams of light filtered through the gauzy curtains and lent an ethereal glow to the old-fashioned room. Brass glinted off bedrails, and shadows hummed along the edges to settle into the corners.

The smell grew stronger.

Smoke. Oh God, it was smoke.

Gasping, Sophie jumped out of bed and leaned one

hand on the night table as the world spun around her.
Several deep breaths had the room righting itself so
she could hurry to the door and pull it open. Smoke
billowed up from the stairway. Flames licked the
wooden handrail.

Panic shot through her.

She slammed the door closed and grabbed her
sweatshirt off the flowered chair to cover the space
under the door. Thank goodness Mrs. Shiller was out
of town. She grabbed her cell and dialed 911, giving
the address to the operator before yanking on jeans, a
sweater, and her boots. Then she ran to the window
and pushed it all the way open before turning back to
the room. The solid door kept too much smoke from
entering, and she figured she had a few minutes to
figure out the safest way down.

She threw out her suitcase and pencils, watching as
they bounced two stories down onto the thick grass
and counting how long it took for them to hit the
ground. Too long. She didn't know the exact distance,
but she'd definitely break some bones if she fell out of
the tree. Smoke wafted out the front of the house to
cover the ground in a fine haze.

From a distance, sirens pierced the night.

Sophie finally swung one leg over the ledge of the
window. "We can do this, baby," she said, eyeing the
nearby thick branches of the statuesque bull pine.
She'd never climbed a tree but had studied gravity in a
physics class. Gravity would win over wishful hopes
any day. She reached for the closest branch, her plan
formulating as she moved.

Flashing blue and red lights stopped her mid-reach
as the sheriff's truck slammed to a stop and both Jake

and Quinn jumped out. More shrill sirens sounded in the night.

"Sophie!" Jake yelled as he barreled across the grass to look up at the window, Quinn on his heels.

"I'm fine, Jake," Sophie called down, her white knuckles on the window frame starting to ache. "Catch these, would you?" She tossed down her sketchbooks, which Jake snatched out of the air and placed near the base of the tree.

Quinn said something into a big black radio just as a red fire truck screeched to a stop and men in full gear scrambled off.

Jake's eyes held Sophie's captive as he murmured something to his brother, who nodded and turned to direct the crew. Then Jake jogged to the tree and jumped to clasp the bottom branch before swinging his legs up over his head toward another branch, crossing his ankles and levering himself into the tree.

Sophie held her breath as Jake easily climbed branch after branch and sent leaves and bark cascading down to the ground.

Suddenly, he stood even with the window. "You ever climb a tree, Sunshine?"

CHAPTER TWENTY

Sophie shook her head, tears surprising her as they slid down her face.

Scratches marred Jake's hands and bark wove through his hair, yet his grin was genuine. "Okay. You're going to reach out to that branch"—he pointed to the branch she had been aiming for—"and inch along until you get even with my hands." He nodded to the spot. "Then, when I touch your wrists, you get ready to move quickly, okay?" His voice stayed soft, soothing.

Sophie jumped as her door crackled into fire. Smoke filled the area behind her.

"Now," Jake coaxed as he shifted his weight on a straining branch.

Quinn took up a position directly below Sophie as she leaned forward and grasped the branch with both hands.

Following Jake's directions, she inched her hands and arms farther toward the trunk of the tree until her knees sat on the windowsill. She couldn't go any farther without putting all of her weight on the branch.

"Good job. Now this is a thirty-year-old tree, very sturdy, very safe. But that branch you're holding won't hold your entire weight for very long. Do you see the branch about three feet below it? The really thick one?" Jake pointed.

"Yes." Smoke filled her nose, and she coughed, her eyes watering from the sting.

"Good." Jake encircled both her wrists with his hands, balancing his weight while standing on two bowing branches. "So sweetheart," he said, speaking with confidence as more smoke spilled out from the window, "you need to hold this branch and swing your feet onto the lower one. It'll hold you all day. Ready?"

Sophie turned panicked eyes on Jake and tried to pull her hands back.

Jake shook his head. "The fire's behind you, Soph. You have to move—now."

"It's okay," Quinn called up from the ground. "I'm right under you. If worse comes to worse, you'll land on me."

Jake tightened his grip as the firemen slammed through the front door armed with axes and an uncoiled hose. "Now, Sophie."

"Jake, the baby." Sophie clenched the branch with a quick look down. Way down to where Quinn stood patiently.

"Babies don't like smoke." Jake's voice lowered. "Besides, ours would love to flatten Uncle Quinn, I'm sure."

Sophie tried to breathe shallowly and not take in too much smoke. With a quick prayer, she seized the branch and swung from the safety of the window, her heart all but beating out of her rib cage.

Her feet hit the lower branch and slid off, her boots scraping for purchase.

Panic squashed the breath from her lungs.

Sophie cried out as her legs dangled, and the sound of a branch snapping in two filled the air. It disintegrated in clumps of bark between her hands. Jake's hands tightened on her wrists as he held her in midair before he swung her so her feet could again find purchase. She caught the lower branch and pressed her legs forward until it balanced in the center of her feet.

She stood for a second, her feet on the branch, her wrists in Jake's broad hands, before he tugged her toward the trunk and wrapped her arms around the tree.

Sophie rested her head against the scratchy bark and her knees began to tremble.

"Okay, almost done now," Jake whispered into her ear as he positioned his body behind hers. "See that branch to the right, about a foot down from you?"

Sophie twisted her head to look. "Yes."

"Hold onto the trunk and just step one foot down to it." Jake pressed even closer. "I've got you, I promise."

Sophie stepped down, her palms scraping the bark as she fought for balance. Then she sighed in relief as she lowered her other foot. The crackle of fire and shattering glass boomed around them. The process continued until they both stood on bottom branches, about seven feet from the ground. At Jake's quiet order, Sophie sat, her hands gripping the trunk while he jumped to the grass.

"Grab my arms and jump." Jake reached up with both hands.

Sophie reached down, clasped broad arms, and let gravity have its way. Her feet met wet grass for a mere second before Jake scooped her in his arms and strode for the paramedic van on the street.

Sophie coughed lightly into his neck, her stomach heaving as Jake lowered her on the tailgate of his truck and a uniformed paramedic placed oxygen over her nose and mouth. Thunder crackled in the distance, and a light rain peppered the ground. Jake pushed Sophie farther into the back of the truck, into dryness.

She closed her eyes and breathed deeply, the scratches on her hands searing. Red and blue lights swirled as the firefighters rolled up their hose and the stench of burned wood filled the air. She began to shake violently, her teeth chattering behind the mask.

"The fire's out," Jake said, his eyes on Quinn and a sooty firefighter as they surveyed the damage from the porch. He shifted so he stood directly between the smoldering walls and Sophie, and she wondered if it were intentional or instinctive. "How are you feeling?"

"Better. I don't think I inhaled much of the smoke. The baby should be fine," she gasped.

"I was worried about you." Jake didn't turn as he spoke.

"How did you get here so fast?" she asked.

Jake straightened as his brother approached. "Poker night at Hawk's. I was there when Quinn got the call."

"The fire was intentional." Quinn didn't waste any words as he reached Jake and cast a concerned gaze toward Sophie. "Most people know Mrs. Shiller is out of town."

"You sure?" Jake lowered his voice.

"Yes. Typical Molotov cocktail through the front window." Both men turned to study her—twin sets of deep onyx eyes with different expressions. Quinn was all cop, curious and hard. Jake's expression spoke of something dark, something heated.

Yet one thing remained the same—both were pissed.

"What?" Sophie scooted to the edge of the vehicle, letting rain splatter against her legs. "You think this was on purpose?"

Quinn nodded. "I know it was. Have you noticed anything odd, anyone following you while you've been here?"

"I haven't seen anyone following me. But…" She took a deep breath. "Somebody has left notes on the Jeep window for me."

Quinn placed a restraining hand on his brother's arm as Jake's eyes narrowed dangerously. "Notes?" he asked.

"Um, yeah. Basically saying that the development was a bad idea," she said.

"And?" Jake growled it.

The notes had seemed silly and not threatening. "And that I should get out of town," she said. "They were more goofy than scary. Well, mostly."

Jake swore under his breath while Quinn cast a glance around at the milling spectators on the street and nearby lawns.

"I don't understand, I mean, the commissioners denied the application." Sophie's temper stirred. "There won't be a golf course."

Quinn shook his head. "The tribe has hired you to build a golf course."

Sophie shrugged, wary of the fury on Jake's face. This wasn't her fault. She turned her attention to Quinn. "I still have the notes. They're over in the suitcase I threw out the window." The muscle ticking in Jake's sooty jaw captured her gaze.

"Stay with her, Jake. Let me do my job." Quinn stepped around his brother and headed for the still smoldering house.

"I want to see them," Jake called to Quinn's re-treating back.

"I know," Quinn tossed back over his shoulder, his legs eating the distance to the pile under the bull pine.

Jake's eyes bored holes in her as his arms slowly crossed over his broad chest.

"I didn't think it was a big deal." Sophie answered his unasked question, snapping the words out.

The muscle in his jaw swelled. "How many notes?"

"Three," she admitted.

"When?" he snapped.

Sophie was saved from answering when Quinn returned with her suitcase in one hand, the other pulling papers from beneath his jacket. Two dark, masculine heads dipped to read the notes in the muted light of the paramedic's vehicle. Sophie shivered at the looks on their faces once they finished reading.

Quinn nodded at her. "Get her home. I'll follow up with questions in the morning."

Jake reached for her.

"No." Sophie moved farther into the vehicle as lightning ripped across the sky.

"You're coming with me." Jake hauled her out of the vehicle and carried her to his truck, where a depu-ty finished loading her possessions into the backseat.

"Damn it, Jake." Sophie fought the urge to kick him. Hard.

Jake didn't reply as he started the ignition and pulled past the emergency vehicles onto the rain-drenched road. Sophie pouted in her seat, determined to ignore him. He drove several miles in silence before speaking. "If you weren't pregnant, you'd absolutely be wearing my handprint on your ass right now."

Her butt actually clenched. "Good thing you knocked me up, then."

His dark gaze set a fluttering in her stomach. "Remind me to Google if spanking will hurt a pregnant woman."

"You don't scare me." Which was a complete freakin' lie. The guy was kind of scary…but he'd never hurt her.

"Why didn't you tell me about the notes?" he asked.

"They weren't really threats," Sophie huffed back.

"So it wasn't a big deal." Sarcasm wove through his every word.

Her arms crossed over her chest as she watched the storm wage outside the truck. "Right. Frankly, I didn't even think to tell you."

"Really," he drawled.

"Yes, really." Heat rose to her face. "This was just a quick fling, remember? A couple of weeks, then I was gone. Out of your life."

As they reached his home, Jake slammed the truck into park and turned off the ignition with a sharp twist of his wrist. "Once you discovered you were pregnant? You didn't think to let me know someone was threatening you?"

Sophie jumped out of the truck and headed for the house. She called over her shoulder, "They weren't threats." Yeah, she felt foolish for not reporting them to Quinn. No way would she admit it.

Jake followed close behind, his long strides putting her between him and the house. He pulled her to a stop, a feral glimmer in his eyes.

The fury of the storm was no match for the tempest rising inside her. "I didn't think to tell you. This was never going to be permanent."

"It is now," he said.

The rain smashed her hair against her face. "Wrong. We're exactly like this storm, Jake. Fiery, hot, even crazy. But you know what? You know the problem with sizzling summer storms?"

"No, what?" Even through the rain, his voice carried the hint of danger. Of wildness that outdid Mother Nature.

"They blow over. You settle back to enjoy the lightning show, the clap of thunder, and poof, they're gone." She yelled above the rising wind. "Blue sky follows along meekly, too quickly."

"We can't have blue sky?" His white shirt plastered against tanned muscle.

"Us? No way." The wind almost toppled her over. "You need to let me go, Jake."

The wind whipped his hair around his face, giving him a formidable, almost primitive look. His ancestry blazed in full force as he stood tall and firm against the gale. "Let you go? I think that's your fucking problem, Sophie."

"Meaning?" Her boots sunk into the mud as she struggled to keep her footing.

"Too many people have let you go." A quick swoop and she was in his arms, struggling against him with all her might as his strong body blocked the driving wind. "Your father, the bastard, left you. The second your mother married, she dumped you in some school. Didn't she?"

Sophie's battle against the strong arms shielding

her from the wind was in vain.

"Even Preston. Mr. Golden Boy with the Rolex. He left you here for me," Jake said grimly.

She fought a shiver at the warm breath against her ear.

One broad boot kicked the door open. He dropped her to her feet and slammed the door against the storm, and his furious face lowered to within an inch of hers. "I'm not letting you go. What's more, you don't want me to." Male outrage blazed through his eyes.

They stood staring at each other, dripping rain onto the stone floor and panting in uneven breaths.

"You are overbearing," Sophie gritted out, fighting a shiver, fighting exhaustion.

"You're an independent pain in the ass." Jake ran a frustrated hand through his sopping hair, obviously trying to control his temper. He took a deep breath.

She glared at him.

His voice softened. "One who has been through an ordeal and needs a hot shower and comfortable bed." He held out a hand. "Truce? At least for the night?" His words contrasted with the hard glint in his eye. He was raring for a fight.

Sophie slowly took his hand, her energy gone. She wasn't up to a fight. At least not right now. "All right. Just for the night."

CHAPTER TWENTY-ONE

The low hum of male voices awoke Sophie the next morning. The night was a blur. She had taken a shower and then fallen asleep in Jake's big bed before her head even hit the pillow. With a moan, she snuggled farther into the bed and tried to go back to sleep.

"It's time to get up." Jake suddenly filled the doorway. "I know you're awake."

"No." The pillow muffled her voice.

Jake moved into the room. "Yes."

"I need sleep," she mumbled, her eyes still closed.

"It seems we've had this discussion before." Jake chuckled. "Quinn is here and has questions for you. Get dressed and come on out."

Sophie groaned.

"Unless you want him to interview you in here," Jake offered.

Sophie glared through one slightly opened eyelid. "Fine. Just give me a minute."

"I will. Get up, sweetheart. We have a lot to talk about." He retraced his steps out of the room.

Sophie sighed and opened both eyes to muted tones of navy and tan and sensual paintings. Her possessions perched against the far wall. Jake must've brought them in earlier. She rolled herself to a sitting position before gingerly standing. The room spun and then settled. She headed for the attached bath.

A warm shower brought some life to her limbs, and she felt marginally better after dressing in comfortable jeans and her favorite green T-shirt. She yanked her curls into a ponytail and ran pink lip gloss over her lips before heading out to face the men waiting for her. All three of them.

They sat in the breakfast nook in faded jeans and long-sleeved T-shirts, thick mugs of steaming coffee on the oak table. The sliding glass door framed thick black clouds rumbling across a grumpy sky. Mineral Lake sat dark and still, waiting to get pummeled. Colton twirled leather gloves in his hand, his gaze idly following a tree branch slamming against the house. Quinn stopped whatever he'd been saying.

"Morning." Jake rose and grabbed a red mug off the counter to hand her, and then gestured her into the seat next to him. Congeniality softened his tone, but his eyes were granite hard. The thick fragrance of Colombian beans greeted her. She sniffed appreciatively as she sat, ignoring the set of Jake's jaw.

"It's decaf," Quinn muttered with a glare at his own cup.

"I told you I wasn't making two pots." Jake reclaimed his seat.

Sophie took a small sip and sighed as warmth filled her. "You three look like you're heading out to work the ranch."

"We are." Jake nodded toward the tumultuous clouds. "We have repairs to make all over the ranch, at least before the next storm hits—which should be late tonight or early tomorrow morning."

"How's Mrs. Shiller's house?" Sophie asked Quinn.

Quinn shrugged. "I went by this morning and met with the fire marshal. The damage isn't as extensive as we thought last night. The living room and stairwell sustained both fire and smoke damage, the kitchen just some smoke. We haven't been able to track down Mrs. Shiller or Lily Roundtree yet, but they'll check in with Lily's niece one of these days. We have repairmen there already."

"Any news on the notes?" she asked and Jake stiffened.

"No. Your prints were the only ones on the paper. The handwriting isn't familiar." Quinn shook his head. "There are a lot of people who don't want any development in the area. The tribe faced organized opposition when we built the casino even though we're autonomous on our own land." He rubbed his chin. "Though this seems like just one individual."

"So was the Unabomber," Jake said soberly. "My money's on the Concerned Citizens Group."

"Maybe," Quinn allowed. "I'll head out tomorrow and talk to Billy Johnson."

"Rockefeller," Sophie said with a small grin. Had her bout with the ketchup pissed off Billy enough that he'd try to kill her?

Quinn leaned forward. "Have you remembered anything? Noticed any strange cars around the neighborhood? Or any people walking or jogging down the street?"

Sophie shook her head. "I haven't noticed anything out of the ordinary."

"That's what I figured. I have deputies going door to door in Shiller's neighborhood. Maybe somebody saw something." Quinn took another drink of the unleaded brew and grimaced.

Silence sat comfortably around them until Colton pushed back from the table, his chair scraping across the thick wood floor. "Come on, Quinn. Let's go saddle the horses. I want to get this done before I head back to school." He nodded to Jake. "We'll meet you at the barn." He dropped a quick kiss on Sophie's head and left.

Quinn unfolded himself to his feet and placed a reassuring hand on her shoulder when he passed her. "We'll find who started the fire. You'll be safe here today, just stay close, all right?" He gave her a gentle squeeze before following Colton out of the room.

"Will you be all right here for a few hours?" Jake leaned forward and took one of her hands in his.

Sophie nodded, his broad hand warming her more than the coffee, his dark eyes smiling at her. "I'll be fine. I thought maybe I'd try out the studio today. I mean, since your mom and Leila went to so much trouble."

A dimple twinkled from his pleased grin. "Do you need help with that?"

"No. And I'm not promising to stay."

"I know." He stood. "We need to talk, but right now I have to go make sure the steers are safely contained."

She wrapped both hands around the warm cup. "It's a nice space to paint, and I may do the exhibit for Juliet."

"No pressure." One knuckle under her chin tipped her face up for his lips to brush hers.

"Right," she murmured with a raised eyebrow as he chuckled and moved across the kitchen.

"I'm not sure how long we'll be, but you call me if you need me. I'll have my cell," he said.

Sophie nodded as he left the kitchen and turned

back toward her coffee. The fire had been meant for her. To harm or just scare, she wasn't sure. Now she was staying at Jake's, right where he wanted her. Maybe she should fly back to California for some perspective. But the canvases and oil paints beckoned her from the bedroom. It wouldn't hurt to at least see how well the studio worked. She could just start one painting, since her day was free. It didn't mean she was moving to Montana for any length of time.

Reassured, she finished her coffee before dodging into the bedroom where she pulled on a pale sweatshirt, gathered her art supplies, and darted out the front door. Her hair blew around her face as she ran toward the garage, climbed the wooden steps to the landing, and pushed open the door. Dim light cut through sparkling dust mites as she slammed the door with one booted foot. The room was as perfect as she remembered.

Smiling, she glanced out the wide southern window to the storm lurking just over the lake. The urge to paint the scene bubbled through her veins, and she set up her easel and settled a pristine white canvas in place. She spread oils onto a board, chose the correct brush, and started to slide paint into a mood.

Several hours later, she ran through the front door as darkness fell early from the oncoming storm. It had held itself at bay the entire day, almost as if it posed over the lake just to assist in her brush strokes. The phone rang as she finished stirring an aromatic beef stew in a Crock-Pot for Jake, who'd called earlier and hoped to be back soon.

"Hi, Sophie, it's Rachel from the general store. The delivery guy just dropped off your new charcoals."

Sophie fought to keep from asking why the petite teenager had known to call her at Jake's. There weren't many secrets in the small town. "How late are you open today?"

"About another hour; we want to miss the storm," Rachel said.

"You think we have an hour until it arrives?" Sophie chewed on her lipgloss.

"Definitely, but no longer than an hour," Rachel said.

Perfect. "Okay, I'll be right there." Sophie cast a wary glance upward and then grabbed her keys and ran to the Jeep. It'd be at least an hour, maybe more, before the storm arrived, and she needed the charcoals to sketch out her paintings for the next day.

The storm held off as she drove the fifteen miles to the general store across from Doc Mooncaller's. She parked, dodged inside, and paid Rachel for the box of charcoals just as the girl was shutting down the lights for the day.

Fat raindrops began to fall as she pulled into the street to head back to Jake's, her new supplies perched safely on the backseat. The passenger door flew open and a lanky teenager leaped inside. Sophie jumped and slammed the brakes.

"Sorry if I scared you." He turned sorrow-filled brown eyes her way.

Fear caught the breath in her throat. "I know you. You were in the crowd at the Concerned Citizens meeting." Sophie eased the Jeep to the side of the road. The slam of drops on metal drowned out the sound of the running engine.

The kid nodded his blond buzz-cut head, his

slender hands running along his dark jeans before he wiped his nose on the back of one sleeve. "I'm Jeremy." He had to be fourteen, maybe fifteen.

"Hi." For some reason, she felt calm.

"Jeremy Rockefeller."

"Ah," she murmured.

"I, um…" A deep red blush stole across his features. "I wanted to apologize. For the fire."

Her heart clutched. "*You* set the fire?"

"Yeah. I didn't know you were pregnant." His eyes filled with tears.

Sophie whirled on the boy. "What difference does that make? It was okay to kill me otherwise?" Fury lit her tone and she stifled the urge to shake the kid.

"Kill you?" Jeremy vehemently shook his head. "Jeez, lady, I wasn't trying to kill you. Mrs. Shiller was out of town, and you had that big tree right outside your window. I knew you'd be all right. Everyone can climb a tree."

Oh. That probably did make sense to a kid. "What were you trying to do?" she asked.

"Be a man. Stand up for what was right." He wiped the back of a hand across his eyes.

"By leaving scary notes and firebombing an old woman's house?" Sophie's voice shook.

His shoulders drooped even more. "Dumb. I know. But your development would've raped the land. I just wanted to do something. For once."

Sophie sighed. The kid's misery was obvious. It certainly couldn't be easy being raised by the odd Rockefeller couple. "So why confess?"

"I can't sleep. I can't eat. I just feel so bad." His words rang true.

Sophie's thoughts reeled. The kid was obviously scared. And remorseful. Finally, sighing, she said, "We have to tell the sheriff."

"I know." Sniff.

She'd been a scared kid with crappy parents at one time, too. "If you promise to channel your aggression better and work for Mrs. Shiller one day a week for the next year, I won't press charges."

"Really?" Hope filled the brown depths of his eyes.

"Really, but I can't guarantee Mrs. Shiller will agree and not press charges, and I don't know what the sheriff will do." She really didn't want to know what Quinn would do.

"It's a deal, anyway." Jeremy held out a skinny hand and they shook.

"Okay." Sophie pulled back onto the road and circled around the fountain to the sheriff's office. Quinn met them at the curb, probably having seen them from his window. Rain curled through his thick black hair and plastered his denim shirt and faded jeans against his body.

Quinn's eyes revealed nothing as Jeremy slowly exited the vehicle. "Are you okay, Soph?"

"I'm fine. Jeremy has a confession to make, and I don't want to press charges," Sophie said.

Quinn's eyes hardened on the boy as he slammed the car door. He rapped three knuckles against the window and waited until she rolled it down a bit. "I'll need a statement from you."

"Nope. I have nothing to say. It's over as far as I'm concerned," she said.

Quinn shook his head. "Jake might have something to say about that."

Sophie shrugged. "It's not up to Jake. It's my decision and I've made it."

Quinn's lips twisted in a wry grin.

"What?" she asked.

"Just glad Jake is the brother who captured you. That's all," Quinn said.

"Funny. Say hi to Juliet for me." With her parting shot, she rolled up the window, gave Jeremy a reassuring nod, and pulled back onto the street. Jeremy, a pitiful expression on his face, watched her drive away. She accelerated and made quick work of the road back to Jake's. Her cell phone rang just as his home came into view.

"Where are you?" Jake's voice barely wove through the crackle.

She fought the urge to sigh. Darn meddling Lodge men. "I suppose you talked to your brother?"

"You should press charges," Jake said.

She rolled her eyes. "No. It's my choice."

"Fine. Where are you, softy?" he asked.

"Pulling into the drive," she said, stopping the vehicle.

She clicked off as the front door opened to reveal him, long and lean in the doorway. The sight of him, tall and sexy and waiting for her, tightened her chest as she jumped out of the Jeep, her charcoals safe in her hands. Jake took them from her as he pulled her inside, out of the misting rain.

"There's a storm coming." Warm arms enveloped her as the scent of horse, dust, and man surrounded her.

"You need a shower." She wrinkled her nose while stepping back.

Jake kept his gaze on her as he gently placed her box by the door. "Sounds like an offer."

"What—" was all she got out before two strong arms whisked her up and carried her toward the master bedroom. "Why are you always carrying me?"

"I like you in my arms." Jake dropped his mouth to nibble along her jawline. Straight to the shell of her ear.

"You like being in control." Breathiness coated her words, and she tilted her head so he had better access.

"I like you safe in my sights. And here"—he tightened his arms, his sizzling mouth now exploring her neck—"is the perfect way to do both." He lowered her to the bathroom tile. Two rough hands lifted her shirt over her head. His eyes hot on her, he yanked his shirt off before his hands unclasped her bra. It fell into the growing heap of clothing on the floor as he unsnapped his dusty jeans. He pushed them down muscled thighs along with his shorts, his eyes warming as she kicked off her boots and shimmied out of her pants.

"Rough day, cowboy?" She nodded to a deep purple bruise across one thick bicep.

He twisted the shower knob. "My mind wasn't on the job at hand." Steam began filling the air.

"What was your mind on?" she asked.

"This." One long tapered finger traced her collarbone and explored south to the peak of one pebbled nipple.

"Oh." Heat filled her.

He stepped forward and backed her into the stone tiled alcove. "And this." Two strong hands went to her buttocks and lifted her against the smooth tile. His mouth dropped to hers, gentle and sweet. The spray beat against his back and cascaded around to mist her.

Sophie wrapped both hands around his neck and both legs around his hips. "And this." His hand slid around to press ever so softly above her left breast. "I want your heart." His mouth dipped to replace his hand. "You already have mine. When I think about that kid jumping in the car with you…"

"He was just a scared kid. Not dangerous." Did Jake just say he wanted her heart? That silly organ fluttered hard.

"You wouldn't know dangerous if it bit you." To prove his point, he bit down into sensitive flesh.

Sophie gasped as sharp pangs of desire shot directly south. "Jake…" Her head fell back as his mouth moved down and engulfed her nipple in heat.

"I told you I'd never lie to you." His rumble against her flesh shot spasms deep within her. "I meant it when I said I was keeping you."

Her hands slid to the powerful strength of his dark chest and down the arms holding her securely, before moving back up to clench in his hair and yank his head to meet hers. Her legs tightened around him as she deepened the kiss. His tongue swept her mouth, one hand cupping the back of her head, the other squeezing her buttocks.

She pressed harder into him.

"Now, Jake," she moaned against his mouth.

With a quick movement, he impaled her against the wall and joined them together.

"Jake." It was too much. Sophie clenched his shoulders and tilted her head against the wall. Jake nuzzled his lips along her neck, keeping them both in place, on the edge of something.

Something amazing.

She swallowed as a tremor shook her. "Have you noticed you always have me against a wall?" she breathed.

He grinned. "This is the perfect position for you." His hands tightened.

She sucked in air, her sex throbbing. Electricity rushed through her veins. Her nerves sparked. "We do seem to fit."

He lifted his head, dark eyes devouring her. "I didn't like you out in that storm."

"I beat the storm home." Her eyes focused on his talented lips. His eyes heated even more. She opened her mouth to qualify the term *home*, only to have Jake swoop in and stop the words in her throat. Unapologetically. He kissed her until her mind reeled, until her heart turned over in her chest, and until she began to move against him, her feet pressing his buttocks with fervor.

Finally, Jake lifted his head and slid torturously out of her before slamming back inside with a twist of his hips, his eyes focused on hers. Sophie clutched his shoulders. A stirring started deep inside. Jake did it again. His grin was pure sin when he stopped moving.

"Promise me you won't go out in a storm like that again." His husky voice wrapped around her with the steam.

"Are you kidding me?" She groaned and struggled to move.

"Deadly serious." And he was. The muscled arms holding her vibrated with the need to move. A fierce muscle ticked in his jaw. His eyes hardened to sparking zinc. His expression showed he'd wait all day for an answer.

Oh, she'd gotten by just fine. "I'll avoid driving in storms." She would've promised just about anything to get him moving again. Quick as a flip of a switch, Jake gripped her buttocks and moved, all strength, speed, and muscle.

She trembled. A tightening in her abdomen compressed her lungs. Tingles of erotic shards rippled up her legs and over her thighs.

She ran her hands over his shoulders to the shifting deltoid muscles. So much strength in such an intelligent man. Throw in the inherent dominance that made her see stars, and every ounce of determination she owned spiraled into wanting to keep him. Forever.

He thrust harder, angling his pelvis to her clit.

She gasped, her hold tightening. Painfully hard nipples brushed his chest, sending sparks of fire to her sex. To her already engorged, ready to explode, aching clit.

Her hands slid farther over solid muscle and deep hollows to reach his vibrating biceps. He was so strong. He could do anything he wanted to her. The thought heated her, and the knowledge that he wanted to take her completely almost sent her over the edge.

His cock stretched her, sliding along firing nerve endings as he pounded.

She ground against him, climbing higher, seeking that detonation only Jake could provide. He hammered into her, gripping her hip, his fingers cupping her head.

A twister whirled through her. She broke. Nerves

flared, and waves rippled through her so brutally she cried out. Holding tight, her body rigid, she clung to Jake to keep her safe.

The prolonged climax tore her world apart, and she whispered his name.

CHAPTER TWENTY-TWO

Several hours after playing in the shower with Jake, eating the delicious stew while arguing over poor Jeremy's fate, and making love again in the big bed, Sophie dropped into an exhausted sleep.

She had odd dreams about skiing through storms all night, and awoke with a start, her eyes adjusting to early morning light filtering through the shades. She rolled over and buried her face into Jake's vacated pillow, filling her senses with the scent of man and musk. Hmm. His pillow was still warm. She snuggled closer and opened one eye on the empty doorway, her mind awakening much faster than her body.

What a night. Jake had been there every step of the way. When she'd been confronted by the Citizen's Group, when she'd needed to climb away from a fire, even when she'd been lost and confused. He was a man who stuck.

She'd always wanted that kind of security. And love.

The thought hit her square in the chest. She loved the man. Completely.

Did he love her? She squared her shoulders. Forget things working out. As a smart woman, as a strong one, she'd make sure things worked out. Whether Jake Lodge liked it or not.

She rolled out of bed with a smile on her face, yanked on jeans and a cream sweater, then padded barefoot into the kitchen. The echo of a clock filled the room as her gaze fell onto a note on the black marble counter.

Morning, Sunshine. There's decaf in the cupboard above the coffeepot. I've gone to meet Colton in the south pasture—steers loose and fence down from the last storm. There's another one coming, so stay inside. Love, Jake

P.S. About the storm, you're mistaken. We'll never blow over.

Sophie noted the signature, and her heart hummed to a deep warmth. He used the *L* word. Maybe he actually meant it.

Thunder pealed directly overhead, and a slash of lightning lit the cheery kitchen. Her stomach rumbled, and her head began to ache. "All right, baby, let's get some food." She filed through the shelves of the pantry. Ah, saltine crackers. Wonderful. A quick look into the fridge discovered butter and strawberry jam, homemade by Loni. The perfect combination.

Sophie placed her treats on the island and munched quietly, her gaze fixed on the dark clouds rolling toward her over the mountains. She finished her plate and looked through the fridge, still hungry. At this point she'd weigh a ton by the time the baby was born. Oooh, cold macaroni salad. Probably Loni's. Sophie took the bowl to the island to eat, enjoying the storm. Lightning jagged across the sky, and she jumped. The lights flickered.

A phone jarred her from her thoughts. Jake's landline. What if were Colton? No. He would've called Jake's cell. Sophie let it ring, listening intently when Jake's deep voice on the machine told the caller to leave a message.

"Jake?" Hysterics lifted Dawn's voice. "You're not

picking up your cell…" Static came over the line. "But…storm…road…there's…blood. I need help." Sophie lost the rest of the woman's words.

She jumped for the phone. "Dawn? Where are you? Dawn?"

"Sophie? I'm…bottom…of Jake's… Call Jake. There's blood. Need help." The phone went dead.

"Dawn? Dawn, answer me," Sophie yelled into the phone. A drumming buzz met her ear. She hung up the phone then grabbed it again and dialed Jake's cell. It went directly to voice mail. What to do? Sophie paced the cozy kitchen. "Okay. Dawn's in trouble. At the bottom of Jake's. Jake's what? The drive?" The drive was several miles long. Perhaps she'd slid off the road below. Sophie jumped at a loud thunderclap. She couldn't leave Dawn at the bottom of the hill. If that's where she was.

Sophie ran into the living room and grabbed a thick flannel jacket out of the closet. "It's okay, baby," she whispered as she buttoned it and rolled the sleeves up to free her hands. "We'll get Dawn and come right back. No problem." She wondered if the baby could hear the rapid beating of her heart. Then she wondered if the baby could even hear yet. Probably not.

After yanking on her boots, she ran into the rain, slipping once in the thickening mud and dropping to one knee. Her jeans shredded, and her skin smarted as blood began to well. With a hiss of frustration, she pushed to her feet and bolted for the rented Jeep, her pant leg stiff with mud and blood. She jumped inside the car, fastened her seat belt, wiped the rain from her face, and started carefully down the drive.

Wind slashed at the vehicle, pushing it to one side of the road where branches scraped the side like fingernails against a chalkboard. Water ran in rivulets across the dark asphalt, throwing the vehicle into a slide.

Sophie gingerly pumped the brakes. "This is bad," she whispered while jerking the wheel to the left. Rain beat against the windshield so hard even the fastest wiper setting failed to clear the view. Lightning crackled across the sky. Sophie screamed as a fallen branch clattered on the hood.

She slammed on the brakes and panted. Maybe this wasn't such a good idea.

"I already know this isn't a good idea," Sophie muttered to the empty vehicle. "But Dawn needs help, and we can make it." No way could she leave Jake's sister hurt and scared at the bottom of the drive.

She pressed on the accelerator while twisting the heat controls to defog the windows. There, that was better.

The road stretched down the hill, empty save for falling pinecones and branches. The wind battered the vehicle like a boxer without his gloves, hard, merciless, dirty. Sophie struggled to keep the Jeep stable on the roadway. The wind shifted, and rain angled straight at her. The cascading heat from the vents failed to warm her chilled bones. Her knuckles white on the wheel, she ventured farther down the road.

She made it about a mile before lightning snapped right in front of her. The crash of a splintering tree roared over the rain. With a cry, Sophie yanked the wheel to the left to avoid the falling white pine, sending the car hydroplaning across the asphalt. A loud crunch of buckling metal rose over the fury of the storm. She shut her eyes as the vehicle bounced twice, spun to the side, and rolled.

Darkness swirled, and then nothing.

. . .

She awoke to rain drumming against metal and pain screaming through her head. She tried to move, opening her eyes and realizing she was upside down. "Oh," she moaned, reaching for her seat belt and pushing the button with trembling hands. She dropped onto her already aching head, her breath whooshed out, and she curled into a fetal position on the inside of the roof.

The Jeep teetered upside down, and branches covered the shattered windshield and blocked her view. Groaning, she leaned forward and tried to open the driver's side door but it wouldn't budge. "Okay," she whispered. "It's okay. I'm okay." She wiped tears and blood off her face and curled into a ball around the baby. "Jake will come."

She pushed the deflated airbag out of her way and concentrated on her body. Her head hurt, and everything else ached. The ignition had turned off, so she didn't have to worry about that. The metal protested beneath her as she shuffled into a more comfortable position. Where was Jake?

Tears filled her eyes as her stomach cramped.

The baby.

She couldn't lose the baby. Until that moment she hadn't realized how badly she wanted the little one. And Jake. She finally had a chance for a real family, for a man who wouldn't leave her. She loved him. She'd known it for a while. As nausea spiraled through her and darkness crept across her vision, she wondered if it was too late.

CHAPTER TWENTY-THREE

The pelting rain, the swirling sirens, the crumpled metal—Jake had been here before. The devastating *déjà vu* of the moment froze his legs in place.

Through the smashed window, the limp body of the woman he loved failed to move. Devastating pain shot through him at the thought of losing her. His chest actually pounded in agony.

Fire lit through him. Not again. He wouldn't lose Sophie.

He jumped toward the upside-down vehicle and grabbed the door handle.

Strong arms banded around him and twisted to the side. Fury leaped through his veins, more powerful than any storm. He pivoted and shoved Quinn. Hard.

His brother slipped in the mud. He growled and pounced, both hands grabbing Jake's arms. "Stop it."

Jake was beyond reason. Only one thing mattered—getting to Sophie. The primitive being deep within him surged to the surface. He shrugged from his brother's grasp and rushed toward the vehicle, shoving a paramedic out of the way.

The tackle from behind dropped him into the mud and away from the car.

Rage heated every neuron in his body. He flipped around, both hands clapping Quinn's face.

Quinn howled in anger and punched him in the jaw. "Fucking knock it off. The car isn't stable—we need to go in through the other side." For good measure, he punched him again. "Let us do our job."

Jake blinked. Reality returned. Mud squished his back, and his heavy-as-hell brother flattened him to the ground. He glanced into his brother's concerned eyes. "She left me."

Quinn yanked them up. "She didn't leave you—not Sophie. This is different."

Maybe. Jake turned toward the car. "I need to know. Is she—"

"I don't know." Quinn shoved him. "Stay here. I'll check."

Jake nodded, helplessness catching in his throat. She couldn't be dead.

He kept his gaze on his brother as he maneuvered around the firefighters trying to open Sophie's door. Quinn leaned in and then slowly stepped back. "She's alive."

Jake hit his knees. Thank God.

Then he leaped forward to tear the car apart and get her out.

• • •

Sophie opened her eyes slowly to a white wall and bright lights. A dull pounding set up in her skull, so she turned her head to where Jake slumped in a chair, his chin on his chest, his hair wet under a black cowboy hat, his shirt and jeans streaked with mud. She shifted to the right.

Loni moved forward in her chair, her black eyes bright with concern, her hair a lopsided mess atop her head.

"My baby?" Sophie croaked, her throat on fire.

"The baby's fine." Loni reached out a hand and smoothed back her curls.

The pain receded to a dull roar as other aches and pains sprang to life. "Dawnie?" Sophie asked.

Loni nodded. "Dawn is fine. Hawk found her at the bottom of the hill. She slid and wrecked her car but only had a couple of small cuts and plenty of bruises. Dawn was more scared than hurt. They're waiting the storm out at Hawk's place."

Sophie glanced over at Jake." I wasn't running away from him." Tears filled her eyes.

"I know. Though you should probably tell him that, sweetheart." Loni nodded toward the midnight dark gaze running over her face. "I'm going to go call Colton. He's worried sick." She hurried from the room.

Sophie's throat felt like sandpaper as she turned toward Jake. "I thought you were asleep."

"I was praying," Jake said.

"I wasn't running away from you," she whispered.

"I know. What were you doing?" His chair creaked as he leaned forward and gently clasped one of her hands in his. Raw cuts and bruises welled from his knuckles.

She gasped at his hurt.

A purpling bruise spread along his jaw. "The Jeep's metal put up a fight while we were getting you out," he confirmed. He stroked his finger down her cheek. "Where were you going in that storm?"

"Dawn called. I thought she was hurt at the bottom of the hill," Sophie said.

"I figured. So you went out into the storm," Jake sighed.

The gathered tears began to fall. "I didn't mean to

risk the baby, Jake. I just didn't know what to do."

"The baby? You think I'm concerned for the baby?" His eyes glowed dark pools of emotion.

"Yes," she said miserably.

"I'm concerned for you. Don't get me wrong, the baby means the world to me. But there isn't any world without you," he said.

Her heart leapt. "What?"

"I love you, Soph. I don't want this life without you in it," he said.

Her mind swirled while heat bloomed in her chest. "I don't understand."

"I thought about it. The whole time you were out. We can live in San Francisco and visit Montana as much as possible. Maybe even get a summer place here." Jake almost smiled.

"You'd move to the city? With Leila?" she gasped.

"I could make enough money in the city to easily travel back and forth. Our kids could have the best of both worlds." He nodded.

Hope exploded within her entire body. "You'd give up your job with the tribe?"

He sighed deeply. "I'd have to."

"The best of both worlds?" she asked, her heart spinning.

"Yes," he said.

"Well then." She smiled, her heart in her throat. "Maybe we should live here and visit the city whenever possible."

He frowned. "I don't understand."

"My children are going to grow up with grandparents. And uncles. And meddling friends. Not alone like I did." This was her decision, and she was making it.

"The law and the ranch keep me really busy. I don't know how often we'll be able to travel." His eyes veiled as if he didn't want to get his hopes up.

She loved the stubborn man. "Jake, didn't I tell you? I'm going to be a famous artist. And a golf course designer. Money shouldn't be a problem."

"You're awfully confident, Sunshine." Dark eyes melted to burnt sugar.

"Yeah, I know. By the way, I love you, too," she said.

EPILOGUE

Ten months later

In the background, the band played a soft tune as children romped along the bridges and yelped when they spotted swimming koi.

"Willa's Garden is perfect, isn't it, Nathan?" Loni crooned to her grandson while deftly lifting him from Sophie's arms.

"Thanks. Man, he's getting heavy." Sophie grinned and stretched her arms over her head before looking around. "Where's my daughter?"

"She's over feeding the koi with Tom. Those fish are going to need a diet by the end of summer." Loni smooched kisses on the baby's nose and then grinned as he giggled. Already, he looked just like his daddy with dark hair and even darker eyes.

"Okay. Where's my husband? They should be finished posing for the picture by now." Sophie scanned the area.

Loni shrugged, her attention focused on the sparkling eyes staring up at her. "I don't know. Probably hanging out with Colton since he's just home for the weekend."

The sound of rapid hooves made both women look toward the main road.

"Oh my!" Loni yelped just as one broad arm leaned down and lifted Sophie onto a rushing black stallion. Two other horses followed close behind, leaving dust in their wake.

"Jake, for Pete's sake," Sophie bellowed from the rushing horse.

She grasped the silky mane in desperate hands, warmth from the familiar body behind her sending awareness through her stomach.

"Hang on." Her husband's deep voice caused chills down her spine as he maneuvered the large stallion through trees with strong thighs. Thighs that gripped hers while hers gripped the horse.

His strong, oh-so-hard body warmed her as they galloped through the damp forest into a meadow filled with light. The horse slid to an abrupt stop and birds took to the air. The arm around her waist lowered her gently before her captor leaped lithely to the ground.

She backed up until a tree stopped her retreat.

"She's kinda pretty," said Colton as he stopped his mount.

"She'll do," Quinn agreed gravely. "What are you going to do with her, Jake?"

"That's my decision," Jake said with a soft grin as he stepped forward. "Now go away, both of you." His eyes remained on the woman watching his approach.

His brothers turned their mounts and took off.

"One more step, and you'll land on your ass." Sophie lifted her chin, fighting a smile. Shafts of sunlight poked through the pine trees all around them, and a quiet descended in the cool forest.

"Is that a fact?" he drawled while taking another step forward. "Think you can take me?"

"I am pretty tough," she agreed, pressing farther into the rough bark.

"So I have to chase you down to get a second alone

with you, hmm? Some captive you turned out to be," he said.

Sophie grinned, her mouth watering at the ripple of muscle over her husband's chest. "Not true. I believe we had several minutes together last night. And early this morning."

"True. But between Willa's spring opening, your designing my golf course, and preparing for another art show, by the time my mouth is in your vicinity, it doesn't want to talk," he said.

"It's not my fault you're insatiable." Love hummed along her veins, through her blood for this man.

"Is, too." One final step and he was but a breath away.

Sophie looked up several inches. "You want to talk, huh?"

"Yes, I believe so." A hand fisted in her hair and warm lips dropped to nuzzle her neck.

"Jake, you didn't answer your brother." She tilted her head to allow for better access. "About what you're going to do with me."

His smile was pure sin as he raised his head and midnight dark eyes captured hers. "I caught you, Sunshine. I'm keeping you."

ACKNOWLEDGMENTS

There are so many folks who help to make sure a book becomes a final product—many behind the scenes whose names I don't even know. So first, to all the hardworking people at Entangled who make the company run so smoothly—thank you!

Thank you to my very patient and understanding family. My husband, Big Tone, you're the best. And I like that you've learned to just nod when a crazy lady at the grocery store asks if the books feature you. Thanks to Gabe and Karly—I appreciate that you pretended I was taking stats at your basketball games and not really plotting out my next scene. You kids rock!

Thank you to my clear-headed, thought-provoking, and loyal agent, Caitlin Blasdell—I'm so glad I found you! Thanks as well to her colleagues at Liza Dawson Associates—you're a wonderful group.

Thank you to my editor, Liz Pelletier, who I had to ply with red wine and sit on in Seattle until she agreed to read my submission. (Note to aspiring authors: this only works once). Thanks for the wonderful edits and the hard work…and I promise next time you suggest I expand a scene I won't add a full twenty pages. Well, probably.

Thank you to my Entangled team: Heather Howland, Misa Ramirez, Jessica Estep, Barbara Hightower, Sarah Weiss, Cameron Yeager, Robin Haseltine, Toni Kerr, Alanna Hilbink, and Curtis Svehlak. Also to everyone who has worked on my behalf whose names I don't know yet. You're amazing!

Thanks to the Inland Empire Chapter of RWA—I appreciate the support and friendship!

Thanks also to my hard-working Facebook Street Team—you're a lot of fun, and you always make me smile. I appreciate the hard work!

Under the
Covers

a Maverick Montana novel

NEW YORK TIMES Bestselling Author
Rebecca Zanetti

This one is for Debbie English Smith, my younger sister, whose gift with horses would've made her fit right in with the Maverick Montana folks.
We just returned from an awesome time in Vegas, and according to the Top Dollar machine,
"You're a Winner!"

CHAPTER ONE

Juliet tensed the second the outside door clanged shut. So much for her brief reprieve. She turned around and sat on the highest rung of the ladder, her gaze on the hard wooden floor so far below her feet. Paintings still hung on the wall, and she needed to take them down. But first, she had to face the sheriff.

She'd known he'd show up after receiving her e-mail. Nerves jumped in her belly as she waited.

He strode into the main room of the art gallery and brought the scents of male and pine with him. Stopping several feet away, he looked up. "Juliet."

"Sheriff." She took a deep breath, trying to keep her focus on his dark eyes.

But that body deserved a second glance. Tight and packed hard, the sheriff wore faded jeans, a dark button-downed shirt, and a gun at his hip. Black hair swept away from a bronze face with rugged features. Not handsome, but definitely masculine and somehow tough. Years ago, she'd liked tough. Many years ago.

He cocked his head to the side and studied her.

For months, he'd been studying her…that dark gaze probing deep, warming her in places she tried to control. But Quinn Lodge was all about control, and the smirk he gave promised she'd be the one relinquishing it. "Any other woman, I'd be worried about that top rung. Not you, though," he murmured.

She smiled to mask her instant arousal from his gravelly voice and resorted to using a polite tone. "You don't care if I fall?"

"I care. But you won't fall. You're the most graceful person I've ever met. Ever even seen." Admiration and something deeper glimmered in his eyes.

She swallowed. "Thank you. Now perhaps we should get to the arguing part of the evening."

"I'm not going to argue." Stubbornness lined his jaw, at home and natural along the firm length. "Neither are you."

While the words sounded like a peaceful overture, in truth, they were nothing but an order. She clasped her hands together and smoothed down her long skirt. When he used that tone, her panties dampened. If the boys from the private school who'd dubbed her "frigid virgin" could only see her now. "Good, no arguing. We agree."

His grin flashed a dimple in his left cheek, and he shifted his weight. "You're not leaving the gallery."

"Yes, I am." She should not look. She absolutely would not look. But she'd recognized his move when he's shifted his weight…yes. A very impressive bulge filled out the sheriff's worn jeans.

She swallowed, her ears ringing. Her thighs suddenly ached to part.

His eyebrows rose. "Juliet?"

Guilt flashed through her even as her eyes shot up. "Yes?"

His smile was devastating. "Would you like to finally discuss it?"

"Your erection?" The words slipped out before she could think. *Oh God*. She slapped a hand over her mouth.

He laughed, the sound male and free. "Here in the

backcountry, ma'am, we prefer the term *hard-on*. But yes, let's discuss the fact that I'm permanently erect around you. Tell me you're finally ready to do something about it."

Her heart bashed into her rib cage. "Like what?" she choked.

"Well now"—he tucked his thumbs in his pockets, his gaze caressing up her legs to her rapidly sharpening nipples—"I've never taken a woman on a ladder before, but the thought does have some possibilities. How flexible are you, darlin'?"

The spit dried up in her mouth, while warmth flowed through the rest of her. He wasn't joking. If she gave the word, he'd be on her. Shock filled her at how badly she wanted the sheriff *on her*. Most men would be at least a little embarrassed by the tented jeans. Not Quinn Lodge. He wanted to explore the idea.

"While I appreciate your offer, I'd prefer we returned to settling the issue of the gallery." Could she sound any less like a spinster from the eighteen hundreds? "I'm unable to pay the rent, and thus, I need to move on." But where? The upcoming art show needed to be somewhere close by or nobody would attend. While she had no choice but to flee town right after the opening, at least she could leave on a triumphant note.

"I don't need the rent. Let's keep a running total, and after you're hugely successful, you can pay me." He ran a broad hand through his hair. "Stop being impossible."

She wasn't a charity case. Plus, the last person she wanted to owe was the sheriff. The man viewed the world in clear, unequivocal lines, and she lived in the gray area. A fact he could never know.

"I'm sorry, but I'm not taking advantage of you." She was out of money, and no way would she stick around.

He sighed. "Juliet, I don't need the money."

The words from any other man would've been bragging. Not Quinn Lodge. He was merely being nice…and telling the truth. His family owned most of Montana, and he'd invested heavily in real estate. The guy owned many properties, including the two-story brick building that had held her gallery for the past few months, since she'd arrived in town.

She sighed. "I'm not owing you."

His chin lowered.

Hers lifted.

A cell phone buzzed from his pocket. He drew it out, frowned at the number, and then looked back up at her. "I, ah, need to take this. Do you mind?"

"No." Darn if his manners didn't make her feel even more uncomfortable.

"Thanks." He lifted the device to his ear. "Lodge here."

He listened and slowly exhaled. "Thank you, Governor." He shook his head. "I don't think so… Yes, I understand what you are saying." Dark eyes rose and warmed as they focused on Juliet's hardened nipples. She'd cross her arms, but why hide? It wasn't like the sheriff was concerned about the massive erection he was still sporting, and she could be just as nonchalant as he. She dragged her thoughts back to his ongoing conversation.

"I would, but I already have a date." That dimple flashed again, this time longer. "Yes, I'm seeing someone—Juliet Montgomery. She owns the art gallery in town. Of course she'll be at the dance as well as at the ride. Thank you very much." He slid the phone into his pocket.

Tingles wandered down Juliet's spine. Several of her fantasies regarding the sheriff included being part of his everyday life. Of course, many more centered on his nights. "We're dating?"

"Well now," only a true Montana man could drawl a sentence like that, "how about we reach an agreement?"

She frowned even as her body sprang to attention. Her raging hormones would love to reach an agreement. "I'm not for sale, Quinn."

He lost the smile. "I would never presume you were. Here's the deal—we both need help. How about we assist each other?"

Without knowing the facts, she knew enough to understand this was a bad idea. No matter how many tingles rippled through her abdomen. "Why did you tell the governor we're dating?"

"He tried to fix me up with his niece, and I needed an out. You're my out." Dare and self-effacing humor danced on his face. "How about we date for the next six weeks, just until the election, and you keep the gallery rent-free? You'd really be helping me out."

Quinn was up for reelection for the sheriff's office. She shook her head. "You don't need to play games. Everybody loves you."

"No. The people in the town of Mineral Lake like me. But Maverick County is a large area, and I need the governor's endorsement. The last thing I have time for is campaigning for a job I love when I need to be *doing* that job."

Considering she'd be leaving soon, maybe she should provide him some assistance. "You have more money than the governor. Buy some ads."

"I'm not spending money on ads. It's a waste of resources as well as an insult to hardworking people."

"Tell the governor you aren't interested in his niece." Juliet narrowed her gaze. Quinn Lodge didn't kowtow to anybody.

"Refusing the governor is a bad idea." He stalked closer to the ladder. "His niece is Amy Nelson, a woman I briefly dated, and she wanted more. Her daddy is Jocko Nelson, and he's more than willing to spend a fortune backing Miles Lansing for sheriff. My already dating somebody saves my butt, sweetheart."

The last thing she wanted to talk about was his fine butt. Nor did she want to think about him dating some other woman. "I'm not your solution."

"Besides," he reached the bottom of the ladder and held up a hand, "aren't you tired of dancing around this? For the last few months, we've danced around this."

"That's what responsible adults do." She automatically took his hand to descend.

Electricity danced up her arm from his warm palm.

"Bullshit." He helped her to the hard-tiled floor. "You feel it, too."

Yes, she did, and the crass language actually turned her on. But he didn't know her, and he wouldn't like her if he did. "I've chosen not to act on any temporary attraction." As a tall woman, it truly unnerved her when she needed to tilt her head back to meet his gaze. "How tall are you, anyway?"

He shrugged. "Six four, last time I checked. How about you?"

"Five ten."

He nodded. "Petite. Very petite."

The man was crazy. She tugged her hand free. "I'm not dating you."

"I know. We're pretending." He glanced around at the many paintings on the wall. "Are these from Sophie's new collection?"

"Yes." The man already knew his sister-in-law's paintings adorned the walls.

"Didn't you promise her an amazing showing for the opening of your gallery?" he asked.

Oh, guilt wasn't going to work. Juliet sighed. "Yes."

"Well, then. This is the only place to have an amazing showing, right?" he asked.

Wasn't that just like a man to go right for the kill? Sophie was Juliet's friend, one of her only friends, and the showing meant a lot to her. "You're not being fair."

He reached out and ran a finger down Juliet's cheek, his gaze following the motion.

Heat flared from his touch, through her breasts, right down between her legs. "Stop," she whispered.

His hand dropped. "I need a pretend girlfriend. You need to keep the gallery open. This is a perfect agreement."

Darn it. Temptation had her glancing around the spectacular space. Three rooms, all containing different types of Western art, made up the gallery. The main room already held most of the paintings created by Sophie Lodge. Rich, oil-based paintings showing life in Maverick, life on the reservation, and the wickedness of Montana weather. The showing would put both

Sophie's art and Juliet's gallery on the Western-gallery map just like the C. M. Russell Museum in Great Falls, or the National Museum of Wildlife Art in Jackson Hole.

She wanted on that map. Perhaps badly enough to make a deal with the sheriff. Plus, she was tired of trying to ignore her attraction to Quinn. Would that attraction explode or fizzle if they spent time together? Frankly, it didn't matter. She had to leave town soon. Why not appease her curiosity? "Okay, but keep your hands to yourself."

"But—"

"No." She pressed her hands on her hips. The man was too dangerous, too tempting. A woman had to keep some control, or Quinn would run wild. No question. "You're creative, and this is your idea. If we pretend to date, you keep your hands off me."

His eyes dropped to an amused, challenging expression. He held out both hands, palms up. "Tell you what. These hands won't touch you until you ask nicely. Very nicely."

"That will never happen," she snapped.

His left eyebrow rose. "I wondered if that red hair came with a temper." Interest darkened his eyes to midnight. "So much passion locked up in such a classy package. I thought so." He leaned into her space. "Be careful, or I'll make you beg."

She almost doubled over from the spike of desire that shot through her abdomen. How many pairs of high-end panties had she gone through the last month, anyway? "Back away, Sheriff."

He stepped back, as she'd known he would, but the knowing desire in his eyes didn't wane. He glanced at his smartphone. "Give me your cell number in case I can't find you at the gallery."

She shuffled her feet. A cell? Yeah, right. Even if she had the money, they were too easy to trace. "I, ah, don't have one."

Watchful intelligence filled his eyes as he glanced up. A cop's eyes. "Why not?"

"I have not had time to find the right one and choose a plan," she lied.

"Interesting." He slipped the phone into his pocket, turned on the heel of his cowboy boot, and headed for the door. "Be ready at six tomorrow night for the Excel Foundation Fundraiser in Billings. The drive will take us an hour."

All tension disappeared from the room as he left. Well, except for the tension at the base of her neck from the land line phone being silent. It had been ringing for almost a week with nobody being on the other side. Surely a bunch of kids just goofing off, but she couldn't shake the uneasy feeling that kept her up at night. Well, when erotic images of a nude Quinn Lodge weren't haunting her dreams.

She sagged against the ladder as she forced herself to relax. Yeah, right. Pretending to be the sheriff's girlfriend would be anything but relaxing. What in the world had she just done?

• • •

The fundraiser was located at the Billings Mountain Hotel, and the grand ballroom sparkled like something out of New York. Chandeliers lined the ceiling, and real crystal decorated the tables.

Juliet willed her nerves to stop jumping.

Just inside the main doors, Sophie Lodge grinned and looked her up and down. "You are gorgeous. Now stop being a chicken. I let you drive in with me earlier so you could avoid Quinn, but your time is up."

Juliet smiled to keep from frowning at her friend. "First of all, we had to come to the city to choose the music for your art show next month. Then, apparently, you needed to shop like you'd won the lottery." It had been fun to shop with a friend again. Although her life had been odd, at one time, she'd had friends she'd enjoyed shopping with. Cool, cultured friends who minded their own business.

Not Sophie. Nobody in the town of Mineral Lake minded their own business. Shopping with Sophie had been more like an inquisition into Juliet's feelings for Quinn.

Sophie flipped her wispy, blond hair over her shoulder. The mass framed her pixie face perfectly. "The menu we chose from the caterer was ideal, too."

Yes, it was. Unfortunately, the deposit for the food included the last dime Juliet owned. Now she had to go through with the sheriff's charade no matter what. It was way too late to turn back.

Sophie teetered on her heels. "It was nice of the hotel to let us change in one of the guest rooms."

The hair prickled on the back of Juliet's neck. Was somebody watching her? She cased the room, and too many shadows slithered around the corners.

"I really like your dress," Sophie continued chattering.

For goodness' sake. Juliet needed to get a grip. Nobody was watching her. She glanced down at the sparkling green dress she'd brought when she moved to Montana. "I think I should've worn basic black."

"Why?" Sophie smoothed her hands over the blue fabric hugging her hips and the very slight baby bump. She'd wanted a fun pregnancy dress, but at only two months pregnant, everything had been too big. Her dress had spaghetti straps, a cinched waist, and great lines. "We work hard and deserve a break. Every woman should sparkle."

The last thing Juliet wanted to do was stand out. "This was such an incredibly bad idea."

Sophie shrugged and peered at the crowd. "If you ask me, it was about time Quinn made a move."

"Your brother-in-law and I are friends. He needed a date, and I said yes." Maybe she should tell Sophie the whole truth. "Anyway, you look fantastic. Do you still think you're having a girl?"

Sophie looked around and then lowered her voice to a whisper. "Actually, I'm almost certain it's a boy. I don't know why, but I think so. Which would be cool, because we could name him Nathan, after my uncle." She all but beamed. "Plus, Leila thinks she'll have a little brother, and I swear, that kid is psychic sometimes."

"True," Juliet murmured. Leila was Jake's daughter from a previous marriage, and the six-year-old was definitely precocious.

Sophie grinned. "You are so good at changing the subject, aren't you? We were talking about you and my brother-in-law, sheriff hottie." Sophie waved. "There they are."

Juliet turned to spot Quinn standing by Sophie's husband, Jake, by the far bar. The men were dressed in black suits. She swallowed. The sheriff looked amazing, tough and sleek, in the suit. It was open at the collar and showed a crisp white shirt. Even then, the sense of contained power vibrated around the man. "Oh, my." Juliet steeled her shoulders.

Sophie nodded vigorously. "I know, right? Those Lodge boys clean up nice. Really nice."

"I see the honeymoon isn't over for you," Juliet said.

"Nope." Sophie started to lead the way through the crowd. "We've been married for a whole month now, and I don't think the honeymoon will ever be over."

Happiness all but oozed from the woman, and a pang of want hit Juliet. What would it be like to have a wonderful husband, a family, and a life without fear? "Please tell me I can drive home with you tonight."

"Nope," Sophie repeated, tossing a grin over her shoulder. "Jake and I are staying at the hotel. I guess you'll have to drive back with Quinn."

Juliet glanced up to discover dark eyes watching her. Her knees trembled, but she gracefully moved between chairs and people on her three-inch heels. While her mother hadn't taught her much, she had taught her how a lady appeared in public. Whether she liked it or not.

Sophie reached Jake first and was instantly captured in a kiss that belonged in private. Juliet ignored them and kept her focus on the sheriff. "Quinn."

He clasped his hands at his back. "You look beautiful. Can I touch you yet?"

She grinned, her heart lightening. How did he know just what to say to make her laugh and relax? "No, but I'm glad you remembered the rules."

He sighed, a woeful frown on his face. "Rules are meant to be broken."

Boy, did she wish he actually meant those words. "You enforce rules...rather sternly, or so I've heard."

"I believe I'm tough but fair." He used air quotes on the adjectives, a smile in his voice.

A round man three inches shorter than Juliet breezed around the bar. "Sounds like a campaign slogan, Sheriff Lodge."

Quinn turned his head and nodded. "Juliet Montgomery, may I introduce Governor Nelson?"

The governor took her hand in his moist one. "It's a pleasure to meet you."

"And you, Governor," she said softly. "Congratulations on getting House Bill 3000 passed. Very impressive."

His wide chest and even wider belly puffed out. "A beautiful woman who follows politics. You're a lucky man, Lodge."

"Yes, I am," Quinn said, his gaze warm on her.

The lights flickered, and the governor released her hand. "Well, I guess it's time to sit down for dinner. I need to make a quick phone call and will meet you at our table." He bustled off.

Quinn stepped close enough for her to smell pine and male, but he didn't touch her. "HB 3000?"

"A new bill allowing Montana residents to trap mountain lions if they're a threat to livestock." She shrugged. "I Googled recent bills before heading into town earlier."

"Googled?" His grin flashed his dimple. "I think I love you."

Her knees trembled with the need to step back.

Even though he was kidding, heat slid through her skin. She smoothed her face into calm lines. "That was easy."

His dark eyes narrowed. "Did I upset you?"

"Of course not." Why in the world did he have to be so observant? She had to get away from him. No way could she spend time in his vicinity and keep her secrets. While she hadn't broken any laws in Montana by using a fake name, she had definitely crossed a line or two. Or maybe having fake identification was a crime. But she hadn't used it, so did it count? Of course, the laws she'd broken back home would land her in prison, without question. She hoped to any God who listened that Quinn Lodge wouldn't be the man slamming the steel door shut.

Quinn leaned closer. "What thoughts are flashing so quickly through that pretty head of yours, darlin'?"

She dropped her eyelids to half-mast. "I was just noticing how sexy you are in a suit, Sheriff." If all else fails, flirt.

"Hmmm." He gestured toward a round table in the center of the room. "How about we go sit down before I press you to be honest with me?"

Instinctively, she batted her eyelashes. "You're talking in riddles." Turning on her high heel, she sauntered through tables and chairs to reach their spot. Her rear end burned from his gaze, and she couldn't help but glance over her shoulder.

She shouldn't have looked. He stood, his focus on her bare skin, fire in his eyes.

The sheriff wanted her—and he had no intention of hiding it.

Grabbing a chair back, she stopped moving before she fell on her face. This was going to be a long night.

CHAPTER TWO

Quinn waited for the bartender to count his change, his gaze on the woman sitting at their table. He'd settled her in her seat before returning to the bar. They had the white wine she liked, and he wanted her happy.

His brother shot him a grin. "Sorry I couldn't ride in with you earlier—my hearing today took longer than I thought."

"No problem." Quinn had always been proud Jake was such a hotshot lawyer.

"I know." Jake eyed the table. "You and Juliet, huh? Finally?"

"Yes."

"How?" As usual, Jake went right for the throat.

Quinn dropped a tip in the jar. "I told her I needed a date, in fact, I needed a girlfriend until the election." Which was the truth. Her sticking by his side would certainly ease the situation with the governor and his niece.

Jake snorted. "Juliet fell for that?"

"So she says." Quinn couldn't stop the wry grin. "She required a push, she's a sweetheart who wants to help, and it seemed to work."

"Maybe she just doesn't want to date you. How many times as she turned you down, anyway?" Jake asked.

"Twenty or so." Quinn lifted a shoulder. "Though she's interested." He frowned and accepted the change.

"There's something about her that seems off. Not dangerous, just off."

Jake took a glass of Scotch and an orange juice from the bartender. "I'd run her."

Yeah, Quinn had thought about a background check. He grabbed Juliet's wine and his ginger ale. "I'd rather she told me the truth."

"I get that." Jake turned toward the table. "My daughter is thrilled you're finally out with Juliet because she's ready for a new aunt."

Quinn almost spilled the wine. "I like Juliet and think we'll have some fun. You need to explain things to Leila." Leila was six years old and way too wise for her years, maybe because her mother had passed away when she'd been so young. But she'd found a new mama when Jake married Sophie, and now she wanted everyone married and happy.

His brother shrugged and kept walking. "Sometimes marriage sneaks up on you. Trust me." He sat next to Sophie and handed her the juice.

Quinn sat down. Nothing snuck up on him, and he wasn't the marrying kind. At least, he wouldn't marry until he stopped being a threat to the people around him. While he had his emotions mostly under control, some nights he awoke from a nightmare, thinking he was in Afghanistan and looking for somebody to hurt. Until reality set back in.

Juliet reached for her riesling and cut him a quick glance.

Next to her, Amy Nelson chattered on about the summer collection of designer shoes she'd just bought. What was it with women and shoes? She should've spent more money on material for a dress. The white one she wore stretched tight against her ample bust and stopped several inches up from her knees. Her boobs pushed out of the sides and up the top, and she'd probably have bruises from the fabric cutting in. Her uncle, the governor, sat next to her texting something on his phone. A widower, he'd apparently brought his niece as a date.

Next to him sat Miles Lansing, one of Quinn's two opponents in the sheriff race. Lansing was a politician, not a cop, and he didn't belong with a gun in his hand. His wife, a brunette with hard eyes and a slinky black dress, sat to his left, her gaze appraising.

Quinn glanced at Juliet again. Her green dress clasped at one shoulder, leaving the other one bare and inviting for his mouth. It cinched at her tiny waist and flared down to her feet. Although the sparkles covered most of her, she was sexy as any dream. An Irish sprite in his Montana world. His cock instantly sprang to attention, which was nothing new when Juliet was near. He leaned over to whisper, "You really do look stunning, Juliet."

A sweet blush rose from her neck up over her porcelain skin.

Sophie's head jerked, and she raised an eyebrow at Amy, the expression a woman got when she was about to defend a friend. Quinn rolled back the last few minutes of chatter in his mind. Oh. Amy had made a comment about homespun dresses and Juliet's sparkles. That was a girl insult, right?

He opened his mouth to say something nice about the dress, only to stop when Juliet patted his hand. The innocent touch shot straight to his groin, and he snapped his jaw shut to keep from groaning.

She smiled. "Oh, Amy, you're so sweet. I bought this at Saks in New York last season. They have the nicest personal shoppers in the designer section. You really must give them a try—they're masters at helping women choose the, well, the right size for their figures." She turned toward Sophie. "How is the design for the golf course in North Carolina coming?"

Delight flashed across Sophie's pretty face. Quinn had a feeling the delight was due to the smack-on insult Juliet had delivered so classily and not from the question about design, but who the hell knew. Women had a language he'd never fully understood, although Juliet had a couple of levels to her he hadn't anticipated. Classy, elegant, and tough. She handled the political situation like she'd done so her whole life. But she came from a small town in Idaho, right?

"I'm almost finished with the practice greens," Sophie said with a grin. Multitalented, Sophie designed golf courses when she wasn't painting. Her first art show would be in a month at Juliet's gallery, and both women seemed to be working hard.

Amy interrupted Sophie, her blue eyes flashing sparks. "When were you in New York, Juliet?"

Juliet took a sip of her wine. "Last year. Every once in a while, I like to visit the galleries in the city to see what's new just so our Western art is up to speed at my gallery."

Her hand shook slightly as she set her glass down. Most people wouldn't have noticed.

Quinn Lodge wasn't most people. The woman lied. Why?

He glanced at his brother to see if Jake had noticed, but Jack was busy tracing Sophie's knuckles with his fingers. Damn newlywed. "Jake, how did your hearing go today?" Quinn asked.

Jake lifted his gaze, his expression knowing. Oh yeah, he'd noticed Juliet's discomfort. "Fine. The hearing was a status one regarding an upcoming trial. Not nearly as interesting as a good election fight."

"Speaking of campaigning" — Miles looked down his patrician nose — "I find it odd Bennington isn't here tonight."

The governor shrugged. "Perhaps he's not as serious about running for sheriff as the two of you." Faded eyes appraising, the governor surveyed the room.

"He's probably busy running his ranch," Quinn said smoothly. He liked Bennington, but the guy had a fierce temper and shouldn't carry a gun or badge. He should stick to his ranch and the wildness surrounding them all.

"Bennington doesn't have much backing." Miles leaned forward. "I've heard the Kooskia Tribe doesn't support him. Frankly, the tribe only supports its own."

Quinn smiled. "The tribe supports the best person for the job, regardless of tribal affiliations. Always has, always will." Right now, the Kooskia Tribe backed him, and he liked to think it was because he did a fine job. Though he was self-aware enough to know it probably didn't hurt that he was a tribal member and his grandfather the chief.

Miles rubbed his Rolex. "I'm sure you could always get a job with the tribal police force."

"I'm sure I could." Quinn met the man's gaze evenly. "I like collaborating with them and still policing the entire county."

Mile's quick smile promised fierce competition.

"Interesting."

Juliet smoothed out her napkin. "Miles, what experience do you have in law enforcement?"

Warmth flooded through Quinn. The pretty redhead had just defended him.

Miles cleared his throat. "I'm more of a financial leader, which we need in the county. Not every sheriff needs to swagger around and shoot people."

Jake snorted. "Have you been swaggering and shooting people again, Quinn?"

"I guess so. Don't tell Mom." Quinn slid his arm around Juliet's chair, careful not to touch. Something in him wanted to tuck her close and hold tight.

Dinner passed quickly and included veiled insults from Amy, classy counters by Juliet, and threats from Lansing about how new blood was needed in the sheriff's office. By the time the waiter removed their dessert plates, Quinn's temples pounded.

Sophie nudged him. "I can't believe you're not drinking," she whispered.

He could use a Scotch. Or three shots of tequila. "I'm driving Juliet home, and I'm on call tonight." Several deputies were out with the flu going around town, and he needed to be alert.

"Bummer." Sophie took a healthy gulp of her orange juice.

Sometimes Quinn wanted to drop his sister-in-law in the lake. At her impish grin, he smiled back. Nah. He adored the pixie-sized smart-ass.

An orchestra in the corner started playing softly, and he pushed away from the table, glad for the reprieve. "Juliet? Let's stretch our legs. Please excuse us, folks."

"I'd love to, Sheriff." She rose from the table, all grace, all beauty, and smiled at the group at large. "Thank you for a wonderful dinner. Enjoy the rest of your evening."

The governor patted his round belly. "We'll see you Saturday at the charity ride? It's for the boys group outside of Missoula and is so important to our constituents."

"We'll be there," Miles Lansing said, a smirk on his lips.

Quinn forced a smile. "Juliet and I wouldn't miss it. See you then."

They needed to get away from the table. Quinn followed her as she all but glided around tables and people to a quiet area by the bar. Tall and curvy, she moved with an intriguing elegance. Her backless dress revealed a sexy spine right down to her tiny waist. Damn, he loved backless dresses. His fingers itched with the need to touch her silky skin, but he'd made a promise.

Juliet stopped, turned, and rested against a three-foot-wide wooden pillar. "Well, dinner was interesting."

His shoulders relaxed for the first time all evening. "Do you understand why I didn't want to escort the governor's niece?"

"Yes. I can't believe you dated her." Juliet's eyes glowed like emeralds in the soft lighting.

"Me either." He glanced over his shoulder to catch their table watching him. He focused back at the stunning woman within his reach. "They're watching us. How about a kiss to convince them we're truly together?"

"We're not." Pink wandered across her high cheek-bones. She'd worn her dark red hair up in a sophisticated twist he wanted to tangle. "There's nothing between us, Sheriff. You need to know that."

He loved a good challenge, so he stepped close enough to smell citrus and woman. "I disagree. There's a lot between us, Juliet. Now, how about my kiss?"

• • •

Juliet had sipped just enough wine, dealt with just enough snide comments from Amy, and fought off enough attraction to the sheriff to pick up the challenge. All night she'd been aware of the heat pouring off the man and of every contained move he made. "You think you can kiss me without touching me?"

"I didn't promise not to touch you. I promised to keep my hands off you." Dare, with more than a hint of male, glittered in his eyes. "One kiss to convince people around us that we're together...and to convince me that you're not interested in me."

She pressed her palms and her back against the smooth wood. For so long, she'd been afraid to date. Most men turned tail and ran when they got to know her. Quinn would never get the chance to run because she'd run first. So why not accept the sexy promise in his challenge? Freedom flushed through her. "All right. Let's see what you've got, Sheriff."

His eyes darkened to a dangerous hue. Slowly, keeping her gaze, he put both hands on the pillar on either side of her head, effectively caging her.

The breath caught in her throat. Desire hummed

awake in her abdomen. The world silenced around her, narrowing to the man suddenly in her space.

He leaned forward until his lips hovered over hers. "Close your eyes." The words brushed against her skin in a soft but unmistakable order.

Her eyelids fluttered closed. For seconds, nothing happened. Then a firm glide of warm lips brushed hers, and she opened her mouth with a sigh. He slanted his mouth and deepened the kiss, all male, all in control. Her head was trapped, her body secured, and his mouth gave no mercy. Gentleness slid into possessiveness. He kissed her hard enough she could do nothing but take all he was giving.

Electricity zipped from her lips to her breasts, zinging around until sparking between her legs.

Her nails dug into the wood in an effort to remain still. Then her hands moved on their own and tunneled through his dark hair, like she'd wanted to do for months.

His tongue brushed hers, rubbing on the roof of her mouth. With a soft groan, she slid her hands over his broad chest to clutch his hair. Her nipples pebbled harder than diamonds when she pressed her body against his. Her clit jumped to life, pounding with a need so great it actually hurt.

He went deeper, making her head spin.

She forgot where she was. For the first time in months, she forgot who she was. As he kissed her, she could do nothing but feel.

For eons, she remained lost in the whirlwind created by Quinn Lodge.

Slowly, he softened the kiss. Finally, he released her mouth.

She gaped at him, her hands in his thick hair, her body pressed against his. *Oh, oh.* She blinked several times and released him to lean back against the pillar. His hands were still flattened against the wall. He'd kept his promise and hadn't touched her. Of course, she'd all but tackled him to the ground to ride like a prized pony.

Expecting triumph on his face, she stilled at the genuine pleasure lighting his eyes.

His cheek creased. "Juliet, I do believe you're one of a kind."

Kindness from the sexy man would be her undoing. She'd tell him to go away…if her voice worked. There was no way her voice worked. What was she going to do?

His dark gaze dropped to her throbbing lips. "Why did you lie during dinner?"

Alarm flared through her mind with the clanging of bells. "I didn't lie."

His gaze rose to pin her as effectively as his lips had a moment ago. "Yes, you did lie. While I couldn't care less why or when you went to New York, I do care that you lied to me."

Then he shouldn't have asked her to be his date. She'd been lying to him since day one, which is why they had to stay apart from each other. The sheriff was too observant. "I don't know what you're talking about, and I really don't appreciate being questioned like this."

"My apologies." His jaw firmed. "Are you in trouble? I mean, do you need help?"

Yes, she was in trouble, mainly from the sexy sheriff. "No."

He sighed. "This isn't one of those situations where you're running from debts, the law, or an abusive ex-husband, is it?"

Close, but not quite. "I give you my word I'm not running from debts, the law, or an abusive ex-husband." It was the truth, and by the way his body relaxed, he believed her.

"Okay." His hands dropped away from the pillar. "Can I touch you yet?"

She smiled, her body roaring with need. If she gave in to it, he'd burn her up. But it might just be worth it. "I'm not interested."

His upper lip quirked. "Darlin' I could have you coming around my cock in three seconds, and you know it."

The rough tone and crass words almost sent her into an orgasm right there. Never in her life had she been talked to in such a manner—who knew she'd enjoy it? Or maybe she just liked Quinn. "You're terribly confident, aren't you?"

"Want me to prove it to you?" he asked.

Yes. Definitely yes. She lifted her chin and glanced around the ballroom. "Where? A nice linen closet somewhere?" Her sniff held just the right amount of derision to darken his eyes.

He leaned in, his heated mouth on her neck. "When I take you for the first time, and believe me, it's going to happen, I want a bed and all night. You're going to scream my name, and you're going to beg, pretty Juliet."

It was a good thing she hadn't worn panties. Why bother? As his confident tone wrapped around them, so did reality. She was leaving, and for the first time, she wondered if she had the power to hurt him. Hurting Quinn was the last thing she wanted to do. "You made a promise—no touching," she whispered.

He levered back, gaze narrowing on her. Whatever he saw made him lean back more. "You're all stubborn Irish, aren't you?"

"Close enough," she murmured.

He nodded. "Okay. You get your reprieve for now. Let's go have a drink next door with Jake and Soph, and then I'll take you home. Tomorrow I work, but on Saturday, I accepted an invitation for us to ride in the Boys Club trail-ride."

Panic heated her. "Ride? Ride what?"

His eyebrow rose. "Horses. Of course. Why?"

She swallowed. "I, ah, I don't ride."

He blinked. Twice. "What do you mean?"

"I don't ride horses. Ever." How hard was that to understand?

"That's impossible. You're from Idaho, right?" He cocked his head to the side.

What did that have to do anything? "Ah, yes," she lied, keeping her gaze open and on his.

"But you don't ride."

She shook her head. "No. Never have."

He slowly nodded, his eyes narrowing. "Okay. I get off work at four tomorrow. Meet me at my house, and we'll go for a quick lesson."

"No way," she blurted out.

"You live in Montana, sweetheart. Sometimes nature makes it difficult to get around, and you need to know how to ride a horse," he said.

By the set of his stubborn jaw, he would not back down. The last thing she wanted to do was pique his curiosity. If he ran a background check on her, she was in for a world of trouble. "Okay. Fine."

Her on a horse. Quinn Lodge being curious. Things were going south...and fast.

CHAPTER THREE

The following morning, Quinn glanced in the rearview mirror of his truck. "Is your seat belt on?"

Leila rolled her eyes. "Uncle Quinn, I put the belt on right away. Are you going to marry Juliet?"

The questions had been peppered at him for the last five minutes as he drove through town. "No. Is the belt tight?"

Dark eyes met his in the mirror. Aware and intelligent eyes. "I axed you a question."

He swallowed. "I answered your question."

"Don't you like Juliet?" Leila asked.

"I like her just fine." In fact, after dropping her at home the previous night, it was all he could do not to break down her door and take another kiss. They'd had a nice drive home, and while she'd been mostly quiet, the silence had been comfortable. But sometimes finesse was necessary. Juliet deserved space, and for a moment in the ballroom, she'd seemed afraid. He couldn't let her fear him, so he'd backed off. Of course, he'd see her for the riding lesson at his ranch later that afternoon.

He drove the truck through the Maverick town archway, heading for a development outside of town, and focusing back on his niece. "I'm not getting married. Juliet and I are just friends."

"Nuh-uh. You always look like you wanna kiss her when we talk about her." Leila tugged on her pink sweatshirt.

He coughed. "I do not."

"Do too." Leila glanced out the window. "Daddy looks at Mom that way." A small flush wandered over her tiny features. "Sophie says I can call her mom. That's okay, right?"

His heart warmed until his chest hurt. "I think it's great, little one. Sophie is a good mom to you."

Leila shrugged and watched the trees flying by outside.

Quinn slowed the truck to turn into the subdivision. The poor kid only had pictures to remember her mother since she'd died when Leila was just a baby. "I remember your mom as someone who loved you with all her heart. She would like you to have Sophie as a mom now, sweetie. This would make your mom happy."

Hope filled Leila's eyes when she turned toward him. "You promise?"

His heart might just break. "I promise. Your mom would want you happy, right?"

"Yes," she said.

"This is a good thing. Love is always a good thing." He waited until she nodded, relief filling her face. Then he turned between stone pillars forming the entryway to the subdivision.

"If you love Juliet, that's a good thing then," Leila said.

There was no way he was winning that debate. He grabbed a silver star from the empty ashtray and handed it over the seat. "You are hereby deputized again to assist me in official sheriff duties."

"Cool." Leila grasped the star and pinned it to her chest. "I'm your favoriest deputy, right?"

"Without question." Though the girl was going to do something safe with her adult life, if he had anything to say about it. Chances were, he didn't. "I need you to keep Mrs. Rush company while I talk to her son." He stopped the truck in front of a newly painted blue house, stepped out, and assisted Leila to the ground.

"I know." She hopped happily next to him, her braids flopping. In her dark jeans, pink shirt, and scuffed tennis shoes, she was the most adorable deputy he'd ever seen. Her black eyes and hair were all Jake, but her delicate bone structure came from her grandmother.

They rang the bell, and Anabella Rush opened the door. Her blond hair was mussed and her eyes tired, but the grin she flashed reminded him of the sweet girl he'd kissed behind the bleachers at fifteen. She hoisted a three-month-old baby to her shoulder, tottering only slightly in the boot cast covering her right foot. "Thanks for coming."

"No problem." Quinn followed her inside the house and stepped over a stuffed bear, three toy trains, and a baby's binkie on the way to the back door. "How many kids do you have now, anyway?"

She laughed. "Very funny. Considering you're godfather to all of them, you know we only have three. It just seems like twenty." Sighing, she patted the baby's back. "I swear, every time Charlie comes home on leave, we end up having another one." Sliding open the glass door, she stepped lightly down four cement steps and over a tricycle before pointing to one of several large trees fronting federal forest land. "Henry is up toward the top."

Quinn glanced down at her. "How did you hurt your foot?"

"I tripped over the tricycle." She chuckled.

"I'm glad you called." Quinn nodded at Leila. "My deputy will take your statement, while I go, ah, climb a tree."

He left the ladies talking on the porch and crossed the wide lawn before arriving at the heavy birch tree. Looking up, he sighed. The kid was so far up, only one dangling tennis shoe was in sight. Shrugging, Quinn seized a sturdy branch and hauled himself up. Branch after branch, he climbed upward, bark scraping his hands and faded jeans. Finally, he reached Henry.

"Hi," Henry said, shoving his glasses back up his nose.

"Hi." Quinn found a heavy branch and sat, making sure the eight-year-old was secure. He seemed fine. "Why are you in a tree?"

"I was thinkin'."

Quinn surveyed the area, smiling as he caught Mineral Lake in the distance. Mountains rose tall and strong around them, while the valley spread out with ranches and homes. "This is a good place to think."

"Yeah." Henry coughed. "My mom called the cops, huh?"

"Ladies don't like when people climb trees and they can't climb up to make sure everything's all right," Quinn said.

Henry rolled his eyes, the blue flashing behind thick glasses. "Dude, my mom can climb a tree. Well, usually."

"That's Sheriff Dude to you, buddy," Quinn said.

Henry snorted. "I heard you're going to marry the art lady."

Quinn stilled. "Where the heck did you hear that?"

"Baseball tryouts." Henry frowned and kicked out a skinny leg.

"I see." Quinn rubbed his chin. "How did tryouts go?"

"Not so good." Henry bit his lip. "Yesterday was warm-up day. Tryouts are actually next week."

Quinn nodded. "I guess tryouts are kinda hard with your dad being overseas, huh?"

"Yeah. He's down range of Afghanistan again." Henry hunched narrow shoulders. "He was supposed to teach me how to throw a curveball, but he had to go…"

Oh, man. "So you're in a tree thinking about the situation?" Quinn asked.

"Yeah. Seemed like a good place to think," Henry mused.

"Why didn't you call me?" Quinn asked.

"I figured you were busy catching bad guys and chasing the art lady," Henry whispered.

Regret slammed into Quinn's gut. "I'm never too busy for you. I played baseball through high school and then college football. I can toss a curveball." He kept his voice calm, while he yelled at himself inside. He should've been checking closer on his friend's family. "Plus, my younger brother, Colton, was the best pitcher in the state for years. It's May, and he's home for summer break from graduate school. We'll get him over here this afternoon."

Hope filled Henry's face. "Really?"

"Of course." Quinn held his hand up for a high five. "Now, let's go get down and make sure your mom isn't mad at us for being in the tree so long."

"Okay." Henry flushed and rubbed a hand through his spiky hair. "That's not the only reason I'm up here."

Quinn settled back down. *God, please don't let it be a sex question*. He wasn't ready for that, but he had offered to help, so he'd figure something out. "You can talk to me about anything. What's up?"

Henry pointed to the wide yard next door. "I was watching Mr. Pearson, just making sure he's okay."

Quinn slowly turned his head to spot a naked, ninety-year-old man plucking weeds away from his fence. "He's naked."

"Yeah." Henry sighed. "He's been making moon-shine in the shed again, and sometimes he samples the goods. Today, I think he sampled the goods."

Quinn strangled on a cough. "Does your mom know he makes moonshine?"

"Nope. She really doesn't climb trees very often." Henry grabbed a branch and started descending. "Do you hafta arrest Mr. Pearson?"

"Well, I at least need to talk to him." Quinn stepped gingerly on a narrow branch.

"Okay. But you gotta know, he'll run. He likes to run sometimes," Henry warned.

Wonderful. Quinn shook his head. He actually wanted to fight for the sheriff position again? As he glanced at the now whistling, stark-nude old guy, he grinned. Yeah. Why the hell not?

• • •

Juliet slowly approached the paddock, wondering how in the world she'd ended up in this particular mess. Sophie had been kind enough to drop her off at

Quinn's ranch house, but at some point, Juliet needed a car. Though licensing a vehicle under a fake name would be too risky, and she really didn't want to break the law any more than she probably already had.

She rubbed her aching eyes. She'd had a sleepless night after the sheriff had dropped her off after the ball, and her exhaustion was all his fault. The kiss had her body on fire and her mind whirling.

Plus, when she'd gotten up to get a drink of water, she could've sworn somebody tapped on the outside door to her apartment. She'd pressed her ear against it, no way stupid enough to open it, but nothing.

The ranch smelled like the wild outdoors with pine, huckleberries, and dust. The barn door opened, and the cause of her restlessness stalked out, leading two saddled horses. Today the sheriff wore dark jeans and a long-sleeved T-shirt that hugged his fine muscles like it was made of horny female cotton.

He tipped his black hat up on his forehead.

Desire slammed through her so quickly she stopped moving. The Stetson shadowed his angled face in a way promising danger and sex, and not necessarily in that order.

She swallowed. "Those are big horses." The biggest one was all black with wild eyes. A stallion? The second was a light tan with a dark brown mane. It was much smaller than the other one, but still huge.

Quinn rubbed the shadow on his jaw. "I've dreamed about you wearing tight jeans. My dreams didn't come close to the reality."

Serious and intent, his deep voice wandered right down her belly to pool in heat. Was it possible to be seduced by a voice? She squared her shoulders. "Why did you chase a naked old man around the Maverick subdivision earlier today?"

Quinn chortled and handed her the reins to the smaller horse. "There are no secrets in Maverick, now are there?"

That wasn't true. Not even close. She frowned at the quiet animal. "No."

Quinn leaned close and brushed a kiss on her forehead. "It's nice to see you, Juliet."

She nodded, her tongue suddenly thick.

His eyes darkened. Keeping his hands on the reins, he tilted his head and his mouth captured hers. Firm and warm, his lips tempted her until she opened for him.

She could've easily stepped back.

Instead, she stepped forward into the heat generated by the man.

He deepened the kiss, taking her under, making her head spin. Finally, he released her and focused on her face. "I've wanted to do that since our kiss last night."

Juliet breathed deep, trying to dispel the crazy need rushing through her body. No way would her voice work.

"This is going somewhere, Juliet," he said.

Panic shoved desire out of the way. She shook her head.

Amusement filtered through his eyes. "Apparently you need time. That's all right. I'm a very patient man."

She glanced around the area in a lame effort to control her libido. His sprawling ranch house held a wide porch, the colors matching the three closest barns. Acreage spread out in every direction, some fields, some trees, plenty of cattle in the far distance. "I like your place."

"Me too." He smiled. "Mom and Tom live toward the north, while Jake and Sophie have a house to the east of here. Apparently Colt wants to build over that way, as well."

"You've combined all the family ranches?" she asked. What would it be like to have family you actually wanted to be around?

"Sure. We all work the cattle and share the profits—and losses." He shrugged. "Are you done stalling?"

She swallowed. "Yes."

He chuckled and drew the smaller horse closer. "This is Mertyl, and she's a sweet mare. I borrowed her from Jake. Put your foot in the stirrup, and I'll hoist you up."

Juliet cleared her throat and tried to ignore her still-humming abdomen. Man, the sheriff could kiss. "I can get up." She'd seen this done on television.

"Sweetheart, let me help." Charming was too tame of a word to describe his smile, and the deepening of his voice was unbelievably sexy. "Just a quick caveat to the no-touching-rule limited to helping you on and off the horse. I promise," he said.

Either she could make a fool of herself and fall on her head or let the sheriff assist her. "Fine."

Quinn grasped her waist and swung her onto the horse. Her butt hit the leather saddle. He instantly released her. Ignoring the heated imprint from his hands, she wiggled into a comfortable position.

"Excellent." Smooth and graceful, the sheriff hoisted into his own saddle. "You've ridden a little, right?"

She considered lying. He had probably been riding

since birth, and he'd figure out the truth. "No. This is my first time."

"How is that possible?" he asked.

"My folks owned a store in Idaho, and we lived in town. No horses." This time she did lie and kept her gaze on the mare's mane. The sheriff needed to quit probing into her past. "Tell me about the naked man you arrested."

"Just a minor arrest for public nudity and being drunk on moonshine," Quinn said. "He made bail, and I took him back home."

Just what she'd thought. "You couldn't give the guy a break?"

"I had to make sure he had a good meal." One dark eyebrow rose. "Plus, the guy broke the law."

No wiggle room with the sheriff and his values. He would never understand why somebody might need to break the law, and she needed to forget this crazy crush she had on him. "You're a hard man, Sheriff."

"So I've been told, darlin'." He held the reins and easily controlled the massive beast. "Are you all right on the mare?"

Besides still being horribly aroused and sitting on a wild creature of death, sure, she was fantastic. "I'm fine."

He nodded, gaze dropping to check the stirrups. "You're a delicate one, Juliet Montgomery. I want you to go slow and take it easy. If you get scared, we stop."

A hard man with a sweet side. A very intriguing sweet side. Juliet couldn't bring trouble down on him. If the truth about her family came out, just being linked with her might hurt him professionally. "I'm not delicate."

"Yes, you are. But I won't let anything hurt you. I

promise." He flashed an encouraging smile. "You can do this."

She came from the city where predators wore fancy suits and drove fast cars. In Montana, the strong wore cowboy hats and didn't care about the rest. Without a question, Quinn Lodge held a natural toughness no city man could match—but he played fair. Those who played fair got hurt. No way would she let him get hurt from knowing her, because her family *never* played fair. "This isn't a good idea, Quinn."

"Sure it is. Just use your hands and legs to steer Mertyl. She's easy," he said.

Had he really misunderstood her? Taking a deep breath, Juliet nudged the horse with her knees. The animal trotted forward.

Ack. Juliet grabbed the reins tighter. She bit her lip while her rear end hit the leather saddle. Slap. Slap. Slap.

Pain ricocheted up her spine.

She whimpered, her mind rushing to the inevitability of her flying over the horse's head and landing on her face. Panic shot through her. Yanking up on the reins, she kicked her feet.

The horse shot into a gallop, straight for the solid ranch house. Juliet screamed, her body flying into the air and slamming back on the saddle.

A low growl echoed behind her before Quinn snapped an order to the horse. The animal halted immediately. Juliet lunged forward onto the pommel and dropped back. Safely.

She hissed out a breath. Her butt ached already.

The sheriff jumped off his horse and strode toward her. The sun slanted across his strong face, highlighting his Native American features in a way she hadn't caught before. Such purposeful steps from such a dangerous man made her want to kick the horse again just to get out of his path.

He reached up and grabbed her elbows, pulling her off the beast. Two seconds later, she stood on the unmoving, rocky, very safe ground. Her legs wobbled as she took several deep breaths.

The mare whinnied and wandered toward some tall grass.

Quinn released her, tipped back his hat, and grasped the reins of his stallion. "I've never seen anybody move exactly the opposite of the horse, before." Shaking his head, he quickly untied his saddle and tossed it on the ground but left the heavy blanket in place. The black horse snorted and twitched its tail.

She stepped away from the monster. "I told you I couldn't ride."

"I know." Quinn's hands circled her waist.

"No." She shook her head and attempted to evade him.

He kept her in place. "Trust me." With a mere shift of his massive shoulders, he tossed her onto the huge stallion.

CHAPTER FOUR

Panic heated Juliet's blood. He'd thrown her on top of a wild stallion. She grabbed the silky mane. "What in the world?"

Planting both hands behind her butt, the sheriff jumped up behind her.

Heat fired down her torso. Desire unfurled inside her with the strength of a tornado. Sparks flew throughout her skin. Instant and unexpected.

He leaned forward, his breath whispering against her ear. "Now relax."

Her nipples hardened to points. Fuzziness filled her mind. A need ripped through her veins so demanding she could barely breathe.

The horse huffed.

Strong, large hands settled into the mane in front of her.

On all that was impossible and holy. She bit back a whimper that wanted loose.

"Okay." His heated breath caressed her ear. His hard chest cradled her back. "Tighten your legs, and you can control the animal."

She swallowed. "I, uh…" Her voice lowered to a huskiness she barely recognized.

"You're safe." His voice slid to guttural.

She tightened her grip. "Okay. What now?"

"Just click your tongue and pull in with your foot," Quinn murmured.

His heated breath licked around her ear, brushing

her face, shooting beneath her skin to warm her. Everywhere. Her eyelids fluttered. Thank goodness he couldn't see her face. Mentally smacking herself, she kicked the horse.

The animal snorted.

Quinn leaned into her, his hardness cradling her back. He dug his boot into the horse's flank, man and beast both rippling with impressive strength.

The horse moved forward.

Flutters that had nothing to do with fear rippled through Juliet's abdomen. She sucked in air scented with male. Her eyelids became heavy, while her limbs tingled. Her breasts ached. Her sex softened.

"Okay. Now you steer him." Quinn's voice was gravel in a cement mixer.

This type of instant desire was unreal. Couldn't be happening. A long shiver wandered down her entire body. He had to have felt it.

"Juliet." He groaned.

Naturally, unwillingly, her head dropped back to his chest. "Quinn."

He stilled and then exhaled. "Juliet, you need to concentrate."

"Can't." Desire reduced her to one syllable, and she couldn't find it in herself to care.

Muscles vibrated against her back. "What do you want, darlin'?"

She groaned low in her throat and shut her eyes. "Quinn."

"Juliet, either start paying attention to the lesson, or tell me what you want."

What did she want? Him. Without question, him. It was a mistake, one she'd probably regret, yet one she wanted to make so badly. "I want you."

He stiffened. The breeze wandered around them with the scents of honeysuckle and pine. "Say the words," he said.

If she said the words, there would be no going back. She'd definitely have to leave town after the art showing. It was only a matter of time anyway. "Touch me."

Sharp teeth nipped her ear, spiraling hunger inside her veins. "Ask nicely."

Her eyes flashed open. His dominant tone trembled through her nerves, sparking around her body until lighting her skin on fire. "Please."

His hand flattened against her stomach, and he pulled her into heat and male. He chuckled, the sound heavy with need. With a slight shrug that moved her shoulders, he slid his palm up to cup one breast over her shirt. "Finally."

Electricity zinged from her chest straight to her clit. A roaring filled her ears. "Don't stop."

He tweaked her nipple, and she exhaled on a sob. How was it possible to be so in need?

Spring sunshine cascaded down, and they sat on a horse in front of his house. Anybody might come by and see. The summer day was warm, but still, she shivered. She struggled to regain some sense of reality. "We're outside."

"I know." He grasped her shirt and ripped it open, sending buttons flying. Warm hands cupped her bra-covered breasts before he flicked open the front clasp, freeing her. A low groan rumbled from his chest as one rough palm caressed her.

He grasped her chin and tugged her head to the

side, exposing her neck. Leaning down, he scraped his teeth along her jugular, kissing and nipping along the way.

He tugged on her nipple.

She arched into his hold, her mind spinning. "Quinn—"

Jeans rustled as he swung his leg and jumped from the horse. Grabbing her waist, he pulled her off, pressing her against the horse's flank until she wrapped her legs around his hips.

His mouth took hers.

Hot, fast, crazy, he kissed every thought out of her brain while pivoting and striding for the house. His boots clomped up the steps, and at the porch, he released her to slide down his body. The entire time, he kept kissing her.

She grabbed his shirt and broke the kiss so she could yank the material over his head. He helped her, his mouth back on hers the second they succeeded. His lips were firm, determined, and he deepened his assault until all she could do was kiss him back.

Vaguely, she heard the clasp of her jeans release. Cool air brushed her bare butt as he pulled them off along with her boots, socks, and underwear.

They shuffled closer to the door, and she grabbed his jeans.

He released her mouth. "Wait."

"No." She shoved his jeans down his legs, taking a quick moment to gasp at the heavy cock straining toward her.

Wow. The sheriff was built.

The jeans caught on his boots. Oh well. She could see what she needed. Slowly standing, she brushed a kiss across his impressive shaft on her way back up.

A low growl rumbled from him.

Both hands clasped her shoulders, and he slid her shirt and bra off. Red spiraled across his rugged cheekbones, and his nostrils flared. "We need to slow down."

"No." She stepped right into heat and male. His broad chest showed a warrior's scars. While she'd heard he had been in the service, she hadn't known he'd been in battle. Defined and muscular, his chest led down to an impressive six-pack. His erection brushed her stomach, and she had to fight to keep from moaning in need. "Please don't treat me like I'm some sort of fragile lady. I'm not."

"You are," he said.

No, she never had been. No matter how badly she'd disappointed her family. Leaning forward, she licked his nipple.

His sharp intake of breath made her smile.

"Quinn, we do this right. Like you want." She lifted her gaze to meet his. Tingles zinged around her from the raw hunger on his dark face.

"Like I want?" he asked, his voice guttural as he shoved open the door and propelled them inside.

"Yes," she breathed out, her heart pounding.

"I need to run upstairs—"

She shook her head. "I'm on the pill—medical reasons."

His eyes flared hot and bright. He kicked the door shut and backed her against the wall. Both hands plunged into her hair, and he took her mouth again. They inched along the wall, hopefully toward a bedroom. She should probably help him out of his boots and jeans so he didn't trip. The wall disappeared, and only cool air ran along her back.

She moaned into the kiss, her body on fire. "Now, Quinn. Please, now." The hunger was so great, she was about to drop him to the floor and take him.

With a growl, he flipped her around, his hand heavy against her lower back. She had a second to appreciate a comfortable-looking dining room complete with hutch. A thick table hit her upper thighs, and she bent over, her torso over the table and him behind her. He shoved papers to the side that cascaded to the floor.

Grabbing both her hips, he gently began to ease inside her.

Whoa. The sheriff was huge. She closed her eyes and willed her body to relax around him. His control was impressive, as he went inch by inch, obviously trying not to her.

She held her breath, her body rioting. "Hurry up, Quinn."

"Hold on," he groaned, finally pushing all the way in.

Sparks flashed behind her eyes, and then she opened them in shock. Pinned against the table, helpless, she breathed out, her nerves firing. So much demand coursed through her, she could barely think.

"You okay?" he rumbled, the hands on her hips tightening.

"Yes," she whispered. She'd never felt like this— never—but that was something to worry about later. After. Way after. Going purely on instinct, she wiggled her butt. "More."

His grip turned brutal. Pulling out, and then shoving back in, he began to pound. Hard, fast, so strong, he thrust. The sound of flesh slapping flesh echoed around the room.

Flames licked inside her sex right where he plunged, filling her almost too full. She clapped her hands against the table, her body straining for release.

Somehow, he increased the strength of his thrusts, propelling her up on her toes. Each relentless drive sent her higher. Her thighs trembled and started to shake. Her sex contracted until pain and pleasure melded together.

A ball of fire exploded inside her, spiraling out through nerves, muscles, and skin. She arched her back and cried out, her eyes closing. Waves of sparking pleasure whipped through her in shattering spasms.

The orgasm lasted forever. Finally, the waves ebbed. Coming down, her body relaxing, she rested her cheek on the cool table.

His fingers left bruises as he ground against her while he came.

She felt the second reality returned to him. His hold relaxed, and whiskers rubbed her neck.

"Juliet?" he asked.

"Hmmm." Opening her eyes and speaking real words would be too much effort. She'd quite possibly never felt this good. Ever.

He withdrew from her body and gently lifted her off the table. Then he turned her around to face him. "Sweetheart? You okay?"

Her eyelids slowly opened. Concern bracketed Quinn's handsome face and glowed bright in his gaze. She managed a tired grin. "I'm excellent."

He shook his head. "I was too rough."

Reaching up, she ran her palm along his jawline.

"You were perfect, Quinn Lodge."

His shoulders relaxed. "That was only round one, sweetheart. Now we get serious—in the bedroom. Where I can treat you right." An expression filtered into his eyes she couldn't identify. Warm and soft, it increased her heartbeat and set alarm bells ringing in her head.

She swallowed, wanting to protest.

He leaned down, the room tilted, and she found herself cradled in his arms. He headed out of the dining room. She snuggled close, enjoying the sensation of muscles shifting in his chest as he moved. Wasn't there something—

Reality hit them both at the same time. Quinn stopped suddenly with a sharp intake of breath.

The jeans were still around his boots.

His eyes widened, he tried to hop, but whatever had tripped him wasn't letting go. The room swirled around.

Juliet yelped and dug her nails into his chest.

He spun midair, changed their positions, and dropped backward onto a coffee table. She landed hard on his chest. For a heartbeat, the room silenced. Then the table gave way. Wood splintered with a resounding crack, and they crashed to the floor. She smacked her head on his chin. He groaned.

Frowning, she rubbed her head while settling on top of him, straddling him. "Are you all right?"

He exhaled, and a table leg rolled out from under his rib cage. "Yes." Both hands ran down her arms. "Are you all right? Did I hurt you? I'm sorry, Juliet."

Warmth flushed through her. "You sacrificed your body for me."

He grimaced. "I like your body better than mine." His hands wandered from her arms to play with her breasts. "Are these okay?"

Heat climbed into her face. Electricity zapped from his fingers to her rapidly awakening core. "Ah, fine."

"Good." His voice roughened. "Though I should check you head to toe in order to make sure. Once we're in the bedroom."

The world disappeared. "Now that sounds like a smart plan." Her worries, her fears…everything except the sexy sheriff ceased to matter. For this one stolen moment in time, life was good. No matter what happened the next day, she was taking this night. Pushing against his impressive chest, she scrambled over his already erect cock and down his legs. "Let's get your boots off first."

"Good idea." He sat up, and pieces of the table rattled.

She huffed out a laugh and yanked off his boots along with his jeans. "There, now. No more tripping."

He shoved himself to stand and kicked the jeans out of the way. They spiraled through the room and hit a Western oil painting on the far wall. The painting dropped to the floor.

Juliet covered her mouth with her hand. "There'll be nothing left of your house when we're done."

His grin was all wolf. "Works for me." Lunging for her, he ducked a shoulder and tossed her over it.

She caught her breath at his speed, her face against his back. He began moving through the house. A calloused hand caressed her butt, and she wiggled. He caressed harder, taking claim, holding her in place.

A tingle wandered through her.

He climbed stairs, and his fingers dipped between her legs.

She gasped out, seeing stars.

Slowly, one finger entered her while another tapped her clit. She gave a strangled cry. "No, stop."

He stopped moving just inside a doorway. "Okay." Another finger slid inside, stretching her.

Oh God. "I meant—"

"I know what you meant." His silky hair brushed her skin, and his teeth nipped her thigh. His thumbnail scraped across her clit. "Control isn't something you get to keep here, Juliet."

Her abdomen quivered. If he didn't cease his playing, she was going to orgasm over his shoulder, completely at his mercy. While the idea was intriguing, she had to keep some dignity. "Being upside down gives me a headache," she said.

His fingers deserted her, and she had just enough time to relax before a hard slap echoed across her buttocks. Fire lanced straight to her sex. "Quinn." She meant it as a protest, but his name came out on a moan.

"No lying—not here and not now. When we're like this, only honesty. Agree or you go home." His muscled shoulders shifted as he took a deep breath. "After I turn your ass red."

She gasped and then slowly relaxed. Lies didn't belong between them when they were together like this. "No lying," she murmured. Then, her hands slid down his back to grab a very impressive ass. "Though I'm getting bored with this discussion."

He laughed and took several steps. Air brushed her skin as he laid her on a bed. His fingers trailed down her abdomen. She gyrated against him, her breath catching.

He released her, and she tensed in protest.

"We have time, sweetheart." Desire spiraled high across his face. Grabbing her hips, he pushed her up the mattress, his body covering hers. He brushed the hair away from her forehead. "You're beautiful."

She blinked. This was about sex. Great sex. She couldn't offer more. "Quinn, I—"

"Shh." He nipped her lips. "I know. No worries."

Well, that might hurt a little. "Oh, okay."

He settled between her legs. "But for the next couple of hours, you're mine."

The possessive tone battered down any defenses she'd been trying to shore. "Maybe I'll claim you, Sheriff." Tangling her fingers through his thick hair, she tugged his mouth down to hers for a slow, long, drugging kiss.

A jangle echoed by the doorway. "Freeze!" a woman yelled.

Then things happened too fast and too slow all at once.

Juliet screamed.

Quinn leaped from the bed and toward danger.

Juliet scrambled under the covers.

"Jesus Christ," Quinn bellowed, jumping back for the bed and shoving under the covers with her.

Juliet clutched the bedspread to her chest, her gaze on the doorway. Quinn's college-aged sister stood with a bat clutched in her hands, her blue eyes wide, and her face extremely pale.

The woman's mouth opened and closed several times. She threw the bat to the floor and ground her fists into her eyes. "Oh my God, oh my God, oh my God. I could've lived my *whole* life without seeing... *that*!"

Quinn growled and threw a pillow at her while remaining safely under the covers. "What the hell are you doing here?"

Dawn ducked the pillow and peered between two fingers. "I wanted to talk to you and found Mertyl wandering down the road. Titan followed right behind her."

"Oh." Quinn sat up but kept the bedspread over the important parts.

"And"— Dawn's voice rose in pitch and volume as she dropped her hand— "I came inside and it looks like there was a big fight. The table is broken, a painting is down, and I heard a noise up here. So, I grabbed the bat and came upstairs."

Quinn stilled. Tension vibrated through the room. "Let me get this straight. You noticed signs of a fight, of danger, and your logical choice was to grab a bat and come upstairs."

"Um—" Dawn took a step back.

Juliet fought the urge to hide her face under the bedspread. "I'm so sorry, Dawn."

The woman shuffled her feet. "No, I'm sorry. I didn't know—I mean, that you and Quinn—well, I mean—"

"Go away," Quinn muttered. Then he frowned. "Why didn't you call for help before coming upstairs?"

Dawn's eyes widened just as heavy boots pounded up the stairs. Jake rushed into the room followed by Colton, their younger brother. Both men wore faded jeans, work gloves, and thick shirts. They'd obviously been working the ranch.

Dawn giggled. "I did call for help."

Oh, no. Heat shot into Juliet's face so quickly her skin burned. She pulled the sheet over her head.

Jake's laugh rang through the room.

"I'm going to arrest all three of you for trespass if you don't get out of here," Quinn barked.

The sound of a door closing was a prelude for a moment of silence before laughter echoed down the hallway stairs. Quinn tugged on the sheet.

Juliet held onto the heavy cotton with all of her might.

"Juliet? They're gone," he said, amusement in his voice.

It didn't matter. She'd never live the last few moments down. Good thing she was leaving town. Soon.

CHAPTER FIVE

Juliet settled more comfortably in the kitchen chair, her gaze on the half-naked warrior cooking dinner. "I think we may have blinded your sister for life."

Quinn chuckled and stirred the scrambled eggs. "I'd prefer not to think about it again." The muscles in his impressive arms shifted as he reached for salt and pepper to dump on the eggs. He wore scars on his back, and it hurt she wouldn't have time to get close enough to ask about them. But she had the night, and she was going to enjoy what she could. He'd thrown on jeans but had left his torso and feet bare. Very masculine. "If I hadn't been nude, I probably would've smashed both Jake's and Colton's heads together for not leaving right away." While the words emerged tough, obvious affection lived in them.

"You and your siblings seem close." Juliet picked at a loose thread on the shirt she'd borrowed.

"We are." Quinn removed the pan and slid eggs onto two plates. Delivering one to her, he grabbed a plate of buttered toast. "You don't have siblings?"

"No." Not really, anyway. She eyed the eggs. "These look fantastic."

"Thanks." He sat and tossed her a napkin. "Eggs are the only thing I know how to cook. Well, besides Christmas cookies."

Juliet unfolded the napkin on her lap. "Christmas cookies?"

He grinned. "Yeah. Leila and I have a tradition of

making Christmas cookies shaped like sheriff stars every year. It's our, ah, thing."

Talk about the sweetest thing Juliet had ever heard. "You're a softy, Sheriff."

"Humph." He dug into his eggs. "Why the gallery, Juliet?"

She paused. "What do you mean?"

"The gallery? There are tons of businesses you could open, and you choose a Western art gallery in a small Montana town. Why?" Lazy intelligence glimmered in his eyes.

The need to confide in him surprised a grin out of her. "I love art. Love paintings, drawings, sculptures— even comic books. No matter how hard I tried, I never had talent." She took a sip of water. "Skill, maybe. But not the talent so few have that amazes anyone who looks."

He nodded. "So you decided to surround yourself with art."

"Exactly." For the first time in a month, her shoulders relaxed. "I do have a good head for business, and I have an eye for other people's talent. That works."

"Do you still paint?" he asked.

"No, but I do sculpt once in a while. Just for me, and just for fun." Her pieces were more functional than inspirational, but that was okay.

The phone rang, and he stretched over his head to grab the handset off the wall. "Lodge." He listened for a moment and then stood to look at his cell phone sitting on the table. "Yes, Mrs. Romano. I understand. Give me a minute." He set down the handset and punched in a number on the cell phone.

Juliet tilted her head to the side. What in the world

was going on?

Quinn waited and smiled. "Hi, Mrs. Maceberry. This is Sheriff Lodge, and I could use Graham's help. Is your son home?" Quinn glanced at Juliet and winked.

Sexy and strong, that wink shot right down to throb between her legs. The man should be captured on film.

"Graham?" Quinn straightened up. "Mrs. Romano's cat is stuck in the tree down the street. I owe you lunch next week if you go and get the darn thing down." Quinn nodded. "You're the best, kid. Be careful and don't fall." The cell phone clicked shut. He lifted the handset to his head. "Mrs. Romano? Graham Maceberry has become my official cat catcher. He'll be there in a few minutes to get Snookie down. Just offer the kid one of your amazing strawberry scones when he succeeds. Yes, ma'am. Have a good night."

With a sigh, Quinn dropped back into his seat. "My job's a dangerous one, darlin'." The smug grin sliding across his face promised both danger and sin.

"I can see that." She licked cheese off her fork.

His eyes flared.

She stopped licking. "Don't look at me like that."

"Like what?" he asked.

"Like you want to eat me alive." She paused as heat filled her face. "You know what I mean."

"I know exactly what you mean." He'd leaned forward to say something that had to be sexy when the doorbell rang. He frowned. "What is up with people today?" Tossing his napkin on the table, he strode into the other room. Voices echoed, and he returned with a plate full of brownies and a casserole dish covered with tinfoil.

Juliet lifted her eyebrows.

Quinn smiled and shoved the plates into the refrigerator. "Mrs. Phillips is missing both of her sons. One is in Idaho at a convention, and the other is overseas. She always makes plenty of food, and I usually get extras when the boys are out of town."

Juliet glanced past him to the myriad of different dishes in the refrigerator. "It looks like a lot of women feed you."

"Yeah, I guess." He shut the door and sat down.

She'd bet her last pair of shoes most of the dishes were made by single women and not grandmotherly types like Mrs. Phillips. "Well, a man has to eat something other than scrambled eggs and cheese."

"Exactly." His gaze wandered over the white dress shirt she'd borrowed. "You look darn nice in my shirt." He shoved his plate to the side. "Why don't we head back to bed?"

She swallowed, caught by the fire in his eyes. "Good idea."

The phone rang again. With a muffled expletive, Quinn answered it. After listening, he took a deep breath. "I'll be right there." Hanging up, he flashed an apologetic grin. "Joan Daniels heard a noise in her backyard. She called me because she's just down the road, and I can get there sooner than the guys on duty in town."

Juliet studied his strong face. "You don't seem worried."

"She hears something every other week or so. It's usually the wind. But, we did have a sighting of a cougar last week, so I need to check it out." He reached for his gun on top of the refrigerator. "Can I borrow that shirt?"

"No." Juliet slid off the chair. Forty-year-old, four times divorced, Joan Daniels wore low-cut shirts and partied in town a lot. *She* was the cougar Quinn should look out for. No doubt she'd called the sexy sheriff for more than a cougar sighting. "I'll clean up while you're gone."

"You're the best." He placed a quick kiss on Juliet's forehead. "I'll make it up to you when I get back." After running upstairs, he returned fully dressed and wearing his hat. "Lock the door behind me." Then he was gone.

How many women did the sheriff rush out to rescue on a daily basis? Juliet shook her head. She didn't have a claim on the man, and she'd insisted on no strings. A quick survey of the kitchen proved the sheriff made quite the mess when he cooked. But hey, he had cooked for her. She dug in and had the room cleaned in short order. The silence ticked around her.

Maneuvering up the stairs, she made the bed. Sitting down, she pressed the sheriff's pillow to her face. Male, wild and free. Yeah. The scent of Quinn. The sense of safety surrounded her in his bed. With a sigh, she lay down and closed her eyes for just a moment.

A strong hand shook her shoulder. "Juliet? Wake up, baby."

She started awake.

Quinn stood over her, lines of fatigue cutting into the side of his mouth. "It's after midnight. I'll take you home before heading to the station to write up my report."

She shook her head and sat up. "Was there something outside of Joan's house?"

"Yes. A fully grown, hungry cougar." Quinn rubbed his whiskered jaw. "Now we have cougars too close to residences. Those animals can be wicked."

"Oh." She flipped back the bedspread and stood. When had she fallen asleep?

Quinn tugged her into his hard body and rubbed his chin on the top of her head. "Thank you for a wonderful night."

"Right back at you, Sheriff." The warm arms around her melted her muscles into relaxation.

He stepped back. "Get dressed, and I'll meet you downstairs. Also, Sophie is driving up to the lodge instead of riding in the trail fundraiser tomorrow. I'll just have her pick you up on the way so we don't risk putting you on a horse again—at least until I can give you more lessons."

His idea of lessons warmed her entire body. She cleared her throat. "I appreciate Sophie picking me up." That way, appearances would be met. The world would think she and the sheriff were dating. Well, they were having sex, but he didn't want her to stay the night. That was all right. She didn't want to stay the night, now did she? Yeah, maybe she wouldn't mind cuddling with his hard body for a while. Hurt spiraled through her, and she pushed the feeling away. "I'll be ready in a moment."

He nodded and headed downstairs.

Well, now. Where exactly had she left her clothes?

CHAPTER SIX

The morning sun trickled weakly through the heavy clouds, promising a rainstorm. Quinn wound twine around the post, snipping the ends into smoothness. The heated summer-storm season was about to hit, and the ranch wasn't prepared. "You're lucky I didn't have my gun on me last night," he muttered at his brother.

Colton chortled and kicked a rock into place to secure another post. "From what I saw, you didn't have anything on you."

Quinn threw the ball of twine at the dumbass. "You're a moron."

"Maybe." Colton tugged his Stetson down against the piercing wind. Even so, his multicolored hair blew around his neck. "But I would've kept the woman all night and not driven her home before midnight."

Jake glanced up from where he pounded in a new post.

Irritation whipped through Quinn stronger than the wind. "I haven't kicked your ass in a while, little brother, but don't think I'm opposed to the idea."

The smart-ass grin Colton shot him nearly guaranteed a beating. "Sounds like fun. I haven't just been studying animal science the last three years, you know."

"Don't think the MMA crap you've been doing comes close to special-ops training, Colton Freeze." Sure, Quinn was proud of his little brother. That didn't mean he couldn't beat the shit out of him now and then.

Jake threw the hammer into the back of the battered Ford where it clanked across the faded metal. "I'm fairly certain the sheriff shouldn't commit battery—especially during an election cycle."

"Stop sounding like a lawyer," Quinn snapped.

"I am a lawyer." Jake grabbed a fence-hole digger and plunged the blades into the moist earth. "As much as it pains me to admit this, I agree with Colt. Your reputation of lovin' 'em and leavin' 'em is ticking off Mom. Let a woman stay the night once in a while."

"Love 'em and leave 'em?" Quinn hefted a fence pole from the back of the truck. "I don't even date anybody in town."

"You don't date, period." Colton moved out of the way for Quinn to shove the pole in the ground. "You have sex and leave. Unfortunately, the city isn't far away from our small town, and everybody knows your cycle."

Jake angled around and grabbed part of the pole to plunge down. "I think Mom has Tom geared up to talk to you. Just a heads-up."

Quinn groaned. While he loved his stepfather and appreciated him becoming a father to Jake and him when they were young, he didn't need a fatherly talk about sex. "Tom has enough to worry about with Dawn." The youngest of them all, little Dawn was plain wild…and in love with the wrong man. "We all have enough to worry about with Dawn."

Colton shoveled dirt around the post. "Nah. The last time Hawk came home on leave, they didn't even talk to each other. She's over him."

Quinn cut his eyes to Jake, who shrugged. "That would be excellent news." Not that he didn't like Hawk, because he did. They'd all grown up together and were good friends. But Hawk's time in the military was wearing on him, and Dawn was way too young to get serious over a man. "What about you, Colton Henry Freeze?"

Colt grinned. "I'm not in love, don't plan on being in love, and am ready to graduate and head home. In fact, I'm going to build over on the east side of the ranch, near the falls."

Quinn yanked his leather glove off to rub his chin. "What about Melanie?"

Jake snorted. "Dumbass here hasn't figured out Mel's a girl."

Colton tossed the post digger onto the truck bed. "Mel's been my best friend since kindergarten. Of course, I know she's a girl."

"And?" Quinn asked.

"And nothin'." Colton jumped to sit on the tailgate. "We're friends. She's dating some banker from Missoula. The guy wears three-piece suits. Three piece." He shook his head.

Colt was a moron when it came to women. But, on the other hand, the place he wanted to build would be perfect for a ranch house. When their mom had married Tom, they'd had Colt and Dawn. When the Lodge boys were old enough to make the decision on their own, they'd combined the Lodge and Freeze acres into one sprawling ranch they all worked. Any profits were split evenly. His biological father had been dead for many years, but Quinn was sure he'd be pleased with how things had turned out. "How is

Melanie's grandpop doing?"

Colton shook his head. "Not good. The doctors say he's terminal."

"I'm sorry to hear that." Quinn ripped off his hat to wipe his forehead.

Jake reached for a thermos and poured coffee for all three of them. "Somehow we got off the subject of Casanova here and Juliet Montgomery."

"We're finished with that subject." Quinn took a deep drink of the unloaded brew and grimaced. Another seven months until Sophie's baby was born, damn it. Jake had switched them all to decaf because he was too lazy to make two pots.

"I know why you either leave or kick a woman out of your bed, Quinn," Jake said quietly.

Of course he knew why. They'd gotten drunk, really drunk, about two years ago and told each other everything they'd seen, everything they'd done, while in service for their country. Then they'd never spoken about it again, which worked just fine for Quinn.

"So do I," Colton murmured.

Quinn narrowed his focus on his brother. *"You* don't."

Colt shrugged. "I may not know the details, but I know you've struggled with PTSD. That's the only thing that would make you kick Juliet Montgomery out of your bed. Period."

Sometimes Quinn forgot his youngest brother was a freakin' genius. Smart as hell, and nothing got past him. "You don't understand."

"I'm not pretending to understand. But, I also know you'd err on the side of caution so as not to hurt somebody, when really you should be taking a chance.

That woman is worth the risk." Colton took a gulp.

Jake staggered back. "Did you just get relationship advice from numb-nuts here?"

Colton laughed and jumped from the truck. "I may be younger, and I may not have fought overseas, but you know what? I'm right."

• • •

Juliet brushed her hair, satisfied with her sparkling-clean apartment. The tiny three-room apartment above the gallery was both quaint and easy to maneuver. She tried not to wriggle on the seat of the vanity in her bedroom.

Her rear end hurt. Mainly from the darn horse ride, but her hips showed slight bruises from the sheriff's grasp.

The thought brought a smile to her face. The man was passionate and explosive, and he'd stopped treating her like glass. Thank goodness.

The phone rang, and her fingers trembled before she answered. Was the sheriff calling?

A throat cleared. "Um, Juliet?"

She exhaled. "Hi, Sophie. What's up?"

"Um, well, don't freak out, okay?" Sophie said.

Juliet's blood pressure rose. "Okay."

"The good news is that the Western Pacific Art Council is sending dignitaries to the art showing, and if they like the paintings, they'll give us a grant for the gallery," Sophie said, her words rushing together.

Hope bloomed in Juliet's chest. "That's amazing. How did you—"

"The bad news is I told them we could have the

showing Saturday in order to meet the deadline for the grant process," Sophie interrupted.

Panic cut off Juliet's breath. She wheezed out. "Saturday is in three days."

"I know, but I've finished all the paintings, and even the charcoals are ready to be hung. We can do this. I promise," Sophie said.

That was crazy. But a grant from the WPAC would guarantee the gallery remained open, even if Juliet had to leave. Sadness compressed her lungs—she thought she'd have more time with Quinn. She sucked in air sprinkled with courage. "Okay. We can do it."

Sophie's happy squeal ripped through the line, and Juliet held the receiver away from her ear. "We need to get to work."

"After the trail ride today, I promise we'll come help you hang the art. We can also send out an email blast and make some flyers for town," Sophie said.

Juliet shook her head, even though nobody could see. "I'm not riding today."

"I know. Quinn asked me to pick you up, and we're on our way now. His mom and I are driving up to the lodge for the picnic. Wasn't that sweet of him?"

"Humph." Yes, it was sweet to get her a ride, and now she could relax. But she was still uncomfortable about the sheriff. "I'll be outside in a few minutes." After saying good-bye and hanging up the phone, Juliet finished with her makeup. She couldn't leave town until after the showing, but a few days wouldn't make a difference.

The phone rang again, and she rolled her eyes. What bombshell would Sophie ring down now?

"Hello?" Juliet chuckled.

Silence.

"Hello? Sophie?" she said.

More silence. Then something shuffled. Somebody breathed. Heavy and somehow ominous.

Juliet cleared her throat. "If this is Tommy Nelcome, your mother told you to stop making prank calls. I'm calling her right now."

The caller hung up.

Okay. That was just a kid. Nothing to worry about. Though he'd been calling a lot lately. Juliet dialed her neighbor, Judy Nelcome, to rat out Tommy. Unfortunately, Judy reported that Tommy was visiting his grandparents in Oregon, and they'd gone to the ocean for the day. So the caller wasn't Tommy.

Juliet hung up and took several deep breaths. Just because the caller wasn't Tommy didn't mean another kid wasn't goofing off. She'd been careful, and she was safe. Her family couldn't find her. An illogical and disastrous need filled her to call the sheriff and ask for help.

It was just a prank call, for goodness' sake. Yet another prank call.

She yanked on cowboy boots, pleased they matched her long skirt. Since she wasn't riding a raging beast, she didn't need to change. After adding several pieces of silver Celtic jewelry, she whipped through the apartment, grabbed her purse and coat, and headed down to the gallery. Tucking her arms in the sleeves, she stepped outside the main door, making sure to secure the locks.

A chilly wind scattered leaves down the quiet street. Their rustling scraped against crumbling asphalt.

The hair on the back of her neck prickled. She glanced at the still storefronts. Her breath burst out in pants. There was nobody there. Her mind was playing tricks on her from a silly prank phone call. An SUV turned the corner, and she sighed in relief at Sophie in the driver's seat, her blond hair up in a ponytail.

Loni Freeze, Quinn's mother, waved from the passenger seat as they paused by the curb.

Juliet waved back and jumped into the back seat. "Thank you for picking me up."

"Of course. You look lovely today, Juliet," Loni said.

"Thank you." Juliet fought to keep from blushing, considering Loni's son had bent Juliet over a table the other day and made her see stars. "So do you."

Loni smiled. Definitely petite, it was a surprise the woman had birthed and raised three large sons as well as energetic Dawn. Quinn had inherited her dark eyes and angled Native American features, but his size must've been his father's.

Sophie signaled and pulled into the street. "Sorry about the huge car. I wanted to bring the smaller one, but you know how Jake gets."

"Yes." A pang of jealousy smacked Juliet between the eyes. What would it be like to have an overprotective husband who cared so much? Sophie had been in a car accident a short time ago, and Jake was a bit obsessive about making sure she drove around in something close to a Sherman tank. "This way we get to stretch out, anyway."

Loni laughed and glanced out the window. "A spring storm is coming, but at least we've moved from snow and sleet to just rain. I hope the rain misses the riders today."

Juliet followed her gaze as they drove through an intersection. A black SUV waited at a stop sign, the windows tinted. She focused, seeking the license plate. There wasn't one.

The vehicle pulled onto the road behind them.

CHAPTER SEVEN

Juliet kept her eye on Sophie's cell phone, just in case she needed to dial for help. They arrived at the lodge within record time. While Sophie drove a big car, she apparently still believed in speed.

The black SUV had disappeared at the base of the mountain.

Maybe her imagination was going crazy. The SUV might've been new, or perhaps a tourist had been in town. There was no indication somebody dangerous had been tailing them.

Juliet slipped from the vehicle.

As a unit, Quinn and his brothers stalked out of the cedar-sided lodge. She swallowed. As a force, they were something to notice. All three stood well over six foot, muscled, and somehow graceful. Dressed in faded jeans, long-sleeved shirts, and cowboy boots, they were every girl's vision of a bad-boy cowboy. Where Quinn and Jake were dark, Colton had deep blue eyes, and a myriad of colors made up his thick hair.

He grinned and kissed his mom on the cheek. "You're late."

Juliet flushed and shuffled her feet. The last time she'd seen Colton, she'd been naked and hiding under the covers.

He leaned in and brushed her cheek with a brotherly kiss. "Hi, Juliet."

"Hi." Her heart warmed.

"Get away from my woman," Quinn growled, a

slight grin tipping his lips.

Surprise filtered through Colton's eyes that matched Jake's lifted eyebrows. That was a bit of a claim, now wasn't it? Juliet frowned.

"My brother is right—for once. You look very pretty, Juliet." Quinn stepped into her space. Then he kissed her. In full daylight, in full view of his family, the sheriff grasped her chin and captured her mouth. His lips slanted over hers, while heat cascaded off his hard body. He took her under, exploring, taking his time as if he had every right in the world to do so.

Liquid lava shot through her, and reality disappeared. It came crashing back all too soon. Her hands flattened against his chest and shoved.

He paused and lifted his head. Darker than midnight and just as mysterious, his eyes focused on hers. "Did you just push me?"

The spit in her mouth dried up. She swallowed. "Yes. We're in public."

"I believe that was the deal." His hold tightened imperceptibly on her chin.

She glanced around, nearly sighing in relief that everyone had gone inside. They'd probably hurried just to escape the inappropriate public display of lust. "Well, we're alone now."

"And?" His thumb swept along her jawline.

"We don't need to pretend." Irritation battled with her unwelcome desire. She needed to distance herself from the sheriff before he discovered her secrets. Or broke her rapidly beating heart—it wasn't like he'd even wanted her to stay the night after the truly excellent sex.

He frowned, his large frame blocking the weak sun.

"What's eating you, darlin'?"

"Nothing." She pushed, and might as well have been trying to shove a cement wall out of the way. "Back off, Sheriff."

He studied her, his gaze serious. "No."

Did he just refuse? Not the polite, follow all the rules, stickler of a sheriff. "Excuse me?" She jerked her head, dislodging his hold.

Her triumph was short lived. Quinn stepped into her, and her butt hit the car. Trapped. "I. Said. No." He rested a hand against the roof. "We'll stay right here until you tell me what has you tangled up."

A roaring filled her ears. "Forget you, Sheriff."

"Juliet."

The low, commanding tone rippled across her skin. Her gaze lifted involuntarily, a shiver wandering down her spine. She blinked twice. Who was this man, and where was the easygoing sheriff everybody thought they knew?

"Now." He leaned even closer, his minty breath brushing her nose.

She wanted to refuse his demand. Maybe kick him in the shin. But that wasn't who she was or how she solved problems. So she wiped all expression off her face and graced him with a kind smile. "I apologize, Sheriff Lodge. I've been a bit out of sorts today, although I'm feeling better now. But I'm cold. Let's go inside and join the others."

His upper lip quirked. "I have a confession, Juliet. When you try to blow me off with that high-society tone, all I want to do is turn you over my knee and spank you to orgasm."

She gasped, and her eyes widened.

He leaned even closer. "Want me to show you?"

"No." The word emerged strangled, while a fluttering heat wandered down her torso. The man would. He'd actually show her right there outside the lodge. "No."

"Hmmm. Then now's your chance to tell me what's going on." He brushed a stray strand of hair off her forehead.

She jumped. "Um. I don't like lying to your family."

"We're not."

"Yes, we are. You just kissed me, and we're acting like we're really dating." She'd stamp her foot if she were anybody else. Though a lingering panic kept her in place.

"After the other night, Juliet, we are really dating," he said.

She shook her head. Dating people stayed the night together after sex. "No."

His eyes narrowed. "That's not what has you wanting to kick me. I have all day, and I can wait."

The man was impossible. A very unusual temper began to swirl at the base of her neck. "Fine. I just, I mean, I know this is temporary, and I don't want to start acting like it isn't." Darn it. The words slipped out.

He cradled her face, brushing a kiss across her lips. "I'm a jerk."

She crossed her arms. "I don't want to talk about it." Yes. She'd put out her lip and pout if she could. The man drove her crazy.

"Too bad." He grasped her wrists and tugged her arms free, sliding them around to clasp at her back. "We need to discuss this further."

Panic heated through her. No discussion. Plus,

pinning her hands was the final straw. She tossed her head, and a satisfying *thunk* echoed when she nailed his chin. Flaring her nostrils, she glared into his dark eyes. "You're messing with the wrong woman here. Back the heck off."

Anger flashed across his face. She'd never seen him mad, and panic had her mouth opening to apologize.

His mouth took hers, shoving the words back down her throat. Then he took. Hard, raw, even angry, he kissed her with a passion that weakened her knees until they trembled. His hands and body kept her trapped, while his mouth destroyed any resistance she might've mustered. With a low sigh, she kissed him back, lost in the electricity generated by a man much more dangerous than she'd realized.

They both breathed heavily when he lifted his head.

She licked her bruised lips, enjoying the flare in his eyes. "I'm sorry I hit your chin."

"I'm sorry I made you feel like this was a short-term, one-night stand by taking you home instead of inviting you to stay the night," he said.

But it was short term. She breathed out. "Okay. We're good now."

"Somehow, I don't think so." He frowned.

"You are the most stubborn person I've ever met," she muttered.

"I've heard that before." He released her wrists and rubbed a finger across her throbbing mouth. "You mean a lot to me, Juliet. I would've asked you to stay the night the other night but, I, ah, can't sleep with anybody."

She stilled, curiosity taking over. "Oh. Why?"

Maybe he snored.

He grimaced. "I have nightmares, and sometimes it takes a little while for me to remember where I am. I can't take the risk of hurting you."

"Nightmares about what?" she asked.

His mouth opened and closed. He cleared his throat. "About my time in the service. Things I saw and did."

The man was confiding in her. She shouldn't like it so much. "Like PTSD?" She'd heard about the diagnosis from movies on television, but she'd never really understood the concept. Feeling for him, she tucked her hands at his waist.

"Yes," he said evenly.

"Have you ever explained that to somebody you wanted to sleep with?" She ran her palm along his whiskers. His five o'clock shadow was undeniably sexy.

"I haven't wanted to stay all night with anybody. Until now." He slid an arm around her shoulders and tugged her toward the lodge. "It isn't an excuse. I haven't found anybody I liked enough to explore the situation with—so it just seemed easier to get out of Dodge. I'm willing to give it a shot now, however."

Hope flared inside her to be quickly quashed. They couldn't have more than right now, because she was out of Maverick as soon as the art show concluded. "Thank you for confiding in me. Now I understand, and I won't push you again."

He exhaled heavily. "Juliet? You're using the high-society tone again."

• • •

Quinn held Amy at arm's length through the dance, fighting the urge to step on her foot and break it. What kind of a woman asked a man to dance who clearly had come with a date? For a split second, he'd considered refusing. But the governor had been watching, and his mama had raised him right, so he'd accepted.

This was the longest song on record.

He glanced around. Someone had decorated the sprawling room with green balloons and purple streamers, lending a party atmosphere to the rough wooden decor. A hand-carved bar made up one wall, a dance floor the other, and tables scattered throughout. A DJ played a collection of country tunes, and a general festiveness filled the air.

His gaze caught on Juliet. Kissing her when she'd arrived hadn't been his plan, but the second he saw her, he'd wanted a taste. The graceful redhead chatted with Colton by the bar. Quinn's heart thumped. Sure, he always figured he'd fall for somebody, get married, and have a family. But his feelings for the woman hit him like a bucking bronc. He figured his ideal mate would be someone suited to the ranch—at least somebody who could ride a horse. Maybe a member of the Kooskia Tribe. Nothing had prepared him for soft Juliet Montgomery, a woman who lost her temper and still didn't swear at him.

He liked her kindness, her gentleness, her odd, inherent classiness.

Confiding in her had been almost too easy, and his heart felt lighter since he'd trusted her with the truth about his nightmares. Had his taking her home the other night hurt her feelings? He hoped not.

Maybe he was ready to take a chance with her.

What if he woke up from a nightmare and hurt her? He'd never forgive himself.

Without question, he wanted Juliet Montgomery in his bed—all night. Maybe it was time to trust not only her but himself.

Though she was keeping something from him. He was well trained, and he had excellent instincts. The fact that she didn't trust him hurt. In fact, it damn well pissed him off. The woman was going to come clean and soon.

She met his gaze and raised an eyebrow at Amy, who was attempting to plaster herself against him. Juliet rolled her eyes.

His instant smile felt good.

Amy tried again to muscle closer. "You smell as good as always, Quinn."

Her perfume choked him. He much preferred Juliet's natural citrus scent. "Thanks."

"Why did we break up, anyway?" Amy asked.

"We didn't exactly date," he said. One foolish night after a fundraiser for Montana forests last year didn't count.

"Why not?" Amy batted thickly mascaraed eyes.

The song ended, and he stepped back. "Thank you for the dance." He made it to Juliet's side just as Colton finished telling a joke. He flashed her a grin. "Juliet, we're dancing."

Juliet pursed her lips. "Loni? Your son is incredibly bossy."

Loni grinned. "He gets bossiness from his daddy and his stepdaddy. I'm an angel."

Colton coughed beer up his nose. "Yeah, Mom. An angel."

"Where are Leila and Tom?" Quinn frowned.

Loni shrugged. "Leila told Tom she hadn't had any Grandpa time lately and was feeling...what was it?"

"Abandoned," Jake said wryly.

"Yeah, abandoned." Loni reached for a glass of wine. "You know Tom—he's a softy. So they planned a day of shopping, an early dinner, and a movie about lost puppies in the city."

Quinn slid an arm around Juliet's shoulders and smiled at Jake. "Your daughter is going to be a dangerous woman someday."

"I hope so." Jake handed Sophie a glass of ginger ale.

The governor and Amy wandered up. He puffed out his chest, and his big belly pushed out the red flannel. "Did you hear about Bennington?"

Quinn slowly turned his head. "What about Bennington?"

"He's withdrawing from the sheriff's race." Amy's eyes lit with glee. "A scandal."

Quinn's gut clenched.

Miles and Shelley Lansing wandered up, no doubt to keep campaigning for Quinn's job. "Did I hear scandal?" Shelley asked.

"Yes." The governor leaned closer to the group, a sly smile on his face, his jowls jiggling as he lowered his tone to a whisper. "Apparently his wife has been growing marijuana in the basement. Five plants. It's still illegal in Montana, you know."

Quinn frowned. "The plants are medicinal, right? I mean, didn't old Mr. Bennington, her father, have cancer?"

The governor shrugged. "I don't care the reason. A

candidate can't be breaking the law and growing pot. The news outlets found out about it, and it's over."

It was almost too obvious how the reporters found out. Quinn studied the governor. The question was, how had the governor found out?

Juliet set down her wineglass. "Why would Bennington have to withdraw from the race if his wife was the one breaking the law?"

Amy rolled her eyes. "Really? A candidate must only associate with lawful people, or he has poor judgment. It's the poor judgment, not the pot growing, that will bring down Bennington."

"Oh," Juliet said, reaching to fiddle with her pendant. "How unfortunate."

Colton slid an arm around Loni's shoulders, no doubt not in the mood for gossip. "Mom? Let's dance." He grabbed her and spun her onto the dance floor.

Sophie slipped her arm through Quinn's. "Juliet, do you mind if I dance with my big brother?"

"Go ahead. Just be careful—he likes to lead." Juliet smiled.

"Yes, I do." Quinn directed his statement at the redhead, while leading his sister-in-law onto the dance floor. Juliet blushed, and he chuckled.

The outside door opened, and two men stepped inside. He didn't know them. Both had riding clothes on, but one of them wore boat shoes. He looked closer. The guy with boat shoes had bloodshot eyes and a red nose.

Quinn caught Jake's eye.

CHAPTER EIGHT

Juliet enjoyed watching Quinn spin Sophie around on the dance floor. She tightened her hand around the wineglass. Her first and only for the day. A lady never had more than one drink, never leaned against anything, and always smiled in social situations. Her mother had drummed such rules into her head from an early age, and even now, she couldn't help but follow them.

Amy leaned against the bar. "So, you and Quinn, huh?"

Juliet kept the smile in place. "Your boots are lovely, Amy."

Amy glanced down. "Oh, yeah. They're from New York." She glanced up, her eyes sparking. "You know, where you said you visited once in a while."

"Yes. I know where New York is." Juliet ignored the trickle of unease wandering along her shoulders.

"Good, but you're not from the city, right?" Amy's smile flashed too many teeth.

"No." Juliet glanced for an escape from the blonde.

"Politics is a messy business." Amy reached for another drink from the bartender.

Juliet took a sip. "Good thing Quinn isn't in politics. He just wants to be the sheriff to do his job and protect people."

"What will he do if he loses?" Amy gulped her drink.

Juliet's face might go into tremors if she smiled any

longer. "Quinn won't lose. He's an excellent lawman."

"Maybe. We'll see." Amy leaned closer. "Our investigators haven't discovered anything about you yet, but they just started looking." With a smirk, she wandered away.

Juliet's throat dried. If her past came out, the news would hurt Quinn. Panicked, she glanced over at him, but he wasn't looking at her.

His focus was on the door.

Two men stood barely inside, their gazes sweeping the area. One wiped his nose on his sleeve. Then he touched the other guy's shoulder and jerked his head toward the bar. The other guy's hands shook, and he sniffed loudly.

Jake grasped her elbow. "Juliet? Please get Sophie and my mom to the restroom." Jake smiled, but the grin didn't come close to reaching his eyes.

An urgency rode his tone and shot butterflies into her stomach. She glanced at Quinn, who gave her an encouraging nod. Numbly, she smiled and glided across the dance floor. Somehow, she gathered both Loni and Sophie on the way.

Sophie leaned in. "What's going on? Quinn sent me to the restroom with you."

"I don't know." Juliet glanced over her shoulder. "Head toward the bathroom, and I'll find out."

"I think you're supposed to come, too," Sophie said.

Yeah, but she might be the problem. While Juliet didn't recognize the guys at the door, that didn't mean they didn't recognize her. "I'll be fine. You're pregnant—get to safety. I'll come get you once I figure out why Quinn is on alert."

They reached the doorway to the restrooms, and

Juliet waited to make sure Sophie and Loni headed inside before turning back around. She tried to appear casual, forcing herself to relax against the wall as if waiting for her friend. Her heart thundered, and her mouth went dry. If anybody was hurt because of her, she'd never forgive herself.

The two guys had reached the bar, probably unaware Quinn and his brothers flanked them. Quinn motioned Colton to the side and angled closer to the really twitchy guy.

Juliet frowned. Why was the guy twitching so much? He looked like he was coming down from a bad high.

Quinn wasn't armed, darn it. Why didn't he have a gun? Didn't most off-duty cops have an off-duty piece? Hopefully, he had a gun tucked in his boot.

The twitchy guy swiveled, big silver gun drawn.

A gasp rippled through the crowd.

Juliet stood up straight. Whatever instincts had told Quinn the newcomers might be dangerous were excellent. She widened her stance. Nobody was getting between her and the bathroom door, gun or not.

The guy with the gun pointed the barrel right at Quinn. "Back off."

Quinn held his hands out, stepping away a foot, shifting his body between the man and Juliet. That probably wasn't by chance. "What do you want?"

"Money." His hand shaking, the guy nodded to his friend. "This is a fundraiser, and we want the money."

"Okay," Quinn said, his voice low and soothing. "Barney, give this guy whatever's in the till."

The bartender nodded, his skinny chin wobbling as he hit the cash register and the drawer slid out.

The second guy threw a bag at Barney, and he started filling it.

The first guy laughed, showing yellowed teeth. "This is a fundraiser, man. We want all the money, not only the bar money."

Jake somehow edged closer to the second guy without seeming to move his feet. "The tickets were purchased weeks ago. The only money here in the lodge is at the bar, and you have that."

Quinn nodded. "Take the cash and leave."

The gunman's face turned a mottled red. His hand shook more. "There's no more money?" he yelled.

Jake shook his head. "Nope."

The guy focused on Jake for the briefest of seconds.

That was all Quinn needed. Faster than a whip and just as deadly, he struck out, grabbing the guy by the wrist and lifting his gun hand. An elbow to the gut, a stomp to the ankle, and the guy went down.

Quinn yanked the gun free.

Jake took care of the second guy with a quick punch to the nose. The guy crashed to the ground, blood spurting.

Colton groaned. "I didn't get to hit anybody."

The guy on the floor lunged up, and Colton nailed him with a sweeping sidekick to the face. The gunman smashed into the bar.

"That's better." Colton grinned, dusting his hands together.

Quinn didn't break a smile. Instead, he removed his cell phone from his pocket and called it in.

Juliet's legs wobbled. She grabbed the wall to steady herself.

Quinn said something that had Jake nodding. Then

Quinn's long strides ate up the distance between them. "Juliet? You're pale, sweetheart. Come and sit down."

The kind tone shot tears to her eyes. "How did they get here?" she whispered.

He frowned and turned toward the men. "I don't know. Why?"

"I thought a black SUV followed us to the base of the mountain, but I wasn't sure. Were they in a black SUV?" She shivered. When had the room gotten so cold?

Sirens echoed in the distance. Quinn slid an arm around her shoulders and gently led her to a chair. "Darlin', deep breaths. You're going into shock, and I need you to hold it together."

She nodded.

Two deputies rushed in from outside.

Quinn leaned down to check her face. "I have to give them orders. Are you okay for a few minutes?"

"Yes." She inhaled.

He brushed a kiss on the top of her head and turned to deal with the deputies. Her hands shook. She glanced around at the stunned partygoers. Lansing and his wife cringed in the far corner. Some sheriff he'd turn out to be.

The deputies handcuffed the robbers. Jake hustled toward the back bathroom to fetch his wife and mother.

Time flew by, or maybe she zoned out for a little while. Finally, Quinn dropped to his haunches in front of her. "I had my deputies bring my truck, so I can take you home. Let's go."

She stood and leaned against him, still in a daze. Within minutes she was bundled up in his truck, seat belt secured, a heavy blanket warming her, while Quinn drove down the mountain. Rain peppered the windows. She swallowed. "Do you have to go process those guys—or interrogate them—or whatever?"

"No." Quinn flipped on the windshield wipers. "My deputies can handle the situation. Tonight is my night off, and I'm taking it."

"Oh." She snuggled under the blanket. "How did you know they were going to rob the lodge?"

Quinn glanced in the rear-view mirror. "I didn't know for sure. The first guy shook like he needed a fix, and I trusted my gut."

"They were on drugs?" she asked.

Quinn's jaw visibly tightened. "Yes. Small town problems are no longer a marijuana plant or Peeping Tom. Now we have meth, drug running, and robberies. To get more money for drugs."

"Any chance those guys will get treatment?" she asked.

"I don't know. They pulled a gun on innocent people, so they should be behind bars. For quite some time," he said quietly.

Why did he have to be so black and white? She sighed.

He smiled at her. "I appreciate you trusting Jake and getting Sophie out of the way."

"Of course." Though, in reality, she'd looked at Quinn before moving. "You were really impressive."

"Those guys were morons. Don't be too impressed." His lips pressed together.

But she was. The way he'd put himself in danger, how quickly he'd disarmed the bad guy impressed her. The rainstorm raged around them, yet Quinn remained a solid island in a dangerous storm. "I like you, Quinn," she said quietly.

He flashed her a surprised look. "I like you, too. Feeling a bit vulnerable, sweetheart?"

Man, he could read her. "Yes."

"I won't let anybody hurt you. Ever." The quiet vow emerged deep and guttural.

No, but she'd hurt him. Quinn Lodge wasn't a man you lied to, and she could never undo what she'd done. "I wish we'd met years ago."

He reached over and smoothed the hair off her forehead. "The robbers drove a small compact to the lodge and not a SUV. Why did you think you were being followed? Did something spook you?"

Wow. Talk about foolish. "It's silly. I had a prank call, and then I went outside and my imagination ran away." She picked a loose string on the blanket. "Overactive imagination here."

"What kind of a prank call?" he asked.

"Just a goofy hang-up." Now she'd created problems where none existed.

He leaned forward to peer through the storm. "I can run your phone number, if you want."

She wrinkled her nose. "No, that's okay. It's silly."

"All right, but if it happens again, promise you'll tell me." His jaw firmed.

"I promise." Her gaze dropped to his capable hands on the steering wheel. Broad, rough, those hands could bring a lot of pleasure.

As if he could read her mind, he tangled his fingers with hers. "How would you like to spend the night tonight?"

Her heart leaped. The town bachelor, the sexy

sheriff nobody could catch, was offering her intimacy. Pleasure coursed through her to be quickly dashed by icy reality. Every time they were together, she came that much closer to blurting out the truth—and that she'd lied to him. But she couldn't help herself. She wanted this. Wanted him. "You want me to stay the entire night?"

"Yes. The whole night," he said, his voice a low promise.

CHAPTER NINE

Juliet settled into the overstuffed chair in Quinn's family room, her gaze on the sparking fire, her hand around the stem of a wineglass. Oil paintings depicting the wild Montana landscape covered the walls, and masculine leather furniture decorated the room. "I don't usually drink more than one glass of wine."

Quinn set another piece of wood on the fire, the muscles in his back shifting nicely. He stood, grabbed his beer, and dropped onto a matching chair. "Why not?"

Her limbs felt heavy. "My mother. She had specific rules about how a lady should act."

"Hmmm." He tipped back his head and swallowed, and the cords in his neck moved with the effort. Sexy and male. "I know from Sophie that your parents have passed on. Was your mother a society-type lady?"

"Yes. Well, she wanted to be." Fond memories lifted Juliet's lips in a smile, and then she grimaced. "My real father was a drunk, and I remember a lot of yelling. My mother divorced him and remarried a man with money, and she started climbing the social ladder. Somewhat." Considering Juliet's stepfather was a criminal, her mother could climb only so far. But she gave the journey a great shot. "She died of breast cancer four years ago."

"I'm sorry, baby." Quinn's eyes softened in the flickering firelight.

A hard man with soft eyes. Dangerous. Way too

dangerous to her heart.

She sipped the cool wine. "How did your father die?"

"A snowmobile accident when I was six and Jake was eight," Quinn said.

Her heart ached for him. "I'm sorry, Quinn."

"Me, too."

"He was full Kooskia, like your mother?" she asked.

Quinn leaned forward on his elbows. "Yes. Is your stepfather still alive?"

"No. He died of liver failure two years ago." While she'd never respected his job, he'd been kind to her, and she missed him. "I'm alone now."

"No, you're not." Quinn leaned back and stretched out his legs. "I promise. You're not alone."

Thunder bellowed outside. The wind whistled angrily above the sound of pelting rain.

Juliet studied the sheriff. The flickering light wandered over his angled face, highlighting his predatory features. Shadows danced along the angles, and suddenly she wanted nothing more than to be his. Even if it was only for the night. She wanted to belong with the sheriff.

Very gently, she placed her wineglass on the table. She folded the blanket and laid the thick cotton on the chair. Her gaze on the quiet man, she crossed the room and dropped to her knees. His thighs pressed in on her shoulders.

His dark eyes darkened further. "What are you doing?" Low, rough, his voice caressed her skin until a fire sparked inside her.

"Taking you." She unbuckled his belt and pulled

the heavy leather free of his jeans. The buckle clanked when she dropped it to the floor. "Lose the shirt."

Keeping her gaze, he yanked off the shirt. Powerful muscles shifted.

She swallowed. "I adore your chest." Ignoring all decorum, she crawled right up on his lap, her thighs bracketing his. Three round scars dotted his left shoulder, and she leaned over to kiss each one. "What are these?"

"Bullet holes."

She stilled, her heart catching. "Oh." She kissed them again. Then her mouth wandered to a long, diagonal scar across his left pec and rib cage. "And this?"

"Knife." His voice lowered.

"I'm sorry." Deep down, something ached for him. She sat up. Her fingers tapped a jagged scar wrapped around his bicep. "What in the world?"

"Barbed wire when I was a kid." He shrugged. "Rode my bike where I shouldn't have."

"You've had a rough life." She caressed the raised flesh.

"I'm feeling pretty good right now." His eyelids dropped to half-mast. "Is it my turn yet?"

Captured by his tone, she nodded.

"Good." He reached behind her neck and undid her necklaces, placing them on the table. Her earrings were next. "This jewelry is pretty."

"The pieces are Celtic—Irish trinity knots," she whispered, her voice going hoarse.

He slid his hands under her wispy shirt, his palms on her flesh, his knuckles raising the material over her head. "I've never seen a woman more feminine than you."

Hard and fast, the sheriff was sexy. Slow and thoughtful, he was downright devastating.

"Feminine, not fragile." She inhaled his strong scent of male and pine.

He traced her clavicle with calloused fingers. "Fragile, too." His gaze stayed on his fingers as he flicked open her bra and smoothed the straps down her arms.

She blinked, exposed to him.

"You're beautiful, Juliet," he breathed, hands palming her breasts.

"I've never felt like this." He made her feel beautiful.

His dimple flashed. "Every once in a while, you're completely bare. Saying what you feel without holding back." His hands firmed, and he lifted his gaze. "That's how I want you tonight."

Vulnerability slithered right down her spine. "I, ah—"

He rolled her nipples.

Heat flooded to her sex.

With just enough of a bite, he pinched. "I told you how I want you. Understand?"

The dominant tone flashed through her and offered an intriguing sense of safety. One she wanted so badly.

To free herself for one night and take all Quinn could give? The idea should be terrifying. But it would be worth the broken heart and sleepless nights after she left town. She'd always have this to remember.

"I understand. One night. No holding back." She ran her hands up the hard cords of his neck. "That goes for you, too. No holding back."

"I hadn't planned on it." Cupping her head, he

lowered his mouth to hers. Firm lips, gentle pressure, so much sweetness in the kiss that tears sprang to her eyes.

Even sweet, a sense of control emanated in his touch. She leaned back and gave in to the need to trace his angular face. "Sometimes, when I've watched you, I wished so badly I was a better sculptor."

He smoothed the skirt up her thighs, his fingers skimming her skin. "When I watched you, I wished for this. For you, in the firelight…becoming mine."

"That's a better wish." She cradled his face and brushed his lips. Her heart jumped even while her mind shut down the fantasy. She couldn't be his. No matter how much she wanted to be. Even if she never broke another law, sometimes a person couldn't negate their past. "I wish more than anything in the world I could be what you want."

"You're exactly what I want." He curved his wandering hands around to cup her rear end. "Someday you're going to tell me what those shadows mean in your eyes, and I'm going to fix whatever is haunting you."

"I wish you could." This whole "holding nothing back" was going to get her into trouble. At least she'd have this image to take with her. A strong man in firelight to remember forever. "But tonight, there are no shadows."

"No shadows." He stood suddenly.

She gasped, her legs tightening around his waist, her hands gripping his shoulders.

"I've got you." The fire in his eyes and low tone of voice held more vow than temporary reassurance. "You're safe."

"You're not safe, Sheriff. Not at all," she murmured.

His dark eyes glittered. "Do tell."

Silky strands tempted her fingers when she threaded them through his hair—and tugged. Just hard enough. "I'm feeling dangerous."

"Juliet," he drawled while carrying her through the room and up the stairs, "I have handcuffs."

She breathed out a combination of heat and humor. "Sounds like a threat."

"Oh no, darlin'." He set her on the bed. "I don't threaten. Ever."

"Really? What was that statement?" she asked.

"A promise." He unclasped his jeans and dropped them to the floor. "I'll take a little teasing from you, beautiful. But you cross me? I'll cuff you and make you beg."

Her breath caught low in her throat. She slanted her lips in a small smile. "You have something I'd beg for?"

His smile was anything but small, anything but sweet. "Let's find out." All wolf, he ripped off her skirt. For a quiet moment, he looked his fill. Naked, exposed on his bed, she remained still. The want in his eyes warmed her—gave her a confidence she rarely felt. So she let him look.

With a low hum of appreciation, he slid his hands over her ankles, up her calves, across her thighs. His mouth followed, pausing at her thigh to nip.

Wait a minute. Panic rushed down her throat. This was something she didn't do. She wiggled, partially sitting up to stop him.

He flattened his hand across her stomach. Firm and absolute. His head lifted, and he pinned her with a look.

She swallowed. "No, er, Quinn. I don't ah, do—"

"I'll get the cuffs." His breath brushed her clit.

A strangled gasp hissed out with her breath. He was serious. He'd actually cuff her. Her mind spinning, she lay back down.

He rewarded her with a soft kiss on her mound.

This was way too intimate. She'd lay still, kind of ignore him, and he'd move on to something else. Something she could enjoy. "This really isn't my thing, Qui—"

He licked her. Slow, sure, he licked her. Electric shocks whipped out from his mouth. Static filled her brain.

Those wide shoulders pressed against her inner thighs, forcing her legs open. "You might as well relax, baby. You taste like honeysuckle and spices, and I could do this all night." He spoke right against her flesh, sending vibrations deep into her body. "In fact, I just might."

Her eyelids fluttered. With a deep sigh, she relaxed.

Slowly, one finger entered her. She arched against his mouth, biting her lip to keep from moaning.

A sharp nip to her thigh narrowed her focus. "No holding back, Juliet." He slid another finger inside her, and crisscrossed them.

A whimper escaped her.

Alternating between licks, nips, even bites, he had her on edge way too quickly. Never quite providing enough pressure to push her over, he kept her at the precipice. Her body stretched tight like a string. Need trembled down her legs. She curled her toes, almost welcoming the cramping pain, just to have something to ground her.

His fingers pumped, his mouth licked, and his deep

baritone hummed against her.

The sheriff was playing and truly enjoying the game.

She wanted to swear at him, but every instinct she had warned her not to challenge him. Not right now. He liked her on the edge, and he liked control. So she let him play until she couldn't take any more.

Sweat dotted her brow, her mind fuzzed, and her body gyrated against him. "Quinn, please—"

He lifted his head, even while his fingers continued to torture her. "Please, what, Juliet?"

She tried to concentrate. "You...know."

His dimple flashed. "No. I really don't. Say the words."

The low growl that rumbled from her chest shocked the heck out of her. "Quinn."

"Those aren't the words." He swirled his tongue around her aching clit with just enough pressure to make her sob.

"Stop torturing me," she ground out.

"Want me to stop? Maybe make a late dinner?" He sank his teeth into her other thigh, sure to leave a mark. His mark.

The thought nearly threw her into the orgasm he dangled out of reach. "I may kill you."

The sharp slap to her clit sheeted the room white. "Now, darlin'...threats aren't nice. Do better."

She very well may hate this side of him. "Why are you doing this?"

"You like it."

The fact that her body was on fire, that she was wetter than she'd ever been and was ready to beg? There was something definitely wrong with her, because she apparently did like it. Like him. All of him.

"Please let me come."

"With pleasure." Wriggling his finger against a spot inside her that had her legs straightening, he scraped his tongue over her clit with firm pressure.

She exploded like she'd swallowed dynamite. Flashes of nearly painful pleasure shot through her veins, rippling through her. She arched into his mouth, both hands clamping on his head, her body undulating in desperate waves.

Somebody screamed, and yes, it was probably her. She rode out the pulses and murmured his name as she came down. Gasping, she released him and pressed one hand on her chest. Her heart beat rapidly against her palm. "Wow."

"That was nice." He shifted against the bed, his shoulders spreading her legs wider. "Let's try that again."

"No." Her head jerked against the pillow. "No more." She sat up to glare at him. Her body was only partially sated…she needed him inside her and now. "That was great. Wonderful. Now get up here."

His eyelids lifted until his heated gaze met hers.

She stopped moving. Frozen, like prey catching sight of a hunter. "Um."

"Beg me." He said the words calmly.

"No way."

"Exactly." He plunged two fingers inside her.

Her body short-circuited, and she flopped back down. He was going to kill her. Finish her off for all time. But, as his mouth got to work again, she had to admit it wasn't a bad way to go.

Quinn took his time and was thorough. Very thorough. It might have been minutes, perhaps hours.

At some point, she was shifting against him, seeking release. Needing to quench the desperate fire he so easily stoked in her. Finally, he moved up her body, taking time to appreciate both breasts.

Then his mouth took hers. Deep, intense, he kissed her like they had forever.

She clasped her ankles across his back, pulling in. His engorged cock lay heavy against the apex of her legs, and she pressed against him, gasping at the exquisite pressure.

He slid inside her, just a bit, and then stopped.

She yanked on his neck, pulling him closer. "Don't stop."

"Don't stop, what?" Sweat sprang out on his forehead. His biceps vibrated as he held still.

"Quinn."

His head dropped, and he sucked her earlobe into his heated mouth. "Tell me what you want."

"You. I want you." She slid against him.

He growled and gripped her hip, holding her in place. "What do you want me to do?"

He was terrible. Truly terrible. "Anything you want. Just do it." She pulled his hair.

His smile flashed dangerous teeth. Pulling her hip up, he shoved inside her with one strong thrust. Her sex squeezed him. Even though she was primed and ready, the shock of his size had her gasping for breath.

Sliding his arms around her thighs, he widened her and began to pound. So strong, so fast, so powerful. He plunged inside her until all she could do was grab onto his defined biceps and feel.

A ball of lava uncoiled inside her.

With a cry of his name, she broke.

CHAPTER TEN

Juliet snuggled her butt closer into Quinn's groin, playing with the hair on his arm, which was lying heavily across her waist. "I like spooning," she murmured sleepily.

He kissed her head.

The storm continued to rage outside, but inside, only contentment reigned.

For now.

"Understand the rules, darlin'?" he rumbled, his body a strong force behind her.

"If you have a nightmare, don't touch you. Don't try to awaken you. I should slide out of the bed and let you wake up on your own," she repeated. Again.

A thick sigh stirred her hair. "I don't like this," he muttered.

"You won't hurt me." She believed the truth in her statement with everything she was. "Believe me. I know."

"I wouldn't mean to hurt you, but you're so small." He shifted as if to slide from the bed.

She grabbed his arm and held tight. "I'm much stronger than you think." Even if he did lash out, she could handle it. Plus, she was only small to him. She had height, and she had strength from lifting more paintings than she could count. "Trust me."

"Hmmm." He relaxed against her.

"I understand how much you like to be in control, and I know this is scary for you." She wiggled a little more. "You're incredibly brave to face this, and I'm honored to be here." It was too bad her demons couldn't be faced down like his. Hers resulted from her own stupidity, and there was nothing she could do but outrun them. "I...care about you, Quinn."

He rolled her over and smoothed hair from her face. His dark eyes felt like they were caressing her face. "I care about you, too. This is going somewhere, Juliet."

Her heart shattered. She blinked and opened her mouth to say something. Anything.

He grinned. "No hurry, sweetheart."

Oh, this wasn't good. She couldn't fight them both, and Quinn Lodge was a force of nature, all by himself. How could she explain everything to him? "I know we're good together. But it doesn't change—"

"Change what?" His eyebrows rose.

"You promised. No shadows tonight," she said.

He studied her. The moment drew on, and she could imagine anybody in his interrogation room just giving up and confessing everything. His upper lip tipped up, and he kissed her nose before speaking. "You're not married."

Her eyes widened. "Of course not."

He kissed her mouth this time with a gentle brush of his firm lips. "Well then, anything else I can handle."

If he only knew. In her past, she ran drugs. Kind of. No big deal. No problem, right? Her heart hurt. "Night, Quinn. Sweet dreams." She rolled over, sure she'd never sleep.

Instantly, she fell into dreams of wild storms, raging water, and money falling from the sky that was more of a nightmare than a hope. A definite nightmare.

Morning arrived too soon, and a fully dressed sheriff shook her awake.

She sat up sleepily. "You didn't have a nightmare?"

"Nope." He lifted a shoulder, his gun strapped to his thigh and his badge at his belt. The man looked like he could handle any problem as easy as most people breathed. "We'll have to try again."

She forced a smile. A second chance wasn't going to happen. Oddly enough, she'd been the one to have bad dreams, instead of him. All of that worrying for nothing. Of course, she deserved it, and he did not. "Why are you dressed so early?"

"I had a call—need to go to work." He leaned down and kissed her. Slow and deep. Finally, he stood back up. "Take your time. There's coffee on, and I think there are bagels in the pantry. Maybe."

She nodded. "I need to get to work, anyway. Sophie's exhibition was pushed up, and we have a lot to do."

He reached in the night-table drawer and secured a knife to slide into the sheath against his calf, below his jeans. Then he stood, his shoulders wide and strong. The man looked every bit as dangerous as he was rumored to be around town. Tough, protective, and merciless if need be. "Tonight, Juliet. We talk." With a hard look, he turned on his cowboy boot and left the room.

Well, that wasn't good.

• • •

The rain drizzled the day into gray. Quinn tipped the brim of his hat to shake off the water, his boots sinking in the soggy weeds. The wind cut through his sheriff's jacket as if it wanted to draw blood. An abandoned barn crumbled behind him, while a dead body lay before him, pale and wan. It had been a while since he'd seen a dead body.

Male, about six feet tall, long, blond hair. Maybe around thirty? "Bullet hole, back of the head," Quinn murmured. "Execution style?"

"Probably." DEA Agent Reese Johnson nodded to the state coroner. "You can take him."

Federal evidence techs bustled around, collecting evidence from grass and dirt.

Reese's phone buzzed, and he looked down to read the face. "Prints found a match. Leroy Vondoni, recently paroled from Rikers. Shouldn't be out of New York state."

"Rap sheet?" Quinn asked.

"Possession, robbery, intent to sell, assault, attempted murder." Reese tapped his phone. "Nice guy."

Why was Vondoni in Maverick? More importantly— "While I appreciate you're calling me in on this, why is the DEA in my county?" Quinn eyed a man he'd trust with his life…in fact, he had at one time. That didn't mean the DEA could set up camp in Montana.

Reese tucked his phone in his back pocket. "We got an anonymous tip the body would be here. An hour later, we were wheels up from LA, and here we are. I called from the plane the first chance I found."

Quinn narrowed his gaze…and waited.

Reese watched the coroner load the body. "I was heading here anyway at the end of the week. Our sources have confirmed there's a large shipment coming down from Canada, and we think Montana will be the entry point."

"Drugs?" Irritation washed down Quinn's throat. What he wouldn't give for a couple of old guys running moonshine.

"Prescription." Reese yanked off his Dodger cap and wiped his forehead. "The new front line. Oxy is more valuable than gold on the streets right now, and I'm hoping there isn't fentanyl thrown in."

"When is the shipment supposed to come through?" Quinn asked.

"Don't know. Gut feeling? Soon. What do you think, Sarge? Your gut has to be humming," Reese said.

"Sheriff," Quinn said absently. His gut was fucking rolling. A dead body in his county was the last thing he needed right now. "Soon is right."

Reese cleared his throat. "Are you going to fight me on jurisdiction?"

"No. I don't have near the resources the feds do. That fingerprint-scanner thing is impressive," Quinn said.

"The machine is yours if we catch these guys." The white scar Reese had earned in Iraq stood out on his forehead. "Though why you don't take one of the many job offers you've received from federal law-enforcement agencies, I'll never understand."

"I'm home, and I like it here." Usually. When there weren't dead bodies dumped on forgotten acreage. "The DEA can have this case, but I want in. I want to know everything," Quinn said.

"That means lunch is on you," Reese said.

Quinn gave a short nod, already forming the

talking points for his meeting with his deputies later that day. "Tell me this is the first body you've seen in connection with whatever's going on."

"Third." Reese rubbed his chin. "These guys use people and then kill quickly. No witnesses."

Quinn headed for his truck. "How efficient of them. Come into town. I have three deputies I want to bring in on this—we'll keep it to a small task force."

"Fair enough. I'll drive with you. Fill me in on the family. Has Colton graduated yet?" Reese followed, turning to toss his keys at another DEA agent before jumping into the rig.

"He has one more year of graduated school and then wants to study international finance abroad for a year." Quinn started the engine. "He has already taken over as COO of Freeze-Lodge Investments, and he's been helping to run the financial end of everything for years." Quinn grinned. "We won't give him the salary or the title until he graduates and is home for good, although he doesn't really care, if you ask me. It's the game of the markets that he loves."

"Is he MMA fighting?" Reese asked.

"No. Though he's a tough bastard. He fought for beer money and just a physical challenge, if you ask me. He's the mellowest of us all," Quinn said. Well, until Colton's very long fuse blew. Then everyone got out of the way.

"I caught one of his fights on ESPN late at night. He was brutal." Reese settled into the seat. "With all the money you've all made with those investments, why do you work the ranch and sport a gun?"

"What else would I do? Sit around and read ledgers?" Quinn mock shivered.

Reese laughed. "Good enough. So, what's new with you?"

Everything. "Not much."

"Seeing anyone?" Reese asked.

Hell, yes. Quinn lifted a shoulder. "You'll meet her, I'm sure. How about you?"

"Hell, no." Reese shifted his gun away from his hip. "I learned my lesson."

Quinn chuckled. Sometimes romance snuck up and bit a guy on the ass whether he liked it or not. "How does a hoagie from Mrs. Johnson's homemade deli sound?"

"Excellent," Reese said.

"Good. Now start talking. I need to know how much danger my people are in." Quinn pulled onto the country road.

CHAPTER ELEVEN

Several hours after leaving Quinn's place, Juliet struggled to align the small painting of horses galloping around the shores of Mineral Lake. She and Sophie had worked all day, and the show was coming together. They'd even harassed Colton into helping them with the bigger pieces.

Juliet hadn't heard from Quinn, but rumor had it a cattle rustling had occurred at the north end of the county, so he'd probably been busy.

He wanted to talk. Perhaps she should come clean and tell him the truth. He deserved the truth, even if he ended up arresting her. Maybe she could talk him out of cuffing her.

Her laugh lacked humor as it echoed around the room. No way. She couldn't talk him out of an arrest.

She finished fiddling and eyed the main room as a whole. Deep jewel tones splashed across the oil paintings depicting tribal scenes, landscapes, and portraits of fascinating faces. The next room held charcoals, and the final room drawings. Without question, Sophie Lodge was incredibly talented. This showing would put the gallery on the map.

Pride filled Juliet. While she wouldn't be able to bask in the success, she'd accomplished her goals. She'd actually set out and done it. Now, she had to go break Quinn's heart. But he deserved to know the truth. It was time to confess everything.

Grabbing her coat, she locked the front door and

hustled out of the building. The rain had stopped, but a tension-filled breeze swirled down the street.

She wandered past storefronts, small restaurants, and a couple of delis before reaching the sheriff's building. Breezing inside the two-story brick building, she nodded at the elderly receptionist, noting that the sprawling reception room was empty. "Hi, Mrs. Wilson," she said.

The receptionist pushed her cat's-eye glasses up her nose. "The day's chilly, Juliet. You here to visit the sheriff?"

Juliet nodded.

"Go on back. He's not doing anything," Mrs. Wilson said.

Juliet doubted that. She skirted the counter and headed down the long hallway, passing several offices and cubicles. His office sat in the northern corner and looked out on the street. She paused at the doorway and gathered her courage.

His unique scent of man and leather hit her the second she stepped inside. The fact that he wasn't alone hit her next. She faltered.

"Juliet. Did we have plans?" He rose from behind a scarred wooden desk. Lines of fatigue spread out from his eyes, but they warmed on her.

"Um, no." She glanced at the man rising from the leather guest chair.

Tall, serious, he held himself with coiled strength. Just like Quinn. He held out a hand. "Reese Johnson. I'm an old friend of Quinn's."

"Juliet Montgomery." They shook. She cleared her throat. "Sorry about the interruption. I'll catch up with you later, Quinn." She pivoted to go.

"Juliet." Quinn's quiet baritone stopped her cold. She turned. He grinned and edged around the desk to lift her chin and brush her lips with his. "You're not interrupting. What's going on?"

A man who had no problem touching her, even around an old buddy. Juliet would bet her last penny the old buddy was from the military, too. She forced a smile. "Nothing. Really. I wanted to see if you had dinner plans."

He frowned. "We're probably going to work through dinner. Ah, Reese is from the DEA."

The Drug Enforcement Agency? The words ripped through her with the force of a sledgehammer. "Oh." She turned another smile on the guest, her posture straightening. Was he in town for her? He couldn't be, so she focused back on Quinn. "I suppose you have a lot of work to do."

"Yes." A puzzled light glimmered in his eyes. He grabbed his coat. "Let me walk you out, darlin'."

She stumbled as he maneuvered her through the doorway.

Hustling her out of the station, he grasped her coat lapels. "What's wrong?"

"Everything is lovely." She donned her smoothest smile.

His dark eyes narrowed. "You're the most graceful woman I've ever met, and you just tripped on a smooth floor. Don't get all society-like with me. Something is bothering you, and you'll damn well tell me what it is."

"Nothing is wrong. I mean, I heard you investigated a cattle-rustling call this morning, and then I didn't hear from you, so I was worried." Not true. Not one word was true. She hadn't worried at all until seeing a DEA Agent in his office.

Quinn cocked his head. "You're right—I'm sorry for not calling you today." He tied her scarf more securely. "The call wasn't for cattle rustling. We found a body on the edge of Miller's northern pasture."

She gulped. "A body?"

"Yes. Shot through the head." He leaned down, his gaze serious. "I don't want you going anywhere alone for the time being."

"I won't." She took a deep breath. "Why is the DEA involved?"

"We think the deceased was involved with the prescription drug trade," he said.

So much relief flushed through her, she nearly swayed. Prescriptions had nothing to do with her. Thank goodness her past hadn't caught up with her. Not yet, anyway.

Quinn tangled his fingers through hers and started down the sidewalk.

She pulled away. "What are you doing?"

"Walking you back to the gallery," he said.

She tried unsuccessfully to free her hand. "That is not necessary. It's barely dinnertime, Quinn. I can walk back by myself."

"No." He tugged her into a sidewalk, his shoulders blocking the wind.

"You're a force of nature, Quinn Lodge," she muttered, stepping over a mud puddle.

He scouted the area on either side of the quiet street. "Thank you."

"I don't believe I gave you a compliment." She sighed. "Is Reese an old military buddy?"

Quinn nodded at a couple of bankers exiting the Maverick Bank for the day. "We served together for five years. He's a good friend."

"You really shouldn't leave him to walk me home. I'm sure you have a lot of work to do," she said.

"He can make phone calls while I'm gone." Quinn slid an arm around her shoulders and tugged her into heat. "You're getting all formal again." He glanced down. "What I don't understand is why."

She was saved from having to answer when they turned the corner and reached her gallery.

Quinn stiffened. "Did you leave the front door unlocked?"

The red door stood slightly ajar. "I don't think so." Had she?

He leaned down. Scrape marks slashed from the lock. He pushed her gently toward the road. "Cross the street and go inside the coffee shop. Stay there until I come and get you." Without taking his eyes off the door, he lifted his phone to his ear and called for backup. Then he pulled his gun free of his waistband.

"Now, Juliet." His quiet order held bite this time.

Startled, she rushed across the road. The bell above the door of Kurt's Koffees & Muffins rang when she hustled into the shop. Turning, she all but pressed her face against the window in time to see Quinn nudge the gallery door open with his foot and step inside, his gun sweeping.

He disappeared from sight.

Every ounce of her control went into keeping still, when all she wanted was to run across the street and make sure he was all right. But she'd distract him when he needed to focus. So she remained at the window, not daring to breathe.

Two police cars screeched to a stop, and a myriad of deputies headed toward the building, guns out.

Thank goodness.

Minutes passed, although it seemed like hours. Finally, Quinn stalked outside.

Relief filled her, and she sagged.

His gaze caught hers, he hurried across the street, and shoved open the door. A thick hand banded around her arm. "Come with me, Juliet."

She nodded, slipping through the doorway. A harsh wind slapped her face. Quinn drew her closer, an arm around her shoulders. "I need you to tell me if anything was taken."

"Okay." She took a deep breath. "Maybe I left the door open?"

"No, sweetheart. You didn't leave the door open." He maneuvered her inside. "Somebody picked the lock."

Dread filled her lungs. "Do you think it was the guys from last year?" Several businesses had been burglarized the previous year by a group of kids from Billings looking for fast cash.

"No. We caught them. Plus, they did the standard smash and grab—broke open the door and grabbed what they could within five minutes. This guy picked the lock carefully. I checked through the gallery, as well as upstairs in your apartment, and didn't discover anything damaged or missing. But you need to check."

The air felt different. Cold and out of sync.

"My laptop is gone." She'd left the HP on the desk by the front door before heading to the sheriff's office. Her heart beating against her ribs, she rushed through the gallery, her gaze on the walls. Sophie's paintings stood bright, dark, and dreamy as silent sentinels to the invasion. But they were safe. No art had been touched or taken.

Thank goodness. Juliet's breath whooshed out. Shaking her hands to release the tension, she followed the sheriff upstairs to her apartment, which appeared untouched. Finally, they ended up in her bright, cheerful kitchen, and she flopped at the table. "I guess they only took the laptop."

Quinn frowned, scribbling in a notebook. "I find that odd."

"That someone would take a laptop? It sounds like a smash and grab like last time." She smoothed out the flowered tablecloth.

He stopped writing. "I'm not sure. Something's bothering me about this. Why pick the lock and leave the door open so you knew? It's like somebody wanted to scare you."

"The entire situation bothers me." She sighed. It seemed doubtful her past had finally found her, but she needed to come clean, anyway. She opened her mouth to spill all, when Reese charged into the room.

He removed his baseball cap. "We have another body."

Juliet's mouth snapped shut. No way would she tell all in front of the DEA agent.

"Over on the south side of the county." Reese glanced at his smartphone. "I have techs on the way. You coming, Quinn?"

Quinn nodded and then grimaced as his cell phone buzzed. He yanked it to his ear. "What?" After listening, he closed his eyes and blew out air. "Is Colton with her? Okay. I'll be there as soon as I can." He hung up and opened his eyes to focus on Juliet. "Rich Jacoby passed away. The ambulance is taking him to the morgue."

"Is Colton with Melanie?" Juliet stood, her eyes widening. Melanie Jacoby and her grandfather were incredibly close and the only living relative either had. Now poor Melanie was all alone.

"Yes. She called him after calling for an ambulance. I guess Rich was unconscious in the barn, and then he died. Colt will help with the funeral arrangements, I'm sure." Quinn grasped Juliet's elbow to escort her to the door. "I'm having a deputy take you to my place. Stay inside until I get home."

She tugged her arm free. Almost. "No. The showing is tomorrow night, and I have work to do."

Quinn's unbreakable grip tightened. "You can finish up tomorrow. For now, I need you safe until I deal with death."

Well, since he put it like that. Juliet grabbed two notebooks off the counter. She could confirm details via phone from the sheriff's home office. "Okay."

Lines cut harsh grooves into the side of his mouth. "When I get home, we're going to talk."

CHAPTER TWELVE

Quinn finished with the scene and left Reese to handle his techs. Another dead body, this guy also tied to the drug trade, according to Reese.

The drug trade in Maverick Montana? No way. Quinn would figure out a way to keep the citizens safe. At the moment, he concentrated his gaze on the watery road outside his truck. The rain had increased in intensity, and his vehicle nearly hydroplaned through Miller's Crossing. The deputies had better hurry up and place those warning signs before somebody got hurt. Night was about to fall, and visibility sucked.

His mind spun, and his gut ached. Who would break into Juliet's gallery and steal the laptop? More specifically, who would want her to know so clearly that she was robbed?

His radio buzzed. "Sheriff? There's a report of a fight tonight at the high school," Mrs. Wilson said.

He sighed and pressed the button. "I'm on my way."

Five minutes and several lightning strikes later, he pulled the truck into the high school parking lot. Teenagers milled around, forming a circle. He hit his patrol lights. They scattered like scared rabbits through the rain.

Biting back a laugh, he jumped out and grabbed the closest rabbit by the collar. "Mr. Benson. Who's fighting tonight?"

Billy's eyes widened, and he gulped several times. "I, ah, don't know."

Quinn did. His gaze caught on the two young men by the bleachers. The juniors stood, guilt on their faces, hands clenched. Pride filled Quinn that they hadn't fled. "Donny and Luke?" He released Benson with a small shove toward the kid's Subaru.

Donny nodded his buzz-cut head, and freckles popped out on his pale face. Luke shrugged and shuffled his feet.

Quinn lowered his voice to his best "don't-fuck-with-me" tone. "Get in the truck. Now."

The boys almost ran each other over to get in the truck.

Quinn eyed the rest of the group. "Everyone else, get home before this storm hits any harder." Pivoting on his cowboy boot, he jumped back into the truck and turned off the patrol lights.

Donny stretched his hands toward the heater. "Are you arresting us, Sheriff?"

Luke cleared his throat. "Um, for what? I mean, we were just standing there. Right?"

Quinn maneuvered the truck onto the road. "You planned to fight."

"Is planning illegal?" Donny asked, hunching his shoulders.

"Could be." Quinn cut him a look. "I'm sure I could find something to book you on."

Luke glanced at Donny. "Your mom is gonna be pissed."

"No shi—kidding." Donny groaned. "My mom is pregnant—very—and on edge."

Luke snorted. "That's an understatement."

"Shut up." Donny elbowed him without much heat. "She's kind of old to be pregnant."

Quinn coughed. "Jesus, Don. She's only thirty-five. That's not old, and your parents started early with you." High school early, actually. But they'd stuck together, and they'd made it.

"Yeah. Old." Donny shook his head.

Quinn took the turn out of town.

"You gonna shoot us and leave us outside of town, sheriff?" Luke asked with a grin.

"I might. You're being such morons, I'd probably be doing your parents a favor." Quinn shook his head.

The tension in the truck abated as the kids realized they weren't headed for the sheriff's station.

"Before I give you hell about planning a fight in my town, especially during a spring storm, why don't you tell me what the fight was about?" Then he'd decide what to do with them. He wasn't finished with them yet.

The boys both shrugged.

"Tell me, or we're heading for booking." Good thing he played poker regularly.

Donny grimaced. "Sierra Zimmerman."

Figured. "You two are fighting over a girl?" Quinn asked.

"Yeah," Luke said.

Quinn increased the speed of the windshield wipers. "Sierra is a great girl. Smart as heck and just as pretty. But you two have been best friends since diapers." He'd caught them once stealing apples from McLeary's farm; they'd eaten so much they'd puked as he'd taken them home.

The boys shuffled restlessly.

Quinn sighed. "All right. Here's the deal. If you like a woman, you fight for her. With everything you are."

Two surprised faces turned their full attention on him.

"However, you don't fight each other. You don't fight your best friend. Show some class, show the girl you're a solid guy who will protect her, and give it all you have. With class, strength, and dignity."

Luke scrunched up his face. "That's confusing."

Quinn barked out a laugh. "Welcome to romance. If you two fight over Sierra and one of you gets hurt or embarrassed, then she's hurt and embarrassed. Do you want that?"

"No," they both said instantly.

"Exactly," Quinn said.

Don frowned. "You're a big war hero who carries a gun. Chicks love you."

To be young again. "Have you seen me use my gun?" Quinn asked.

"No," Luke said.

"Exactly. I have a gun, I have training, and I'll use it if I have to. But I certainly wouldn't use it against my friend." Quinn turned into the Maverick subdivision. "If anyone ever comes after your family or your woman, you go after them with absolutely no mercy." He was probably going to get his butt kicked by their mothers for giving such advice, but he'd always been honest with the kids and given them his best. "Other than that, you fight fair and don't scare your girl. Ever."

"Fighting scares girls." Don nodded sagely.

Quinn shrugged. "Frankly, I'm not sure if it scares them, but fighting ticks them off. For the most part, they're a lot smarter than we are."

"That's for sure," Luke muttered.

"So, what are you going to do with us?" Don asked, his gaze on the lightning zigging across the sky. "We know you have something in mind." Luke nodded next to him.

Now he'd become predictable? "Tomorrow you're both offering to clean up leaves and debris for Mrs. Rush and her neighbor, Mr. Pearson, after this storm blows over."

"Pearson's making moonshine again," Luke said.

Quinn shook his head. "We dismantled his still. If he starts walking around naked again, I expect one of you to give me a call."

"He likes being naked," Donny said. "I mean, he's not crazy or anything. He just said that at his age, the sun feels good on his wrinkles."

"Man, does he have a lot of wrinkles," Luke chortled.

"He's over ninety." Quinn snorted. "So, do you two have any questions for me now that we've talked?"

Donny settled against the seat. "Are you going to marry the art lady?"

"She's pretty," Luke said.

That was not the type of question Quinn had invited. He sighed. "She is pretty, and I just started dating her." He pulled his truck into Luke's driveway. "Marriage is a long way off for me, kids."

Donny glanced at Luke. "As men, we're stupid."

"Morons." Luke leaped out. "Want to come in and play Xbox?"

Donny glanced at Quinn, who nodded. "Sure. I just gotta call my mom. Thanks, Sheriff."

"Make sure you explain everything to your parents, because I will be talking to them." Quinn forced a stern frown. "I'm sure I don't need to tell you what happens if you two decide to fight again."

"Nope," Donny said while Luke shook his head vigorously.

"Good." Quinn waited until they'd hurried inside before pulling out of the driveway. He grabbed his radio. "The high school is all clear, Mrs. Wilson."

"Who was fighting, Sheriff?" she asked, her voice high with curiosity.

"Donny Wilcox and Luke Merryweather were thinking about dusting it up, but they changed their minds. They both like Sierra Zimmerman." He gave her the full story, knowing it'd be all over town the next day anyway.

Mrs. Wilson chuckled. "Sierra is dating the Silvia boy. I saw them at the movies last night." She clicked off.

That figured.

He maneuvered the truck through the storm, his shoulders relaxing when he arrived back in town. After a quick stop at his office, he wanted to get home to Juliet. It was time he followed his own advice and fought for the woman—even if he had to fight with her to get to the truth.

His radio buzzed. Shaking his head, he lifted it. "Yes?"

Mrs. Wilson cleared her throat. "Shelley at Babe's Bar called and asked for you to drop by."

"Me? Why?" He hit his blinker to turn.

"Well, apparently Hawk and Adam are getting into it." Mrs. Wilson sniffed. "Though I doubt it. Hawk just got back in town, and he and Adam have been buddies for years."

"Thank you, Mrs. Wilson. I'll report in as soon as I figure out what's going on." Quinn scowled. He was finished giving speeches about friendship for the night. If Hawk and Adam were being assholes, he'd throw them both in cells until morning.

He double-parked in front of the bar. The scents of tequila, perfume, and sawdust pummeled him as he walked inside. Country music played over the speakers, although the band dais remained empty. Good. Last thing he wanted to deal with was watching his baby sister sing in a bar, while she was home for spring break. Although the girl could sing.

Hawk and Adam stood over by a pool table, beer bottles in hand. Well, no one had thrown a punch yet. Quinn made his way to the back, his gaze on his friends.

"What's going on, gentlemen?" he asked.

Hawk gave him a look. "Nothing."

Hawk owned the ranch to the south of Quinn's and had been Colton's best friend since birth. Half Kooskia, he had dark hair, green eyes, and Native features. Quinn considered him another younger brother and was tempted to smack him just like he would've Colton.

Adam cleared his throat. "Just a little disagreement about my band, Sheriff." He was Colton and Hawk's age. After graduating from college with a business degree, he'd bought the bar in town. He also played in the band and was a fairly decent guitarist.

Quinn shoved impatience down. "Tell me you're not fighting over a girl."

Adam coughed. Hawk stilled.

"You have got to be kidding me." Quinn shoved his hands in his pocket to keep from slamming their heads together. "Tell me you're not fighting over my sister."

"Not like you mean." Hawk took a deep swallow of his beer.

"Explain before I kick your ass, Hawk," Quinn said. So much for niceties.

The outside door opened, and Colton shoved inside. Surprise lifted his eyebrows as he hustled toward them. "What's going on?"

Hawk groaned, while Adam grinned.

Quinn settled his stance. "Somebody was about to explain that to me."

Adam's eyes filled with amusement. "Hawk objects to Dawn singing in the band when she's home during weekends."

Colton nodded his head toward the waitress. "We all object." He smiled when she brought him a long-neck. "Not that we don't like your bar or your band, Adam. But Dawn is too young to sing in a bar. Besides, she should be staying at college and having fun each weekend instead of driving home."

"She's legal to drink," Adam said. "I think she's old enough to make up her own mind."

Quinn was more interested in why Hawk felt the need to object on Dawn's behalf. He eyed his old friend, who met his stare evenly and without blinking. "How long you in town, Hawk?" Quinn asked.

"Just a week," Hawk said.

Quinn rubbed his chin. "While you're here, let's all meet up to secure the fences on both our properties before the next storm hits." That way, he and Hawk could have a little discussion.

Hawk's full lip quirked. "I look forward to it, Sheriff."

Yep. Quinn was going to have to smack him a good one.

"Sheriff?" the bartender bellowed. "Mrs. Wilson is on the phone. She said you left your radio and phone in the truck."

Quinn took a deep breath and focused on the bar. "And?"

"There's been a wreck out on the interstate, and they need more spotlights," the bartender said.

"This night is never going to end." Giving anyone within his vicinity a hard look, the sheriff turned on his heel and headed toward the door and his next disaster.

CHAPTER THIRTEEN

Juliet glanced at the dark storm outside and hung up the phone. The caterer would be early the next day to set up, and he'd assured her everything would go smoothly. More than anything, she needed the show to go perfectly. Sophie deserved astounding success.

Wiggling her feet back into an awake state, Juliet surveyed the sheriff's home office. Dark walls lent a masculine atmosphere while the tumbled stone fireplace offered coziness. She could picture him sitting at the solid oak desk, filling out the ranching ledgers. The room even smelled like him. Sexy and strong.

The doorbell rang.

She pushed back from the desk and wandered through the sprawling house to the front door. Glancing in the intricate window set in the middle, she groaned. Then she pulled open the door. "Hi, Joan."

Joan Daniels opened her mouth and closed it quickly. She stood on the porch, casserole dish in hand. A low-cut blouse enhanced impressive breasts. Her jeans were tight enough they had to be cutting off oxygen to her feet, which were crammed into four-inch heels. "Hi, Juliet. Is Quinn home?"

"No." Ingrained manners forced Juliet to step aside. "Would you like to come inside?"

"Sure." Joan drifted by in a rose-scented cloud. She'd piled her blond hair high in a series of tumbling curls to compliment sultry and dark makeup. She sauntered through the hallway and into the kitchen as if she'd been there many times. "I brought dinner for Quinn as a thank-you for rescuing me from a wild cougar the other night." She set the dish on the granite island. "He had to come out late at night."

"I know." Juliet slid her polite smile into place, wondering who'd save the sheriff from the cougar now in his kitchen. "I was here when the call came in."

"Oh." Joan maneuvered around the island to perch on a bar stool. "Well, you're not the first woman to spend time with the sheriff. He's a handsome man."

Had Joan "spent time" with Quinn? Juliet took the dish and placed it in the refrigerator. Hopefully the woman would leave since Quinn wasn't home. Her manners got the better of her. "May I offer you something to drink?"

"Absolutely. He keeps Wallace Brewery beer on the bottom shelf." Too many teeth flashed when Joan smiled. "I'd love one."

Sure enough, there were several bottles of Wallace Pale Ale on the bottom shelf. Juliet grabbed two and handed one to Joan. Twisting off her cap, she shoved the fridge shut with her hip. "Cheers."

Joan removed her cap and lifted her bottle. "Cheers." She tipped back her head and took a healthy swallow. She hummed. "It's so thoughtful of the sheriff to keep these in stock. He likes the Robust Red, you know."

Actually, Juliet hadn't known that. "Really? He always drinks Scotch when we're out."

Joan frowned. "I wonder why he's so formal with you. The man likes beer." She leaned forward, elbows on the counter, false interest in her eyes. "Maybe he's not comfortable with you."

Juliet took another sip. "I'll have to ask him when he gets home tonight."

Joan's eyes narrowed. "We'll both ask him."

The doorbell rang. Again.

Juliet set her beer on the counter. "Excuse me." She hustled through the hallway to the door. Hopefully Sophie or Jake had decided to drop by and check on her. She opened the door and smiled with every bit of manners she owned. "Hello, Amy. How nice to see you."

Amy Nelson arched an eyebrow. "Where is the sheriff?"

"Out on a call." Juliet stepped to the side, amusement and irritation battling for control inside her. "Would you like to come in? A neighbor and I are having a drink in the kitchen."

"For a moment." Amy swept by Juliet and headed down the hallway. She charged into the kitchen and zeroed in on Joan. "Hi. I'm Amy Nelson."

"Joan Daniels." Joan glanced at Amy's dress. "That is a stunning dress."

Juliet reached for her beer. The dress was stunning. Sparkling red, the material shimmered and hugged Amy's curvy figure perfectly. "I agree."

Amy smiled. "Thank you. We had a fundraiser for my uncle on the north side of the county, and I introduced him before his speech."

Juliet cleared her throat. "Amy's uncle is the governor. He's running for reelection."

"As is Quinn." Amy squinted at Juliet. "I'm here to talk to him about the rest of his campaign. The man needs to get smart and start campaigning."

"Nobody can beat Quinn. I mean, he is our sheriff."

Joan finished off her beer.

"True." Juliet gestured toward the bottle. "Would you like another?"

"Sure," Joan said.

Juliet turned toward Amy. "Would you like a beer?"

"No, thank you." Amy eyed the beer bottle like it might explode. "When will Quinn return?"

The doorbell rang. Again.

"Excuse me." Juliet carried her beer down the hallway this time. "You have got to be kidding me," she muttered. What other woman from Quinn's not-so-distant past would be visiting now? She yanked opened the door and stopped short.

Loni Freeze and Leila Lodge stood on the porch, holding hands. Leila jumped up and down. "Hi, Juliet! Uncle Quinn said you'd be here."

Juliet grinned. "Hi, Leila. Loni. There's a small get-together in the kitchen. Come on in."

"Whoo-hoo," Leila yelped, releasing her grandmother to skip down the hall.

Loni crossed the threshold, her head tilted. "Quinn sent us to check on you. They've set Jacoby's funeral for the day after tomorrow. Poor Melanie."

Remembered sadness washed through Juliet. Being alone made the world a darker place. "Melanie has you and your family, Loni. She'll be all right."

Loni slipped an arm around Juliet's waist. "You have us, too. Don't forget that."

Temporarily, it felt nice to belong. "Thank you."

They entered the kitchen as Leila dropped to one knee, her gaze on Amy's sandals. "Are those Manolo Blahniks?"

"No." Amy glanced down at the three-inch heels.

"They're Christian Louboutin."

Leila gasped, her eyes widening. "They're so pretty." She stood and ran to her grandmother. "I love shoes."

Loni ran a hand down Leila's dark hair. "I know, sweetie. I do, too." She glanced around the kitchen, a small smile playing on her face. "Well, this is nice, isn't it?"

"Very." Joan took a healthy swallow of her beer, her disgruntled gaze wandering again to Amy's dress.

Juliet sipped more of her beer. The only thing missing from the party was—

The door to the garage opened, and Quinn Lodge stepped inside. He stopped, his gaze on the gathering of women. A laugh bubbled up in Juliet, but she quashed it. If a "holy shit" expression existed, Quinn was wearing it.

Leila leaped for him. He caught her easily against his chest and smacked a kiss on her forehead. "Hi, Uncle Quinn. Juliet's having a party."

Loni bustled forward and pecked him on the cheek. "We stopped by to keep Juliet company, and turns out she had some visitors. Isn't this wonderful?"

He settled his hand on the butt of his gun in a natural pose. "Ah, yes. Very nice. I, ah, dropped by to grab the spotlight I left in my garage. There's a wreck on the interstate." He set Leila down, his gaze on Juliet. "I might be late."

She nodded, her face heating. Maybe the blush resulted from Loni's delighted grin. Maybe it resulted from the heat in Quinn's gaze. Or maybe it resulted from the glares from the other two women in the room.

Quinn had already shut the door behind himself and escaped to the garage before she regained her voice.

• • •

Juliet awoke from a deep sleep to glance at Quinn's bedside clock. Three in the morning. Something shuffled at the bathroom doorway, and Quinn strode into the room with that male grace she had begun to recognize.

She sat up and clicked on the lamp. "I'm awake."

Wet hair curled around his ears, and he'd tied a towel around his masculine hips. Lines of exhaustion cut into the sides of his mouth, and dark stubble covered his chin. "Sorry if I woke you up."

"I didn't even hear the shower." She shoved curls out of her face. "You okay?"

"Fine." He dropped the towel and slipped under the covers, reaching over his shoulder to turn off the lamp.

Instant heat radiated toward her. Should she go back to sleep? Perhaps give him some space?

He made up her mind for her by rolling onto his back and tugging her on top of him. Gentle hands smoothed the hair away from her face. "The wreck was a bad one, but the ambulance arrived in time. I think everyone might be all right."

"Good." She settled more comfortably against his hard body. Soft moonlight filtered in through the shades, and his eyes blazed through the dim. "You were gone a long time."

"Just a couple of hours. After clearing the scene, I

had two DV calls to take. I hate those." His hand wandered down her back and cupped her butt.

Heat spiraled through her abdomen. "That means domestic violence, right?"

"Yep. Worse calls ever. I arrested several people tonight—both men and women." He caressed her rear. "Let's talk about something else. How long did your party last?"

A grin tickled her cheeks. "You mean the get-together of women who want Quinn Lodge? Everyone left after you made your appearance."

He snorted. "Funny."

"Not really." She wiggled against his groin just enough to cause his eyes to flare. "This is an awkward question, but I feel the need to ask it. Are you, um, seeing either Joan or Amy?"

"No." He tugged her T-shirt over her head, leaving her in flimsy panties. "I have never dated Joan but did have one unfortunate night with Amy about a year ago after a fundraiser. We all make mistakes."

Jealousy zinged in a weird electric arc into her heart. "She still likes you."

"I like *you*." His voice deepened to a dark tone that wandered right through her skin and warmed her. Everywhere.

"I like you, too." She pressed a gentle kiss against his nose and then looked closer. "Is that a bruise on your chin?"

"Probably." His hands flattened on her butt, pressing her onto his rapidly hardening cock. Even his thighs felt powerful and strong against her. "One of the guys didn't want to be cuffed. We, ah, scuffled."

She took a deep breath, not really having

considered the danger he faced every day. "Are you hurt anywhere else?"

"You'll have to discover that for yourself, darlin'." He grinned. "Why don't you start with my mouth?"

"Why don't I," she murmured, brushing his lips with hers.

His mouth captured hers. Deep, strong, he commanded the kiss like he did everything else in his life. Liquid fire rippled through her. Wetness coated her thighs. Her lips trembled and parted for him. He angled his head, depending the kiss.

A click resounded inside her head. Fire and home. She was home.

At the frightening thought, she lifted her head. Her breath panted out. Tingles erupted on her lips.

"I wasn't quite done kissing you, Juliet," he rumbled, his dark gaze on her mouth.

"What makes you think you're always in charge?" She slid her knees up to straddle him.

He grinned and slipped his fingers in the waistband of her panties. "If I were in charge, you wouldn't still be wearing these." A quick tug, and he yanked them off.

She settled back into place and lifted an eyebrow. "I'm no longer wearing those."

"I guess I am in charge." He flipped them over and began easing inside her, going slow but not pausing, until he thrust the final inch inside her with one strong push.

With the shock of his entry, she cried out, her body arching into his. Mini-explosions rocketed through her sex. Flashes of light erupted behind her closed eyes. Need cut into her with sharp, demanding blades.

She tangled her hands in his hair, rearing up to kiss him. Hard.

He returned the kiss, his movements slow and drugging. Sexy and deep, he kissed her, consuming all her fear and uncertainty. She relaxed into the safe cocoon created by Quinn Lodge, melted into him with a sense of trust she'd never shared with another person.

His body impaling hers, his mouth destroying hers, he stripped her of any lingering defenses.

Finally, he lifted his head. "You are the most perfect creature I could've ever imagined."

She swallowed, her eyes widening, her heart softening. "Quinn—"

"Shh." He kissed her again, pulling almost out and then sliding back home. "Just feel."

So she did. She slid her hands down to his shoulders. Muscles bunched against her palms as his mouth wandered along her jawline and down her neck.

He pushed hard into her, his pelvis slanting against her clit. Heat zipped up to her breasts, pebbling her nipples. His chest brushed the sensitive buds as he increased his speed, pounding into her until the headboard banged the wall.

Her thighs clasped his, and she tilted up to take more of him. To take all of him.

He thrust harder, his fingers digging into her hip. A ball of fire slowly uncoiled inside her. Then, with a flash of lightning, it detonated into a series of explosions that arched her back. She cried out his name, her nails digging into his skin. Wave upon wave of electric pleasure pumped through her until finally, she went limp.

With a growl of her name, he ground against her and came.

After several deep breaths, he dropped his forehead to hers. The friendly intimacy slid contentment into her smile. She patted his shoulder. "Sorry about the fingernails."

"I'll wear your marks any day." He withdrew, smiling at her brief whine of protest. Rolling to his side, he spooned her in safety and warmth. "I like having you here, Juliet."

"I like being here." She rubbed his arm. "I'm sorry you had a rough night."

"The night just got a lot better…and drop the society tone. I'm not too tired to spank you." Lazy amusement colored his voice, yet an edge always lived within Quinn.

She swallowed. "That's how I speak."

"Only when you're uncomfortable or trying to control a situation." He tightened his hold. "Before I forget, I was hoping you and Sophie would take Anabella Rush out this weekend. Maybe to a dinner and movie or something like that. My mom agreed to babysit her kids."

Juliet snuggled into the pillow. "Sure. I've met Anabella quite a few times and really like her. Why are you her social organizer?"

"I think the woman needs a night out. Her husband is still overseas, and she needs a break."

The tough, gun-toting sheriff was a softy. "I'd be happy to help." A sudden vision of what life could be like if she stayed with Quinn filled Juliet's mind. She'd be called upon to help with the community, to be a part of so many lives. The sharp desire to be included in such a way stunned her.

"Thanks." He pressed a kiss to the back of her head, his voice slurring with exhaustion. "I'm excited for your showing tomorrow night. You're my date, right?"

Her smile heated her cheeks. "Yes. I'm your date."

"Excellent."

Time to tell him everything.

Quinn began snoring in her ear. Poor guy was exhausted. Well, she'd take the reprieve and tell him all in the morning. Yes, she was a coward and was just fine with that.

She closed her eyes, but her mind kept wandering to the showing. Had she gotten everything ready? What if she'd forgotten something? And where the heck was her laptop? While she'd backed everything up, having her gallery invaded gave her the creeps. Was her past catching up with her?

Finally, she dropped into sleep.

She'd slept for a while before something startled her awake. Her heart smacked against her ribs. She gazed around the unfamiliar room.

A low growl jerked her head up. She slowly turned and scooted up in the bed.

Quinn lay on his side, sweat dotting his upper back. The bedcovers had been shoved to his waist. A tortured groan roiled from his gut.

She forgot his instructions and reached out to place a cool hand on his shoulders.

He moved faster than she could've imagined, rolling over, forcing her down, and pinning her with his body. One broad hand wrapped around her throat. His heart beat hard enough she could feel it through her chest.

"Quinn," she whispered, her trembling hands caressing his chest. "Quinn? It's me, Juliet. Wake up, baby."

His eyes shot open. They weren't focused. His hold tightened.

"Quinn, wake up." She put more force into her whisper. "Wake up, now."

Awareness filtered into his dark eyes, followed quickly by horror. He moved his hand. "Jesus, Juliet. I'm sorry." He made to roll off her.

She shot her legs around his waist and her hands onto his shoulders. "Don't move away."

He closed his eyes and his body vibrated. "Let go of me."

"No." She caressed his chest. "I'm okay. You're fine. You had a nightmare, and you didn't hurt me." She rubbed his whiskers. "Open your eyes."

He did, and the regret in them broke her heart. So she smiled. "I'm fine. You move like an old, slow mare."

An unwilling smile lifted his lip. "I'm neither old nor slow."

His grin relaxed her shoulders. "Unfortunately, you were so slow, I was afraid I'd hurt you, Sheriff. We might need to get you a personal trainer."

He snorted. "A trainer?"

"Don't worry. I took a karate class years ago. I'll protect us," she said.

He lowered himself onto his elbows. "Are you sure I didn't hurt you?"

"Nope. Not at all." She could help him through this—she really could. "I promise."

"Did I scare you?" He lost his smile.

"No." She kept hers in place. "Honest. I knew you'd never hurt me—and you didn't."

Uncertainty had him pausing. "All right." His phone buzzed from the table. He grabbed and pressed it to his ear. "Lodge." He sighed. "I'll be right there." Hanging up, he dropped a kiss on her mouth. "Home invasion on the south side of the county. Gotta go, darlin'." He kissed her deeper until all her bones turned to mush. "I'm looking forward to our date tonight and your amazing gallery opening."

"Me too," she said.

He sat up, his back to her. "Juliet? This, um, means a lot. That you're here and willing to work on this. That you trust me."

The words slammed her in the stomach. She trusted him not to hurt her, but she hadn't trusted him to still care about her once he knew the truth. "I do trust you—and I, ah, have a lot to tell you."

He looked over his shoulder. "Now?"

"No. You have to go, and I need to finish getting ready for the show. Tonight, after the show, I'd like to tell you about my crazy family and the trouble they've gotten me in."

He smiled and somehow, the world brightened. "I look forward to it."

Juliet forced an answering smile. "Me, too."

CHAPTER FOURTEEN

The gallery opening and art showing was a huge success. People still packed the gallery, although the show would end in less than ten minutes. Juliet wound through bodies, her cheeks flushed.

Reaching Sophie's side, she leaned over to whisper, "I've had six offers on *Storm over Maverick*." The incredible oil was alive with dark thunderclouds and jagged lightning. "You're going to need to meet with your tax guy to plan next year."

Sophie beamed. "How wonderful." She tipped back her head and finished her non-alcoholic apple cider and set the glass to the side. "A reporter from Los Angeles interviewed me. He's doing a piece on Western art and how the modern paintings compare with the early Remington, Gollings, and Seltzer work."

Juliet clapped her hands. "I'm so happy for you."

"I, of course, mentioned the Maverick Gallery at least ten times," Sophie said.

Juliet grabbed a flute of non-alcoholic cider from a bustling waiter and handed the bubbly to the star of the hour. "You're a good friend, Sophie Lodge."

"Ah, Juliet…I'm hoping we end up more than friends." Sophie glanced over to where Quinn and Jake huddled near an open window. "That man is in love."

"So am I." Juliet's gaze ran over the sheriff. Even in the dark suit with a crisp white shirt, a sense of wildness surrounded the man. Contained wildness.

The caterer waved Juliet over.

"Excuse me," she murmured to Sophie. Turning on her decadent three-inch heels, she glided around people to the makeshift kitchen. "How are things going, Raul?"

The stooped man tossed a white braid over his shoulder. A former chef from France, Raul had retired to Montana years ago. He had to be in his mid-eighties at the earliest. "Excellent. It's time to cut off the champagne and collect the empty trays."

"You're the boss." Juliet laughed and headed into the chaos of the empty kitchen.

"Now that's a laugh I've missed." A low voice echoed from around the corner.

Fear made Juliet's ears ring. "Freddy," she said.

"JJ." Her stepbrother came into the room, his smirk baring sharp incisors.

"Darn it, Fred. How did you find me?" Her hands trembled.

He rubbed his nose. "I may not be as smart as you, but I can figure some stuff out."

"Get out of here, or I'll call the cops." Would her past ever leave her alone? She forced herself to keep from running for the hills.

"The cops? Or Sheriff Snuggle-Bunny?" Freddy asked.

Freddy knew about Quinn. Her knees weakened. "There's nothing snuggly about Quinn Lodge. He'll take you out back and skin you like the weasel you are."

"Don't call names." Freddy flashed the diamond in his incisor. A Third Street hooker once told him diamonds in teeth were cool. His tailored leather jacket, black jeans, and spotless cowboy boots couldn't be more out of place in Maverick, Montana. Of course, he only wore the boots because they gave him a couple extra inches in height.

"You look like *My Cousin Vinny*. Without the charm," Juliet muttered.

"I kinda like that movie, Juliet Jennifer Spazzoli." He snorted. "*Montgomery* suits you better."

Montgomery had been her maternal great-grandmother's maiden name. "Why are you here?"

"What? I can't meet up with family? It's been too long." He shoved an entire canapé in his mouth.

If she screamed, Quinn would come running. "Did you break into the gallery yesterday?"

Freddy lifted a narrow shoulder. "I needed a computer and figured my little sister would lend me one."

"What's the truth, Freddy?" she asked.

"I need help." His beady eyes beseeched her. "For old time's sakes."

The door opened, and Quinn stepped into the kitchen. "Hey? Are there any more of those shrimp deals—" His chin lowered as he took in the situation with one glance. "Who's your friend, Juliet?"

Freddy coughed and leaned forward to extend a hand. "Fredrick Spazzoli from out of town. I, uh, collect Western art and was hoping to acquire a couple of the, you know, the amazing pieces here tonight."

They shook hands, and Freddy winced.

Quinn cut his eyes to Juliet. "Juliet?"

She took a deep breath. "His name is Fredrick Spazzoli, he's my stepbrother, and the last thing he wants to collect is art."

Surprise flashed across Freddy's face, while no

expression marred Quinn's. He focused back on Freddy. "And?"

Juliet clasped her hands together, drawing dignity around herself like a wool coat. "He's a criminal who has never been caught. I don't know why he's in town, but since there seems to be DEA activity, my guess is Freddy's up to his old tricks of moving drugs."

Freddy flushed a deep red. "I'd watch yourself, JJ."

Disbelief rippled through her so quickly she swayed. "Did you really think I'd lie to him? For you?" The man had never understood her.

"Why not? You've been lying to him since you got here." Freddy snorted snot up his nose.

"Not for you," she muttered.

Quinn squared his stance. "What exactly are Freddy's old tricks?"

"They run the gamut from illegal betting, extortion, petty theft, grand theft, and most recently, drug running." She was dropping her own coffin into the ground, but it was too late to turn back now. "My mother married into the Spazzoli crime family. They were small time...nothing like the mob people you see on television. But, they were into crime."

Wounded outrage pursed Freddy's lips. "I think that's slander, little sister. I mean, since you have absolutely no proof, and your Cuddles here can't arrest me just on your say-so." He edged closer and stopped when Quinn's shoulders went back. "Besides, if there was a family crime enterprise, you're in the family, now aren't you?"

Quinn turned his focus to her.

She swallowed. "Yes," she whispered. "I'm sorry, Quinn. We moved drugs."

• • •

Quinn paced his office, confusion and anger mingling inside him until he wanted to hit something. Juliet was a criminal along with her weak and slimy stepbrother? How was that possible? "I want in on the interviews."

Reese sat in a guest chair, his legs extended, and his new cowboy boots crossed at the ankles on Quinn's desk. "I figured." He read from his phone. "The DEA has suspected Freddy Spazzoli of running drugs since the death of his father a few years ago, but so far, we haven't nailed him."

"Why not?" Quinn dropped into his chair, a thousand pounds weighing him down.

"Anyone able to testify against the guy ends up dead," Reese said,

"The guy seems like a moron to me." No way had the scared dork killed people.

Reese cracked his knuckles. "He *is* a moron. We're fairly certain he's being directed by somebody, but we haven't nailed down who it might be."

"No wonder Juliet escaped." Of course, her statement that she'd run drugs made it entirely possible she'd created a new life to escape the law.

Amusement lit Reese's normally serious gaze. "Speaking of your love, how long are you going to let her stew in the cell?"

"At least she's safe in the cell." Quinn had arrested both Juliet and Freddy the second Juliet had dropped her bombshell, hustling them out the back door and to the station. "Until I arrest her for running drugs. Or until you do." This still wasn't possible—there had to be a logical explanation.

Reese's phone beeped, and he read a message. "There's no record whatsoever on Juliet Spazzoli. Her mother married Dominique Spazzoli when Juliet was ten and changed Juliet's last name at that time."

Quinn frowned. "Spazzoli didn't adopt her?"

"No. Just the name change. Dom Spazzoli owned several illegal betting operations but didn't run drugs. For a criminal, he was one of the decent guys. I mean, sure, he killed once in a while, but he didn't sell drugs to kids."

"Unlike Freddy." And maybe Juliet.

Reese's brow furrowed. "We don't have any proof against Freddy. Even if Juliet provides proof, according to her own statement, she's a coconspirator. We can't arrest Freddy just on her word."

Quinn shoved a hand through his hair. "I'm not using Juliet's statement against her until I talk to her officially." The woman had clammed up the second he'd arrested her, regally lifting her chin. She was the most graceful prisoner he'd ever cuffed and escorted into a jail cell.

Reese shrugged. "We're talking federal law here. Her statement doesn't hurt her any more than it hurts Freddy…unless we get corroborating evidence against one of them. Considering she just confessed, I'd bet my shiny new boots she has some evidence we could use against both of them." He leaned forward. "How well do you really know this woman?"

"Apparently not well at all." Quinn was 100 percent in love with a woman he didn't know. How crazy was that? Love or not, if she'd been involved with the drug trade, she wasn't who he thought. "I wish we could tie

Freddy to the murders. Then he'd give up his partner or boss or whoever the guy is."

"The operation is believed to span several states. We're talking federal trafficking here," Reese said.

Dread slammed into Quinn's gut. Juliet would to go jail for life if she'd been involved in the drug trade. "There has to be some mistake."

"There's no mistake," Reese said slowly. "I definitely want Freddy and his partner on the trafficking and murders. Maybe we could talk to the federal prosecutor about some sort of deal with Juliet—if she has proof that hurts Freddy, or if she knows who Freddy is working with and is willing to testify."

Hope commingled with fury inside Quinn, but he kept his face impassive. "I'm sure that will be an option—once we find out the entire truth. So far, I'm not believing Juliet willingly trafficked drugs." He couldn't be that horrible a judge of character, could he?

"Are you thinking with your head or your dick?" Reese asked.

That the question was valid pissed off Quinn more than he would've believed possible. "Don't make me shoot you."

Reese lifted a shoulder. "The DEA has waited long enough, and now I'm going to interview my suspect. You in or out?"

Quinn clenched his hands. "I'll get her." He stomped from the room, taking deep breaths to maintain control. It'd been years since he felt on edge like this, and he needed to hold it together. The long hallway stretched forever until he reached the first cell. Still wearing her sexy black dress with the sparkly silver shoes, Juliet looked like a captured princess in the dismal cell.

A feminine and fragile princess.

Keys jangled against the old lock as he released the bars. "Come on, Juliet."

Her pale face whitened further, but she rose gracefully from the single cot. "Where?"

"Interrogation." Every instinct he owned wanted to reach out and gather her close for a hug. "The DEA wants to interview you about your statement to me."

She nodded, regally lifting her head and gliding past him into the hallway. "Your friend, Reese?"

"Yes." Quinn relocked the door. He'd put Freddy in a cell at the far end of the cell block and had every intention of leaving him there until Reese wanted to talk to him.

She stopped. "Quinn, I—"

"Save your statement for the DEA. I don't want to hear it." Quinn motioned her ahead of him, his gut clenching at how her hands trembled. Didn't she know he'd have to testify about anything she said to him?

"Of course," she said formally. "I apologize."

For the first time in eight years, he hated the fact that he was the sheriff.

CHAPTER FIFTEEN

Juliet shifted on the cold metal chair in the interrogation room. Chilly and intimidating, the room was small with unadorned, dingy, white walls. "I understand my rights as you've read them to me."

Reese nodded from across the scarred wooden table. "All right. Let's get started."

Quinn leaned against the far corner, his massive arms crossed. "No. Not yet."

Reese raised an eyebrow. "Sheriff Lodge, if you're going to be difficult, I'll ask you to leave."

Fire lanced through Quinn's gaze. In the loosened white shirt and black suit, he looked like a panther ready to strike.

Panic lanced Juliet's chest. Two old friends might fight because of her. "I'm ready to get started, and I'll answer anything you ask."

"No, you won't," Quinn ground out.

"Why not?" Reese asked, irritation curling his upper lip.

The door slid open. "I assume it's because my client is waiting for her lawyer." Smooth as silk, Jake Lodge stepped into the room. He'd donned a slate-gray Armani suit and carried a hand-stitched leather briefcase. "Would you gentlemen please excuse us so my client and I can confer?"

Reese slowly turned his head to glare at Quinn. "You called your brother?"

Quinn headed for the door. "She has a right to a

lawyer. I figured, why not get the best?" He disappeared into the hallway.

Reese stood and rounded on Jake. "You have ten minutes."

Jake smiled. "I'll take as long as I want, Agent Johnson. Now get out." He slid into Reese's vacated spot.

"Fine. I'll go talk to Freddy now." Reese swore under his breath as he left the room. The door slammed shut.

Jake's face gentled. "How you holding up?"

Tears pricked the back of her eyes. "Not so well. Quinn is mad at me."

"Ah, yes. But we need to be concerned with the drug charges right now, Juliet," Jake said.

"He's really angry with me." Who cared about drugs? She wanted Quinn to look at her like he did yesterday.

Jake coughed into his hand. "I need you to focus here."

"Of course." Relying on years of experience, she drew dignity close. "What do you want to know?"

Jake lifted one dark eyebrow in an expression Quinn often wore. "Everything."

Juliet took a deep breath. "All right, but I'm only telling the story once. Please ask Quinn to come back."

"Sheriff Lodge will be subpoenaed to testify as to anything you say. Let's bring him into this conversation after I figure out our best move," Jake said, gently.

Juliet straightened. "I'm going to tell him everything, anyway. You're my lawyer, and you have to follow my wishes."

"Your wishes are going to land you in federal

prison." Jake rubbed his scruffy jaw. Apparently he hadn't had time to shave when changing clothes. "It's well after midnight, you're tired, and you might not be thinking clearly. Trust me on this. You don't want Quinn in here quite yet."

"I can't do this twice, and he deserves to hear the full truth." He'd given her his trust, and she owed him. So she had to tell the full truth and not hide behind the law.

Jake shook his head. "You're acting against the advice of your lawyer."

"I know," she whispered.

Jake stood and ripped open the door. "Quinn?"

Quinn appeared immediately. "What?"

"She wants to include you in this meeting." Still shaking his head, Jake retook his seat.

Quinn frowned. "That's crazy."

"I know, but she only wants to tell the story once." Jake grabbed a legal pad from his briefcase to slide onto the table.

Juliet looked at Quinn. "Do your job and listen to my story, Quinn."

His jaw tightened until it had to hurt. "You're putting me in a terrible position."

She sighed. "Let's get this over with."

Anger blazed in his eyes, but he retook his position in the far corner. Of course, he'd followed duty. She'd counted on his sense of honor.

"I lied to you, and I'm sorry." Clearing her throat, she focused her gaze on her hands. "When I turned ten, my mother married Dominique Spazzoli. He was a criminal. Mainly illegal betting operations, but probably some blackmail and extortion. He took me in, gave me a home, and I loved him." She swallowed and glanced at Quinn's expressionless face. "I know he was a criminal, but he was good to me." Not even to get out of a federal drug charge would she say anything bad about Dom. He was the closest thing she had to a father, and he'd loved her, too.

"Did you partake in any illegal activity growing up?" Quinn asked.

Jake jerked his head toward Quinn. "You're invited to listen and not ask questions, Sheriff."

"Bullshit." Quinn's arms uncrossed. "I'm here, and I'm partaking. Deal with it, counselor."

Wonderful. Now the brothers were going to come to blows. Juliet cleared her throat again. "No. Dom kept me as far away from the criminal activities as possible. He didn't deal with drugs. Freddy entered the drug trade when Dom died."

"You entered with him?" Quinn asked.

"Of course not." A shiver racked her.

"It's too cold in here." Quinn yanked off his suit jacket and dropped the heavy material over her shoulders.

Instant warmth and the scent of male surrounded her. Something inside her stomach softened. "Not on purpose. The Children's Art Clinic of New Jersey hired me to teach a couple of classes a week to kids. I had so much fun teaching those kids how to sculpt." Her hands trembled, so she clasped them together. "The CAC is a nonprofit that exposes underprivileged kids to the arts. The job didn't pay much, but I loved it."

Jake tapped his silver pen on the pad. "The CAC was a drug front?"

"Not at all. Freddy put the drugs in my trunk, I

drove from New York to Jersey, and somebody would take the drugs out while I taught classes."

Quinn dropped into the one vacant chair by his brother. "Did you know?"

"No." She allowed her own stupidity to reflect in her voice. "For six months, I ran drugs, and I had no clue."

Quinn shook his head. "The kind of danger you must've been in…"

She nodded. "I'm a moron. How could anybody have no clue they were trafficking drugs across state lines for six months? But really, how often to you look in your trunk if you're not storing stuff?"

Quinn stared at his brother. "If she had no idea, if she had no intent to traffic, there's no crime, right?"

Jake slowly nodded.

Juliet shook her head. "Seriously? I'm Dom Spazzoli's stepdaughter and Freddy Spazzoli's stepsister. No way would a federal prosecutor or jury believe I was unaware of the drug transfer. Period."

"She has a point," Jake said.

"Besides"—she picked at a sequin on her dress, wanting to get it all out there—"I didn't call the cops once I found out. I called Freddy and yelled at him. He had me look at a building across the street that had a camera pointed right at me. I was on camera for six months. Freddy believes in insurance policies."

"Did the cameras ever catch you looking in the trunk?" Jake asked, scribbling on his notepad.

"Not until the day I discovered what was going on," she said quietly. Crap, she really needed to tell the whole story. "So, I got out of town. I mean, I acquired false identification and got out of town."

Jake held up a hand. "I believe what my client means is a friend of hers supplied her with false identification. She neither purchased it, nor has she used it since."

Juliet frowned. "No, I—"

"Good enough," Quinn growled. "We can revisit the false-identification issue later. For now, I want you to tell me everything you learned about Freddy's drug business."

The door opened, and Reese pushed a rickety cart holding an older television on top of a DVD player. "Freddy was very cooperative and supplied me with a video that is quite intriguing." He plugged in the electronics and grabbed a rusty remote.

Jake slammed his pen down. "We're in the middle of something."

Reese flashed a dangerous smile. "I understand what you're doing. However, why don't we watch this video? Afterward, I'll leave so you can confer with your client on how she wants to plead this out."

Ice-cold fingers traced Juliet's spine. This was so not going to be good. Her shoulders straightened, and she flashed Quinn an apologetic grimace. "Push play, Agent Johnson."

Reese engaged the television and player before starting the video. Several minutes went by that showed several wrapped white packages put into her trunk in front of her apartment in New York and then taken out of her trunk in New Jersey. The men involved were Freddy's lackeys, but not once did Freddy make an appearance.

Quinn wandered to lean against the far wall.

Jake stretched his neck. "First, there's no proof

those are drugs. Second, not once has Juliet been on screen with the trunk open. You've got nothing, Agent."

Reese pressed a button. "Let's fast-forward to the end, shall we?"

Juliet briefly closed her eyes. "Good idea."

The tape scrolled forward until it showed the events of the day that changed her life forever. The camera captured her leaving the art clinic just in time to see a man slam her trunk closed. She stilled, and he ran away. A frown marring her face, she'd hustled forward and opened the trunk.

Cash. Tons of wrapped and stacked cash lined her entire trunk.

The interrogation room went deadly still.

Even with the grainy camera, there was no question that a lot of money sat in her trunk.

She'd whipped out her cell phone and called Freddy, who'd laughed his head off when explaining the cameras. She'd turned to look directly at the camera while still on the phone. Slowly, she'd ended the call, torn her cell phone apart, and left the shattered pieces on the pavement. After slamming the trunk shut, she'd gotten in the car and driven off.

The recording went fuzzy and then black.

Reese turned off the television. "As you can see, counselor, your client drove off with full knowledge her trunk was full of cash. She had enough knowledge of her family to know that it was probably drug money. She neither called the police nor the DEA. What she did do is disappear from town with the money. That's theft at the very least, and more than likely, accessory after the fact on the drug charges."

Juliet opened her mouth, and Jake shook his head. "Don't speak."

She nodded. Her driving away with all of the cash looked horrible for her.

Reese continued, "I think I can get her on trafficking drugs, however. A jury is unlikely to believe the 'I-didn't-know' defense. They rarely do." He slammed the remote down on the table.

Juliet jumped.

Reese leaned in. "I understand why you ran. Stealing so much money from Freddy and his cronies certainly put a hit out on you. I'm going to leave now, and you and your attorney are going to figure out how to turn the money over to the DEA and what type of evidence you can come up with to send your brother to jail. It's your only hope."

"I have no evidence against Freddy." She ignored the warning flashing in Jake's eyes. "Besides, the money is gone. Every last dollar."

Jake motioned Reese to back up. "Okay, we're going to talk in hypotheticals now. Does everyone understand?"

Slowly, both Quinn and Reese nodded.

"Good." Jake peered at her. "Hypothetically, even though you have no knowledge of any money, what would a woman in the situation like the one you just saw on the tape have done with all of that money?"

The moment seemed a bit late for hypotheticals, but what the heck. Juliet lifted her chin. "Hypothetically? I suppose the woman would've had some fun giving all the money away. Maybe some to the Art Clinic, some to the First Baptist Church on Delaney Street that needed a new roof, some to the Catholic

Church around the corner, some to the boys baseball club in southern New York for new backstops. I suppose then the woman would give money to charities and churches as she drove west to safety. Until it was all gone."

Reese staggered back. "All gone?"

Jake chuckled. "I don't suppose the woman would've kept track of where all the money went?"

She plastered on her sweetest smile. "I would assume a woman like that would've kept track. Definitely."

Reese shook his head. "You had start-up money for the gallery. That was drug money."

She clasped her hands together. "If you check my bank records, you'll see I emptied out my savings as I left town. I used my own money to start the gallery." All of her money, in fact. She hadn't used one cent of Freddy's drug cash.

Jake pushed back from the table and stood. "My client and I are leaving."

Reese held up a hand. "Wait a minute."

"No." Jake skirted the table and assisted Juliet up. "She has cooperated fully with you. All you have is a mistaken statement made to her current lover when she was under extreme duress. While the video of her finding something in her trunk is interesting, it has neither been authenticated nor truly examined. We're not even sure that's Juliet, much less money in the trunk. Even if you do somehow prove that was cash, nobody has reported cash being stolen. Therefore, you can't prove whose cash it was. Hypothetically, of course."

Wow. Juliet stumbled along with Jake to the door.

He really was an amazing lawyer.

Jake paused. "While I have no doubt you'll be meeting with the federal prosecutor soon, Agent Johnson, you don't have probable cause for an arrest. You know it."

Quinn cleared his throat, looking so big and dangerous he seemed to take up all the space in the room. "She's in danger, Jake. We don't know who's in town with Freddy, and we don't have anything to hold him on."

Juliet tried to catch Quinn's eye, but he kept his focus on his brother. Hurt cut into her heart. In trying to keep him, she'd lost him.

Jake nodded. "She's staying with Sophie and me. We'll keep her safe, and we'll bring her to the Jacoby's funeral tomorrow."

"Good. I'll talk to you later." Just as smooth as that, Quinn Lodge excused her from not only the room but his life.

Juliet's chin rose, and she followed Jake away from interrogation and Quinn Lodge.

CHAPTER SIXTEEN

Rain pattered around the gravesite. Juliet shifted her boots in the wet grass and edged closer to Sophie under the sprawling umbrella. While she wanted to be respectful and keep her focus on the preacher or the coffin being lowered into the ground, her gaze kept straying to Quinn.

He stood next to Melanie as they said good-bye to her grandfather. He'd left his Stetson in the truck, and the rain slid down his angled face unchecked. Sadness darkened his already dark eyes, and his black hair curled at his nape. A calm in the storm, he maneuvered closer to Melanie when she trembled.

Colton flanked Melanie's other side, an arm around her shoulders. The woman's thick, brown hair curled down her back. The rain only added to the wild curl. Her brown eyes glimmered with tears, and, sandwiched between Quinn and Colton, she appeared breakable. She clutched a bouquet of pink roses. Colton whispered something into her ear, and her lips tipped in a small smile. She leaned into him as the coffin came to a rest.

The preacher finished his eulogy, and Sophie tucked her arm through Juliet's. "I'm glad Colton can be here for Melanie right now."

"Me, too," Juliet said softly. "Though I thought Melanie was dating a banker." The man in the three-piece suit was nowhere to be seen.

"She is, for now. I guess he's at some conference in

London. Apparently he's flying home tomorrow." Sophie turned toward the cars. "Let's head to the wake early to make sure everything is set up."

Juliet stumbled in her high-heeled boots. "Actually, do you mind dropping me at home? I think I'll skip the wake."

"Juliet Spazzoli." Sophie tugged her through bodies toward the road. "You are not hiding just because your boyfriend hauled you down to the station for questioning. Grow a pair, girlfriend."

Jake snorted next to her. "I truly wish you'd stop using that expression, Sunshine."

Sophie shrugged. "You grow a pair, too, counselor." Then she yelped as Jake snaked an arm around her waist and lifted, turning her midair to face him.

Juliet grabbed the umbrella handle before a spoke pricked her forehead. She paused as Jake easily held his wife a foot off the ground, determined amusement darkening his eyes. Sophie's eyes widened. Yeah, the Lodge brothers didn't take kindly to challenges.

With a shrug, Juliet left the couple. "I'll meet you at the car."

She picked her way around gravestones and the hilly terrain. As she reached the car, a strong hand banded around her arm. The scents of pine and male surrounded her, and her heart galloped into motion. Slowly, she turned. "Good afternoon, Sheriff Lodge."

He ducked to keep from getting smacked with the umbrella. "I'll give you a ride to Mel's house."

"That's kind of you, but I'm going back to my apartment." She fought a wince at how formal she sounded.

"No, you're not." Quinn took the umbrella and,

keeping her head shielded, led her to his truck. "We had to cut Freddy loose, and I'd rather keep an eye on you until I figure out what he's doing."

"While I appreciate your concern, I've been taking care of myself for quite some time." Yet her legs kept moving right alongside his. Might as well poke the bear sooner rather than later. "Let go of my arm, or I'm going to kick you in the knee."

He opened the passenger door and glanced down at her boots. "Those are kind of pointy."

"Yes, they are. I assume they'd do some damage." She grabbed the umbrella and closed it.

"You've already been to the jail once. Do you want another trip for assaulting a police officer?" His head cocked to the side, but no expression filtered across his rugged face.

"Not really. However, if I'm not under arrest, you can't make me get in your truck," she said.

Predictably, he did exactly what she wanted him to do. Both hands grabbed her waist, and he lifted her into the truck. At the one touch, desire flared awake through her entire body. Several deep breaths did nothing but make her abdomen ache more.

She waited until he'd shut the door, crossed in front, and jumped into his seat before speaking, "I knew you were going to do that."

"Darlin', we both knew I was going to do that." He started the ignition. "We obviously need to talk."

Her stomach ached. "You're mad at me," she said.

"Furious." He nodded at a couple of people walking along the road toward the long line of cars. "Put on your seat belt."

"Does this mean we're over?" Something in her

chest splintered.

"Right now? I have no clue. I need to deal with making sure Melanie is all right, making sure Colton doesn't screw up his future, find out why drug dealers are killing people in my county, fight to keep my job, and get your stepbrother out of your life for good." His knuckles turned white on the steering wheel. "You lied to me. There have been times in my life when trust was the only thing I could rely on. I…need time to figure things out."

The splinter in her chest exploded. "When I was eighteen, I fell in love with a guy named Sonny Mitchsi."

Quinn's nostrils flared. "He was a criminal?"

"No. Sonny was a genius—got a full ride to business school," she said.

"All right," Quinn said.

"The second he found out about my family, he dumped me. Said he couldn't be involved with somebody like me—somebody with a family like mine." Remembered hurt slithered down her spine. "I didn't want you to do that."

Quinn growled low. "You didn't give me the chance."

She sighed—he was right. "I didn't ask to get in your truck."

"I know." He glanced in the rearview mirror. "Jake and Sophie needed a moment, and so did you and I."

"Am I going to go to jail?" Juliet asked quietly.

"No. You have the best lawyer in the world, and frankly, you didn't do anything wrong." Quinn pulled the truck onto the main road. "Well, anything illegal. You didn't do anything illegal."

Oh, but lying to him was wrong. Lying to him and then sleeping with him, that is. If they'd remained just acquaintances, the lying probably wouldn't have mattered much. Now it seemed like everything. "I'm sorry, Quinn."

"Me, too." He tossed his black Stetson on the dash. "You didn't trust me, Juliet."

There was the crux of the problem. Everyone leaned on and trusted Quinn Lodge, yet she was the only person he'd opened up to. No wonder he was so mad.

"I am curious. How long were you planning to stay in town?" he asked.

Chills cascaded down her back. "I was planning on leaving after the showing."

His firm jaw snapped shut. "I see. Where were you going?"

"I thought I'd go to Utah or Wyoming." Somewhere there were mountains, cowboys, and a community. But no place would have Quinn Lodge. "I'm sorry."

They rode the rest of the way in silence, finally pulling to a stop in front of Melanie's white farmhouse. A porch wrapped around the entire first floor, the planks faded and a few in need of repair.

Quinn frowned through the windshield. "I hadn't noticed Old Man Jacoby needed help. Apparently I should've paid closer attention." He stepped out of the truck and crossed behind it to open Juliet's door.

She allowed him to assist her to the gravel. His hands lingered at her waist, and his eyes darkened.

"Sheriff?" someone called out.

They both turned and a flash went off. Several flashes peppered the air. With a growl, Quinn stepped in front to shield her.

The photographer rushed toward a parked car and sped off.

Juliet pursed her lips. "What was that all about?"

"I don't want to know." Quinn closed her door and took her elbow to escort to the porch.

"But, if that was a reporter, do you think they found out about me?" Oh, no. Any scandal could destroy Quinn's campaign.

"Maybe." He released her. "I'll see you inside." Without another word, he hurried to where his mother emerged from a truck, her hands full of dishes. After pecking Loni on the cheek, he reached for the bundle.

A lonely chill squeezed Juliet's chest. She would've liked having been part of the Lodge-Freeze family. Sighing, she went inside for the wake.

• • •

The morning after the funeral, Juliet poked her head outside the gallery door. "Deputy Baker? Would you like some coffee?"

The young officer shook his head. "No thank you, ma'am." He turned his red head back to survey the quiet street.

"How about you come inside and warm up? You can guard the gallery just as well from inside." She fought guilt—the poor guy had been outside all night, just trying to protect her from her own family.

"Thank you, ma'am, but the sheriff left strict instructions for me to stay right here until my replacement arrived." The kid didn't change his focus.

Sighing, Juliet closed the door. Quinn was

punishing her for her decision to return to her apartment and not impose any longer on Sophie and Jake. She punched in numbers on her landline and asked to speak with the sheriff. Mrs. Wilson said she'd take a message, but that the sheriff was out on a call. Juliet decided not to leave a message.

Instead, she hustled to her desk in the corner to balance her books. After the exhibit the other night, she was finally in the black. Thank goodness.

An hour passed.

Then another.

Suddenly, the door blew open. She yelped and jumped. The sheriff stood in the doorway, gun out, his face a concentrated mask. "Juliet?"

She pressed a hand to her chest. "Why is your gun out?"

He frowned and set his gun back in the shoulder holster. "I got a report of screams coming from the gallery."

The young deputy sidled in from the other gallery. "There wasn't anybody in the back entrance, sheriff."

Quinn's gaze narrowed. "You didn't hear any screams?"

"No, sir," the officer said.

"I think it's a hoax," Quinn muttered.

"Who called it in?" The deputy scratched his chin.

"I don't know. It was a call to dispatch. Take point outside, Baker. Phillips will be here in five to relieve you." Quinn waited until the deputy took his leave to focus on Juliet. "I also had a message you called."

She ran her hand along the back of her chair. "I'm refusing police protection. Please keep your deputies off my property."

A veil dropped over his eyes. "You're in danger, now there's a prank call regarding you, and you don't get to refuse police protection."

She glowered. "You're trespassing, Sheriff Lodge. Please leave."

"No." He crossed his arms.

For the love of all that was holy. Stubbornness lived in the man, at home and comfortable. "We broke up." She understood exactly what "I need time to think" meant. "As such, you no longer need to concern yourself about me. All of the truth is out, and Freddy probably has no interest in me. Especially since Jake explained to him that the money is long gone."

"Regardless of the status of our relationship, you're a citizen in my county. If you're in danger, you get police protection." Quinn leaned against the door. "Deal with it, Juliet."

Anger rippled through her veins. So she plastered on a polite smile and straightened her shoulders. "Well, then, I thank you for your diligence, Sheriff Lodge. The citizens of Maverick are fortunate to have you protecting us."

Temper rippled across his face.

His phone buzzed, but his dark gaze kept her pinned while he answered. "I'll be right there." Turning on his heel, he yanked open the door to reveal a different deputy at guard. "Stay with her and report in hourly." Without looking back, he strode out of sight.

The door drifted closed.

Her phone rang, and she cleared her throat before answering, "Maverick Gallery."

"Hi, Juliet. This is Mrs. Hudson, from down the

street?" an elderly voice chirped.

"Hi, Mrs. Hudson." Juliet took another deep breath. The sweet widow lived in a small cottage a block down the street, and Juliet often dropped off groceries or goodies for the woman.

"What can I help you with?"

"Oh, Juliet. I dropped my favorite earrings—you know the ones Arthur gave to me right before he died? Well, they slid behind the stereo," Mrs. Hudson said.

"Oh." Juliet glanced at the clock. "You need me to fetch them for you?"

"No, dear. I grabbed them," Mrs. Hudson said.

Juliet frowned. "Well, good."

"But then the stereo dropped on my leg," the elderly woman said.

"What?" Juliet sprang to her feet. "Are you all right? Do you need an ambulance?"

"Oh, no, dear. I'm fine. Well, not fine. My foot is bruised, and I can't stand on my tiptoes." Mrs. Hudson sighed.

"Do you need me to bring bandages or, well, anything?" Juliet asked.

"No. But I do need you to come and get my yellow bowl—the one with flowers on it—off my top shelf. I can't reach that high, and I'm going to Betty Adam's for Bunko tonight," Mrs. Hudson said.

Relief flooded Juliet. "I'd be happy to help. In fact, I could use a walk right now. Give me a minute."

"Thank you, dear." The elderly lady hung up.

Juliet chuckled. Now that was a confusing conversation. She slid her arms into her coat and headed for the door. "Deputy Phillips, I take it?"

Phillips nodded a buzz-cut head. He stood to about six feet and was built like a truck. "Yes, ma'am."

"How do you feel about a walk?" she asked.

"You walk, I follow, ma'am," he said with a smile and twinkling brown eyes.

"Excellent." She stepped into the chilly day and frowned at the gathering clouds. Not another heavy summer storm. She hustled down the block to Mrs. Hudson's white bungalow. She knocked on the door. The elderly lady hollered for her to come in.

Juliet left Deputy Phillips on the porch and hurried inside. "Mrs. Hudson?"

"In the kitchen, dear," Mrs. Hudson said.

Juliet removed her coat, entered the sparkling clean kitchen, and stopped short. "Quinn."

"Juliet." He sat at the round table, a large bowl of oriental chicken salad set on the crocheted tablecloth in front of him.

Juliet raised her eyebrows at Mrs. Hudson.

The woman smiled and all but pushed Juliet into the chair across from Quinn. "The sheriff was kind enough to get down my bowl, but now I need a couple of testers for the salad I want to take tonight." She dumped another bowl of oriental chicken salad in front of Juliet and smoothed her purple, velour pantsuit. "Now you two eat up, take notes, and I'll be right back. I promised Henry Bullton next door some salad." Humming to herself, she all but skipped out the back door.

Juliet's stomach knotted. "I thought she'd injured her foot."

Quinn took a bite of the salad. "Nope. She's interfering."

Juliet's hand stopped halfway to the fork. "Interfering?"

"Yep." He took another bite. "The word around town is that we broke up, and apparently, the news doesn't sit well with Mrs. Hudson."

Heat climbed into Juliet's face. "Well, it sits just fine with me."

"Does it, now?" Quinn polished off his salad. "Good to know." He stood—a strong man with a hard jaw. "I have a meeting in five minutes. Please tell Mrs. Hudson that I enjoyed the salad very much and to mind her own business."

"You tell her that." Juliet lifted her chin.

"I will." He halted at the kitchen door. "Make sure Deputy Phillips is with you all day, Juliet. I'd hate to fire the guy." Whistling a smart-ass tune, the sheriff sauntered out of sight.

CHAPTER SEVENTEEN

A raging headache set up camp behind Quinn's left eye as he shoved open the door to the station. While he adored Mrs. Hudson, he didn't need any help in figuring out his life. He needed time.

The silence in the station shot his blood pressure into overdrive.

Stopping at the reception counter, he pinned Mrs. Wilson with a hard look. "What's going on?"

"Don't you speak to me in such a tone, young man." She shoved her glasses up her pointy nose, giving him the same glare she had when he'd stolen tulips from her garden to give to a girl. He'd been eight.

He fought the urge to shuffle his feet. "I apologize, Mrs. Wilson. Why is it so quiet in here?"

"I think everyone is upset about this." She flashed a sympathetic grimace and slid the Missoula paper across the counter.

Dread dropped into his gut. He turned the paper around to see a front-page picture of him helping Juliet out of the truck at the funeral. The caption read: "Sheriff Lodge Escorts mob-daughter Juliet Spazzoli."

He scanned the article. Some of it touched on his reelection bid, but most of the article detailed the DEA's case and offered speculation about Juliet's crime family. Quinn handed the paper back to Mrs. Wilson. "Throw the entire thing away, would you?"

"Will this hurt you in the election?" she asked.

"I don't know." Right now, he didn't have time to worry about the election. As he entered the main hub of the station, all of a sudden, everyone was either on the phone, typing, or out of sight. With a sigh, he stalked between people who wouldn't meet his eye until entering his office.

"We could sue the paper." Jake sat in a guest chair playing *Angry Birds* on his phone.

"Why? Most of the article seemed to be somewhat factual." Quinn skirted his desk and dropped into his chair.

Jake shot another red bird into the air. "You'll need to campaign now."

"I don't have time." Quinn shoved papers out of the way.

Jake clicked his phone shut. "Do you want to be the sheriff or not?"

Right now? "Not."

"Liar." Jake stuck his phone in his pocket. "I've booked you on two radio stations next week. The interviews will go quickly, and you need to do them."

"Fine."

Jake grinned. "You and Juliet make up yet?"

"No," Quinn said.

"Stop being such a stubborn bastard," Jake said without heat. His eyes darkened with sympathy.

"She lied to me," Quinn grunted.

"Yeah. People make mistakes, Quinn. Even you." Jake cleared his throat. "Officially, I'm here to report that my client will testify to anything she has knowledge of regarding Freddy Spazzoli's drug business in exchange for both state and federal immunity."

Quinn lifted an eyebrow. "Does your client know

anything she hasn't already shared?"

"Er, no." Jake grinned.

"Then not only is her testimony useless, she doesn't need immunity." Quinn doubted the DEA would waste time prosecuting Juliet without any proof.

The grin disappeared. "I still want the immunity. The money concerns me…and there's a decent accessory-after-the-fact charge if the DEA wants to make an example out of her. Push your friend for the deal, Quinn," Jake said.

"Dealing with the DEA is your job, Jake." Quinn settled back in his chair. He didn't deserve to be sheriff if he called in special favors. "You might also want to concentrate on the possession of false identification charge that will be heading Juliet's way soon. The local prosecutor will love the case."

"What false identification?" Jake asked.

"She brought false ID from New York to Montana," Quinn said.

Both of Jake's dark eyebrows rose. "Did she use any identification?"

"Don't know." Quinn crossed his arms.

Jake picked at his faded jeans. "Have you either seen this identification or applied for a warrant to search her home or place of business?"

Quinn scowled. "Obtaining a warrant is on the agenda for today."

Jake flashed the smile that made other attorneys quake. "Feel free. You won't find any identification."

Quinn gripped his desk. "You told her to destroy evidence?"

"Of course not. I didn't tell her a damn thing." Jake stood.

"Tell me you didn't destroy evidence," Quinn said, his breath heating.

Jake loped toward the door. "I believe I'll take the Fifth on that one, Sheriff. Have a nice day."

"You're an officer of the court," Quinn bellowed after his disappearing brother. Son of a bitch. The relief sliding through him pissed him off more. With a growl, he started punching in letters on his keyboard. Those reports wouldn't write themselves.

An hour passed and someone tapped on his opened door. The scent of wild citrus hit him right in the solar plexus. Smoothing his face into interested lines, he focused on the door. "Hello, Juliet." Standing like his mama had taught him, he gestured her into a chair.

She gracefully crossed and sat. Her pale face and trembling hands made him feel like an ogre.

"How can I help you?" He retook his seat before he could grab her up and cuddle her close.

Her forehead creased. "I, ah, well, you requested my presence."

He leaned forward. "Who called you?"

"Mrs. Wilson." Juliet glanced at the door, no doubt seeking a quick exit.

"Mrs. Wilson?" Quinn yelled.

The file clerk poked his head inside the office. "Mrs. Wilson took a half-day sick day, Sheriff."

"I'll bet she did," Quinn muttered. He rubbed his whiskers. Had he forgotten to shave again? "I'm sorry, Juliet. Apparently I need to fire my receptionist."

"You're not going to fire Mrs. Wilson," Juliet said, her lips tilting slightly. "Anyway, I wanted to say how sorry I am for the newspaper article. I wish I could do something about it."

"Not your fault." Her scent was driving him crazy.

The file clerk returned to place a box on Quinn's desk. "From Shelby's bakery." The kid disappeared, shutting the door behind himself.

Quinn frowned at the box and flipped open the lid. Inside lay several cookies, all shaped as hearts and decorated with a Q + J.

Juliet covered her mouth, her eyes lighting with amusement. "You have got to be kidding me."

Quinn cleared his throat. If the old biddies in town thought they could force him into anything, they were freakin' crazy. "I'm sorry about this, Juliet. Their interference is ridiculous."

She lost her smile. "I'm sorry, too." She rose, looking small and fragile.

He stood. "I, uh, am probably going to get a warrant to search your place later for the doctored identification." Damn it. He had no right to warn her.

"Oh." She tugged open a monstrous purse and rummaged inside. "I'll give the identification to you now."

"No." He hadn't wanted to set her up. Not at all. "Don't do that."

"No more hiding, and no more lies, Quinn. Take the ID. I bought it off a guy in the Village." She yanked out a wallet and searched through it. "I don't understand."

Relief dropped him back onto his seat. "Don't tell me—it's gone?"

"Um, yes." Juliet frowned. "I don't understand."

"I do." He shook his head. While part of him strongly disapproved, the other part wanted to buy his brother a drink later. As a thank you. "You should probably talk to your lawyer. Either way, there's no reason to search your place."

She nodded and turned toward the doorway. "Very well. Good-bye, Sheriff."

"'Bye, Juliet."

The door shut behind her with a sad sense of finality. Quinn Lodge glared at the cookies. What now?

• • •

Although early, the country-western bar was already hopping. The band blared a quick tune, and several couples two-stepped across the sawdust-covered dance floor. Juliet eyed the clear liquid in the shot glass from her table near the bar. "I'm not sure doing shots is such a good idea."

Sophie shrugged and sipped her ginger ale. "Why not? I wish I could."

Anabella Rush tipped back her head and downed her shot. "Yeah. Why not?" Then she sputtered, her eyes watering.

"That's why," Juliet said slowly. What the heck. She grabbed the glass and poured the heated alcohol down her throat. The liquid rushed down and exploded in her stomach. She gasped and coughed.

Sophie smacked her on the back. "There you go, girlfriend. Now, did Quinn eat one of the heart-shaped cookies?" Her laugh competed with the band.

Juliet flushed. "Not while I was in his office. They just ticked him off." She sighed. "I don't think he'll let anybody push him into forgiving me. This whole plan by the town is going to backfire."

"I told Loni that." Sophie's eyes widened, and she slapped a hand over her mouth. "I mean, I, uh—"

"Loni's in on this?" Juliet gasped.

"Yep." Sophie nodded. "She likes you. A lot."

That was just sweet. Her heart warmed. "Well, that's nice." Juliet brushed sawdust off the table.

The fast song stopped, and Dawn Freeze stepped up to the mic to sing a country ballad. The entire place quieted. Low and sexy, the young woman's voice crooned around the room, creating a cocoon of intimacy. Several couples slid onto the dance floor.

Juliet leaned forward. "Wow. She can really sing."

"Yeah." Sophie grinned. "The guys hate her singing in a bar. Jake keeps trying to get her to sing more in church."

Considering his little sister was wearing tight jeans and a black half T-shirt that showed very smooth skin, Juliet imagined none of the brothers liked it much. Her gaze caught on a man across the bar watching Dawn with heated green eyes. "When did Hawk get back to town?"

"Last night. He's on leave for a week." Sophie turned as Colton plunked down a beer in front of Hawk. "Oh, great. There's our babysitter."

Juliet waved. "Don't be silly. He's here to hang out with Hawk and watch his sister."

Sophie frowned. "Colt can multitask, believe me. Darn protective Lodge-Freeze men."

"I miss my husband." Anabella hiccupped. She motioned to the waitress. "Another round, Milina."

Juliet's eyes widened. "Oh, I forgot to tell you. I went into my purse to give Quinn the false identification stuff I bought in New York, and it was gone. I have a terrible feeling my lawyer did something he shouldn't have done."

Sophie snorted and reached for her newly delivered plate of nachos. "That was me, girlfriend."

Juliet gaped. "Destroying evidence is illegal."

"So my rather angry husband explained in great detail when I told him what I'd done." Sophie reached for the bowl of pretzels. "Though, he kind of looked relieved, too."

"He yelled at you?" Anabella gasped.

"Nope. I'm all pregnant and delicate, you know?" Sophie grinned.

Juliet shook her head. "You broke the law."

"Prove it." Sophie's smile turned a bit lopsided. "No proof, no crime."

Anabella took another shot and sputtered. "Remind me not to tick you off."

Sophie nodded. "Yeah. Don't tick me off. I know stuff."

For some reason, all three women thought that was ridiculously hilarious. Their laughter brought interested looks from both Colton and Hawk. Sophie gestured toward them in what could only be called a smart-assed wave.

They laughed harder.

• • •

Juliet sighed deeply right around midnight. "I think I'm too sad to get drunk."

Sophie sighed heavily. "Not me—I miss drinking."

"I'm not drunk." Anabella rubbed her nose. "But I can't feel my nose."

Sophie patted her hand. "You don't need your nose tonight."

"True." Anabella nodded wisely. "So true. But when my husband gets home next month, I hope I can smell him. He always smells so good."

Juliet sighed and scooted out of the booth. "I think it's time for water." She headed over to the bar and skidded through sawdust. Regaining her balance, she stopped short as a woman stepped in front of her. "Amy?"

Amy Nelson nodded, her gaze sweeping Juliet's jeans and boots. "Nice outfit, career killer."

"Thanks." Juliet glanced down at Amy's short skirt and vested top. "You look like a high-priced hooker." Oops. Maybe the alcohol had affected her.

Amy put both hands on her ample hips. "Why are you still in town? Time to leave."

"Why?" Juliet asked.

"Because you're already ruined Quinn's chance of being sheriff again," Amy said.

Juliet struggled to maintain a polite smile. "I don't think so. Quinn will still win."

"No he won't." A fierce smile split Amy's face. "Which is all right and in the plan. With all his money and all his charisma, the man could go much higher than sheriff, if he had the right partner directing him."

Juliet snorted and then covered her mouth in embarrassment. Taking several deep breaths, she clasped her hands. "Quinn doesn't take direction from anybody."

"I admit I've had to be careful. But now that he's out of the sheriff race, he can enter the Senate race next year. I'd love to live in DC." Amy frowned at Sophie and Anabella as they laughed back at the booth. "I'll have to get him out of this podunk town and away from his family. They are definitely holding him back."

Anger danced spots in front of Juliet's eyes. "Wait a minute. You're the one who alerted the Missoula paper?"

"Yep." Malicious glee danced in Amy's eyes. "I can't tell you how helpful you've been."

"This conversation is over." Juliet lifted her head and turned to sidestep Amy.

The woman dug sharp nails into Juliet's arm. "Get out of town before I destroy you even more than I already have."

"Let go of me." Juliet used her most regal voice.

Amy dug deeper and then shoved.

The world disappeared. Temper roared through Juliet so quickly she staggered. Clenching her fist, she swung and nailed Amy right in the jaw. The woman flew into the bar and slid down to the floor.

The front door opened to reveal the sheriff.

Juliet's eyes widened. Fists bunched and slightly drunk, she stood over the sheriff's ex-lover after having just clocked her one.

Oops.

CHAPTER EIGHTEEN

Quinn had stuck Juliet in the same jail cell as last time. The wool blanket on the one cot shifted as she settled against the concrete-block wall. The man had taken one look at the scene in the bar and handcuffed both Amy and her. Handcuffed!

About an hour had passed before Quinn appeared on the other side of the bars. Even with anger warming her chest, her gaze ate him up. Tonight he'd donned faded jeans, scuffed cowboy boots, and a long-sleeved, dark green T-shirt. He'd tucked his gun at his waist, and the deadly weapon looked right at home. A deep shadow covered his jaw, and pure irritation shone in his black eyes.

She lifted her chin and refused to talk first.

"How's your hand, slugger?" he asked.

She crossed her arms. "Fine."

"Good. Amy Nelson has decided not to press charges." Quinn wrapped his hands around the bars.

Juliet lifted one eyebrow. "Really? That's surprising."

"Not after I explained that witnesses saw her push you before you laid her out, and that if I arrested you, I'd have to arrest her, too. I doubt the governor would appreciate bad press right now."

"Good." If the floor would open up and swallow Juliet, she'd be fine. "So, I'm free to go?"

"Maybe." The sheriff didn't twitch, apparently in no hurry to allow her out of the cell. "When I asked you to help out Anabella, I didn't mean to get her drunk and then get into a bar fight."

"I'm aware of that fact, Sheriff. I do apologize for my part in the disaster that became our night out." She stood. "Now, unless you feel I deserve more jail time, I'd like to go home."

His eyes darkened. "What you deserve is a good walloping that keeps you from sitting for the next week."

Her head jerked up. Nails bit into her palm when she clenched her already aching fist. "I do beg your pardon."

"Oh, you'd beg." He stepped closer to the bars. "Enough of the nonsense, Juliet. I don't have time to chase you all over town, break up bar fights, and drive home drunk women who cry the entire time because they miss their husbands. Either promise you'll behave, or I'm leaving you in the cell for the night."

Her spine straightened one angry vertebra at a time. "While I know you have no reason to believe me, most of those issues weren't my fault. Now either let me out, or allow me to call my attorney."

He kept her gaze, and she fought the very real urge to step back. Finally, with an irritated male sigh, he unlocked the door and slid the bars open. "I'll drive you out to Jake and Sophie's. They're waiting for you."

"No, I—" Her protest caught in her throat at the flare of anger in his eyes. "That would be fine. Thank you." Frankly, she didn't want to go home alone.

He escorted her out of the station and to his black truck, waiting until her seat belt had been fastened before pulling out of the parking lot. They drove in silence through town and toward the reservation.

The moon caressed his rugged face, enhancing his hard jaw and full mouth. Every once in a while, his Native heritage stood out in primitive relief. Tonight was one of those nights.

Her glance caught on his large, capable hands on the steering wheel. "Sorry you have to drive me home." His grunt in response had her rolling her eyes. "Your sister is an amazing singer."

"Humph." Quinn glanced out at the clouds rolling across the moon.

Fine. The sheriff didn't want to talk. Juliet shoved hair out of her way and glanced at the darkening forest outside as the moon disappeared. Thunder rumbled in the distance. The sky crackled and opened up. Rain pelted the truck.

Quinn flipped on the windshield wipers with a flick of his wrist. "Are you warm enough?"

"I'm fine." She hugged herself with her hands and chastised herself for not wearing a coat.

A cop's gaze raked her head to toe. Without saying a word, he increased the heat. "Stop being stubborn."

"Me, stubborn?" She glared at him. "You're the most stubborn person I've ever met."

His cheek creased.

Suddenly, he veered the truck toward the trees. Swearing, Quinn hit the brakes and yanked the wheel. Only his quick reflexes kept them from hitting a huge lodgepole pine. They rolled to a stop. Quiet descended.

He eyed her. "You okay?"

"Fine." Except her heart might've been bruised from beating so hard against her rib cage. "What happened?"

"Deer. I want to make sure I didn't clip him." He

jumped out of the truck and into the rain.

Clunks sounded from the back. Quinn shone a bright light into the forest. Juliet released her seat belt, leaped from the truck, and hurried toward the sheriff.

Quinn looked over his shoulder. "Get back in the truck."

"No." She stepped gingerly off the road. "Two pairs of eyes are better."

He wiped rain off his forehead. "Juliet, the rain is freezing, and this will just take me a minute. Now get your ass back in the truck."

"I am so finished taking orders from you, Quinn. Kiss my butt. Twice."

He barked out a laugh and turned to shine the light into the trees. No animal stared back. With a shrug, he turned and was on her before she could take another breath. Hands on her hips, he lifted her easily, walking backward until he'd opened the door and plopped her on the seat.

Enough was enough. She kicked out with all the frustration and anger she'd stifled for days. And nailed him right in the thigh.

They both froze for a second. She opened her mouth to apologize, but he was faster. He pulled her toward him, his mouth smashing hers with what must be the anger and frustration *he'd* stifled for days.

Sharp teeth nipped her bottom lip, and she opened her mouth in surprise.

He dove in.

Gone was the congenial sheriff and the gentle lover. In his place stood a primitive man she wanted more than her next thought. His fingers threaded through her hair held her in place. His hips kept her legs apart, and his mouth took what he wanted. No finesse, no kindness, just pure, raw lust.

Sharp pangs of need ripped through her. Her body ached. She moaned deep in her throat.

He released her, his eyes blazing. "If you want to stop, tell me now," he rumbled.

"I don't want to stop." She ripped open his shirt, needing to feel him. All of him.

His free hand grabbed the bottom of her shirt and hauled it over her head. The second the flimsy material was free, his mouth took hers again. One flick of his finger released the front clasp of her bra, and his hand, calloused and demanding, palmed her breast. Her nipples peaked. He tweaked one, and she whimpered with raw need.

He released her hair and grabbed her jeans with both hands. The button zinged against the windshield, and the zipper ripped free. Strong hands dragged off her boots, the jeans, and her panties. Jerking down his jeans, he gripped her ass, lifted her, and impaled her.

She gasped in shock.

He was too big…too much.

Rain slid down his torso, and she rubbed her hands into the wet hardness.

He stood in the rain, at home in the dangerous storm. Droplets pelted him, matting his hair and dripping over the hard angles of his face. Hard hands kept them groin to groin. His easy strength in bearing her weight cascaded tingles through her abdomen. Hot and sexy, those tingles had nothing on the flaring nerves where his cock stretched her.

His gaze pinning her, he ran one hand up her spine to secure the back of her neck. Then he lifted her and plunged her back down along his length. His groin slid against her clit.

Spikes of pleasure rippled from where they were joined. Her mouth opened wide on her exhale.

A satisfied smirk creased his face.

Need and want shot through her. She grabbed his shoulders to lift herself, to get him moving.

The hand on her hip and the one at her nape prevented her movement. His watchful gaze kept her captive as he stood in the storm, holding her. Controlling them both. Then he waited. Determination sharpened his cheekbones, hardened his jaw. The man would wait until day broke.

Something feminine stretched awake inside her. She took in the dangerous warrior, seeing him finally for the primal being he was at heart. The sheriff tempered his wild nature with good humor and a protective embrace encompassing the entire community. For the first time, she glimpsed the predator inside.

Feminine instinct took over. She smoothed her palms on his shoulders and relaxed her body. Relaxing into his strength, to his will, she allowed him to take her wherever he wanted to go.

A masculine gleam lightened his eyes.

He shifted until they both stood in the rain, her back to the truck. Then he thrust inside her, pounding with a ferocity wilder than the storm. The coolness of the water contrasted with the heat from the male taking her, throwing her into a maelstrom of sensation. The hard pounding, the chilled rain, the warm man, the love bursting through her heart…swirled together until her mind shut down.

His fingers gripped her hips, his hard shaft pounded inside her, leaving his mark as completely as he'd left his brand in her heart.

With a cry of his name, she broke. Splinters of shooting pleasure cut through her, and she rode them out, lost in the sensations. He ground against her with his own release. Her orgasm lasted forever. Finally coming down, she relaxed against him. He held her tight.

Quinn walked them back to the open truck door and set her gently on the seat.

Her heart clutched. Not a word had passed between them. Without looking at him, she grabbed her shirt off the steering wheel and scooted over to the passenger side.

What now?

• • •

Juliet frowned at Sophie sitting across the scarred wooden table in their booth. The scents of grease and burned toast coated the air. "I don't care how bad your cravings are. I shouldn't be out in public today."

Sophie rubbed her baby bump. "Come on. Leila is at Loni's, and I needed a greasy breakfast from the Dirt Spoon. Nobody will recognize us here."

Juliet shook her head. "I appreciate you letting me stay the night, but we should've remained at your house for breakfast."

"The guys had to fix fences after the storm last night. It was easy to get away so we could talk." Sophie studied her. "You were rather disheveled when Quinn dropped you off last night."

Disheveled and heartbroken. The sheriff hadn't said a word after handing over her clothing and dropping her off. Well, nothing but an order to stay at Jake and Sophie's until he fetched her the next day. "I don't want to talk about it," Juliet muttered.

Sympathy curled Sophie's lip. "I understand. I'm married to a Lodge, remember?"

"Yes, I know. But Quinn and I aren't married. Heck, we're not even talking." Sure, he'd mounted her like she was a prize mare the previous night, but without talking, there was no intimacy. "I could just shoot him."

"Been there, seriously considered doing that." Sophie took a deep drink of an herbal tea before grimacing. "Shooting Jake, I mean. I never wanted to shoot Quinn. Until now." Loyalty lifted her lips in a sweet smile.

"I've probably broken enough laws lately," Juliet said wryly. "I'll be right back." She headed to the restroom, filing through the room filled with several people she'd seen at the bar the previous night.

She reached the door, and the hair on the back of her neck prickled. Slowly turning around, she already knew who she'd see.

"Morning, JJ," Freddy said.

She took a breath to scream and halted as he drew a gun. A shiny, almost too big for his hand, silver gun. It wavered.

"You have a choice." Freddy glanced toward the busy restaurant. "Either come nicely with me, or I'll take both you and your pretty friend. Please, JJ. I just wanna talk to you."

"Go where?" She edged toward the bathroom. If

she could get inside, maybe there was a lock.

"My partner would like to discuss the missing millions with you." Freddy grabbed her biceps. "Please. It'll just take a minute." Desperation creased his forehead.

"There's no money," she admitted.

"Nobody is stupid enough to give away that kind of money." He swung her around and dug the gun into her ribs. "If you want, you could make a lot of money with us. You'll need to relocate and start over, but hey, you're good at pretending to be someone you're not." Kicking a back door open, he pulled her into the chilly morning air.

"Fine. I'll go with you." She could scream and struggle, but there was a good chance the gun would go off. Even if the idiot didn't shoot her, he might shoot somebody else. It'd be a lot easier to jump out of a moving vehicle when he drove past the police station.

"Thank you. I promise, you'll be happy you did." He dragged her around the corner to the alley. "I can't believe how clean the alleys are in this stupid town. Who has clean alleys?"

"I think it's a county ordinance." She stumbled over a puddle, splashing mud on her jeans. "You know the sheriff is going to skin you alive for this, right?" Quinn might not like her any longer, but a woman kidnapped in his county would truly anger him.

"Jesus, JJ. The guy fucks you, and you think he's invincible?" Freddy's hold tightened. "He's a stupid hick—one who'll end up dead if he comes after you."

"Who's your partner, Freddy?" She eyed the end of the alley. Maybe she could trip him and make a break for it.

"Oh, you'll meet him. He's got some real good ideas for making money," Freddy said.

A black SUV slid into the alley, and a man jumped out. Much bigger than Freddy, the guy wore guns in a shoulder holster, leg holster, and at his waist. He reached them in two strides. Dead blue eyes stared into hers. "Where's my money?"

The moment changed from an irritating one with Freddy to a deadly one she wasn't likely to escape. Her mouth went dry.

A truck sped by the other end of the alley.

The guy tugged something from his pocket. He grabbed her hands and zip-tied them, pulling too tight. She bit her lip to keep from giving him the satisfaction of knowing he'd hurt her.

Getting in the car would be disastrous. She jerked away and opened her mouth to scream. He manacled her around the waist and yanked her into his body, slamming a hand over her mouth. She struggled, kicking and twisting, but he hauled her to the car and tossed her in the back, where she smashed into another man. The first jumped in beside her. "You drive, Fred."

"No problem, Luis." Freddy lifted himself into the front seat and put the truck in drive.

Trapped. Her hands bound, she sat between two large men. Screaming seemed like a good idea. She sucked in air—

"If you scream, I'll have to knock you out," Luis said calmly.

She paused. If he rendered her unconscious, she wouldn't be able to get away. She glanced at the man on her right. Several scars lined his face, and he kept his gaze on the buildings outside. Guns and knives were tucked into his pants and leather vest. A man in the front passenger seat was similarly armed and also keeping watch of the world outside.

She swallowed. "You guys going to war, or what?"

Luis chuckled. "No. We have a shipment coming in and like to be prepared."

Freddy drove through the archway to town and turned the vehicle toward the mountains. The safety of Mineral Lake disappeared behind them.

CHAPTER NINETEEN

The cabin smelled like mildew. Juliet twisted her wrists. The zip-tie dug into her skin, holding tight. Luis had pushed her into the cabin and chair thirty minutes ago, and her arms had gone numb. So much for her big escape plan.

A chill from the wooden chair swept up her spine, and she eyed the small area. The place was more of a shack than a cabin. A rough fireplace set into one wall, a dingy kitchen the opposite. In the middle sat a round table with four rickety chairs. One wall held doors to what looked like a small bedroom and bathroom. The final wall showcased a medium-sized window that probably had a decent view of the mountains behind the soiled blue blanket covering the panes. Her laptop perched on the table, humming softly.

Luis nodded to Freddy. "Go scout the south perimeter while I chat with your sister."

Dread settled in Juliet's gut.

Freddy stilled and then eyed Juliet. With a sympathetic grimace, he nodded and dodged outside, shutting the door.

Luis grabbed a large envelope off the table and twirled it with long fingers. End over end. Again, end over end, his gaze on her, thoughtful and somehow more menacing than if he were angry. "Where's my money?"

"The money I found in my trunk is long gone." She met his dark scrutiny without flinching.

He drew a picture from the envelope to toss in front of her. The photo depicted Quinn standing on the steps of the sheriff's station, his eyes narrowed, his body alert.

"I believe the sheriff has excellent instincts." Luis pulled out another picture. "He apparently felt me watching. However, had I decided to shoot him, his instincts wouldn't have helped." With a twist of Luis's wrist, the next photo landed on the table.

Juliet barely kept from gasping. The new picture showed Leila and Sophie walking hand in hand out at Sophie's ranch. "You spent some time taking pictures."

"I like to be thorough." He yanked out several pictures to throw on the table. Pictures of Juliet, pictures of townspeople, pictures of her friends. "I could've ended the life of any one, or all, of these people at any time. And I will."

"I believe you." She slid her most polite smile into place.

"Good. Where's my money?" Luis asked.

"I'm telling you the truth," she said evenly.

He drew a wicked-sharp knife from his back pocket. "You have a very pretty face."

"That's kind of you to say." She might throw up now.

He grinned. "While I enjoy a complete smart-ass, I will cut you."

Her stomach knotted, but she kept his gaze. "That doesn't change the fact that the drug money is long gone."

His eyes hardened. He skirted the table and slid his hand around her throat, lifting her head and squeezing just enough to make breathing difficult.

"I'm losing my patience."

She swallowed through the constriction. If he moved a little to the left, she could knee him in the groin—she'd have one shot. Somehow, she had to get him out of his head. So she focused on him and... winked.

He blinked. Admiration slid into his gaze. "I'm really regretting we couldn't go into business together, Juliet."

Surprise slid through her. "Freddy said you have another plan to use me as a front."

Regret twisted Luis's lip. "You were set up perfectly in Maverick to front my operation. Unfortunately, when you went clean with the sheriff, you destroyed any chance of our working something out."

"Oh," she murmured. "So if I tell you where the money is, I'm pretty much finished."

"You're a lot smarter than your brother," Luis said.

"The doorknob is smarter than Freddy," she muttered.

Luis threw back his head and laughed, the sound slightly maniacal. "I like you. A lot. So here's the deal. Tell me how to find my money, and this will go smoothly." He leaned in, his minty breath brushing her skin. "If you don't cooperate, I'll hurt you like you can't imagine."

Bile rose up her throat, but she shoved it down. Her smile hurt. "I'm not that tough, Luis. I promise." If she gave him the file in her computer that showed where all the money had gone, he'd kill her. If she didn't give it to him, he'd torture and then kill her.

His hold loosened. "I'll help you decide. If I have to work at getting the information, when I'm finished with you, I'm going to start on the people in those pictures. Probably with pretty Sophie Lodge. I usually prefer blondes." He tucked his face into Juliet's hair and took a deep breath. "Though maybe I'll switch to redheads."

She gagged.

He backed away, irritation bracketing his mouth. "Tell me the truth."

Her mind scrambled for a way to stay alive. "Did you kill the two men on the outskirts of the county?"

Luis shrugged. "They tried to steal from me, and a man does have to keep control of his employees."

Luis liked to talk, and for some reason, he seemed to enjoy talking to her. She had the oddest feeling he wanted to impress her. Well, before he tortured her. "Did you kill them with that knife?"

His smile flashed sharp teeth. "Juliet, you don't seem to understand that there's no need to gather evidence for your boyfriend."

The mention of Quinn pricked tears at the back of her eyes. "I was just curious."

He slid the knife closer to her face. Light glinted off the sharp blade. "Yes, this is the knife." His voice dropped to a croon. "Isn't she pretty?"

Wow. Whackjob.

The door banged open, and Freddy stalked inside with a tall, skinny man who had more pocks in his skin than freckles. And he was seriously freckled.

"The first shipment is here." Freddy glanced at Juliet, his shoulders relaxing.

Had the moron been worried about her? Not worried enough to stop Luis, though. Juliet glared at the weasel.

Luis jerked his head toward the bedroom. "The money's in the green duffel."

Freddy hustled into the bedroom and returned to hand the duffle to the freckled guy. "It was a pleasure."

The man left without saying a word.

Freddy rubbed his hands together. "One more shipment, and we're out of here."

Juliet cleared her throat. "You know, Fred, I've noticed Luis doesn't seem tolerant of employees screwing up."

Freddy frowned. Luis smiled. Juliet tried to keep from puking.

Freddy eyed Luis and then focused on her. "And?"

"You screwed up. You lost his money, and now you lost his chance to use my gallery as a front. Frankly, I'm shocked you're still standing." She tilted her head toward the deadly knife. "Something tells me you'll be rather intimate with that blade in the near future."

Luis chuckled. "I swear to God, Fred, I think I'm in love with your sister." He twirled the knife like a gunslinger playing with pearl-handled pistols. "Look at her try to cause a rift between us. She's stalling, and I find it adorable." His gaze raked her down to her boots. "Though if she doesn't tell me where the money is, I'm going to kill her."

Freddy stilled. "Tell him, JJ. He promised not to hurt you if you just told him."

Juliet shook her head. "You're such a moron. He lied to you."

Freddy's mouth opened and shut like a guppy out of water. "No, he didn't. You're safe. I promise."

"He's going to kill you, too, Fred. Get a grip," she said.

Luis tucked away the knife and drew a gun, point-ing it at Freddy. "I'm done. Tell me where the money is, or I shoot him."

"What the hell, man?" Freddy backed away, both hands up.

Luis flipped off the safety. "I'm counting to three."

Juliet's brain scrambled.

"One," Luis said calmly.

"T-tell him, JJ," Freddy sputtered.

"Fine." She didn't want to see Freddy's brains splattered all over the wall. "I kept track of where the money went. The document is called 'Robin Hood' in my laptop."

Keeping the barrel aimed at Freddy, Luis punched keys with his left hand. His eyebrow lifted as he seemed to read. "You gave all of my money away…to Lost Cats of Spokane?"

She shrugged. "I only gave them ten thousand. But those cats needed catnip, Luis."

His eyes widened, and his pupils narrowed. Shifting his aim from Freddy to her, he drew back his lip. "You're going to pay for this in ways I can't even imagine right now."

• • •

His back to a Ponderosa Pine, Quinn shook his head at his brother. "We can't wait for backup."

"I know," Colt said grimly, yanking off his work gloves. "You armed?"

"No—except for a pocket knife in my boot." Quinn eyed the shotgun secured in a holster on Colton's horse. "I think that's it for guns."

Hawk shoved through the brush to the secluded area. "There are four men patrolling, plus whoever's in the cabin." Nodding toward a ridge to the north, he rubbed his chin. "That area has vantage over the valley—should take me five minutes to be in place. I'll need Colt's shotgun."

Quinn took a deep breath to keep from running full bore toward the cabin. "Hawk, we've never talked about—"

"I'm a sniper. The best." Hawk's odd-colored green eyes darkened.

That's what Quinn had figured. "Okay. Take the northern ridge."

Jake shoved his way past the bushes, a wicked knife in his hand. "I took this off the guy patrolling to the east."

"Is he dead?" Quinn asked calmly.

"No. Out cold." Jake tucked the knife at his waist. "I sent Sophie back to town, although she wanted to stay and help."

The little blonde had seen Juliet kidnapped and had followed in her car, calling the guys on her cell phone. Quinn's gut swirled. "Thank God we were working on the northern pastures."

Hawk tilted his head. "I'm heading to the ridge. Give me five." He loped over to the tethered horse and yanked the shotgun free. With a grim look at Colton, he broke into a jog and disappeared from sight.

Quinn peered around the tree at the quiet cabin. A heated ball of dread slammed him. Was Juliet all right? What if they'd hurt her? His legs trembled with the need to storm the cabin.

Jake grabbed his arm. "Give Hawk a moment to get into position."

Quinn grunted. "She thinks I'm still mad at her."

"You are." Colton removed his jacket.

"Doesn't mean I don't still love her." Sure, he'd been a complete asshole and should've worked things out after he fucked her by the side of the road. But he was a stubborn bastard, and his anger had kept him silent. If anything happened to her, he might as well shrivel up and die.

"Get it together, Sheriff." Jake's eyes darkened with concern and anger. He cared about Juliet, too.

Drawing on years of experience, Quinn shoved emotion out of the way. Cold, methodical, he came up with the plan to save the woman he loved. It was risky, and chances were somebody would be shot, but it was all they had.

"Let's go," he said grimly.

• • •

Juliet eyed the man who wanted to harm her. Her mind buzzed, but her shoulders relaxed. Maybe this was what shock felt like.

Luis twirled the knife. "The good news is that I'm not going to kill you right now. The bad news is that you're coming with us, and I'm going to take my time with you tonight." His eyes lightened to a creepy leer.

Juliet lifted her chin regally. The longer she stayed alive, the better the chance of escape. "Sounds like a lovely plan."

The window shattered, and a large mass crashed through the blanket. Quinn! The door banged off its hinges a second later, and Jake barreled into the room followed by Colton.

Luis pivoted and shot toward the window.

Juliet screamed.

Quinn rolled into a somersault and cut Luis off at the knees, knocking him down. The gun spun across the floor. The men grappled, their punches landing hard.

Jake grabbed Freddy and shoved him face-first into the wall.

Colton viewed the bedroom and bathroom. "Clear," he said.

Blood flowed from a wound in Quinn's right shoulder. Luis shoved his knuckles in the injury.

Quinn hissed and elbowed Luis in the nose, following up with a cracking uppercut.

The drug dealer shook his head, snot and blood pouring from his nose. He punched Quinn hard in the wound.

The sheriff grunted, his face paling. His damaged arm hung limp by his side.

Luis smiled through bloody teeth and yanked back his fist.

Quinn dropped his head forward in a classic headbutt. Luis's nose broke with a terrible snap. He howled in pain. He grabbed Quinn's arms and fell onto the floor, throwing the sheriff over his head.

Quinn landed with a muffled curse.

Juliet's gaze darted to Jake and Colton, where they calmly watched the fight. What was wrong with them? Why weren't they moving to help?

Quinn rolled to his feet and came down hard on Luis, banging the man's head on the floor. With a grim smile, the sheriff flipped Luis onto his stomach, straddled and cuffed him.

"Are you all right?" Quinn turned toward her, his eyes hard and assessing.

She nodded, unable to speak. Tears swelled and blurred the room.

Quinn yanked Luis to stand and pushed him toward Colton. "Secure them in the back of the gray truck."

Luis chuckled through a split lip. "I have men around the perimeter, Sheriff. Let me go, or we're all dead."

"We found your men." Quinn wiped blood off his forehead. "My sniper is in place in case we missed anyone. I'll bet my sniper against your guys any day."

Luis spit blood and a couple of teeth onto the floor. Colton grabbed him and shoved him outside.

Jake pulled Freddy away from the wall and smashed him back into it. "Oops," Jake said, grinning and tugging again. "Come on, buddy. Let's go outside." They disappeared into the cold.

Quinn reached her in two strides. "Are you sure you're all right?"

"Yes," she said between hiccups.

"Take it easy, sweetheart." He tugged a knife from his boot and cut the tie holding her hands. Then he growled at her scratched skin, rubbing gently.

"I'm fine," she said, standing. Her knees gave out.

He eased her back into the chair. "Take a couple of deep breaths. The adrenaline is kicking in now." Big, gentle hands massaged her legs and then her shoulders. "You're fine, Juliet. Deep breaths."

She nodded and inhaled, exhaling slowly. "How did

you get here?"

"Sophie saw Freddy take you." Quinn dropped to his haunches. "I almost had a heart attack when she called. We were just a couple miles away working on a downed fence and headed right here."

She sniffed. "I'm glad you did." Her eyes widened at the blood coursing down his arm. "He shot you."

Quinn frowned and ripped his shirt over his head. A deep, red gash welled on his upper arm. "The bullet scratched me. No biggie." He wrapped his shirt around the wound and pulled tight.

Sirens sounded in the distance. He grimaced. "I'm sorry about last night. I was a jerk who couldn't figure out what to say."

She blinked through tears. The man had just saved her life after she got him shot, and he was apologizing. "This is my fault." The sirens got closer.

He stood and assisted her up. "We called for backup." Not that Quinn needed backup.

Juliet squared her shoulders and slid her feet along the wooden floor. Her knees still wobbled. "I'm sorry about all of this."

He dropped a kiss on her forehead. "I know. We'll figure it out, Juliet. I promise."

When they reached the doorway, she peered outside. "Um, do you really have a sniper somewhere?"

"Hawk was with us fixing fences." Quinn gave some weird military sign. "Don't worry. He rarely shoots the wrong person." A grin quirked the sheriff's lip.

"Very funny." She gingerly stepped onto the muddy walkway. Red-and-blue lights swirled as deputies gathered several cuffed men into police vehicles.

A black SUV screeched to a stop, and Reese

Johnson jumped out. "Is she all right?"

"Yes," Quinn said, helping her along the rough trail to a police vehicle. "Did you get the drug runners?"

Reese grinned. "Yep. We caught one with a shitload of cash and another one with a truck full of drugs." He nodded at Juliet. "I've gotten the okay to offer you full immunity for everything if you testify as to what you witnessed today."

Jake shoved away from a police car. "While my client doesn't need immunity because she hasn't broken any laws, we would still like the offer in writing from the federal prosecutor."

"Sheriff Lodge? Over here." A camera light flicked, and a man with a microphone stepped closer. "What happened here?"

Quinn growled and moved toward the reporter.

"Stop." Jake grabbed his arm and hitched him back. He opened the back door of a cruiser and reached for Juliet's hand. "Get in." Juliet scooted over, and Quinn dropped next to her.

Jake smiled. "I'll meet you two at the hospital."

Quinn moved to get out of the car. "I want the reporter out of here."

Jake leaned in. "I called him, dumbass. Trust me." After shoving his brother, he slammed the door.

A deputy slid behind the wheel. "To the hospital we go, Sheriff."

CHAPTER TWENTY

Juliet leaned her head against the chilly wall and tried to get comfortable on the plastic orange chair. Even in quaint Maverick, the hospital smelled like bleach, antiseptic, and despair.

The doctors had rushed Quinn into a room upon their arrival, and a petite but rather forceful nurse had directed Juliet to the waiting area. In the corner, a television played an old sitcom.

Her stomach hurt. She closed her eyes, allowing peace to wash over her. Everybody was safe, and the bad guys had gotten what they deserved.

What about her? What did she deserve? She sat up as Quinn's mother hustled into the room.

Loni Freeze gathered her into a vanilla-scented hug. "Oh my goodness. You worried me." She patted Juliet's back, offering maternal comfort.

Tears welled in Juliet's eyes. She leaned away and blinked. "I'm fine, but Luis shot Quinn."

"I poked my head in the examination room. Quinn is barking orders at the poor doctor." Loni shook her head, sending her gray braid flying. "That boy. I don't know where he gets such a temper."

Tom Freeze, Loni's husband, rushed into the room with Dawn. "I know exactly where he gets his spirit." He dropped a kiss on Juliet's head. "I'm glad you're all right, sweetie." Then he sat and slipped his hand over Loni's.

As a pair, they fit. Tall with gray hair and deep blue

eyes, Quinn's stepfather contrasted with Loni's black eyes and sharp features.

Dawn was a perfect blend of the two, with blue eyes and black hair. Those eyes lit up when Hawk and Colton stalked into the room.

Juliet clasped her hands. "Thank you. Both of you."

They nodded.

Dawn frowned. "I didn't know you helped rescue Juliet, Hawk."

He shrugged. "I provided backup and let the sheriff do his thing."

Did Dawn not know Hawk was a sniper? Juliet raised an eyebrow. The young man met her gaze evenly, without expression. Her small nod promised she wouldn't tell.

Sophie ran into the room next, skidded to a stop and tugged Juliet out of her chair for a big hug. "I was so worried. I saw Freddy take you, and I didn't know what to do, so I followed in my car and called the guys for help, but if I didn't get them, I wasn't sure what—"

Juliet hugged her hard. "Take a deep breath. Thank you, and I'm fine."

Sophie stepped back and surveyed Juliet head to toe. "You look all right."

"I'm fine." She forced a smile. "Quinn got shot, not me."

Colton nodded toward the television. "Is this your doing, Jake?"

The film clip showed Quinn escorting Juliet out of the cabin amid deputies arresting the drug runners. Reese Johnson stood next to the reporter, thanking the Maverick County Sheriff for assisting with the biggest drug bust in recent history. He claimed justice was served only because Juliet Spazzoli put herself in danger to help authorities.

Jake grinned. "Someone has to make sure the sheriff gets reelected. Can you imagine if he worked the ranch full time?"

"No. He's bossy enough as it is." Colton gave an exaggerated shiver.

Hawk slowly nodded. "Amen."

Jake rubbed his chin. "I think the DEA will offer a deal to Freddy, Juliet. Just so you know."

A relief that made her feel guilty swept through her. "I know I shouldn't be, but I'm glad."

Jake's eyes filled with understanding. "Family is still family."

The room started to crowd with concerned citizens and police officers. Excusing herself, Juliet stepped outside. She figured she'd walk home and do some thinking, as well as make herself some lunch. Shouldn't she be hungry? Perhaps the next day she'd talk to Quinn.

Did childhood insecurity hold her back?

A deputy smoked outside his car. "Ms. Montgomery? Would you like a ride home?" He tossed the cigarette into a mud puddle and opened the back door. "The sheriff would kick my butt if I let you walk home with a storm coming."

A chilly wind swept through her thin sweater. With a grateful nod, she slipped into the warm patrol car. "Thanks."

The deputy glanced over the seat. "This way the sheriff will know where to find you when the doc is finished stitching him up." At his cocky grin, he pulled the car into the road.

Juliet rolled her eyes. Now even his deputies attempted to matchmake. If they only understood that nothing swayed the stubborn sheriff. Nothing.

• • •

Juliet stretched her arms, much more comfortable in her yoga outfit. She'd changed the second the deputy had dropped her at home. It was a good thing she'd accepted the ride, considering her knees had started trembling within seconds of sitting down. Apparently the adrenaline rush took a while to dissipate.

Flipping on the local radio station, she tried to relax.

The empty apartment mocked her. She should eat lunch, but nothing seemed appealing right now.

Her heart ached an actual, physical, thumping of pain. Oh God. She was truly, absolutely, completely in love with Quinn Lodge.

She wondered how Quinn was doing. Maybe she should've stayed at the hospital.

Shame heated her face. The guy had taken a bullet for her, and she'd fled because she was too chicken to talk to him. She'd run away. Like always. Too afraid he'd reject her.

But she'd needed to get away and think…the same way Quinn had said he needed time to think.

Maybe he wasn't finished with her—he just had needed a second to breathe.

A broadcaster interrupted a Garth Brooks song with an update about the sheriff being shot and a promise that there would be a press conference in a few minutes. Sheriff Quinn Lodge would be outside the sheriff's building shortly.

He'd gone back to work? After being shot? Irritation heated her skin. The man needed a keeper. In fact, he needed her.

Sure, she'd lied to him—and she'd been stupid not to trust him. But everyone made mistakes.

He'd said he loved her.

People who loved each other were supposed to forgive each other. Look at the meddling, pain-in-the-butt town. Everyone tripped over everyone else.

But they forgave each other. Because they loved each other.

Quinn Lodge was a good man—a good man who should be fought for.

Juliet Spazzoli was a heck of a fighter.

She ripped open the outside door and stomped into the early evening. If the sheriff thought he could just screw her and dump her, then he was as stupid as Freddy. As she reached the curb, she almost collided with Mrs. Hudson and Henry Bullton.

"Well, hello, dear." Mrs. Hudson smiled, her powdered skin wrinkling. "Henry and I wanted to drop by and see if you'd like to go for a walk." She pushed Juliet toward the sidewalk.

Henry nodded. "The sheriff is about to give a talk." Sliding a bony arm through Juliet's, he tugged her away from the door.

Two uniformed deputies jogged over from Kurt's Koffees.

Juliet stumbled. "Deputies Phillips and Baker? Are you looking for me?"

"Yes, ma'am," Deputy Baker said. "We grabbed coffee and were headed to your place to escort you to the press conference." He elbowed Deputy Phillips, who just shrugged.

Juliet frowned. "How did you know I was going?"

Phillips grinned. "We didn't, but we thought we might talk you into it."

She narrowed her gaze. "I appreciate the support, but—"

A SUV screeched to a stop, and Sophie, Loni, and Dawn hopped out.

Dawn hustled over to assist Mrs. Hudson. "Oh, good. We thought we'd have to drag you to the sheriff's station, Juliet."

Juliet dug in her heels. "Why are you all pushing me there?"

Loni smiled. "I love my boy, but he's a stubborn one. He's hurt, you're hurt, and there's no time like the present to fix things."

Sophie skipped over a mud puddle. "Plus, he won't exactly yell at you in front of cameras. Well, probably only one camera. But still."

Juliet's mind spun as the group herded her down the street. They passed several blocks and picked up an even bigger crowd. Finally, they arrived at the sheriff's office.

Quinn stood on the top step, wearing a clean shirt and jeans. Several reporters and one cameraman had set up in front of him. His wet hair curled over his collar. His eyes were hard, his jaw set, and his shoulders impossibly wide. Slowly, one dark eyebrow rose when he noticed her.

She stepped closer to him. "Can we talk?"

The camera swung to her.

"Now?" A crease deepened between his eyebrows

as he took in the gathering townspeople.

Loni nudged Juliet up the rest of the steps.

She steeled her spine. "I'm sorry about getting you shot." There. She'd said it.

Jake slid into view. "I believe the sheriff would like to thank you for your help in setting up the drug dealers, Juliet." Several people in the crowd nodded.

Quinn loomed over her with an intimidating stance, apparently not giving a hoot about the election, cameras, or crowd. "You forgot to apologize for disobeying me and ending up in danger. I told you to stay at Jake's until I picked you up today."

She glowered. "I don't take orders from you, Sheriff." Her gaze caught on the white bandage peeking out of the neck of his shirt. "Though I am truly very sorry you were shot." She winced.

"What part of 'Don't leave Jake's until I come and get you' did you not understand?" He was mad. Beyond mad. Fury filled the sheriff's eyes...fury at her.

Jake interjected again. "The woman wanted to help you catch a drug dealer. She's a hero."

The crowd roared with a chorus of, "She's a hero."

Good Lord. She swallowed. "I know. But you're not perfect, either."

His gaze softened. "I know, and I really am sorry about last night."

"What happened last night, Sheriff?" a reporter asked.

Juliet's face heated.

Quinn glared at the reporter. "None of your damn business."

Juliet put her hands on her hips. A feminine instinct she hadn't realized she had awakened. Determined.

Ready to fight if necessary. Fight with him. More importantly—fight for him. He was everything she could ever want in this life…or the next. She leaned up and whispered into his ear, "You said you loved me."

"I do love you. Why didn't you tell me the truth?" he whispered back. Something besides anger flashed in his eyes. Hurt. She'd hurt him.

"We can't hear you, Sheriff," a reporter called.

"No shit." Quinn lifted his voice.

The crowd rustled. A photographer flashed pictures.

Juliet leaned into him. "At first, you were just the hard-core sheriff, and I didn't know you. Then, when we became close, I'd already lied for so long. I didn't want to lose you. Didn't want to disappoint you." She kicked her foot and watched a pebble roll away. "I'm sorry."

"Look at me, Juliet," he ordered.

The low tone tingled through her body. Gathering her courage, she looked him right in the eye. "I really am sorry."

"Do you love me?" he asked.

"Yes. I love you," she said easily.

"No more lying?" he asked.

"No." Hope bloomed in her chest. "I promise."

"I love you, too." He brushed a curl off her cheek. "I was heading to your place after this stupid press conference."

Tingles lifted her smile. "You were?"

"Of course. I'm not letting you get away, Juliet." He tugged her close, and his mouth took hers.

The spectators erupted in cheers.

EPILOGUE

Quinn parked the truck against a lodgepole pine, looking dashing in a black shirt and faded jeans. Maybe not dashing, but definitely handsome and stronger than the mountains around them.

"My stomach is in knots." Juliet smoothed her skirt.

He glanced toward Loni and Tom's sprawling ranch house. "Either I won or I lost and will run for sheriff next time. If I lost, I wouldn't mind working the ranch a little harder. The guys seem to be slacking a bit."

Juliet smiled. "You're overbearing."

His cheek creased. "So you've told me."

"Thank you for your help with the DEA." She'd gotten immunity for anything she might have done and had supplied affidavits against Freddy and Luis. Freddy had made a deal to testify against Luis in exchange for a lenient sentence. Luis had pled out since the evidence was so strong.

The criminal issue was over.

Unfortunately, maybe Quinn's career was, too.

He slid from the driver's seat and crossed around to open her door. After assisting her to the ground, he shut the door. "I thought this would be a nice place to chat."

She wobbled in her new boots. "Chat? Are you stalling, Sheriff? Let's go inside to the party and see if you've been reelected or not."

"Yes, chat." He shuffled his feet and cleared his throat. "My family means a lot to me and will always be in my business and in my life."

"Okay," she said.

"So will the town, the reservation, and the entire county." He tugged on his already open collar. "You need to understand my life."

Where in the world was he going with all of this? Perhaps he was more nervous about the election than he'd let on, but he wasn't telling her anything she didn't know. Of course his family and the town would always be a part of him. "I do understand."

"Good." He breathed out in relief. "In that case"— he dropped to one knee and yanked a small box out of his pocket— "will you marry me?"

The world stopped spinning. Completely stopped. Nothing moved, nothing breathed. Juliet froze, her mind blank. Her knees quivered.

Quinn opened to box to reveal a spectacular square diamond surrounded by intricate Celtic knots—all in platinum. It was the most beautiful ring she could've ever imagined, offered by the most amazing man on the planet.

Her breath whooshed out. Birds sprang to a loud chirping. The wind rustled around them. Joy filled her so completely she swayed. "Yes."

Relief filled his eyes followed by a huge smile splitting his face. "Yes." He slid the ring on her finger and stood, gathering her close for a kiss that started sweet and ended deep.

A roaring filled the early evening. They broke apart to find his family, deputies, and half the town spilling onto the porch.

"Woohoo." Loni clapped her hands. "Get out the posters."

Several "Congratulations on Your Engagement" posters and banners were taped along the house by many pairs of willing hands.

"How did you know?" Quinn frowned and drew Juliet closer to the crowd.

Leila shook her head. "Uncle Quinn. Just 'cause you bought the ring in Billings don't mean we don't know people there." She smiled, revealing a gap in her front teeth. "Duh."

"Yeah, duh." Jake reached out and shook his brother's hand before grabbing Juliet for a hug. "Welcome to the family."

Hugs, kisses, and congratulations surrounded them until everyone finally piled back inside. Quinn held Juliet's hand, keeping her on the porch. "Life is going to get crazy, sweetheart. My job doesn't have normal hours, and I'm involved in more than just keeping order."

She smiled, running a reassuring hand down his arm to gaze up at his dark eyes. "I know, and I like being part of the community. Besides, I still get free rent at the gallery, right?" Her lips curved as amusement filtered through her. She was already planning another art showing for Sophie.

He chuckled. "Well, how about I let you *earn* free rent?"

"Hmmm. Sounds kinky." Turned out Juliet liked kinky. Who knew?

"You know the whole pretending-to-date plan was a setup to get you right where I wanted you?" He brushed a kiss across her nose.

"Maybe you ended up right where I wanted you." She levered up on her toes and slid her lips along his.

"You're everything I could ever want."

Quinn tucked her closer and took over the kiss, going deep. They both breathed heavily when he released her.

Jake poked his head outside. "Preliminary numbers are in. Looks like you're the sheriff again." He turned back toward the party. "Damn it, Colton. That was my plate of nachos." He disappeared from sight.

Quinn tangled his fingers with Juliet's. "Well, sweetheart? Welcome to chaos."

She grinned and slid into the family home and into a chaos where she belonged. "I like it here."

"Good thing." His hold tightened. "I love you, Juliet."

"I love you, too." She leaned into his strength. "Forever."

ACKNOWLEDGMENTS

There are so many folks who help to make sure a book becomes a final product—many behind the scenes whose names I don't even know.

Thank you to my very patient and understanding family. Thanks to my husband, Tony, for the amazing support, laughs, and fun. It's nice you don't think I'm crazy for talking to the character voices in my head. Thanks to Gabe and Karly—I'm so proud of both of you!

Thank you to my spectacular agent, Caitlin Blasdell—I'm so glad I found you. I've used almost all of the really good adjectives to describe how awesome you are…I'm going to have to think up some new ones for upcoming books. Thanks as well to the gang at Liza Dawson Associates—you're a wonderful group.

Thank you to my editor, Liz Pelletier, who gives excellent editorial advice and always has a terrific sense of humor. I hope we have many more books together in the future…and many more chances to meet up in person. I love those times!

Thank you to my Entangled team: Heather Howland, Misa Ramirez, Jessica Estep, Barbara Hightower, Sarah Weiss, Cameron Yeager, Alethea Spiridon Hopson, Jacki Rosellen, and Robin Haseltine. Also to everyone who has worked on my behalf whose names I don't know yet.

Thank you to the Lethal Ladies for the support and help through the years. Thanks to the Inland Empire

Chapter of RWA—I appreciate the support and friendship. Thanks also to my hardworking Facebook Street Team—you're a lot of fun, and you always make me smile. I appreciate the hard work!

Finally, thank you to my constant support system: The Englishes, Smiths, Wests, Zanettis, Chapmans, and Namsons. You're the best!

Rising
Assets

a Maverick Montana novel

NEW YORK TIMES Bestselling Author
Rebecca Zanetti

For Stephanie Cornell West, the most loyal person I know. I love you.

CHAPTER ONE

"She can't be working here. No way." Colton Freeze leaned forward in his chair and slid his nearly empty beer on the battered wooden table. A jukebox belted out Garth Brooks, peanut shells lined the floor, and longnecks took residence on almost every table in the bar. Unfortunately, the sense of home failed to relax him.

"I'm only telling you what Mrs. Nelson said at the bank." His friend, Hawk, turned toward the long, oak bar. "If she is working here, I wish she'd show up so I can go home to bed."

"Soon." Colton shook his head. "There is no way Melanie works at the coffee place in the morning, her ranch all day, and Adam's bar at night." She hadn't bothered to tell him. He'd been overseas finishing his securities degree, and nobody had thought to tell him his best friend was working herself to death? A fear he hadn't experienced in over ten years, when she'd become ill with pneumonia, slammed him between the eyes, nearly bringing on a migraine. He shoved the sensation away.

"I didn't know, or I would've called." Hawk gazed thoughtfully across the smoky room, his odd green eyes narrowed.

"You've only been home a day." Colt frowned. He cocked his head as the bartender called into the kitchen with a, "Hi, Mel."

Unbelievable. She *was* working in the bar. Colton

steeled his shoulders and schooled his face into a pleasant expression. If he yelled at her right off the bat, she wouldn't talk to him, and that would get him nowhere.

He needed to speak with her. While they'd grown apart a little bit during their teenage years, when they'd moved on into the world, they'd kept in touch as he attended school. After her grandfather had died two years ago, they'd reconnected, and Colton had made sure to call, text, and email while he studied.

After a short time, he couldn't sleep without talking to her and sharing his day. Maybe he should've been home instead of pursuing knowledge.

As his best friend, she was needed. He'd almost lost her once to the pneumonia, and he'd never allow himself to feel such fear again. She'd been what? Maybe twelve years old? From that day, he and Hawk had always made sure she had a coat nearby, although she hadn't gotten sick again. Now his gut churned that she hadn't shared her problems with him. "Where in the world is she?" he muttered.

She emerged from the kitchen and stepped out from behind the bar. Colton straightened in his chair. "What the hell?"

Hawk emitted a slow whistle. "Wow."

Yeah, wow. Melanie's customary outfit of faded jeans, scuffed boots, and a working T-shirt was absent for the night. "Adam must have made her wear the outfit." Son of a bitch. He'd kill the bar owner.

Hawk leaned forward, elbows on the table. "She looks good."

She looked better than good, and shock sprang Colt's cock into action. A tight tank top showed off perfect breasts, while a skirt curved along her butt to stop a couple of inches away. Long, lean legs led down to high-heeled boots. She was a wet dream come true.

Melanie wobbled a full tray of drinks to deliver to a table of rowdy farmers.

"Maybe the medical bills from her grandpop's fight with cancer added up, and she needed the extra money?" Hawk rolled his shoulder and finished his beer.

Colton exhaled but couldn't look away from the sexy brunette. Sexy? Jesus. It was just the shock of the new look. She was still Mel, still his best friend. "Now I need to worry about both of you."

Hawk sighed. "Tell me you didn't ask me out for a beer my first night home to lecture me."

Colton turned toward his oldest friend. Lines of exhaustion fanned out from Hawk's eyes, and a dark purple bruise mottled his left cheekbone. He was usually battered when he returned home from active duty, but this time a hardness had entered Hawk's eyes. Now wasn't the moment to bug him, however. Colton shrugged. "Nope. Just wanted to catch up. I'll push you tomorrow on leaving the SEALs."

"Fair enough." Hawk took a deep swallow of his beer as his gaze remained on Melanie. "I'm glad you called. It appears as if things might get interesting tonight."

Doubtful. Colton turned his attention back to the woman who hadn't trusted him enough to let him know she was in trouble. Something in his chest ached, and he shoved the irritant aside with anger. While he was known for a slow-to-burn temper, especially in comparison with his two older brothers, when he exploded, it was legendary.

There would be no temper tonight. First, he had to figure out what was going on, and then he had to solve the issue. Logically and with a good plan. When Mel glanced his way, he lifted his empty glass.

She hitched around full tables to reach him. "Why did you cut your hair?" Her face was pale as she tried to tug her skirt down.

He knew she wouldn't be comfortable half nude in public. "When did you start waitressing in a fucking bar?" The words slipped out before he could stop them.

"Smooth," Hawk muttered into his beer.

Melanie arched a delicate eyebrow and released the bottom of the skirt. "Last I checked, my grandfather was dead and you weren't my keeper. Do you want another beer or not?" The tray hitched against her hip—a hip that wasn't nearly as curvy as it had been the previous year. She'd lost weight.

Even so, he wanted to grab that hip and... "What time do you get off?" he asked.

A dimple twinkled in her cheek. "It depends who I take home with me."

He couldn't help but grin back. "You are such a big talker."

"I know." She shoved curly brown hair away from her face. Hair wild and free. "Why are you asking? Think you'll need a ride home?"

"I'm taking you home, and we're talking about your three jobs." He tried to smooth his voice into charming mode, but the order emerged with bite.

"The last time you tried to boss me around, I hit you in the face and you cried for an hour." She nodded at a guy waving for a drink from a table on the other side of the dance floor.

Colton glared at the guy. "I did not cry."

"Did too," Hawk whispered.

Colton shot a look at his buddy before focusing back on Mel. He'd been seven years old, and she'd almost broken his nose. "My eyes watered from the punch. That wasn't crying." They'd been having the argument for nearly two decades, and the woman never let up. "You've cried on my shoulder many a time."

She reached for his glass. "That's because men are assholes, and you have great shoulders."

Every boy or man who'd ever hurt her had ended up bashed and bloody afterward because either he or Hawk had made sure of it. "You're right on both counts. Which begs the question, if you're in trouble, why aren't you crying on my shoulder now?"

Sadness filtered through her deep eyes. "You're my friend, not my knight. It's time I stood on my own two feet."

He wanted to be her knight, because if anybody deserved protection, it was Melanie. "I'm mad at you."

"I know." She smacked his shoulder. "You'll get over it. You always do."

Was it his imagination, or did regret tinge her words? He tilted his head and studied her.

She smiled at Hawk. "I'm glad you're home. You staying this time?"

Hawk lifted a shoulder. "We'll see. It's nice to be among friends, I can tell you that."

Mel fingered Colton's short hair, returning her attention to him. "Why did you cut it?" she asked again.

That one touch slid down his spine and sparked his balls on fire. What in the hellfire was wrong with him? He shifted his weight. "I thought it was time for a more mature look since I'm taking over at the office." Of course, last time he'd grappled at the gym, his opponent had gotten a good hold on Colton's hair. At that point, a clipping had become inevitable.

Mel smiled. "You do look all grown up, Colt Freeze."

He'd love to show her just how grown up. At the odd thought, he mentally shook himself. Friend zone. Definite friend zone. That was it. "Part of being a grown-up is asking for help."

She rolled her eyes. "I'll be back with another beer." Turning on a too-high heel, she sauntered toward the back corner.

Colt's gaze dropped to her ass. The flimsy skirt hugged her flesh in a way that heated his blood. While Mel was small, she had always been curvy. More than once, he'd wondered.

For years he'd gone for wild girls...fun, crazy, and not looking for forever. During his life, he'd avoided anything but friendship with Melanie, who was a keeper. A good girl, sharp as a blade, and kindhearted.

Hawk cleared his throat.

"What?" Colton asked.

"You're looking at Mel's butt." Hawk set down his beer. "How long have I been out of town, anyway? Has something changed?"

Colton shoved down irritation. "No. Besides, what's wrong with Mel's butt?"

"Nothing. In the world of butts, it's phenomenal." Hawk leaned to get a better view. "Just the right amount of muscle and softness. In fact—"

"Shut up." Colton jabbed his friend in the arm. Hard. "Stop looking at her ass."

Hawk chuckled. "If you're finally going to make a move, let me know. I have a hundred bucks entered in the town pool."

Colton's ears began to burn. "Town pool?"

"Yep. The exact date you and Melanie finally make a go of it." Hawk pushed back his chair. "Now that you're home, get ready for some meddling."

"Mel and I are just friends." He'd kill himself if he ever hurt her. In fact, he'd beat the crap out of her first boyfriend in high school because the prick had cheated on her. So the fact that she had an ass that made Colton's hands itch to take a hold of was something he'd ignore. Again.

"I may stay home for a while, because this is going to be fun." Hawk stood. "Mind if I head out? I need sleep."

Colton shook his head. "No problem." Hawk did require sleep if he was thinking Colton and Mel could be anything more than friends. The three of them needed each other, and things had to stay the same. "I'll see you at your southern pasture at dawn. The order of twine finally came in earlier."

"Can't wait." Hawk turned and headed out of the bar, seemingly oblivious to the several pairs of female eyes tracking his progress.

A voluptuous pair of breasts crossed Colton's vision before a woman plunked down in Hawk's vacated seat. "Well, if it isn't Colton Freeze," Joan Daniels said before sliding her almost empty wineglass onto the table.

"Hi, Joan." Colton forced his gaze to her heavily made up eyes and away from the twins being shoved up by a bra worth twice whatever the woman had paid for it. "How are you?"

Joan pouted out red lips. "Almost empty."

"We'll have to get you another." Colton slid a polite smile on his face. While he may be single and definitely horny, he was far from stupid. The four times divorced cougar leaning toward him represented a complication he neither needed nor wanted. Talk about not fitting into his plans. "Are you out by yourself tonight?"

"Yes." She clasped her hands on the table and shoved her breasts together in a move as old as time. "How about you since Hawk took off?"

"I'm waiting until Melanie is off shift." It wasn't the first time he'd used his friendship with Mel as an excuse, and it probably wouldn't be the last.

Joan sniffed. "Why? She's still dating the oldest Milton son from Billings, right? The banker?"

Colton lifted a shoulder. If Mel was still dating the banker, it was the longest relationship she'd ever had. The idea shot a hard rock into his gut, one he'd have to figure out later. His unease was probably due to the fact that any banker wearing three-piece suits and allowing his woman to work three jobs wasn't good enough for Melanie. Though using the word *allow* around her would end in a broken nose. Colton smiled at the thought.

Melanie slid a beer in front of him and leaned over to pour wine into Joan's glass.

Joan narrowed hard eyes. "How did you know what kind of wine I want?"

Melanie recorked the bottle. "You're drinking red.

This is our red."

Colton bit back a grin. Adam's wasn't known for a fine wine selection, but beer was another matter. "Did you bring me a nice beer?" He glanced closer at the thick brew. "Looks hearty."

"Suck it up and try the new beer, wimp." Mel nudged his shoulder.

Joan leaned closer to Colt. "We were discussing you and Brian Milton."

Melanie eyed Colton. "Is that a fact?"

The tone of voice held warning and had the unfortunate result of zipping straight to Colton's groin. He felt like a randy teenager all of a sudden, and enough was enough. "I wasn't." If all else failed, throw the cougar under the bus. "Joan brought up Milton."

"Why?" Melanie turned her formidable focus onto Joan.

"Curiosity." Joan's caps sparkled even in the dim light. "You've been dating for quite a while. Is it serious?"

"It's personal." Melanie dropped a couple of beer napkins on the table. "I have a ride home, Colton."

"Yeah. Me." He took his drink and gave her his hardest look—one that wouldn't faze her a bit. "Either agree, or there's gonna be a memorable scene in the parking lot when I toss your butt in my truck."

Sparks flashed in Melanie's eyes. She leaned in, and the scent of lilacs and woman almost dropped him to his knees. "Threaten me again, Freeze, and I'll make you cry for hours."

He'd never been able to refuse a challenge, so he turned his head until their lips hovered centimeters apart, his gaze piercing hers. "Sounds like a date."

CHAPTER TWO

Melanie stretched her calves in the front seat of Colton's truck and bit back a wince as his headlights illuminated a downed fence on her property. Then another—both nearly covered by snow.

"What's going on here?" he asked.

"I've been busy," she said.

He glanced her way, a new tension cascading off him. "What about your crew?"

"Let them go. No money to pay them, but I do contract with Hawk's crew whenever I need help on a case-by-case basis." Her feet pounded in pain, and goose bumps covered her bare arms. She hated working in the bar outfit with a passion rivaling a Freeze temper.

"Is that why you're working three jobs?" he asked quietly.

"Yes, and don't even think about offering me money." Her neck prickled. Sure, he was rich. She didn't want his money—she never had, and she sure as heck didn't want to discuss her reasons for needing money. Not now, anyway.

"How's the ranch doing?" Colton asked.

"Great. I have fifty head in the south pasture, the Angus bulls in the north pasture, and all of my foals to the west." She loved ranching and never considered another career. Montana was home, and she had no problem mucking out stalls when necessary.

"Crops?" Colton asked, his genius mind obviously

doing calculations.

"Winter wheat, barley, and Camelina." The oil seed crop was used in biofuel, and it had been Colt's recommendation she plant it last year. "The money will come in, and I'm not worried." Right.

He rubbed his chin, settling back in the seat. "How about a loan?" In the moonlight, the many colors of his hair still shone, even though the mass no longer touched his shoulders. It seemed like the finest genes from both his Native American and Irish ancestry had combined into a hair color women paid a fortune for.

"I don't want a loan." She studied his angled profile. Hard and sharp, his even features showed a rugged toughness he'd lacked as a cute teenager. Now he was all man.

A pang hit her that someday he'd settle down. Finally become one woman's man. Lucky wench. The man planned his entire life down to exactness. His future wife was probably some PTA president with as many college degrees as he had.

Melanie hadn't had time for college, and she liked her boots muddy. Dirty boots didn't belong at PTA meetings.

His muscled shoulders rolled, and he kept his gaze focused out the window. "Working three jobs is too hard and too stressful." Colt stopped the truck in front of the porch she'd painted the week before.

Thank goodness something looked fresh.

Distant or close by, he'd always been overprotective, and she could take care of herself. Time was short, and she needed money, not protection. "Stop worrying." She slid from the truck. "Thanks for the ride home. I'll talk to you tomorrow." Slamming the door shut, she loped up the steps and unlocked the front door.

The engine cut behind her. A door slammed, and heavy boot steps echoed behind her. "I can't help but worry. You're going to work yourself to death."

There was no alternative. She needed to get out of the skimpy clothes. She hurried inside, kicked out of the heels, and dropped her purse on the sofa table.

"Why do I get the feeling you're not telling me everything?" He remained on the porch.

Sighing, she allowed her shoulders to drop as she turned to face him. The man had excellent instincts. "I'm not telling you everything."

Colton stilled. "Excuse me?" he asked softly.

She swallowed. The tone of voice was something new. "Some parts of my life are private."

He blinked. "No, they're not. If you're in trouble, Hawk and I are here. The three of us."

Exactly. This was a problem the three of them couldn't solve. It's not like she'd ask either one of them to impregnate her. "I know, but I'm on my own with this one."

"There is no *on your own*. It's not how we work." Colton vibrated with a rare display of temper.

Irritation crawled up her throat. "Listen, Colt. I know you're used to meddling family members and the security that comes with that, but back off. I'm alone, and I need to figure this out by myself." It was a low blow, considering he'd always felt badly about her lack of family and his abundance of it, but she had to get him off the topic of money and her need for it.

"You're kidding me. I can't believe you said that." His chin lowered.

She'd known him her entire life and had seen him truly angry twice. Maybe three times. The man had an incredibly long fuse, but if it blew, everyone scattered.

As he stood in the doorway, blue eyes blazing, there was no question as to his fury.

She lifted her chin and casually moved toward the nearest chair, suddenly feeling vulnerable in the tight outfit that revealed way too much. "I don't need your help."

"Sit down." The order held bite and rumbled in a deep tone she'd never heard. Yeah, she may have poked a slumbering bear. Her butt hit the cushion even before her mind clicked into gear. Instant anger swelled through her at how quickly her body had followed his order. She shot to her feet.

"Too late." Long strides propelled him so close she could feel his heat. "Stick with your instincts and not with that stubborn mind."

She turned slightly to outmaneuver him. "I don't take orders from you, Colton Freeze."

He mimicked her motion and stepped into her space. "If you're not smart enough to take care of yourself, you damn well *do* take orders from me."

Anger and a well-earned nose for self-preservation battled for dominance inside her. She took a step back. "Get out of my house."

He mirrored her step. "No." Crimson angled across his high cheekbones, enhancing the dangerous hollows beneath them. As a kid, he had been adorable. As a teenager, handsome. As a fully grown, tough, battle-scarred man, he was all predatory male.

One she was smart enough to back away from, even as her nipples sprang to attention from his

intense gaze. Oh, this couldn't happen. *Down nipples.*
Down. Several steps later, her butt hit the wall.

A second later, they stood toe to toe. His palms
flattened against the cedar logs, caging her. "We're
about to come to an understanding here, Melanie
Murphy Alana Jacoby. Got it?"

Heated air filled her lungs with delicious tingles.
She breathed out slowly, trying to control herself.

He'd been her best friend for decades. She knew
how to appease him, how to make him laugh. The right
words were there and would smooth everything over.
For two seconds, she considered saying them. But she
was past that. He'd come into her home, he'd ordered
her around, and now he wanted things his way.

Not a chance.

So she said the one thing guaranteed to push him
over the edge. "Fuck you, Colt—"

His mouth was on hers before she finished saying
his name. Heat and power slammed from the kiss, and
her mind swam.

Fire lashed through her so quickly her knees
weakened. Her nipples scraped his chest, and lava
consumed her. Her eyes fluttered shut, and she fell
into the storm created by a man much more dangerous
than she'd known.

She kissed him back, her body alive, her mind
shutting down.

There was nothing but the whirlwind of impossible
need cascading around them, through her, into her,
beyond her.

The kiss was hard, angry, and more passionate than
she could've dreamed.

Many times they'd come close to kissing, but one of

them had always backed away. With a grin, or a joke, they'd escaped ever taking the chance. The one thing Melanie knew for sure was if Colton ever kissed her, if he ever showed her that side of him, there'd be no turning back. Ever.

As he released her mouth to pin her with a dark gaze, there was no question he knew it, too.

Determination filtered through his eyes, and his jaw firmed. Something new and intriguing fluttered alive in her abdomen. Her eyes widened, and satisfaction lifted his lips.

Holy crap. Colton Freeze didn't want to turn back.

CHAPTER THREE

After a restless night, Colt kicked the post into place, his stomach empty, wind slapping his cheeks and scattering snow across his boots. "The weather is supposed to warm up in March. Where's the sun?"

Hawk rubbed a well-worn glove across his forehead. "It's only five in the morning. Give the day a chance."

"Whatever," Colton muttered.

His brothers glanced up from tying off twine around a fence post.

"What's eating you?" Quinn asked. As the sheriff in town, Quinn often stepped in before anybody threw a punch. Well, unless it was Quinn aiming the fist.

"Nothin'." Colton shook his head. One sleepless night didn't mean a thing.

His oldest brother, Jake, leaned into the back of a battered truck to grab a thermos. "What's up, Colt? Is your detailed plan for this week off track?" Jake shared a look of amusement with Quinn.

"I don't plan everything," Colton said.

"Do too," his brothers muttered right back.

"Whatever. I'm just chomping at the bit to get into the office later." Not true—not true at all. His mind still spun from the disastrous kiss the previous night. What had he been thinking? Kissing Melanie was not in any plan.

Even worse, his body didn't regret it nearly as much as did his mind. In fact, his body wanted to march right back to Melanie's and finish what they'd started.

His body could shut up. "How's Sophie?" he asked Jake.

"Great." Jake grinned like he always did when talking about his spunky wife. "She's starting to show and having some fun shopping for maternity clothes."

"I think this time you're having a girl," Quinn said, reaching for another fence post.

"Either would be great, but I do think it's another boy," Jake countered. "Just a gut feeling."

"Twins," Colton said with a grin. It was nice seeing both of his older brothers married and happy, although he had no intention of joining them anytime soon. Jake had married an artist and already had a baby boy, and Quinn had married an art gallery owner, and their wives had become instant friends.

Hawk scratched his head. "What is she, about five months along?"

"About that," Jake said. "This pregnancy was a complete surprise considering Nathan is only fifteen months. We could find out the sex but decided it'd be fun to wait and see. Our daughter is hoping for a girl this time."

Little Leila was from Jake's first marriage, which had left him a widower. It was wonderful seeing both Jake and Leila happy with Sophie in their lives now.

Leila would be a great big sister no matter what. At eight years old, the sweetheart was more fun than imaginable. "Tell her to be ready after dinner for our movie night," Colton said. He liked to take his niece to the movies every time a new Disney came out.

"She already picked out her outfit." Jake grinned. "She won't tell me what you two have planned for the

St. Patrick's Day float."

Colt reached for a hammer. The family always entered a float in the Mineral Lake St. Paddy's Day parade, and this year, he and Leila had volunteered to create the design. "Let's just say it involves wolves and bears that are cuddly versus scary."

"Sounds good." Quinn stretched his back. "Let us know when we need to show up and pound nails."

"It's a plan." Jake cut a look toward Hawk, his gaze intense.

Colton nodded imperceptibly.

"All right." Jake threw a hammer that clanked in the back of the truck. "Quinn and I will head over to the northern pasture and check on the fences before going into town. I have an early meeting with some clients." As a lawyer, Jake often had early meetings.

Quinn slowly gazed at Colton and then Hawk. "Good idea. See you two later." Sliding into the front of the Ford, he waited for Jake to jump into the passenger seat.

As the brothers drove down the bumpy field, leaving them alone, Hawk turned toward Colton. "That was subtle."

"Huh?" Colton asked, stretching his neck.

"I figured all three of you would discuss my options with me." Hawk wiped grime off his forehead.

Colton shrugged. "We didn't want to gang up on you." They would if they had to. Hawk was family, and when family needed help, you jumped in. "I can call them back if you wish."

"No thanks," Hawk said. "Get the prompting over with."

"When do you need to decide on re-upping?"

Colton asked.

Hawk sighed, his green eyes narrowing. "A month. I leave on another mission any day, and then I have a month to decide."

"Want to talk about the mission?" Colt asked quietly.

"Can't." Hawk kicked a post into better alignment.

Figured. Colt's gut ached whenever he thought about Hawk's time as a sniper in the service, but he understood they couldn't talk about it. "I need another partner in my business, and I want it to be you."

"You don't need another partner, and I doubt you have a partner to start with." Hawk grabbed the post with both hands and twisted the base deeper into the earth.

Colton reached for more twine. "I want you and Mel as partners. It'd be more fun, and you have capital."

"You're richer than dirt and don't need my capital," Hawk said.

"Come on. You've given your time, and you've done a lot of good. It's eating you alive, and that won't work. We always talked about owning a series of fighting gyms, and now is the time." Colt set his jaw. He'd enjoyed MMA fighting while in college and wanted to bring fighting and different martial arts classes to gyms throughout Montana.

"Don't you think you'll be busy with running Lodge-Freeze Enterprises?" Hawk asked.

"Sure, but I want this business for the three of us." He'd never planned on only working as the CEO for the family companies, and even as young kids, he, Hawk, and Mel had planned to work together. Of course, as teenagers, he and Hawk had thoughts of owning a Hooters-type bar until Melanie had vetoed the idea.

As adults, they had different priorities than just fun. Colt's current one included getting his oldest friend home in one piece. "You look tired." Obsessed. Dangerous. Haunted.

"I'm fine." Hawk rolled his shoulders and glanced down the row of repaired fences that protected cattle and didn't delineate any division between their ranch lands. Since his mother had died, they'd worked the ranches as one. "One more mission—something I need to take care of, and I'm out. I promise."

Colt paused. "The mission sounds personal."

"Missions are always somewhat personal." Hawk's face lost expression in a way that pissed Colton off.

He hid his irritation. "So, about our partnership?"

"You're the financial genius. If you think we can make a go of it, I'm in." Hawk finally smiled. "What's the plan, anyway?"

"I thought we'd start with a gym in Mineral Lake and one in Billings…and expand from those locations. Teach martial arts, some fitness classes, and self-defense. Should be fun, and it's not like we lack training." Colt finished with the last tie-down. "What do you think?"

Hawk straightened his back and looked toward the snow-covered mountains to the north. He rubbed his chin. Finally, he turned toward Colton, dark eyes somber. "After this month, I'm in."

Relief whipped through Colton so quickly he turned away to throw tools in the back of the remaining truck to hide his expression.

"How about now you tell me what's bugging you?" Hawk loped toward the vehicle.

"I kissed Melanie last night." Colt had never kept a secret from Hawk, and he had no intention of starting now.

Hawk halted and swiveled around. "Holy shit."

That pretty much summed it up.

"Did she kiss you back?" Hawk shoved his hat further up his head.

Colton paused. Yeah, she'd kissed him back. With fire, with tongue, she'd pretty much blown his world. "Yes."

Hawk rubbed his chin. "Well, it was either that or punch you in the face. What does this mean?"

Heat roared through Colt's chest. "Nothing. It means nothing. The kiss was a temporary moment of craziness. I hadn't seen her in too long, she wore that dress, and I was, ah, pissed." Right? That was it.

"Um, okay." Hawk stepped into the passenger's side of the truck and waited for Colton to get in. "But why? You guys are great together."

"The three of us are good together." Colton slid into his seat and ignited the engine. Where one went, the other two showed up. The security of their friendship had made for a good childhood for them all, and they couldn't leave Hawk out. He'd lost everybody but them.

"I'm not into threesomes," Hawk drawled.

Colton snorted. "Did you just make a joke?" His buddy had been way too serious for much too long.

"I'm funny," Hawk said.

Hawk was many things, but funny wasn't one of them. Laconic. Serious. Deadly.

Colton nodded, steering the truck around potholes. "You are hilarious."

"Thanks." Hawk wiped dirt off his forehead. "The three of us are great friends, but you and Mel have always had something…separate. Something just for you."

Colton jerked his head. Had they abandoned Hawk?

Hawk cut him a look. "It's a good thing, and I have never felt left out."

Was he telling the truth? The friendship with Mel and Colt had been all Hawk could hold on to for so many years. Hawk had never known his father, and he'd lost his mother as a teenager. Colton would never exclude him. "Mel and I are good friends." No male-female stuff. Well, until last night. "We know everything about each other. No intrigue, no surprises, nothing to take us further." Plus, he wasn't ready for forever, and he'd just hurt her.

Then he'd have to kick his own ass.

"Hmmm." Hawk pressed a button on the radio. "We all didn't hang out as much as teenagers. Ever wonder why?"

"We were busy with sports and dating. We still hung out a lot," Colton said.

Hawk shrugged. "Maybe you two didn't want to watch each other date other people."

That was just silly. "Whatever."

"Aren't you tired of bubble-heads?" Hawk asked.

Colt skirted a sprawling hole and headed for the nearest ranch road. "Bubble-heads? Shawna was an anthropologist with a doctorate."

"Yeah, but she was dumb." Hawk shrugged and

then winced as the soundtrack for *Grease* belted out. "Perhaps book smart, but the woman couldn't hold a conversation to save her life."

Colt thought back to the voluptuous blonde. "We didn't talk a lot."

Hawk snorted. "Exactly."

Like Hawk talked very much. This conversation included more words than Hawk usually used in a week. Colton shoved a rough hand through his hair as the music continued. "Apparently Melanie was in the truck earlier. Why does she still like those soundtracks, anyway?"

Hawk shrugged. "*Grease* was the first movie the three of us watched together. Remember? We snuck the VCR tape from her grandpop's movie stash right after she moved here."

That was right. Mel had only been four, a chubby little girl with sad eyes. Her parents had died in a small plane crash, and her grandpop had instantly brought her home to raise.

Colton had taken one look at her and decided they were going to be friends for life. The idea that she still loved the music because of him and Hawk was a sweet one, and she was a sweet woman. "I remember."

Hawk rolled down his window. "Mel's all grown up. How do you feel about her marrying somebody else and building a life?"

A possessive edge cut through Colt and brought him up short. "Marry?"

"Sure. She's a doll, and hot to boot. She'll get married and settle down," Hawk said.

Colton frowned, not liking the panic heating his blood. "Humph."

"I figured you hadn't thought it out." Hawk leaned an elbow on the window. "You might want to do so."

Colton's mind spun. "I'll give it some thought. For now, what do you think about Melanie working to oversee the construction of the gyms as her part of the start-up costs?"

"Great idea." Hawk peered through the windshield as the sun finally appeared.

"She doesn't have experience," Colt said.

"So?" Hawk asked.

Colton nodded. "She'll look out for our interests, and the contractors I'll hire will have experience."

Hawk nodded solemnly. "I'd feel better with Melanie keeping an eye on things."

Now that was a friend. "Me too. Um, I think something's going on money-wise with her."

"More than the ranch and her grandpop's bills?" Hawk asked.

"Yes." Colton rubbed his eye. Melanie wouldn't spend money frivolously or just lose it. Something had to be going on.

Hawk tapped his gloves on his knee. "Ask her."

"I did," Colton said.

"Then give her some space. She'll ask for help when she needs it." Hawk wiped condensation off the window.

"Maybe." Colton shook his head. He wasn't great at giving space—never had been.

Hawk chuckled. "When are you breaking ground on your new house?"

Colton shrugged. He'd been planning to build a house on the other side of the ranch and was now living in one of the small cabins skirting the west side.

It suited him as he got settled. "Not until we get the gyms going." His plan made sense, and he'd stick with it.

"Do you think Mel will agree to supervise the construction?" Hawk asked.

"Yes." Now all Colton had to do was convince Mel she was needed, and she truly was. He needed her to stay healthy, relax, and make some money...and her watching over the construction would be an added bonus. "Wish me luck."

"Luck," Hawk drawled.

Colton ignored the amusement in his friend's voice. He'd convince Melanie to oversee the construction, and they'd go back to being buddies like always.

How hard could it be?

• • •

Melanie bussed coffee cups from another table, her mind still spinning. She'd kissed Colton. He'd kissed her.

Boy, had he kissed her.

"Hi, Melanie," a chipper voice said.

Melanie turned to see Colt's young niece standing behind her. "Hi, Leila. I just cleared a table for you."

Leila shook out her long hair. "I got a haircut. See?"

Melanie smiled and shared a look with Leila's grandmother, Loni. "You look beautiful, sweetheart," she said.

"Thanks." Leila slipped into the nearest seat. "Uncle Colt is taking me to the movies tonight. Do you wanna go?"

Heat flushed through Mel until her cheeks ached. "I would, but I have plans." Somewhat true. Since she had the night off, she planned on cleaning her house and catching up on laundry. Even watching a movie if she had time to rent one.

"You gotta date?" Leila asked.

"Nope." Melanie straightened her back, her vertebra cracking. "What can I get you two?"

Loni reached out to brush a motherly hand across Melanie's forehead. "You look flushed. Feeling okay?"

Sure. Except Loni's youngest son had kissed Melanie senseless the night before. She forced a grin for the woman who'd stepped in years ago and taken Mel bra shopping when her grandfather had needed assistance. At that point, noticing how lonely the teenaged girl was, Loni had checked in often. "I'm fine. Just bustling around," Mel said.

Loni's black eyes sparkled in her pretty face, her Native American heritage creating an interesting combination of smooth angles. "Good. I've been worried about you working so much."

Not for the first time, Melanie wondered about her own mother. What would it be like to have such concern for every hour of every day? She cleared her throat. "Hey, Loni. I wanted to say thanks."

Loni lifted her head, dark eyes wise. "For what?"

Melanie shook her head. "For being there for me... always. I needed you, and you were there."

Loni patted her hand. "Of course I was there... we're family."

Yet they weren't. Not really. "I know." Melanie smoothed down Leila's dark hair. The girl had inherited her grandmother's delicate build and thick hair.

Leila grinned. "When are we gonna have another *Grease* marathon at your place?"

Melanie laughed. "Any time, and you know it. This time we can sing along loudly because I bought the karaoke system we found on the internet. Now, what can I get you two?"

The outside door clanged, and the air changed. Not in a perceptible way, but with a way that raised the hair on Melanie's arm. She knew who'd walked in before she turned around.

Her heart dropped to her knees.

Colton walked in dressed in a full blue suit with striped power tie.

She gulped, her hands clutching on the rag. They'd known each other their entire lives, and she'd never seen him in a full suit. Even for school dances, he'd looked more cowboy than savant.

Today he looked like exactly what he'd become: one of the most influential and powerful financial geniuses in the Pacific Northwest. His hair was ruffled, enhancing the perfect angles of his handsome face. A powerful build filled out a suit costing more than her beat-up pickup.

His ideal mate definitely wore designer heels and not scuffed cowboy boots. The chick probably even spoke French. Or Italian. Or some fancy language that educated people knew.

His gaze warmed when it raked her. "Morning, Mel."

Shivers cascaded through her stomach. "Mornin'." Why was she looking at him so differently? One kiss, one that was a colossal mistake, shouldn't change anything.

The kiss *hadn't* changed anything.

He nodded at Kurt behind the counter. "*To go* today, thanks."

Kurt tipped his bushy head and ducked to steam some milk.

Colton pressed a kiss to his mom's cheek and reached to drag Leila up for a hug. "How's my favorite girl today? Ready for our date?"

Leila smacked him noisily on the nose. "Maybe."

Colt's eyebrows lifted. "Maybe?"

Leila pouted. "I don't know."

Mel cleared her throat, and when Colton glanced her way, she tugged on her hair.

Colt grinned and snuggled his niece closer. "But you have such a new pretty haircut. We have to go out and show it off."

Leila gasped in delight. "You noticed."

"Of course—you look all grown up." He settled her back in her seat and mouthed a *thank you* to Mel.

A pang shot through Melanie. Someday Colton would have kids and a life of his own, and she'd be relegated to the status of old friend. A surprising hurt spiraled through her.

"You okay?" Colton asked.

"Sure." Melanie smiled as Kurt sauntered over to hand Colton his drink.

"Good." Colton slid cash to Kurt and kept his focus on Melanie. "Because I was wondering if you'd mind driving into Billings to the office today—perhaps for lunch? I have a business proposition for you."

"What a lovely idea," Loni said with a smile.

Melanie narrowed her gaze. Loni and Leila being in the coffee shop simultaneously with Colton was no accident. The manipulative man had arranged the situation. "Oh, I—"

"I already know you have the night off, and I sent one of our crews to take care of your downed fences today." The smile Colton flashed was filled full of dare. "So I think you have time."

Irritation slivered across her skin, but she couldn't very well let him have it in front of his mother. "But I—"

"Oh," Loni exclaimed, digging into her purse. "Since you're going into Billings, would you do me a huge favor and return this brooch to Jillison's jewelry store? I would go, but I'm not up to par today, and today is the last day I can return the piece for full value."

Melanie faltered as she accepted the high-end bag and took a good look at Loni.

She looked great. Fantastic, even. Bright eyes, good color, sweet smile.

Even so, there was no way Melanie could refuse. "Of course. I'm happy to help." She'd planned to go into the city at the end of the week for an appointment, so maybe she could change the day, anyway. She shot Colton a look promising retribution, and his smile widened.

"It's a lunch date, then." Amusement twinkled in his blue eyes. "I will see you ladies later."

Melanie forced a smile as he loped from the coffee shop. She had just been expertly maneuvered by the best. And…had he said *date*?

CHAPTER FOUR

Colt shoved a stack of manila file folders to the side of his desk, his mind on emerging markets. He'd invested the family holdings heavily in a start-up green science company out of Seattle, and six months ago, he'd been convinced it was a good idea. It had fit his grand plan perfectly.

Now he wasn't so sure, although the owner was a buddy from college. Had Colton invested too much? He'd been so confident—maybe to the point of cockiness?

Colton had still been overseas studying international markets, although he'd unofficially taken over for his father as CEO of the company long ago. Now his dad took care of the main ranch and enjoyed semi-retirement with Loni.

Colton pressed both hands against the heavy wooden desk. How many times had he played around the desk while his father had worked deals sitting in the very chair Colton now sat in? How many school reports had he finished in the office, always enjoying the dealing and financial aspects?

His dad and Jake and Quinn's dad had been business partners long ago. In fact, the desk had originally belonged to the boys' father. He'd died in a snowmobile accident when the boys were young, and after a couple of years, Tom and Loni had fallen in love, gotten married, and had two more kids—Colton and Dawn.

They'd combined the ranches and family business into one. One that now rested on Colton's shoulders. For now. In a couple of months, Dawn would graduate with yet another degree, this one in business. Right now, she was finishing up her graduate degree at the university, and then she'd head to Europe for six months to study international finance until early December. Then, finally, she'd come on board at home. Their little sister loved school.

A blond head poked inside his door. "Mr. Freeze? Your sisters-in-law are here to see you."

Colton glanced up at his new secretary and grinned. They had to be about the same age, and the formality had to go. "Thanks, Anne. And please... call me Colton. The *mister* makes me feel old and decrepit."

Anne smiled. "Fair enough. I'll send them in." She disappeared from view.

Sophie, Jake's wife, was the first through the door, all energy, even in her fifth month of her second pregnancy. "Hey, bro. We were in town shopping, and I thought I'd drag you to lunch since Juliet has to get back to the art gallery." Her wispy blond hair feathered around a cute, pixie face.

Juliet followed gracefully behind Sophie, her red hair curling around her shoulders. She'd married Quinn last year, and her calm nature made the sheriff relax in a way he hadn't in eons. She glanced around the stately office. "Are you going to decorate more to your tastes?"

Colton frowned and looked around at the paintings that had adorned the walls for decades. "Probably not. Although...I'm thinking of moving headquarters to Mineral Lake."

Sophie clapped her hands together. "Great idea."

Juliet pursed her lips. "With the internet and so many people working from home, there's no reason you'd have to drive to the city. When are you thinking about moving?"

He shrugged. "I wanted to talk to the family first, but I was thinking within the year."

"That's a great plan." Sophie bounced up on the balls of her feet. "Now come feed a starving pregnant lady, would you?"

He grinned and crossed around the desk. "Melanie should be here in a few moments, so why don't we wait for her?" Then he could butter Mel up with good food before hitting her with his business proposal.

Sophie's eyebrows lifted. "Mel's coming into town?"

"Yes," Colton said.

"Oh." Sophie slipped an arm through Juliet's. "Well, now. In that case, I'll just grab something on the way home." She started dragging Juliet from the office. "I wouldn't want to impose."

Colton hustled to follow them to the doorway. "You're not imposing." Not that Sophie had any problem inserting herself in any situation if she deemed it appropriate. "Mel should be here any minute."

"No, no, no." Sophie waved as they reached the outside door.

Juliet halted their progress and looked down several inches at Sophie. "You have a day this week in the town pool, don't you?"

Sophie snorted. "Of course not."

Juliet glanced toward Colt, her eyes sparkling. "I

think we should accompany them to lunch."

"Nah." Sophie tugged harder. "I know you have sometime in next month for their get-together date."

Juliet's eyes widened. "I most certainly do not."

Sophie laughed. "When you lie, you sound like a countess."

Colton shot them both a hard stare. "Please tell me you're not in on some Maverick County bet that involves me."

"Nope," they said in unison.

Sophie won the struggle and yanked open the door. "The bet only involves the town of Mineral Lake and not the whole county. Bye, Colt. I'll talk to you later." The door closed behind them.

He had to find out more about this stupid town pool. Colton cut a look at Anne. "That was interesting."

Anne smiled, all professional. "Your sister-in-law has a lot of energy."

Now that was the truth. Scratching his head, Colton turned back toward the stacks of work on his desk. "When Melanie Jacoby gets here, please send her in. Thanks."

The entire town of Mineral Lake needed to get the heck out of his business.

• • •

Melanie wiped damp palms along her faded jeans. She should've worn a dress, but jeans were her normal look. Yet as she entered the stately brick building that housed Lodge-Freeze Enterprises, she wished for a different style.

One that fit with a gazillionaire like Colton.

Then she shook her head. Man. They'd been friends since preschool, and he knew everything about her. Well, almost. He didn't give one hoot how she dressed.

She pushed open the door and stopped short.

"Hi," said a gorgeous blonde from behind an antique desk.

Yeah. Melanie's biggest nightmare skirted the desk in a pretty pink suit, green eyes sparkling, hair perfectly styled. Colton's exact type, right down to the plus-sized boobs.

"You must be Melanie," the stunning woman said.

"Yes." She held out a hand to shake. The woman's manicure matched the smooth suit. "Nice to meet you."

"You too. I'm Anne, the office manager *slash* secretary *slash* receptionist." The woman gestured Melanie toward a plush chair in a stylish waiting room. "Colt said to send you right in, but he's on the phone with a broker from Taiwan—something about emerging markets—so how about I give you a heads-up when he's finished?" The smile was genuine and the tone gentle.

"Thanks." Melanie tried not to leave boot marks in the thick carpet as she crossed to take a seat. Next to Anne's style, Mel looked like a cousin from the freakin' boonies. From *that* branch of the family tree.

"I love your boots." Anne leaned over for a better look. "Where did you get them?"

Mel glanced down at the Lucchese hand-tooled boots. "My grandfather gave them to me for my birthday a few years back."

Anne smiled. "They're amazing."

Yeah, they were. Melanie smiled her thanks. What the heck? The perfect blonde who was lucky enough to work with Colt all day needed to be snotty or arrogant, not *nice.* Melanie wanted to dislike her. A lot. Instead, she was very much afraid she'd just made another friend.

The outer door opened and a miniature bundle of pure energy ran inside. "Mama!"

Anne stood, her eyes widening. "Tyler. What's going on?"

A robust woman followed through the doorway, a kid's backpack over one shoulder, a stack of haphazard papers in the other. "I'm so sorry, Anne, but my daughter was in a car accident, and I need to go to Seattle. Immediately." The woman dropped the bag on Anne's desk and turned back to the door. "I'm so sorry."

Anne gulped. "It's okay. Let me know how your daughter is."

The woman left.

Anne swallowed, turning pale. Her lips faltered as she smiled. "So it's you and me today, baby."

Tyler smiled and nodded before zeroing in on Melanie. "I'm Tyler. I'm three."

Melanie grinned at the little cherub. He had his mom's green eyes and spiky, crazy blond hair. Pudgy cheeks showed a couple of dimples. "I'm Mel."

Colton's door opened, and he stepped outside.

Anne hurried around the desk. "Mr. Freeze, I'm so sorry, but my day care lady had an emergency." She brushed hair from her face. "I know this isn't a place for kids—"

"Tyler," Colton said with a grin. "Dude. How's it going?"

Tyler launched himself at Colt, who swung him up in a wide arc. "Good. I ate goldfish."

"Yum." Colton tucked the toddler more securely into his side. "Tell your mama to call me Colt, and tell her you can work here any day. Always."

The moment hit Melanie square in the abdomen. Colton was a natural with kids. In fact, he was a natural with this one.

Anne fluttered her hands. "It's just that—"

Colt rolled his eyes and set Tyler on the desk. "Stop sweating the small stuff, Anne. Kids have always run amuck in this office, and I wouldn't want it any other way."

The woman nodded, blinking rapidly. She obviously needed the job.

Melanie attempted a reassuring smile. "There's a spot in Colton's office where we carved our initials when we were seven. Over by the wooden file cabinet." Of course, it had been Tom's office at that time. And he'd decided to leave the initials in place, even through several repaintings of the office.

Anne grinned. "I saw those—there are three sets."

Hawk had been there, too.

Colton strode forward and slung a friendly arm around Mel's shoulders. "We're heading out to lunch. If you need to take a half day and go hang with Tyler, no worries. If you want to stay here and work together, no worries. So…no worries."

The last was said with a firm note that caused the oddest fluttering in Melanie's belly. And he wasn't even talking to her.

"Thank you," Anne said quietly.

"See ya later, Colt," Tyler called out.

"Bye, buddy." Colton all but propelled Melanie out of the door and through the building. "I'm starving. Besides the latte earlier, I haven't had a thing to eat. Tell me you're hungry."

Melanie lifted a shoulder. "I could eat before we fight."

"We're not fighting." The firm tone returned.

Melanie glanced at his hard face. "Does anybody ever win a negotiation with you?" Those Taiwanese businesspeople didn't stand a chance.

Colton's natural grin made him seem even more approachable, if that was possible. "Yeah. You, Hawk, Dawn, Leila...family always wins." He casually switched their positions on the sidewalk so he walked between her and the street. "Well, unless I'm right. Then I win."

"Are you ever wrong?" she asked, trying to bite back a smile.

"I'm sure it has happened." He opened the door to a quiet deli.

Mel nodded and chose a table near the window to sit. The quaint restaurant had checkered tablecloths on the tables and movie posters on the walls. "What's up with your receptionist? Cute kid." Hopefully Anne was married.

Melanie didn't want to analyze why that mattered to her. Not now.

"She's a single mom and is the best organizer I've ever seen." Colton glanced at the specials scrawled across a chalkboard.

"Anne is very pretty." Melanie studied the hand-printed menu.

"Huh?" Colton focused back on Melanie and

shrugged. "I guess, but I need a good assistant, and she's excellent. I don't care what she looks like."

Right. "You're not blind, Freeze."

The bubble-gum-popping waitress showed up to take their orders.

Colton smiled, instantly sending the teenager into swoon-mode. "I'll have the roast beef on sourdough, and the lady will have turkey on whole wheat with extra pickles."

The teenager nodded and bopped away.

Melanie kicked Colton under the table. "Turkey isn't what I wanted."

He lifted an eyebrow and studied her. The seconds ticked by until she couldn't stand his gaze any longer. "Okay. Turkey may be what I wanted…this time. But you might've been wrong."

"This is a great sandwich place, and turkey is your favorite sandwich," he said.

She lifted her chin. "You don't know me as well as you think."

"I know you kiss like a goddess."

She could only stare. Yep. That was Colton. If there was an issue, a problem, he charged head-on into it. No coyness, no subtlety, no hidden agenda. "I can't believe you said that," she finally choked out.

He took a sip from a sweating water glass. "I figured we should talk about the kiss."

"Why?" She shook her head, panic heating her lungs. She couldn't lose Colton as a friend, not now. Definitely not now. "We're friends. We slipped. It's over."

"I know." He rubbed his cut chin. "But, well, I liked kissing you. It felt—"

Right. It felt right. She nodded. "I know, but we've been best friends forever. I mean, *forever.*" He and Hawk were the certainties in her life. The limited stability she could claim. Of course she was attracted to Colton—the guy was all hard angles and good nature. He also had gone through women like toothbrushes for a long time…and she didn't want to be relegated to an old drawer in the bathroom.

Plus, his girlfriends were usually blond, beautiful, and buxom. Melanie didn't fit into any of those slots. The mere idea of Colton seeing her naked sprang hives over her chest.

The waitress slipped their baskets before them and hustled off to wait on a group of boys who'd just sat down.

Colton eyed his large sandwich. "Is it Milton? Are you serious?"

Melanie reached for a chip. No. She and Brian were more like buddies, but it was nice having somebody as a plus-one. "I don't know. We've been dating for a while, but I'm not sure where we stand." In fact, she probably would know more later after her doctor's appointment, but she didn't want to go into her problems with Colton. Yet.

"Okay." He took a bite of his food. "Remember when we talked about owning a business together as kids?"

She grinned. The boys had wanted to own a strip club, and she'd wanted a horse farm. "I do remember."

"Now's the time," Colt said.

"No." She shook her head, shoving down hope. "I can't invest right now."

"I know. Hawk and I will bankroll the start-up

costs, and your third will be in labor—overseeing the construction and the publicity for the first two martial arts gyms. One in Mineral Lake and the other in Billings," he said.

She tapped her fingers on the table. "I appreciate the vote of confidence, but I don't need a handout."

He grinned, and at that point, she empathized with the Taiwanese broker.

Leaning back, he sighed. "Listen. We need somebody on the front lines, and I'm too busy taking over the business, and Hawk will be overseeing the fighting. It would set his mind at ease to know you were looking after things."

Fire flushed through her. "Don't you dare use Hawk as an emotional point." She hated that he had to leave again for danger so far from home.

Colton shrugged. "I'm just telling you what he said. Plus, we'd have to pay somebody to oversee the construction, so we might as well pay you. We trust you, and now you don't have to work three jobs. Win-win."

"No." She shook her head. "You're not planning my life. Period."

He sobered. "Believe me, I'm not planning anybody's life right now."

She frowned, concern focusing her. "What's wrong?"

He shrugged, an odd vulnerability darkening his eyes. "Maybe nothing. I invested heavily in a business, and it may have been a mistake."

Colton Freeze making a financial mistake? Melanie raised both eyebrows. "Ouch. Can I help?"

"Yes." His upper lip quirked. "Please come on board to oversee the construction of my baby. I need somebody I can trust so I can concentrate on the other matter."

He was impossible. Talk about going for the jugular. Or heartstrings. Owning a business with Colt and Hawk had always been one of her dreams, and there had to be a way to make it happen. She would like to help him, and this might be fun. "If I do agree, then that's my buy-in. No salary."

"We need the salary because we already included the line item as a cost in the construction loan," he countered.

Oh, he had an answer for everything, didn't he? She bit her lip. "I wouldn't mind burning the outfit from Adam's bar."

"Now that would be a pity," Colton said.

She focused on Colton. "Stop flirting with me."

"Can't help it. I know how you kiss." His tone rumbled guttural low.

She rolled her eyes. "I would love to call your bluff, Freeze."

"Not bluffing."

He wasn't. She knew him, and if she made a move, he'd meet her more than halfway. "Our friendship is the only stable thing I have right now. The only stable thing in Hawk's life. I'm not going to ruin it," she said.

"Why haven't we ever gotten together?" Colt's brows drew down in the middle.

She kept herself from squirming on the chair. "By not sleeping with you, I remained in your life. Special." Which was the absolute truth.

He grimaced. "I'm not that bad."

"No, you're not." In fact, he was freakin' amazing.

"You've never wanted to get serious or settle down, and usually whoever you were dating did. So when it ended, you avoided them." If Colton ever avoided her, it would break her heart.

"I'd never avoid you," he said, his eyes flaring.

"I never wanted to take the chance." Now she winced. "Plus, now we're too different."

His cheek creased. "We both own ranches and love it. How are we different?"

"You're loaded with a ton of degrees. I only took one class in college." She squirmed in her seat.

"Seriously?" His amusement fled. "Degrees are just degrees and have nothing to do with intelligence, work, money, or anything else." He shook his head.

She smiled. "Said the guy with a bunch of degrees." Sure, she was smart. But still.

"That's the dumbest thing I've ever heard. If you want a bunch of degrees, go get them. You're one of the smartest people I've ever met, and you thinking this is crazy," he said.

Warmth flushed through her that he realized she was just as smart as he was...even without diplomas. "Maybe. Even so, I'm staying in the friend arena," she said.

"Like I said, you're an intelligent woman." Even so, regret filled his eyes for the briefest of moments. Then his cell phone buzzed, and he glanced at the face, quickly returning the text. "Hawk's in town looking for us. He should be here in a minute."

In less than a minute, Hawk strode in, wearing flak and not cowboy boots.

Melanie's heart dropped. "You're heading out."

"Yes." Any peace or relaxation Hawk had earned

while on leave had fled, leaving his face a hard, cold mask. "Just got my orders. Wanted to say good-bye."

Mel skirted the table to duck into a hug. "Be careful, and come home."

He hugged her back, longer than usual. "I will. You be safe, take care of Colton, and protect my business interests while I'm gone."

She leaned back to smile. "You planned this."

"Nope." A small smile flirted with Hawk's lips. "But I want everything in place when I get back. Please."

"Okay." There was no other answer she could give. "I promise if you come back safely, I'll take care of the construction."

"Excellent." He released her and turned as Colton stood.

Never afraid to show emotion, they hugged, and a lump settled in Melanie's throat.

"Come back." Colton stepped away.

Hawk yanked an envelope from his back pocket. "Just in case." Long strides took him from the room.

Concern bracketed Colton's face as he watched his friend leave. Then, tucking the envelope in his pocket, he sat.

Melanie sat back down. "What's in the envelope?"

Colton shrugged. "He leaves one with me every time, and it feels like a bunch of letters. I'm assuming they're for us, probably my mom, and my sister. I never look and just give it back when he gets home. Like I will this time."

Melanie stilled. "A letter for your sister Dawn?"

"They're good friends," Colton said.

Dawn and Hawk were a lot more than friends, but now wasn't the time. So Melanie nodded and tried to smile. Why did it seem like things were changing? She glanced at the rest of her sandwich, no longer hungry.

She considered asking Colton to accompany her to the doctor's appointment later but quickly discarded the idea. There had to be some personal distance between them if they were going to remain friends and now business partners. Inviting the man to her appointment required an intimacy they didn't have and never would.

Something in her wanted that closeness with him.

For the first time, she wondered if their childhood friendship could last into adulthood when deep down, she was beginning to want more.

CHAPTER FIVE

Colton pushed back in his chair and surveyed his office. Dark paneling covered with landscape paintings of Montana, and more specifically, Maverick County. When he relocated, he'd take the same paintings.

They were home.

Quiet ticked around him since Anne and Tyler had gone out for a late lunch. His shoulders felt like boulders perched on them. Hawk had left for his mission, Dawn was still at school, and now Melanie was dating a banker. One not good enough for her. Plus, the idea of her really falling in love with somebody else turned him cold.

The idea that he needed her so much worried him. This didn't fit in with his life plan for the next few years.

His phone buzzed, and he smiled when he saw it was Sophie. "Hi, Soph. What's up?"

"Colton?" her voice emerged high and frantic. "I'm ten minutes out of the city, and something's wrong."

"Whoa." He stood, already crossing his office. "Wrong with what? The car?"

"No," she whispered. "The baby. I can't find Jake, and I'm an hour from home, and the sheriff, and Doc Mooncaller. You're the closest one to me right now. I don't know what to do."

Panic rushed through Colton to be immediately squashed. There wasn't time for panic if Sophie needed help. He calmed his voice into a soothing tone. "Where are you?" He loped into a run through the office and outside to his truck.

"I pulled over at the Exxon gas station outside of Billings." Tears filled her voice.

Colton started his truck and drove into the street. "Okay, Sophie. Here's the deal. You sit in the car, take deep breaths, and try to calm down. I'll be right there, and I'll take care of everything."

"Okay." She took an audible deep breath.

"Give me an idea of what's happening," he said.

Her voice caught. "I had a bad twisty zing of pain, and now I'm spotting."

That couldn't be good. "Where's Jake today?" Colton asked, his mind calculating the best scenario.

"He's at the federal courthouse in Billings, but his phone is off, so he must be in court," she said.

"Okay." Colton pulled onto the interstate. That was good that Jake was in the city. Very good. "I need to hang up for a second and make a couple of calls, and then I'll call you right back. Okay, sweetheart?"

"Okay." She sniffed.

He hung up and dialed one of his financial clients, the best gynecologist in Montana, and received quick reassurances that they'd see Sophie as soon as he got her there. Then he dialed the courthouse and was told that Mr. Lodge was in court.

"I'm sure, but I need you to get a message to him," Colton said to the curt woman on the phone.

"I'm sorry, but not while he's in court." Derision dripped from the woman's tone.

"Listen lady, we have a family emergency, and you need to get my brother out of court. Now." Colt's rare temper began to compete with the panic sweeping him. "Believe me, while you don't want to face Jake's wrath, you *really* don't want to deal with me. Tell him to meet me at Rollings Women's Center. *Now*."

"Well," she huffed. "I'll see what I can do." She clicked off.

Colton fought a growl and took the exit for the gas station. He found Sophie sitting in her car, tears on her face, pure terror in her eyes.

Instantly, he shot into calmness. "Any more pain?" he asked casually as he helped her from the car.

"Um, no." Her face relaxed marginally. "It's too early for the baby to arrive." Panic reasserted itself as the color slid from her cheeks.

"The baby is not coming." He lifted her into the truck. "This is a glitch, happens all the time." What did he know about pregnant women and babies?

She grinned, her lips trembling. "Been studying the issue, have you?"

No, but he should've been. He shut her door and jogged around to jump in the driver's seat, his mind reeling. "Sure. This is just fine, but we're going to see a doctor anyway. The best in the country."

"The entire country, huh?" Sophie's shoulders relaxed even though her hands shook in her lap. "How fortunate that he lives in Montana."

"Where else would he live?" Colton fought for a reassuring tone as he pulled back onto the interstate, forcing himself to only drive a few miles over the speed limit. Okay, twenty. He cleared his throat. "Did anything like this happen with your last pregnancy?"

"No," she said.

He glanced over, not liking the dark circles under

Sophie's eyes. She looked way too delicate and frightened. "This will be fine. Take another deep breath."

They arrived at the clinic in record time, and Sophie started to open her door.

"Wait." Colton jumped out and crossed around to lift her from the truck.

"I can walk, Colton," she protested.

"No." He hustled into the clinic and marched up to the receptionist. "Doctor Jordan is waiting for us."

The door flew open behind them, and Jake ran inside.

Oh, thank God. Colton turned and deposited Sophie in her husband's arms.

Jake snuggled her close. "Are you okay, Sunshine?"

A nurse opened a door by the receptionist and motioned them inside. "The doctor is waiting for you."

They disappeared after the nurse. Colton swallowed and walked over to sit, dropping his head in his shaking hands. What if he hadn't gotten there in time? Had he driven too quickly and hit too many potholes? What if—

He lifted his head and took several deep breaths. Enough. He'd just sit in the plastic chair and wait for the good news. It would be good news. He wanted to call Quinn or their dad but decided to wait until he heard something. Anything.

So he called the ranch and gave instructions for somebody to drive out and fetch Sophie's car.

Then he waited.

Alone in the waiting room, he watched as woman after woman, all in different phases of pregnancy, went in for an appointment and then left. Some were accompanied by men, some by other women.

Finally, Jake and Sophie exited the mysterious land of pregnant women.

Colton stood and schooled his face into calm lines. "Well?"

Sophie smiled, weariness in every line of her body. "I'm okay."

His butt hit the chair. Thank God.

She touched his shoulder. "Deep breaths, Colton."

He chuckled and stood to hug her. "That's excellent advice." Then for good measure, he hugged his older brother. "We're sure?"

"Yes." Jake clapped him on the back, black eyes still worried. His power tie was askew, and he'd removed his suit jacket. "They can't explain the twinge. I guess a lot of weird stuff happens in pregnancy, but the spotting is normal. We had an ultrasound, and the baby appears healthy—although the doctor has ordered bed rest for Soph the second we get home."

Sophie leaned in. "It's another boy."

He knew it. Colton smiled as his shoulders dropped from up around his ears. "I figured."

"At least we can use Nathan's clothes again." Sophie pressed her hands together. "Now I need to get back to work on the sketches for the sports complex we're building across town."

"No," Jake and Colton said in unison.

Sophie's eyebrow rose. "Huh?"

"Home to bed. The doctor said bed rest." Jake shoved a hand through his thick black hair.

Sophie nodded, still way too pale. "I know, but I can sketch from bed."

Jake nodded. "I guess that makes sense, so long as you sleep a lot, too. We'll need to figure out what to do with your car."

"I had somebody from the ranch go get it," Colton said.

"Thanks," Jake said, his gaze intense.

"No problem," Colton said.

Jake stepped closer to him. "No, I mean *thanks*. Really."

Colton nodded, his throat closing.

A nurse in pink scrubs bustled out from behind the receptionist with a purple box in her hands. "Mrs. Lodge? These are the new prenatal vitamins we're recommending and giving to all our pregnant patients. Run them by Doc Mooncaller when you see him, but they have a better balance of the calcium and iron, and we really like them."

Sophie took the box with a big smile. "Thanks."

Colton escorted them outside and to Jake's truck. "I have to close down the office but will head home afterward. Call me if you need anything."

They drove off, and Colton stood for a moment, letting the cool breeze calm him. Across the street sat a bar, and he really wanted a drink. But he probably wouldn't stop at one, and the last thing he needed was Quinn arresting him for a DUI once he'd driven back to town. So, he headed for the ice cream store next to the bar. It was probably too cold to eat ice cream, but he didn't care at the moment.

He greatly enjoyed his double scoop of mint chocolate chip and was almost calm by the time he'd finished the cone. Buying a small vanilla cone in case Tyler still played at the office, he turned toward the door.

Right in time to see Melanie exit the gynecologist's office—with a big purple box of prenatal vitamins in her hands.

He faltered and dropped the vanilla ice cream on the floor.

CHAPTER SIX

Melanie tucked the box of prenatal vitamins in her purse and ducked her head against the wind as she headed toward the jewelry store to return Loni's brooch. She texted Brian to meet her at the store, hoping they could grab a latte.

She returned the brooch and turned around to run straight into Brian's mother. Ugh. "Hello, Mrs. Milton."

Mrs. Milton slid her designer sunglasses off her Botoxed face. "Melanie." She glanced around the store. "Looking for rings, are we?"

Melanie forced her smile to remain in place. "No. Are you?"

"Of course not. A lady doesn't buy herself rings, dear." Condescension dripped from the woman's tone as she glanced down at Melanie's jeans and boots, which were an obvious contrast to Mrs. Milton's designer knit suit. "I've been meaning to have a talk with you, anyway."

Well, that was just great. "About?" Melanie asked, eyeing the door.

Mrs. Milton leaned in. "About your obvious attempts to secure child support for the next eighteen years."

Melanie took a deep breath. "Excuse me?"

"Brian told me about your medical condition, and I have to say, good effort on your part." Mrs. Milton clucked her tongue. "You wouldn't be the first to try to enter my family in such a way, but your manipulations aren't going to work."

Apparently the gloves were off. Melanie leaned down toward the shorter woman. "I believe that's how you became a Milton, right? Knocked up with Brian's older brother?"

Red suffused the woman's pampered cheeks. "Well, I never."

"Oh, I believe you must have." Melanie edged toward the door.

Of course, Brian chose that moment to walk inside. His three-piece suit hung nicely on a fit frame, and his blond hair appeared ruffled. He took one look at the women and sighed. "Afternoon, ladies. What's going on?"

Melanie chuckled. "Well, your mom is ordering me to stay away from you, and my response could be accurately characterized as telling her to bite me."

Brian's grin emerged quick before he sobered, rubbing the smile off his clean-cut, handsome face.

"Brian, I absolutely forbid you from seeing this gold digger. She just wants to raise her station," his mother intoned, obviously not caring who heard.

Melanie snorted. "Station? Listen lady, you live in Billings, Montana, and not upstate New York. High society…you're not."

"I will not sit here and be insulted like this. Brian, I'll see you back at the bank." With a loud sniff and her nose in the air, Mrs. Milton swept from the jewelry store.

Brian grimaced. "Did you have to get in a fight with my mom?"

Melanie shrugged, starting to feel guilty. "She started it."

Brian eyed the lone woman behind a counter showcasing sparkling sapphires. "Hi, Maisey. I don't suppose there's any way you could keep this little family argument quiet?"

Maisey pushed cat-eye glasses up her nose and patted her long gray hair. "Not a chance, Brian. Not even a remote of a chance." Her grin sported fancy dentures.

"That's what I figured. Have a nice day, ma'am." Slipping an arm across Melanie's shoulders, he escorted her back into the weak sunshine. "My mom does have her good points, you know."

The poor guy didn't even sound like he was convinced of that. "I know, and I'm sorry I let her bait me. Why did you tell her about my doctor's visit?"

"I didn't. I researched endometriosis on a computer at the bank, and she saw it. So I kind of had to explain." He sighed. "What did the doctor say?"

"Nothing, yet. He took eggs, and I'll find out tomorrow if they're viable to be frozen. So someday I may have my own genetic kid. Maybe." She tried to keep her voice light. The medical bills were killing her, but what choice did she have?

"Getting pregnant right now might be the solution," he said, stopping the walk.

At that second, her relationship with Brian clarified with a sharpness in her mind. She smiled. "Please don't tell me you're willing to knock me up just to escape your mother."

He chuckled, his brown eyes twinkling. "The idea does have merit. But, no. I was thinking we should give it a shot for us. For a good future together." As proposals went, it was as lukewarm as possible.

"I like you." Which was the absolute truth. When she envisioned her future, he wasn't in it. Or rather, he was in it as a friend—a good one. "We're not in love."

"Are you sure?" Brian sobered. "Give me a chance, Melanie."

She didn't love him—and tying them together with a child would hurt them both. "I'm sorry."

He sighed, the sound full of regret. "So this is it?"

"Yeah." Dating him had been fun and comfortable, but after one kiss with Colton, she wanted that feeling again. Maybe not with Colt, but with somebody. Somebody who could knock her socks off. "I'm sorry."

Brian's head lifted while his lips pursed. "Don't be. I'm fine."

Even so, she'd hurt his ego and not his heart. Speaking of which—"I wish you'd follow your heart." *Lame line, Mel.*

"I have a heart?" Brian asked.

"Of course." She tugged on his lapels for the last time. "You left it on a beach in Malibu during college. Go back there…start a surf shop…and enjoy your life. It's too short to spend behind a banking counter when you don't want to be there."

A faraway look came into his eyes. "But my family—"

"Will understand you have your own dreams. Besides, you have three brothers. Statistically, one of them will like numbers." If not, they should all go find their bliss, as far as she was concerned.

"I'll think about it." He brushed a good-bye kiss on her forehead. "So, friends?"

"Absolutely," Melanie said, meaning it.

A slightly insulting expression of relief crossed his

face. Breaking up would probably help him with his family, especially his tyrant of a mother.

Melanie turned away to head for her truck, her mind spinning. Her boyfriend was now her friend, her sexy best friend was now occupying her dreams, and her body was betraying her.

Fate had a cruel sense of humor.

• • •

Late afternoon, after driving back home, Melanie finished the last of her hot chocolate while walking down the main street of Mineral Lake. She'd had to dig for change in her empty pocketbook, but she'd found enough for the small treat. Folks strolled along storefronts, emerging from restaurants and coffee shops, all bundled up against the Montana spring weather. Warmth was a myth this early in March, and a day could go from full sunshine to hail to snow to rain in less than an hour.

One woman pushed a baby stroller, and Melanie's heart thumped hard. She saw babies everywhere now. Freezing her eggs so she could someday have a baby was a logical decision, even though it emptied her pocketbook.

"Melanie?" a low voice called from behind her.

She turned to find Colton and Leila standing hand in hand.

"Hi, you two." Her lips faltered as she tried to swallow. Colt had such a way with kids.

Colton grinned. "We're glad we spotted you. Join us for an early dinner."

"Thanks, but I know it's your special night. I'll let

you two get back to your date." She grinned at Leila, who'd worn a pretty yellow jacket and jeans for the big night. Her long black hair was up in pigtails, and she'd put on pink lip gloss. "Your date is lovely, by the way."

Leila grinned. "You're pretty, too. Come to dinner and then a movie with us."

"Oh, no. I wouldn't want to impose." Melanie needed to get the heck away from her too sexy friend. Just let her libido die down a bit, and things would get back to normal.

Colton reached for her elbow. "Have you eaten since lunch?"

"Well, no. I'll grab a burger or something on the way home," Melanie said.

"No." He propelled her into Sally's Restaurant. "You need to eat healthier, Mel."

She swallowed. "What in the world is wrong with you?" Colton Freeze had never given one fig about her eating habits.

He glanced at Leila and then back at Mel. "We can talk about it later. For now, we're here, and we're all eating a healthy dinner." He turned toward a row of long booths by the window. "Pick a table, Leila, my girl. Any table you want."

Leila danced ahead and scooted into the booth. "I get to sit by Mel," she called out.

Colton waited patiently.

Melanie thought about arguing, but suddenly she was hungry. And curious. Very curious as to what had gotten into Colt. Maybe the new health kick had something to do with opening up the gyms. "Fine, but you need to stop acting so weird."

"I'm just getting started," he muttered as they slid

into the booth across from each other.

The waitress bopped up to take their drink orders.

"Pop?" Leila asked hopefully.

"Lemonade or water," Colton said. "For all of us."

Melanie frowned. She could use come caffeine, but understanding Colton's need to steer Leila into a healthy zone, she nodded. "The lemonades here are fresh."

"Good." Colton leaned forward. "How's your garden at home?"

She smiled, relaxing. "Excellent. I had a great crop last summer and canned a bunch of fresh fruit and vegetables." She loved gardening—from the planting to the harvesting. As a hobby, it was a productive one.

Thus began an interesting dinner of Colton pointing out the healthier alternatives to just about… everything. He even managed to cover the necessity of sleep and exercise.

By the time they walked down the street toward the old-fashioned movie theater, Mel was more bemused than irritated. "Have fun at the movie."

Colton slipped an arm around her shoulder. "You have to finish the date with us, right Leila?"

Leila grinned up. "Yes. We get popcorn at the movie."

Colton faltered. "Well, the salt might be too much."

Melanie stopped cold. Last time he was home, she'd caught him with what could only be termed an orange lunch. Cheeseburger, Cheetos, and macaroni 'n' cheese. "What in the living daylights is wrong with you?"

He shrugged, color filling his high cheekbones. "Salt makes people retain too much water."

Melanie glanced down at her jeans. "Do I look like

I'm retaining water?" She shrugged out from under his arm and looked up into his face. "Be very careful with your answer here, Colton Freeze. I have no problem kicking your butt in front of your niece."

Leila giggled. "That sounds fun."

Colton backed away on the slushy ground, his hands up. "No. You look great." His gaze swept her head to toe and warmed enough to heat the air around them. He swallowed, and his voice lowered. "Really great."

A ball of need unfurled in Melanie's abdomen. How did he do that just with his voice? "Okay. So, let's go to the movie, have popcorn, and even candy."

"Yay!" Leila jumped up and down.

Colton opened his mouth and quickly shut it. "Good enough."

They started back down the street until Mrs. Hudson stopped them. Single, elderly, and sweet, the widow lived at the end of Main Street and was always present. "Why hello, young folks. You out for a date?"

"Yes," Leila answered for all of them.

Mrs. Hudson nodded her gray head and smoothed down her fluorescent green coat. "I heard you broke up with the Milton boy, Melanie. He's a nice boy, but probably not the right one for you."

"They haven't broken up," Colton said slowly.

Mel cut him a look, not surprised the gossip had already reached town. "Actually, we broke up this afternoon, but we're still friends. It's all good." Then she stepped back at the fire shooting through Colt's blue eyes.

His jaw hardened, making him look dangerous. Deadly even. "Why didn't you say something?" The soft tone of voice was all the more frightening for the anger behind it.

Melanie blinked. "I don't know. It actually wasn't that big of a deal. We've been just friends for a while, really."

Loni and Tom Freeze suddenly emerged from the coffee shop. While Loni was dark and petite, her husband was broad with sparkling blue eyes that Colton had obviously inherited. They'd both bundled up in colorful scarfs.

"Off to the movie, folks?" Tom asked, his gaze focused on his youngest son.

"Not a big deal?" Colton asked, his gaze remaining on Melanie. "I'll kill him. I swear to God."

Melanie stepped back from the fury. "Why? I'm telling you, we're fine. What is wrong with you?"

"Son?" Loni asked, sliding her hand along his visibly vibrating arm.

"This isn't okay, not at all." Colton gentled his voice. "I'll talk to Milton tomorrow and work everything out. I promise."

Aliens had abducted her best friend, because there was no way Colton would act like this. "Have you had a stroke recently?" Melanie spit the words out between clenched teeth, her temper awakening. The conversation in the middle of the street with onlookers was just too much.

"Funny, and no." Colton lifted his chin. "There is no way you're breaking up, and Milton is stepping up if I have to beat him senseless."

That was it. "You have lost your freakin' mind. Get the heck out of my business and right now." She put her hands on her hips.

"No." He continued to ignore everyone around them.

Enough. She jerked away from him. "I'm out of here. Call me when you regain your sanity."

"You're not going anywhere by yourself. You're upset, and I'll take you home." Colt's voice went guttural with temper as he whirled her back around.

"Why would I need a ride home?" she yelled, her temper springing loose.

"Because you're pregnant," he yelled right back.

The world halted. Several couples turned around from various positions on Main Street to stare. Mrs. Hudson slapped a hand over her mouth. Tom went still. Loni whirled toward Melanie, and Leila clapped her hands together with glee.

Melanie's mouth opened and closed, but no sound came out.

CHAPTER SEVEN

"You are one stupid dumbass," Melanie said on the way to Billings the next day.

"That's the general consensus," Colt agreed from the driver's seat of his Ford pickup. "Again, I'm so sorry I announced to the town that you were knocked up by Milton."

She hunched her shoulders. "It's not just that. Now the whole town knows I'm having female problems. Jimmy Balbie at the bank asked if I needed to sit down while I was waiting to make a payment earlier this morning. When I turned around, he actually stepped back like I was going to hit him."

Colton's lips twitched. "I'm sorry. Again."

"Whatever. You know the only reason I'm letting you drive me to my appointment today is because I couldn't say no to your mother," Melanie muttered.

"I'm fully aware of that." Colton eyed the rearview mirror and signaled to exit the interstate.

Loni had quickly stepped in the previous night to sort out all of the confusion. Then she'd made sure everyone in town was clear that Melanie was not pregnant.

Colton cleared his throat. "Did you know there's a town bet on what day we get together?"

Melanie glanced up. "*We* as in you and me—we?"

"Yes," he said.

"Are you kidding?"

"No, and I almost didn't bring it up, but I figured

you'd want to know. I'm not sure who's taking bets, but I will find out." Colton parked the truck at the clinic. "What's going on today? Exactly?"

Melanie took a deep breath. Might as well tell him the truth. "They harvested eggs from me yesterday, and today I find out if they are strong enough to be frozen for future use."

"Um, okay." Colton unfolded his large frame from the truck and crossed to open her door. "This explains the money problems you're having."

She nodded. "No health insurance, and these tests cost a fortune. You're right—I'm dead broke."

One eyebrow rose. "You could've asked for help."

"This is personal." She couldn't believe he was even here with her. "Although it is nice of you to bring me to my appointment."

He helped her from the truck. "You're not getting naked or anything today?"

"Nope." Just his saying the word *naked* made her want to strip.

"I'd like to come in with you to talk to the doctor. I have questions." Colton shut her door and pressed his hand to her lower back in a touch that was both reassuring and possessive.

The touch zinged right between her legs. What was wrong with her? She had enough problems without getting turned on by Colton Freeze. Well, she'd tell him anything the doctor said, so why not? "Okay."

"Great. So why do you have prenatal vitamins, anyway?" Colton asked.

Melanie shrugged. "Just in case, I guess. They're giving them to anybody even considering getting pregnant."

"I see." They checked in, and the petite twenty-something receptionist smiled at Colton like they were old friends.

"Back again?" she asked.

He returned the grin. "Can't stay away."

"With your wife this time?" The woman appraised Melanie.

"She's the only woman in the world for me," Colton returned easily. He ran his hand down Melanie's arm as they turned for the seating area in a way that sped up Melanie's heart while asserting a connection.

As if they were a couple—a real couple.

He'd filled Melanie in on Sophie's adventure the previous day on the way into Billings. How frightened the woman must've been.

"I'm glad Sophie is all right," Melanie whispered, although the waiting room was currently empty.

"Me too. Though she may kill Jake if he doesn't stop hovering," Colton said.

"Poor Sophie," Melanie said, keeping her voice level. What she wouldn't give to have a hovering husband who cared about her health, about her future. She eyed Colton. He'd make a great husband someday.

He caught her glance and reached down to twine their fingers together. "Stop worrying. It'll be all right."

His palm enclosed hers in warmth and security, sending electricity up her arm to zing through her chest. She glanced down at his darker skin against her much smaller hand. While she was by no means petite, compared to Colt, she was small. Feminine. Her nipples peaked. Thank goodness she'd worn a bra today.

She had to get herself under control. One little kiss,

and she was looking at Colton under a different light. One that included nude, moving parts. Although a part of her was beginning to think…what the heck. Why not make a move and take a chance?

The nurse broke her from her internal musings by calling her name and escorting them back into a doctor's office with two leather chairs facing a massive teak desk. A plethora of diplomas decorated the walls along with a couple of pictures of the doctor holding a huge rainbow trout.

Dr. Jordan leaned forward, his gray eyes serious and matching his beard. "Please have a seat." He smiled. "I didn't realize you'd be here, Colton."

Colt settled Melanie and then sat down. "I'm here for moral support."

"Good." The doctor paused to read papers in an open manila file.

Melanie's pulse quickened, and a rock dropped into her stomach. She shifted uneasily.

Colton took her hand, and the world settled.

The doctor pushed his glasses up on his forehead as he finished reading. "None of the eggs were viable for cryopreservation. I'm sorry, Melanie."

Cold washed through her. She blinked and then nodded. Pain lanced along her empty abdomen.

Colton leaned forward while keeping her hand. "Why not?"

The doctor steepled his fingers under his chin. "Tons of reasons. It might be premature ovarian failure, but I won't know why or how without genetic research."

"Even then, you probably won't know, right?" Colt asked.

Melanie's head was in a cloud as she turned his way.

"I researched fertility," he said.

"Maybe." The doctor's glasses dropped back into place. "We may have harvested too early, however. We can try again, but I'm still concerned about the endometriosis. Even if we successfully harvest eggs, you have a small window where I believe you'll be able to carry a child."

"Right now," Melanie said quietly. The emptiness in her grew to pain.

"More than likely, and you probably have about a five percent chance right now." The doctor winced. "Although new treatments are coming forth every day for infertility and endometriosis. I wouldn't lose hope."

"Thank you." She had to get out of there before breaking down. Tears choked her throat. She retrieved her hand and stood. "I need to think about options and will be in touch." As if in a dream, a bad one, she hitched through the office and out the door. She was tough, and she could handle this.

A sharp wind slapped her in the face.

She made it about halfway down the walkway before stopping.

Colton stopped beside her and lifted her chin with one knuckle. "It's okay, Mel. We'll figure this out."

It was the gentle tone that broke her. She burst into tears and barely had a moment to appreciate Colton's *oh shit* expression before he gathered her close, tucking her into warmth and safety.

"I know I shouldn't have hung my hat on cryopreservation, but…" She started crying harder, her face against his strong chest.

He held her easily, gently rubbing her back, his voice reassuring. A strong, masculine calm in the middle of a wild storm. "Let it out."

So she did. Holding on, allowing him to shield her, she cried for the future she'd never have.

• • •

Colton half-pivoted to put Mel between the brick building and his body when the wind picked up in force. He kept his movements smooth and gentle, tamping down on pure frustration.

He'd stand between her and any danger, but he couldn't protect her from this. Helplessness didn't set well with him. At all. His mind calculated the way to fix things. To get her to stop crying. He had money, and he'd take her to every specialist in the world.

Winding down with a small shudder, she lifted her head.

Tears clung to dark lashes over her pretty brown eyes. Tracks showed on her smooth skin, and suddenly she felt small and delicate in his arms. Vulnerable. Emotion ripped through his heart with the force of an anvil.

He moved without thinking, stepping into her and covering her mouth with his. The kiss was supposed to be calming, to be gentle.

But as she moaned and pressed against him, his mind shut down. He stilled for one tiny second and then gave in. He fisted her hair, tilting back her head, and went deep. Sweeping inside her mouth, taking, claiming.

Need roared through him, and he grabbed the back of her leg, lifting against his hip and pushing her against the brick. Pressing his cock against the heated apex of her legs.

She sighed deep in her throat and rubbed along his length, tilting her hips for better friction. He had to get inside her. *Now.*

His hand was on her breast before he remembered where they were. Who they were.

He levered back, his breath panting, his chest heaving.

Shock and desire comingled in her dark eyes. His gaze dropped to her swollen, pink lips, and he groaned. He'd give everything he owned to have those wrapped around his cock. Just once.

She gasped and let her foot drop.

A couple of ladies passed by behind him, twittering.

Red bloomed across Mel's smooth cheekbones. He stepped back, his brain swirling, his dick trying to punch through his zipper.

She swallowed. "M-my hair."

His hand was still clamped in her hair. Slowly, he disengaged, trying not to pull. She winced as he untangled himself.

He should be a gentleman and apologize. The words stuck in his throat. While he may be feeling a lot of things, sorry wasn't one of them. Not even close. But he retreated and gave her some room.

A myriad of expressions crossed her face, and he read each one clearly. He'd always been able to read her, even when she hadn't wanted him to. Desire, confusion, embarrassment, need…every emotion he was feeling flickered in her eyes.

He took a deep breath. "I promise I'll fix this, Mel. Trust me."

CHAPTER EIGHT

Trust me. Melanie shook her head as she left the coffee shop in town the next day. The man was certifiable — there was no way he could fix her situation. He'd driven her home the previous night, and they'd each stayed lost in their own thoughts. The silence had been heavy with way too much thinking, but neither had broken it.

He had to be regretting attending her appointment and then kissing her. Of course, it was the emotion of the moment. No way did Colt want more from her than friendship.

But he sure hadn't kissed her like a friend.

Loni Freeze stepped out of Millard's Mercantile across the street and waved. "Hi, Melanie." Hustling across the quiet road with several packages under her arms, the woman smiled. "What's up?"

Melanie grabbed a package before it hit the slushy ground. "Nothing. Just wandering and thinking."

Loni scrunched her nose. With her smooth skin and dark hair sprinkled with gray, she looked too young to have two grandchildren with another on the way. "About anything in particular?"

Melanie shrugged. "About everything."

"Ah, I've been there. Sometimes you just have to relax and let your subconscious take over." Loni eyed Paul's Pizza Joint, which proudly took up several window fronts next to the mercantile. "Let's grab pizza and figure this out before it starts snowing or raining or sleeting again."

On cue, Melanie's stomach rumbled. "Okay." She followed Loni into the restaurant, and they agreed on a loaded veggie pizza.

Loni yanked out her phone and typed in letters. "Let me text Sophie to see if she wants a pizza. The poor woman is going crazy on bed rest."

Melanie smiled. "I'm sure. In fact, I don't think I've ever seen her rest." The blonde was a whirlwind.

"Yeah—she's struggling, but that baby will be worth it. I have to say, being the grandmama is a lot easier than being the mom." Loni took a sip of her iced tea. A glint of amusement lightened her dark eyes.

Melanie probably wouldn't be either. She swallowed and tried to smile. "I bet."

Loni's eyes softened, and she reached out to pat Mel's hand. "Everything will work out, sweetheart. I promise."

Melanie flashed back to the third grade when Loni had stepped in. "Do you remember that teacher, Mrs. Simpson? My third grade math teacher?"

Loni sniffed. "I would hardly call that woman a teacher. She sure didn't last long here."

No, she hadn't. Melanie had been staying with the Freezes while her grandfather was on a cattle run, and she'd brought home a math paper with some pretty harsh grading and a request for Melanie's *guardian* to visit the teacher.

Loni had dressed to kill in a business suit and accompanied a quaking Melanie to the school. Then she'd politely waited until Mrs. Simpson, a twice-divorced redhead who spent more time on the single male teacher-parent conferences than anyone else in the history of the school, finished complaining how Melanie couldn't concentrate on numbers and just daydreamed. That maybe she should be put back to the remedial math program of the previous grade.

Melanie, dressed in her best Sunday-school dress, had hung her head, ashamed Mrs. Freeze would realize how dumb she was.

Then Mrs. Freeze had let loose.

Without raising her voice, without using swear words, Mrs. Freeze had calmly explained if there was a problem, it was with Mrs. Simpson's lazy, irresponsible approach to teaching, which was more in line with speed dating. If Mrs. Simpson wanted to catch husband number three, trolling in the elementary school was the wrong tack.

It had taken Melanie several days to figure out what *trolling* meant.

Then Loni had expressed, in great detail, how intelligent and hardworking Melanie was, and that she would someday be highly successful. Loni had wound down with strongly encouraging Mrs. Simpson to try harder as a teacher.

There may have been a veiled threat or two in there, but Melanie didn't read between the lines for several years.

They'd marched out of the school with both of their heads held high. It was in that moment Melanie figured out two things: one, Colton had the best mom in the whole world. And two, she'd never be alone. She was safe.

Then they'd spent several afternoons after school learning multiplication in a way that involved horses, cookies, and hair barrettes. Melanie had gone on to excel in math and even took college math classes while in high school.

Even years later, Loni was Melanie's hero. Melanie smiled. "You took care of Mrs. Simpson, didn't you?" The woman certainly had the clout to get a teacher removed.

Loni shrugged, her eyes sparkling. "Don't know what you mean."

"Thanks for standing up for me."

"Your grandfather would've done the same thing if he'd been in town, although, I do have my own style." Loni laughed. "Plus, you were a great kid, and that teacher was rotten."

It was nice to have people in her corner. Melanie had missed the fun times at the Freeze house when she and Colton had gone their own ways as teenagers. Somewhat, anyway. Colton and Hawk had always been her backup, even when they'd all been dating other people. "Thanks."

Loni leaned back as the pizza was brought to the table. "No biggie. So, how are you holding up?"

"Good." She realized it was true. Sharing her problems and bawling all over Colt had actually made her feel better. "I wish the whole town didn't know, but…oh well."

"Ah, sweetie. The town always knows." Loni slipped slices onto their plates. "It's good that you and Colton are there for each other. I like that."

Melanie took a bite and chewed thoughtfully. Warm, gooey cheese landed in her stomach, and she sighed in pleasure. "By the way, have you heard anything about a bet involving Colton and me?"

Loni coughed and quickly took a sip of iced tea. "Bet? What bet?" Her eyes opened wide.

"Oh, come on." Melanie snorted. "You're terrible at bluffing. Please tell me you haven't actually bet."

"Of course not." Loni grinned. "I wouldn't jinx things that way."

Now that was just sweet. Loni had never hidden her affection for Melanie nor her wish that she and Colton would get together. She'd also never meddled or tried to push them together.

Melanie sighed. "How much is the pot?"

Loni leaned forward and dropped her voice to a whisper. "I heard the kitty is at about five grand."

Melanie gasped. "Are you joking?"

"Nope."

"Who's the bet taker?" Melanie asked.

Loni shrugged. "I'm sure I don't know."

Yeah, right. The town always knew.

• • •

Colton drove into town and slid into a slush covered parking slot before unfolding from the truck.

"Colton." Mrs. Hudson emerged from the coffee shop, her gray wool coat swallowing her, and a bright pink knit scarf wrapped around her neck several times. "Do you have a minute?"

He hustled toward the elderly lady. "Yes, ma'am. What can I do for you?" Last night he'd already apologized for the mix-up with Melanie.

Mrs. Hudson slipped her bony arm through his. "We can chat while you escort me toward my car." Her worn boots matched her scarf, and he made a mental note to make sure she got some new boots before next winter. Maybe he should find her some rain boots for the rest of spring. Yeah. Good idea.

"I'd love to escort you." He angled his body to protect her better from the wind. The woman lived at the end of Main Street and had driven three blocks instead of walking. Rain or snow, the woman normally walked, probably so she didn't miss anything on the way. "I noticed you drove instead of walked today. Are you feeling all right?"

"Yes, I felt like a drive today. Plus, it's going to sleet, and I didn't want to get caught." She twittered and patted his arm. "You're such a fine young man. My niece, Beatrix, is visiting at the end of the week, and I was hoping you'd take her out and show her the town."

The woman had always been a matchmaker. He smiled. "That's kind of you, and I appreciate your thinking of me, but I have plans."

Mrs. Hudson slowed down. "Well, she'll only be here two weeks, and I have to admit, she's quite easy."

He coughed out air and glanced down at tight, gray curls. "Excuse me?"

She looked up and squinted faded blue eyes. "Beatrix. She gets around, a lot." Mrs. Hudson shrugged. "I thought you two might have some fun for a couple of weeks before she leaves. Just two weeks."

Colton stopped. What in the world? Realization smacked him in the face stronger than the wild wind. "Mrs. Hudson. You wouldn't have entered a bet regarding Melanie Jacoby and me, would you have?"

Mrs. Hudson brushed invisible lint off her coat. "Of course not."

Colton bit back a laugh. "Tell me the truth, or I'll go propose to Mel right now."

Mrs. Hudson gasped, her head shooting up so she could meet his gaze. "You wouldn't."

"Oh, I would," Colton said.

"Fine." Mrs. Hudson sighed. "I have St. Paddy's Day as my date, and I sure could use the money, Colton Freeze. If you'd just declare your love that day, I'd really appreciate it."

He couldn't believe she'd tried to bribe him with a slutty niece. Mrs. Hudson was a pimp. He laughed. "I will certainly keep your date in mind. Who's taking the bets and keeping the money, anyway?"

"Can't tell you," she said sadly. "When you make the bet, you have to swear not to tell, or you forfeit your money."

When he found the bet taker, he was going to kick some ass. "What happens if your chosen day passes?"

"You get to make a new bet." She tugged him back into moving toward a blue compact with new tires. "Then you give new money and have to make the promise again."

"Those are lovely tires, Mrs. Hudson." Colton escorted her around to the driver's side.

"Thank you. I won the raffle for new tires at the sheriff's station," she said proudly, opening the door and slipping inside the driver's seat.

Quinn had made sure she won after having bought the tires for her in the first place. "You're a lucky one," Colton said.

She nodded. "Have a nice day, Colton, and remember who covered for you in the fifth grade when you picked flowers from Mrs. Leiton's garden. She's still wondering who took her prized tulips, and as you know, she has a terrible temper." Shutting her door, Mrs. Hudson drove down the street at least ten miles under the speed limit.

Good lord. Mrs. Hudson was a blackmailing pimp.

CHAPTER NINE

Melanie gave one last chance at arguing with Loni about the check for lunch. "It was my turn to pay."

"I don't think so." Loni stood and then stopped. "Oh. Colton's here."

Melanie turned, still in her seat. Colton had obviously been working the ranch, dressed in faded jeans, cowboy boots, a dark T-shirt, and a black Stetson. As he strode toward her, he looked more sexy villain than smooth good guy.

Hence the black hat.

Heat spiraled into her abdomen.

He kept his dark blue gaze on her, but he kissed his mama on the cheek.

Loni patted his arm. "I have an appointment, but I think Melanie was considering dessert."

No, she hadn't been.

"Good." Colton took Loni's vacated seat and removed his hat. "We need to talk anyway."

Loni all but beamed as she exited the restaurant.

Melanie focused on him. "I'm handling my own life."

Colt slowly lifted one eyebrow in a curiously dangerous way. "There's nothing wrong with leaning on friends."

Frustration heated her lungs. "When did you start seeing me as some helpless female?"

He studied her for a moment. "I've never seen you as helpless, and I've *always* seen you as a female. You were a cute little girl, a pretty teenager, and now you're a sexy woman."

Heat climbed into her face, sparking her breasts on the way. "You're giving me a headache."

He grinned. "That's the opposite effect I want."

"What do you want?" The words rushed out of her, and she both wanted to know and didn't want to know the answer.

"Right now I want to help you have a baby," he said.

The waitress gasped as she approached the table. In her twenties, she'd dyed her hair a fun purple to match her eye shadow.

Melanie took a deep breath. The statement would be all over town within minutes. "Julie, I'll take the chocolate sundae with extra chocolate, please." The pizza place didn't sell liquor, or she'd order tequila.

"Vanilla scoop in a bowl," Colton said without flicking his gaze from Melanie's face.

Julie almost tripped over her sensible shoes as she hurried from sight. Probably to start texting friends.

Melanie shook her head. "I-I don't, I mean, you—"

"Not with me." Colton grinned.

A surprising disappointment swirled through her. "Oh. Of course not."

Colton sat back and blinked. "You don't want to, ah, have a baby with me, do you?"

Okay. The complete alarm he was trying to hide wasn't exactly complimentary. "No," she said. Having his kid and just being his good buddy would only cause heartache for her, especially when Colt finally fell for somebody. Somebody *not* her.

He frowned. "Okay." The word sounded a bit disgruntled.

She cleared her throat. "Um, I'm fairly certain the waitress misinterpreted your statement and is now texting everyone in town you offered to knock me up."

Surprise lifted his eyebrows. "Are you sure?"

"Oh, yeah. Definitely," she said.

"Hmm. You wouldn't classify the statement as a declaration of love, would you?" Colton asked.

Goodness, her friend had lost his freakin' mind. "No."

His expression cleared. "Good."

She blinked several times, searching for reality. "Why?"

"The bet. When I declare my love for you, the bet ends." He stretched his neck.

Flutters cascaded through her stomach. Love? No. No way. "Says who?"

"Mrs. Hudson. She needs me to do so on St. Paddy's Day and tried to bribe me with an easy niece." Colton grinned.

The flutters turned into wild batwings. His smile was too much…just too much. Melanie swallowed. "That's terrible."

"Maybe." Colton leaned forward and grasped her hands.

Fire shot through her with an electric arc. "W-what are you doing?"

"I called the doctor for more information earlier, and your window is short, Mel. If you want to have a baby, now is the time," he said.

She was the last Jacoby alive, and she'd wanted to have a baby. To keep her family alive. But at what cost? She'd felt all right freezing eggs, but to get pregnant right now? There was no other choice if she wanted to have a child. "I may go to the sperm clinic in Seattle." Sure, a lot of women did it, but being a single mom running a ranch would definitely be difficult.

"Perfect. I have a list of specialists you can see in Seattle, as well." His thumb stroked her palm, and she bit back a groan of need. The touch was light, sensual, and way more erotic than she would've dreamed.

"Well, I guess I might head to Seattle." Right? She hated that her body was forcing her into this decision when she wasn't ready. But deep down, irritation welled at how accepting Colt was about her becoming pregnant. Maybe it was because they wouldn't know the sperm donor? Or maybe he really did only see her as a friend and didn't wonder a little bit about them, like she did.

Colt released her and leaned back when the waitress delivered their desserts. "I'll see if we can lease Hank's plane for the ride."

Private plane? Hank's car dealerships succeeded all over the Pacific Northwest, and he owned a private jet that flew him around when he wanted. At about ninety and crotchety, the guy didn't travel much any longer. "Um, *we*?" Melanie slipped her spoon into the chocolaty mess.

"Sure." Colt tried his ice cream, his gaze thoughtful. "You shouldn't go alone, and I can combine the trip with some business. I'm still worried about that firm I invested in so heavily, so I'd like to see if I can fix the situation."

Melanie started. "How heavily?"

He sighed. "Enough to have me concerned, but I'll take care of it. Plus, on the plane, we can review the plans for the gym. I'm picking them up from the architect later today."

A plane ride, in a private jet, with sexy Colton…to go get inseminated with somebody else's sperm? Gee. Now that sounded like a vacation come true.

Melanie forced a smile. "Can't wait."

• • •

Thunder bellowed across the wide Montana sky outside, and Melanie hustled around the ranch house to grab flashlights and candles. She loved a good winter storm. Since the temperature had warmed up, they probably wouldn't get full snow. But sometimes the rain became spectacular.

The house had stood proudly in place for generations and would easily weather the storm. Two stories, it held three bedrooms on the top floor, while the living areas were on the main floor. Her grandfather had raised her in the family home after her parents had died in a plane crash, and sometimes she still felt his presence.

Today while she'd mucked out stalls, she'd sang his favorite Garth Brooks tunes. She loved ranching. Love the smells, the sights, even the uncertainty. She'd never want to do anything else.

She flicked off the kitchen lights and wandered into the large living room. A stone fireplace took up one wall, while a wide bank of windows framed majestic mountains out the back. It was barely dusk, but soon the clouds would cover any remaining sun.

She'd donned comfortable yoga pants and a heavy shirt for the evening show. Placing her warm coffee with brandy on a table, she tucked herself into an overstuffed chair with an ottoman to watch the storm.

As if Mother Nature had waited just for Melanie, lightning sparked a fluorescent purple over the white-capped mountains.

Beautiful. Absolutely stunning.

The skies opened with a crack, and icy rain slashed down. She fetched her mug and sipped thoughtfully.

Lightning jagged across the sky again, illuminating the creek outside the window. She gasped and rushed to the window. Waiting. Another flash, illuminating a massive heifer tangled and kicking ice.

Panic coughed up Melanie's throat, and she slid her cup onto a table. The creek wasn't frozen all the way through, and if the cow didn't stop kicking, it'd plunge to an icy death.

How did it get so close to the creek, anyway? Grumbling, she threw on a jacket, hat, and gloves before grabbing a flashlight and wire cutters from the entryway table. She opened the door and ran smack into Colton.

He grabbed her arms to keep her from landing on her butt. "Where are you going?"

"To save a heifer." She eyed the raging storm as her garbage can slammed up against the side of the nearest barn. "Want to help?"

"Of course." He shut the door. "Where?"

"This way." She led the way down the porch and jogged around the house toward the almost frozen stream. Rain pounded down, soaking her hat. She shivered and plunged along the snowdrift. "What are you doing here, anyway?" she yelled over the violent wind.

"Came to talk about the trip tomorrow," he yelled

back, shielding her from the storm.

Melanie swung the flashlight toward the flailing cow. Crap. It was one of the few pregnant cows, so not a heifer. She couldn't lose both the cow and the calf. The cow bellowed in anger as its powerful hoofs smashed ice in every direction.

"Whoa there," Melanie murmured, sliding through snow. "Calm down, baby." Barbed wire cut into the cow's neck as it fought, its eyes a wide, wild brown. "She must've fallen through the fence up the hill."

Colton wiped rain off his forehead, peering closer. "She brought part of the barbed wire with her." He squinted, focusing up the hill. "Mud slide with a side of ice."

Melanie turned to shine the flashlight up the hill just as the cow broke away from the bank. With a bellow, the animal leaped toward them. Melanie caught her breath on a stifled scream.

Strong arms wrapped around her, throwing them both to the side. They impacted icy slush and mud, sliding several feet. Colton rolled them over, holding her tight, taking the brunt of the damage, the side of his face smacking against the ground.

Snow and dirt whipped around them.

Melanie coughed out air and lifted her head, her body flush on top of Colton's.

"You okay?" he asked, brushing pine needles from her hair.

She blinked, her heart racing, her breath caught. Everything had happened so quickly. The body beneath her felt harder than the frozen ground. His scent of musk and male overcame the smell of pine and storm, and warmth spread through her chilled skin. "Yes."

"Good." Blood flowed from a cut above Colt's right eyebrow. He rolled them over and stood up. "Stay here." Taking the wire cutters from her stiff hand, he stood and stalked over to the cow, now fighting with a pine tree that had caught an edge of the barbed wire.

Melanie scrambled to her feet, her boots sliding on the mud.

Without wasting a moment, Colt dodged in and tackled the cow, one knee to its neck, the other on its flanks, careful to avoid its belly. Sure movements had the barbed wire snipped in several places and removed. "Stand back, Mel," he called over the storm.

She retreated against the side of the house.

Colton jumped back, and the cow struggled to its feet and snorted. For the briefest of moments, they looked at each other. Then the cow turned and ran toward the nearest pasture. "We'll probably have to hunt her down after the storm," Colton yelled, turning around.

Melanie nodded again, her body rioting. She could only gape as she focused the flashlight beam on her best friend.

He stood in the rain, blood and mud mixing with water across his chiseled face. Wet cotton clung to his hard frame, and passion all but cascaded off him.

He turned her way and…grinned.

Her heart clutched. In that very second, two things became frighteningly clear. One: she didn't know her best friend as well as she thought, because his smile masked the nature of a truly dangerous man. And two: she was completely and forever in love with him.

CHAPTER TEN

Colton forced his hands to unclench and his voice to remain calm. "Are you all right, Mel?"

She nodded, her eyes too wide in her too pale face. "Yes."

Frustration swept through him, and he fought to keep calm. The sight of her frightened face would keep him up for nights. She shouldn't be managing a ranch all by herself—accidents always happened.

He strode through the storm, grasped her arm, and began leading her back to the house. "Are you sure you're okay?" he asked, once he stepped onto the covered front porch.

"Me?" she laughed, the sound slightly off-kilter. "You're bleeding."

He wiped blood off his forehead. "Just a scratch." Clearing his throat, he tried to stomp mud off his boots while tugging a clean bandana from his inside coat pocket to wipe his hands clean. "I, ah, need a shower."

She stepped toward him, and he lifted an eyebrow. After what seemed like a small mental debate, she grabbed his destroyed shirt and tugged. Stretching up on her toes, her mouth slid against his.

Fire lashed through him so quickly he swayed. A million thoughts exploded at once, and he shut them down. Completely.

Groaning, he hauled her close and took over. The fear, the storm, the fury all comingled into raw need inside him. There were no more thoughts, no more uncertainties.

There was only this woman and this moment.

So he took both as deep as he could. He angled his mouth, and she drew a sharp breath, holding it.

Her lips softened beneath his as he explored her, learning her taste. Wild huckleberries and brandy? The most delicious combination in existence. She moaned deep in her throat, the sound sparking down his torso to his balls.

Her grip on him was strong and sure. He bent her, his hands full of woman. Brushing a hand across her firm ass, he shuddered. "Do you know how long I've wanted you?" Punctuating his words, he cupped a handful. Firm and tight, her flesh was better than he'd dreamed.

He shouldn't have said that. But the connection between his mouth and brain had disappeared.

She sighed against him, pressing closer. "Hurry."

"Not a chance." He reached behind them to shove open the door, backing her inside. Heat blasted them. His hold tightened, and he lifted her to sit on the rugged entryway table, legs spread, shirt now muddy and wet.

The storm raged outside, rain clashing down past the covered porch. He kicked shut the door. Even so, the wildness inside him overtook any sense of caution. Of reality. Letting go of any doubts, he fisted her hair and twisted, putting her right where he wanted her. She returned his kiss, gyrating against him, the calm Melanie turning into a wildcat.

Her nails bit into his coat. She unclenched her hold and released him in a primitive display of trust.

He wouldn't let her fall. This was Melanie. He gentled his touch, leaning back. Slowly, he ran his knuckles across her smooth cheekbone. "You're beautiful," he breathed. The woman mattered, and he'd take care of her.

She blinked, freezing for a second. Then her eyes darkened, and she yanked on the hem of his coat and shirt, pulling both up and over his head. He ducked his head and allowed her to tear it off. The cold wind slapped his skin right before her warm palms slid across his pecs.

She breathed out and pinched his nipple.

He stilled. Heat spiraled through him, and he allowed himself one small breath. Control. He needed control. Glancing down at her upturned face through heavy lids, he felt the first snapping of it spinning away.

Her eyes were melted chocolate and glazed with need. He'd bruised her lips, and they pouted pink and gorgeous. But he needed to slow down and show her how much she meant to him.

Much more than he'd be willing to admit to either one of them.

This was crazy, and he should stop them both, but it was too late. Keeping her gaze, he slid a hand over her undulating abdomen and down into her yoga pants, not stopping until his fingers touched a very thin cotton barrier. Swallowing, he moved the material aside and found her.

Hot and wet, her soft skin almost dropped him to his knees. Tapping his fingers in place, he wrapped his other arm around her waist and lifted her. She slid both arms around his neck and pressed closer, her thighs hugging his hips, her core tilting against his hand. A soft moan of need escaped her, and his cock zipped to full attention.

Holding tight, he headed straight for the sofa to sit her on the back. A quick twist, and he yanked her shirt over her head.

She was perfect.

Small, white, and sweet, her breasts tempted him. Teased him. He dropped and licked one pink nipple, circling the bud until it was hard as glass. The intimacy of the moment caught his breath.

She dug her hands into his wet hair, holding him close. His Mel wasn't shy.

He tried to restrain his strength, but she pulled on his hair, and gentleness became a dream. She keened when he scraped his teeth across her nipple.

So he turned to the other one and gave it the same attention before standing upright and grabbing the waist of her pants. Her hands drifted down his body to his belt. "Lift," he whispered.

Releasing him, she balanced on the back of the sofa with both hands and lifted. A cloud, a tinge of uncertainty crossed her girl-next-door face as he removed her pants and thong.

That wouldn't do.

He dropped them to the ground and kissed her, hard and complete. She moaned against him, and he pressed against her sex, sliding one finger inside a warmth too hot to be real.

Her breath caught even during the kiss, and she pushed against him.

He released her and waited until her eyes focused before speaking. She was amazing. "Hold yourself up, Mel. If you fall, I stop."

Confusion clouded her features until he dropped to his knees and his mouth found her.

Her entire body went rigid, and for a moment, he thought she'd fall onto the sofa cushions on the other side. But her thigh muscles tightened, and she remained in place.

He grinned against her, his finger working her G-spot, his tongue lashing her clit. She tasted like the forest, wild and free. Those spectacular thighs trembled, and her internal walls gripped his finger.

The minx was fighting it.

Amusement and determination filtered through him at the same time. Only Mel would try to control when and how she orgasmed. She was about to learn that any control in the bedroom belonged to him.

He sucked her clit into his mouth, and at the same time, he slipped another finger inside her to twist.

She cried out, her back arching, as she came. Her abdomen trembled while she rode out the waves. He lashed her clit, prolonging her orgasm as long as he could.

Finally, with a murmured sigh, she came down.

And fell over the back of the couch.

• • •

Melanie sprang to her knees and shoved wild curls away from her face as she gaped at Colton on the other side of the sofa. That had been the most amazing orgasm of her life. By the pleased look on his face, he knew it. She had no words.

Mud coated his pants, and his cheek had swollen with a purple bruise. Even so, she wanted him inside her. Now.

As if in total agreement, he unbuckled his belt and drew it through the loops. The hills and valleys of his rigid abs compared to those of the mountains around them. Powerful and dangerous. Then his jeans and boxers hit the floor. He held a condom in his right hand. Good. Definitely a good idea.

She swallowed, not sure where to look. Now that she'd orgasmed, reality was threatening to return. She dared a peek.

Holy crap. The rumors whispered by lucky cheerleaders in high school were true. Beyond over the top, true.

Colt was built. Gifted. Freakin' huge.

She swallowed. "Um—"

"Stop thinking." He reached for her waist and lifted her over the sofa.

"Man, you're strong," she muttered, that fluttering setting up in her abdomen again. He'd lifted her like she was one of those delicate, fan-waving women in the city.

"Strong enough." He spun her around to face the couch. Seconds later, he pressed her against the leather.

Panic and desire swooshed through her. "Colt—"

"Shh." He nipped her ear, his body enclosing her, his heated breath warming her skin. "Open for me, Mel." A smart slap echoed before her ass radiated an erotic pain.

She opened her mouth to protest—probably—and he cupped her sex, his index finger tapping her clit. *Oh God, Oh God, Oh God.* She tried to push up, to do anything, and was stopped by his free hand flattening across her upper back.

"I want you like this," he whispered into her ear, sending tendrils of lust through her skin from behind her. "Just like this."

A crackling filled the air as he must've slipped on the condom. Grasping her hips, he plunged inside her with one strong stroke.

She cried out and levered up on her toes, taking all of him. He was too big—too wide—

He reached around and tugged on her clit, and she dropped down. The fiery need lashing through forced her to push against him, to gyrate, to do anything to ease the pressure.

"Relax." He slid his hands over her bottom, caressing where he'd smacked her. "I've dreamed of my palm print right here." Then those dangerous fingers slid around and up to her breasts to play.

He tugged and caressed, sending sparks of electricity to where they remained joined.

"Colt," she ground out. Emotion swamped her. Colton Freeze was inside her. Completely. Her heart jittered, and she tried to control herself. "Move or I'll kill you."

"Hmmm." He licked along the shell of her ear. "Like this?" Slipping his hands down, he grasped her hips and slowly slid out of her to smoothly slide back in.

"M-maybe a bit faster," she panted, her vision going gray. "So I don't have to murder you later."

"Ahhh." He nipped. "Okay." Dark amusement lowered his voice. Digging his fingers in, taking control, he slid out and then back in with force. Increasing his speed as well as his strength, he began to pound.

Hard, angled, and in perfect timing, he thrust into

her. They moved in tune with each other, instinct and history whispering something neither would accept right now.

She arched and tried to take him deeper. So deep he'd never find his way out.

He chuckled and planted his hand against her upper back. She tried to push harder, to get him to quicken his thrusts, stilling only when a hard slap across her buttocks shocked her.

Wetness spilled from her, coating her thighs.

"I don't like that," she hissed against the cushions.

"Liar," he whispered, his grip strong and sure.

With his hand holding her in place, and his body thrusting, she could do nothing but take what he was giving. Helpless, she couldn't move, she couldn't even see him behind her. Damn if that didn't turn her on more.

The moment held a powerful truth. He controlled more than her body.

With a low growl, he pounded harder, his dick swelling inside her.

She sighed, arching, trying to reach the pinnacle. "Colton."

He slowed, and her eyes flipped open.

Then he paused.

She shook her head. No stopping! Digging her nails into leather, she shoved back against him.

He chuckled at her ear and slowly withdrew to turn her around so she could face him. "I want to see your face," he murmured.

The tenderness and fire lighting his amazing eyes stole her breath. The shift from wildness to Colt's natural sweet disposition threw her, and she swallowed.

He threaded both hands through her hair and leaned in. The kiss started soft and instantly spiraled to lava. She rubbed against him, the ache inside her almost unbearable. He lifted her to slide them both to the other side of the sofa. The second her butt hit cushions, she manacled his hips with her legs, securing her ankles.

One strong thrust, and he embedded himself inside her.

She opened her mouth on a strong exhale. "I've always wondered," she whispered.

A gentle smile curved his lips. "Me too."

One more soft kiss to her mouth, and he reached down to grab her hip. Slowly, he started to move.

Electricity ripped through her. "More."

His eyes darkened with an emotion she couldn't read. His pace increased along with the force of his thrusts.

She curled her fingers around his rib cage, digging in. Her thighs clenched. But she couldn't look away. A part of her wanted to look away, to sever the intimacy binding them tight, but he held her gaze captive.

All or nothing.

That was Colt.

A spiraling whipped through her, slamming hard in her cervix, and she cried out, her back arching. Waves of intense electricity rippled through her, and she held on, riding them out. His name was the only sound on her lips.

Finally, with almost a sob, she went limp.

Colton ground against her as he came. Enfolding her, he kissed her cheek. "Melanie."

CHAPTER ELEVEN

Colton checked his blackened eye in the bathroom mirror after wiping away fog. Dark and purple. Yep. He'd had worse, but it was still a shiner.

Melanie combed out her wet curls next to him, her silence speaking volumes.

After having sex, they'd washed up in her tiled shower, and it was all he could do not to take her again. But he'd been rough, and although Mel thought she was tough, she had a delicacy that had always concerned him.

The moment held intimacy, and a part of him wanted to dive right into it. Sex with Melanie was different. Better than anything he'd felt before...more real.

But this was *Mel*. And they'd had *sex*. He made sure the towel was fastened tightly around his waist before turning toward her. "Are you all right?"

She started and glanced up at him. Pink wandered across her cheekbones. "Fine. You?"

The crisp tone nudged his temper. "Yes. Did I bruise you?"

She whirled toward him, fire lancing through her eyes. "You mean when you *spanked* me?"

She was pretty. Stunning even. The challenge all but shooting from her had the dual benefit of ticking him off and amusing him. The woman was trying to deflect the situation, and a part of him didn't blame her. So he stepped into her space. "If I had really spanked you, darlin', you'd know it."

Her outraged intake of air was his only warning before she smacked his thigh with the hairbrush.

"Ow." He rubbed his skin. "You're a brat."

"Maybe." She went back to brushing her hair, her teeth sinking into her bottom lip. "I don't know what to say."

Neither did he. His usual urge to run after sex was nowhere to be found. Instead, he wanted to grab her again and spend the day playing in her bed. All day. "What do you want to say?"

She frowned. "I'm not sure. Part of me is freaking out, part is happy, and part is wondering if I just betrayed Hawk."

Colton swallowed. "Hawk?" His mind reeled. "I mean, you and Hawk haven't—"

Melanie snorted. "Of course not. Jeez. But the three of us make a friendship."

"I know." Colton's shoulders relaxed. The idea of Mel and Hawk had hit him in the gut. Hard. "He told me to go for it before he left."

Mel arched an eyebrow. "Go for it?"

Heat rose through Colton's face. "Not in a juvenile way, but in a good way. He likes our friendship but has always thought you and I might become more."

"Are we? Becoming more?" she asked, chocolate eyes darkening.

"I don't know." Well, if she could dig deep and be honest, so could he. "Do you want to become more?" What was he asking? What did he want? He needed to step back and think a little. Come up with a good plan.

She grinned. "Look at your mind spin."

He settled. "What do you want, Melanie?"

She blinked. "I, ah, well, things are a little odd right now. With going to the sperm bank and all."

No shit. "I know." He rubbed the bruise at his eye. "For now, why don't we just take it easy? I mean, let's keep this between us until we figure things out."

She nodded, sending curls flying. "Definitely keep it between us. The last thing we need is gossip."

"Exactly." He expelled a deep breath.

"Um, do you still want to come to Seattle with me?" she asked.

Frankly, he had mixed feelings about the sperm bank. "I wish there was more time to figure this all out."

"Me too." She slid the brush onto the counter. "At first, I was just being smart by wanting to freeze the eggs. But now, if I don't give in vitro a try, then I might never have a child."

"What about adoption?" he asked.

She shrugged. "That's certainly an option, and a good one, but I'd still like to get pregnant. Just once. Maybe see my mother in a baby, you know?"

He nodded. "I'm definitely going to Seattle with you."

"Because of the business problems." She nodded.

He shook his head. "Because you need support. Dealing with the business problems is a bonus."

She grinned. "Stop flirting with me."

"I'm not flirting." Although he appreciated her attempt to lighten the mood.

"You don't even know when you're flirting." She grabbed his towel and pulled.

He reached for the material, only to have her laugh and run out of the bathroom, leaving him buck-assed naked. If she thought that would stop him, she didn't know him at all.

Grinning, he leaped after her with his battle cry echoing.

Her laughter turned to near giggles as she ran through the house in her towel, almost tripping but never quite slowing down enough for him to pounce. Figured that intimacy with Melanie would be fun as well as sexy. This was new.

The front door shot open, and Colton turned to block Melanie from any threat.

Quinn stood framed in the doorway, water dripping from his hat.

Colton choked back a laugh. "Hi, sheriff. What's up?"

"I heard a scream." Shocked would be an accurate description of Quinn's expression. "Where are your clothes?" Slowly, he turned his head as Melanie padded out from the kitchen, still wearing her towel. "Oh."

Melanie clutched the towel to her breasts. "Morning, Quinn."

Quinn flushed ten shades of red. "Mornin'."

Colton bit his lip to keep from laughing out loud. "What's up?"

Quinn tapped his hat against his leg, sending droplets flying. "Um, some of Melanie's cattle wandered down to our eastern pasture, and I thought maybe she had a fence down."

"She does." Colt scratched his head and caught the towel Mel threw at him. He wrapped the material around his waist, keeping his gaze on his brother. "Go get dressed, Mel." Suddenly, he really didn't like anybody, even his brother, seeing Melanie half dressed.

Relief crossed Quinn's face. "Good idea. Then we can, ah, figure out which fences need repairing." Quinn waited until Melanie headed into the bedroom to pin Colton with a hard stare. "What in the hell are you doing?"

Colton lost his grin. What was he doing?

CHAPTER TWELVE

Melanie straightened her seat belt in the private plane as they prepared to land. There were four rows of plush leather seats, each with a table in front of it. She and Colton were the only passengers, and he sat across from her and to the left. After a long morning of mending fences on both ranches, they'd swung by his cabin for clothes, and they'd headed for the plane.

Where Colton had plunked furiously on his laptop.

They hadn't talked, and she wasn't quite sure what to say, anyway. He was all but obsessed with his meeting, and she studied him as he pounded away on the laptop even now.

She'd never seen the business side of him—not really.

He'd made several phone calls during the short flight, and the financial numbers he'd rattled off had been impressive. For once, the charming cowboy had been replaced with a genius shark now wearing a suit.

A black suit that emphasized his size and strength in a way that dampened her thighs. She glanced down to make sure her bra was working. Yep. Any evidence of her arousal was safely hidden. Thank goodness.

He clicked the laptop closed, and she jumped.

One dark eyebrow rose. His mask of charm had disappeared and left a man staring at her with an intensity that sped up her breath. In the darkened plane, the blue of his eyes took on a midnight hue. "We should talk about last night," he said.

"No." The word emerged—an instant defense against anything he could say. She settled her hands on her flowered skirt. "Thank you, though."

His unwavering gaze remained on her. "Yes. We're involved, and now you're heading to a sperm bank. I used a condom last night—"

"Of-course-you-used-a-condom." She breathed the words out as quick as she could. "Colton. I'm not asking you to get me pregnant."

He wet his lips. "I know. But things have changed, and I, ah…"

Things were certainly complicated. Melanie cursed her body for putting her in this position. Her heart ached. "Are you saying if I have somebody else's baby you don't want to see me? I mean, we're not really seeing each other. One night…that wasn't even a night. I mean, it was one orgasm. Okay, two for me and one for you. But—"

"Jesus, Mel. Take a breath." He leaned back. "I care for you, I—"

"Stop." The last thing she needed was him to let her off easy. Hurt flowed through her, and she shoved the pain away. "Last night was just sex, Colt. One time, and it's over. There's no need to feel obligated, nor is there a reason to ruin our friendship. Let's forget it."

He finally blinked. "I don't want to forget it."

Her head jerked up, and her lungs heated. Unwelcome and warm, hope coiled through her chest. "Huh?"

"I just want some time. To ease into this and figure out what it is. I mean, it's *us,*" he said.

She forced her shoulders to relax. There was no logic here. "I know."

"So let's explore the new us." He straightened his understated tie. "I've dated a lot of women—"

"I know that, too," she said dryly.

He shot her a look. "None of them have meant an iota of what you mean to me."

Her heart thumped. Hard. "The problem is I don't have time. Not really." If she ever wanted to have a baby, now was the time. Even so, chances weren't good. At the thought, she finally accepted this path. She'd do everything she could to have a baby.

He shoved his hand through his hair. "I know. But—"

The wheels set down with a minor thump, and they were on the ground. He sighed and unbuckled his belt, waiting until the plane taxied to the private hangar before standing and swiftly opening the door. He held out a hand. "I have a car waiting."

She halted in standing and then took his hand. He wouldn't have a limo, would he? No way could she go to a sperm bank in a limo. No way. "My life is becoming a bad sitcom." She followed him down the steps.

"What?" Colton asked, turning around.

"Nothing." Relief filled her at spotting the black Camaro waiting by the plane with its top already down. Seattle had been experiencing a very nice March with an ever-present sun, unlike Montana. "Nice car."

He grinned. "I thought you'd like it." Accepting their overnight bags from one of the pilots, he tossed them in the trunk.

Melanie slipped into the passenger seat, taking a moment to appreciate the smooth leather. "I still don't understand why we needed to bring overnight bags.

We're heading home today, right?" In addition, she might leave town knocked up. She blinked. No matter what Colton said, her becoming pregnant would put a damper on whatever they were starting together. If they were starting something. Chances were—

"Stop thinking so hard." Colton unfolded his length into the driver's seat. "My meetings may go late, and we might have to stay the night. I promise I'll make it worth your while." The deep timbre of his voice slid right under her skin to spring nerves to life.

"Stop flirting with me." She buckled her seat belt.

"I'm not."

Goodness help her if he started. She sighed. "Now isn't a good time for us to start something."

"Yet we did." He ignited the engine and smoothly drove the powerful car through the quiet private airport to the main road. "It's not like you're getting inseminated today, anyway. This is a preliminary consultation, right?"

She swallowed. "Normally, but with my circumstances, they said they'd expedite the process if I want. I made the appointment months ago in case the embryo freezing didn't work, and they would have all of my files and history by now."

"Oh." His hands visibly tightened on the steering wheel. "I'll cancel my meeting and go with you."

"No." Panic tasted like acid. "If I'm going to do this by myself, be a single mom, then I should do it all by myself." The idea of Colton sitting outside the door while she had her feet in stirrups, changing her entire life, made her head spin. "Thanks, though."

He cut her a look that shot straight for her panties. What was wrong with her? She couldn't arrive at a sperm back turned on.

Life had gotten too weird too quickly.

Would she go through with it? For the first time in weeks, she wasn't sure.

• • •

Colton ignored the spectacular view of the Seattle skyline outside the conference room window, his mind spinning. He shouldn't have dropped Melanie off at the sperm bank. But she'd insisted, and he really didn't have a right to accompany her.

Melanie. Pregnant. Not with his kid.

Which one of those statements bothered him the most? He hated to admit it, especially since they'd never even been on a real date, but if there was a kid in there, he wanted it to be his.

What was going on in his head?

The last thing he'd planned at this stage of his life was settling down. Sure, it worked for his brothers, but he was just getting started in his career. Frankly, he'd liked playing the field. A lot. His plan was his plan, and the idea of altering it sent chills down his back. Plus, well, it was Melanie. She deserved somebody established in life, somebody ready to take care of her.

He'd be that guy if his plan went along the correct course, but not for a while. Right now, he was just starting out—and he may have already screwed up.

But when he thought of forever, when he thought of something real, the only face he saw in his head was Melanie's.

There wasn't anybody else he wanted to plan life with. To wake up with every morning, and to grow old and cranky with. Only Melanie.

And he'd just dropped her at a sperm bank alone.

"So what do you think?" Mark Manning, the CEO of Greenfield LLC asked, shoving his wire rims up his pointy nose.

Colton frowned at the only other person in the conference room. "About what?"

Mark sat back, his scrawny neck moving. "About our financial shortcomings. Can you invest more money?"

Colton leaned forward and made sure he had Mark's attention before replying. "No."

Mark sighed. "Then I'm not sure what we'll do."

Colton flipped open the report in front of him and grabbed his pen. "You'll reallocate these resources here…and these here." He proceeded to step-by-step show Mark how he'd not only climb out of the red but start making money.

Mark finally sat back. "I think you're right."

Colton smiled while keeping his eyes hard. "I know. Also, you should be aware if you ask me for more money again, I'm going to shoot you."

Mark laughed and quickly sobered, his light brows slanting down. "Are you serious?"

"Yes." Okay, he wouldn't shoot Mark, but he might beat the crap out of him. "I told you not to invest in the other natural-oil company, and you didn't listen. Now I have to go back to my board of directors and tell them times are going to be tight for the next year." His board was his family, and he hated letting them down. But after the tough year, he'd work his ass off until times would be flush again, hopefully.

A flush time he'd like to spend with Melanie. The

woman had never traveled. He'd love to take her somewhere warm for a winter vacation, somewhere they could find a private beach and play nude. Those breasts would probably burn. He loved her breasts.

His head jerked up. He had to stop her. If she needed a baby, he'd give her one.

Standing, he quickly shook Mark's hand. "I have to go. Send me weekly reports until we're back on track." Ignoring Mark's look of surprise, he hustled out of the office and all but ran for the car parked on the street.

Would it be too late?

The curse words he hissed as he maneuvered in and out of traffic compiled into a crazy flow of expressions. Where did people learn to drive? Finally, he double parked in front of the skyscraper housing the sperm bank.

Running inside, he scanned the kiosk near the elevators. Fifth floor. She was on the fifth floor.

He skipped the elevator for the stairs, taking them two at a time. He burst into the waiting room, and several people glanced up from filling out forms. Lots of forms.

Long strides propelled him across the room to the receptionist's granite desk. "I need to see Melanie Jacoby. Now."

The receptionist, a buxom middle-aged redhead with deep frown lines, shook her head. "I'm sorry, but she's in a procedure room."

Oh, hell no. His brain had shut down hours ago, so his body took over. He shoved open the door next to the desk and hurried down a long hallway lined with closed doors. His boots echoed on the fake wooden floors.

"Melanie," he bellowed, trying doorknobs.

One door opened to reveal a nude fat guy holding a plastic cup, and Colton yelped, slamming the door. "Sorry, dude. Lock the door." That image was burned in his retinas for life.

"Melanie Jacoby," he yelled louder.

A door opened farther down, and Melanie stepped out, pamphlets in her hands and her eyes wide. "What in the world?"

He took a deep breath. "Don't do this. Have my baby instead."

CHAPTER THIRTEEN

Melanie took a sip of her wine in the small alcove of the restaurant. The scent of garlic and roasted peppers wafted around. "You are out of your flipping mind," she repeated.

Colton drew air in through his nose, his hand around a glass of some man drink. "I know." He grinned. "You should've seen the face of the guy I stopped mid-jack."

Laughter bubbled up in Melanie, and she snorted. "I bet you weren't looking at his face."

Colton groaned. "Don't remind me."

After hurrying from the clinic, Colton had driven them to his favorite pizza joint in the outskirts of Seattle. "So you didn't get inseminated."

"No. Even though I'm ovulating right now, I couldn't do it." Frankly, she had been having doubts and was no way prepared to make such a monumental decision. Well, not true. She'd decided to hold off because of Colton. She didn't have to admit the truth to him, but she couldn't lie to herself. "I don't know what to do."

Colton nodded. "Well, I was thinking. Say you get a baby from a sperm bank, and you have a boy. Who will teach the kid baseball?"

She hunched her shoulders. "Well, probably you, though I'm not bad." Although Colt had been the best pitcher in Montana in high school and part of college before he'd turned to MMA fighting.

"Right. And who will attend those embarrassing *your body is changing* nights at school with him?" Colt took another drink of the clear liquid.

"You." Melanie nodded.

"In other words, if you had a baby, I'd step in anyway," Colt said reasonably.

She sighed. Truth be told, any time she pictured a little boy, she pictured him with Colt's intriguing hair and eyes. "I know." Now she felt selfish for even considering having a baby. She wasn't the only one whose life would change.

"So why not give the kid superior genes and a whole lot of cousins and family?" Colton showed a rare dimple in his right cheek.

Melanie lifted an eyebrow. "Superior genes?"

"I'm glad you agree." Colton finished his drink as the pizza arrived.

She shook her head. "The timing is terrible. I mean, after we—"

Colton slipped pieces on their plates. "I know. The fact that we slept together does muddy the *let's have a baby* waters."

Melanie rubbed her eyes. "Life has gotten out of control." It'd be smoother if she could take that night back, but deep down, she didn't want to. "I can't ask you to become a father right now. I know that's not in your big plan."

"My big plan?" he asked.

Self-aware, he was not. Melanie chuckled. "Sure. You plan everything. Go to school, check. Get masters, check. Study international business transactions, check. Take over family company, check. Talk Dawn into working there when she comes home for good in

December, check. Open businesses with childhood friends, check. Play the field and have fun for a decade, check. Find hot, big-breasted blonde and settle down with three point two kids…"

He chewed thoughtfully and then sipped his water. "You know me pretty well, do you?"

"Yes." The pizza warmed her belly, and she finally relaxed for the first time that day.

His gaze heated hotter than the pizza. "You believe in fate, right?"

She shrugged. "Sure. I live in Mineral Lake, Montana. Fate and destiny are in the waters."

"So, let's proceed as if we just started dating, which frankly, we have, and see where fate leads us." Colt signaled for another drink. "We ditch the condoms and let destiny decide."

She coughed and then quickly took a drink of her wine. Colton—inside her—bare and hard? Heat slammed between her legs, and she shifted restlessly. Sex anywhere and anytime with Colton?

She tried to sound normal. "Let destiny decide? That is so unlike you. For years, I've watched you plan every relationship, up to and including the probable breakup."

"I've never been with you before," he rumbled.

Warmth spread right around her heart and settled in. If he didn't stop being so sweet, she was going to fall even deeper in love with him. She cleared her throat. "What if I do get pregnant?"

"Then we proceed from there." Colton accepted his new drink and didn't seem to notice the waitress all but pressing her boobs against his shoulder and flirting.

Melanie waited until the woman had left. "If I get pregnant, you'll convince yourself you're in love with me, and then you'll want to get married to fulfill your plan. I can't take the pressure." Even worse, what if he fell in love with somebody else down the line, and she was left alone? Because from the moment lightning had struck her the other night, it had become abundantly clear that Colton was it for her—and he still saw her as a buddy he wanted to help out.

The sides of his eyes crinkled. "I'd hate to pressure you, so let's make a deal."

Even she knew better than to make a deal with Colton Freeze. "What kind of a deal?"

"If I get you pregnant, I promise not to pressure you to marry me." He leaned back, confidence in his eyes. "In fact, I'll wait until you ask me."

• • •

Colton opened the door to their hotel suite, smiling at Mel's gasp of surprise. A stunning sunset illuminated the Seattle skyline outside the wide span of windows, and she hurried past the sitting room furniture to get a better view.

His manic rush through a Seattle sperm bank had showed him one thing in exact clarity. He cared for Melanie too much not to be there for her and whatever baby she had. As always, he could plan this out. The woman reminded him of a skittish colt he'd trained as a teenager, all big eyes and hot temper.

This whole health problem made her even more reluctant to start up with him, so he'd proceed carefully until he figured out what was best for all of them.

For now, they'd proceed slowly and have some fun.

He yanked his tie loose and tugged the silk free, unbuttoning the first couple of buttons on his shirt.

Melanie turned around as he was rolling up his sleeves.

Her eyes darkened and widened.

He bit back a smile. The expression crossing her face was one he'd never seen on her. Wary and intrigued. So he continued rolling up his sleeves and stalked toward her.

Slowly.

She swallowed. "I'm not sure about this side of you." Her words emerged just breathless enough to awaken his cock.

"What side?" He continued toward her.

"You know."

He knew exactly what she meant. But she was going to say the words. He reached her and grasped her chin to tilt her head. "What's throwing you here?"

She blinked. "You've always been a bossy and protective pain, but this *edge*, is almost too much."

She was so sweet. He liked that she didn't play coy, even when he kept her off center. Nor did she attempt to hide the desire now spiraling through her and darkening her stunning eyes. No other woman had ever come close to this one.

"I have never been bossy." He ran his thumb along her lower lip, letting the softness entice him.

She rolled those eyes. "Baloney. If not bossy, then what?"

"In control." He tightened his hold and slid his lips against hers. Once, twice, a third time. "I like to be in control in the bedroom, and you like giving it up."

She gasped and jerked away. "I do not."

Oh yeah. Cat and mouse. One of his favorite games—and one he'd bet Melanie had never played. He leaned in until his mouth rested against her ear. "Sure you do. I bet you're wet right now."

Her hiss accompanied a two-handed push against his chest. The intrigue crossing her face didn't lie. "I am not."

"Prove it," he suggested.

"You are such an ass." She bit her lip against a half smile.

He grabbed her and kissed her hard until she pressed against him, little moans chorusing from her chest. Then he released her. "Watch that language, or I'll do more than one little spank this time."

The clouds slowly slipped from her eyes until they narrowed. "I don't think so."

"I do." He ran his knuckle down the side of her face. "We both know I could have you begging, totally at my mercy, within minutes."

Her gasp should've warned him. "Mercy?"

"Yes." He kept his gaze on her smooth skin.

And thus didn't see her leg shoot out to hook his. She took him down in a quick move he'd taught her about four years previous, turning them until he landed hard on his chest, her strong thighs straddling his back.

Her ass hit his just as she slipped an arm under his neck and pulled.

Then, against all logic, he burst into laughter. Not chuckles, not light amusement, but full-bore belly laughs that came from deeper than his heart.

Her execution of the move was beautiful.

He could barely breathe, his neck pulled back, her

arm cutting off his air. The cold wooden floor chilled his skin, while his blood heated with lust.

"Stop laughing," Mel hissed, pulling harder.

He couldn't help it. Tears gathered in his eyes, and even with her chokehold gaining strength, he couldn't stop laughing.

Until she released his neck, grabbed his hair, and smashed his forehead into the floor.

Pain radiated through his entire skull. He stopped laughing.

She. Did. Not.

Using his knee, he flipped over, grabbed her arms, and rolled until she lay flat on her back beneath him. "That last move is supposed to knock an opponent unconscious," he ground out, his head aching.

She rolled her eyes. "You're fine."

"I didn't teach you those moves to use against me." He fought to tamp down on a temper that suddenly wanted to roar.

"You shouldn't laugh at people. There are consequences." She glanced up at his pounding forehead and blanched.

His temper settled. "You believe in consequences, baby?"

She stilled, her gaze flashing to his. "Uh—"

He reached down, spun them around, and ended up in a position he never thought he'd see, with Melanie Murphy Alana Jacoby over his knee, ass in the air. He brought his hand down hard to gain her attention.

She yelped and tried to scoot away. "Colton!"

He easily kept her in place and laughed, his good humor restored. "You're staying here until you apologize for trying to bash in my skull."

"I should've tried harder." She half laughed and half bellowed. "Now let me go."

He smacked her again. "No."

"Hey, butthead." She kicked out her legs. "This isn't right."

He paused. "You're right. This is all wrong." He reached for the waist of her skirt and yanked it off her legs, almost groaning at the sexy black thong that left her pinkening buttocks exposed. He ran a finger along the seam of material. "This is pretty."

"I am so going to kick your ass—" She shrieked as he smacked her again. "Damn it, Colt—"

Smack. "Apologize, Mel." *Smack.* "Though this is fun." *Smack. Smack. Smack.*

His dick pulsed in agreement with each playful hit. He settled her more comfortably across his thighs and bit back a harsh groan at the contact. If he didn't get inside her soon, he might explode.

"You're getting turned on by this?" She gurgled, laughing while struggling with all her strength.

"Oh yeah." His palm print was outlined on her gorgeous ass. "I could do this all day. So you might want to apologize." He smacked her again for good measure.

"I should've knocked you out. You're a pervert." She wiggled her butt in a move to slide from his lap, and he groaned out loud this time.

"Pervert?" He palmed her heated ass, grinning at her sharp intake of breath. "You're as aroused as I am."

"Am not," she predictably hissed.

"Lying gets you spanked in earnest." He slid his palm over her butt, between her legs, and fingered her wet slit. Hot and wet, she'd saturated the material.

The sound she made was full of need.

His eyes almost rolled back in his head, and his balls drew tight and said *hello*. He slid up and ran his nail over her clit.

She gasped, her muscles tightening. "Colton."

"Ah, Mel." His voice emerged guttural. "I think I'll make you come just like this. While being spanked."

She shoved her torso up from the floor. "I'm *sorry*. Way, way, way, *sorry*, so *sorry* I smashed in your head, not that you need your brain. *Sorry*, a thousand times *sorry*."

He laughed out loud and then hissed as his cock brushed her underbelly. Well, fair was fair. So he lifted her up.

She turned and tackled him, wrapping her legs around his hips and slamming her ass down on his groin. They both groaned at the contact, and then her mouth was all over his.

Hot, greedy, demanding.

He fell back, taking her with him, his mouth working hers the entire time. Her hands were frantic as she ripped open his shirt, sliding heated palms along his skin.

She fumbled with his zipper, and he kicked off his pants and boxers at her urging.

Levering up, she grabbed him and tried to lower herself. Fire all but shot from her eyes as she failed. "You're too big."

Basketball. Football. Television sitcoms. He fought to keep sane as she gripped him tightly. "No, I'm not." He ripped her shirt over her head for good measure. "Go slower. Take your time."

"Okay." She took a deep breath and rolled her hips while taking him in.

His heart pounded in his ears, and every muscle he owned tensed with the need to flip them over and pound into her. He fought the urge, letting her play, allowing her to set the pace.

Finally, decades later, her ass finally hit his groin.

"Oh." Her mouth pursed, and her eyes widened. Both palms flattened on his chest as she angled her pelvis.

Heat surrounded him. Pulsing, caressing, taking... her internal walls gripped him with impressive strength. The neurons in his brain may have misfired. Any control he owned was a sliver from snapping completely. "Melanie? You want to start moving now." His voice was raw gravel as he held tight to the reins, uncertain he'd succeed.

"All right." She threw back her head and lifted up.

He manacled her hips and slammed her back down.

Their groans melded together. Then he did it again, setting a pace she easily jumped right into.

He glanced up at her, wanting to stay in this moment forever. Her wild curls cascaded around her classic face, her brown eyes focused elsewhere, and a light blush wandered from her breasts to her cheeks. She was fucking perfect.

Gripping her hips, he set up a fast rhythm. She met him thrust for thrust, her thigh muscles constricting with each movement.

He wanted to slow down, to get lost in her. But electricity sparked down his spine to lash his balls, and he was too close to ending the moment. So he reached down and slid the calloused pad of his thumb along her clit.

She cried out, back arched, nails digging into his chest as the orgasm overtook her. Pumping harder, faster, she yanked him right into heaven with her.

He held her tight, coming like a teenager on prom night.

Finally, she took a deep breath and collapsed against his chest. He slid his palm down her spine to caress her still warm ass. "We're gonna have to do that again," he said with a smile.

Contentment wandered through his blood, warming him. He wanted to spend all night with her in his arms, instead of needing to ease away after sex. Instead of freaking out or worrying about the new feelings, he allowed them to take root.

His phone dinged from across the room. The ding pointed to a programmed alarm. Setting Mel to the side, he yanked on his jeans and scanned his phone.

A chilling dread slithered down his spine. Melanie lifted her eyebrows in question, and he shook his head, standing and leaping for the laptop perched on the table. Typing furiously, he double-checked the cash accounts. "Son of a bitch."

"What?" Melanie asked.

"I had an alert set on our accounts with Manning, and it looks like he just took the money and ran." Colton would kick the crap out of him…if he found him.

"Call the police." Melanie reached for her clothes.

Colton sighed and rubbed his eyes. "If we turn him in, the money will be tied up forever as they build a case against him."

"Oh." Her breasts jiggled as she tugged her shirt

over her head. "What's your plan?"

"I go after him." This was a clusterfuck of tremendous proportions. Sure, they could survive without the money for a year by tightening their belts, but at some point, his family needed the money back. Especially before next calving season.

"Okay." Melanie wiggled her butt and shimmied into her skirt.

His dick sprang alive. He was facing a complete financial disaster, and his body wanted to play. "You are way too tempting."

The smile she flashed him heated right through his blood to his heart. Man, he needed to get a grip. Turning away, he quickly dialed his assistant. "Anne? Sorry to disturb you. This is what I need." Giving her details, he ran through his itinerary. "Thanks."

Shaking his head, he ended the call and focused back on Mel. "I have to go get our money back."

Melanie nodded. "You will."

"I thought he was my friend. Guess not." How could he have been so stupid? So sure of himself he didn't stop to think. Colton eyed the flushed brunette he'd much rather be playing with right now. "You take the plane back home. I have to track Mark down—if he went by car, I'll follow him, or I can get a commercial plane ticket."

"Is this man dangerous?" Melanie asked.

"Not as dangerous as I am," he said, grimly.

"Oh." Melanie eyed the door. "I'll get ready to go."

He reached for her and drew her close. "When I get back, we need to talk." Maybe by then he'd figure out what he wanted to say.

CHAPTER FOURTEEN

He'd been chasing Manning for three frustrating days. A biting rain slashed down, competing with the blustering wind. About an hour outside of Fargo, North Dakota, Colton sat in his rented Jeep, gazing on the quiet fleabag motel. Room 117 to be exact.

His contacts at the security firm he often used had confirmed Mark had used a credit card to rent the room. Whoever the firm used as a contact had some serious info, which is why he never balked at their fees.

Colton rubbed his scratchy chin.

A pudgy man following two hookers had entered a room at the farthest end of the motel, but other than that, there hadn't been any life. If Mark was in the room, he was being quiet.

Enough was enough.

Stepping out of the Jeep, Colt's boots splashed in a mud puddle. Striding the distance to the door, he calculated the best approach.

Planting his boot near the knob, he kicked in the flimsy door. The cheap metal swung open, banging off the side wall.

Mark turned from sitting on the bed—and reached for something in his bag.

Colton was on him that fast, hands fisted in Mark's shirt. "What's in the bag?"

Mark swallowed, his glasses askew on his face. "Nothing."

"Right." Colton tossed the asshole across the room

with minimum effort and reached for the barely visible silver gun.

Mark smashed into the dresser and dropped to the floor.

Colton frowned, twisting the gun in the meager light. "This is a Lady Smith & Wesson." He frowned at Mark. "You bought a girl's gun?"

Mark shoved himself up from the grimy carpet and straightened his glasses. He wore a faded T-shirt and dress pants. "You just committed a battery."

Colton grinned and moved to shut and lock the door. Well, shut the door. The lock no longer worked. "You committed theft, fraud, and the worse crime of pissing me off." Turning, he leaned back against the damaged door. "Why are you in North Dakota?"

Mark's Adam's apple bobbed up and down. "I have an investor here and am trying to get all of your money back." He eyed the window and seemed to listen for help.

There was no assistance coming to this dive. Colt clicked his tongue and stepped forward to grab Mark by the neck. "Try again."

Mark's skinny arms moved up to block, and Colton swatted them away. The guy wasn't even worth it. "I thought we were friends," he said quietly.

Mark sniffed. "We are friends."

"Think so?" Colton threw him into one of two mangy chairs by a Plexi board table. Then he drew Mark's laptop from the gun bag and set the computer before his former friend. "Where's the money?"

Mark shook his head. "The money is gone."

Colton pushed the laptop into place. "Where is my money?"

Mark wiped his snotty nose on his sleeve. "Gone."

Colton sighed and shrugged out of his coat. "I know you, you little prick. You have an overseas account set up, and now you're going to transfer every cent from that account to this one." He drew a piece of paper covered with a series of numbers from his front pants pocket.

"I can't." Mark sighed, his hands trembling on the table. "You'll never kill anybody over money. Other reasons maybe, but not money."

"You're right." Colton shoved a rough hand through his hair. "I won't kill you."

Mark's shoulders relaxed.

"I will break every single bone in your body, one by one." He kept his gaze steady. "You think you know me? Keep in mind not only have you stolen from me, you've stolen from my family. That's a hard line you've crossed."

Mark paled. "I'm sorry, but I needed the money. I made some bad bets, and I'm being chased."

"I don't care." Colton leaned down, holding Mark's gaze. "Your problems are yours. Now transfer the money."

"I can't," Mark whispered, his gaze dropping to the silent laptop.

Colton shoved up the sleeves of his T-shirt and sat down at the computer. He hadn't hacked an account since his early teens, but some gifts just stayed with a guy. Even so, it was going to be a long night.

• • •

Darkness without stars surrounded Colton as he jogged down the airplane's steps in Maverick and tossed his duffel in his truck. Rain smashed down, just as cold as the one in North Dakota.

It had taken several hours for Colton to hack into the accounts, another hour to realize that the actual money was gone, and then two hours to transfer the patents to his family's corporation. The cash was gone, but the patents would pay off. Eventually. For now, he had bad news for his family.

Very bad news.

Man, Colton was tired. Threatening people didn't set well with him, and he hadn't slept in nights. The idea of slipping into a warm bed with an even warmer Melanie propelled his foot down on the accelerator.

His phone buzzed, and he frowned. Who would be calling in the middle of the night? A quick glance showed it was Quinn. "Quinn? What's up?"

"Hey. Where are you?" Quinn asked.

"Heading into Mineral Lake," Colton said.

"Good. I'm glad you're home," his brother said.

Colton stilled. "What's up?"

"It's Hawk. His helicopter went down two days ago downrange of Afghanistan." A slight tremor vibrated in Quinn's voice.

All thought, all emotion, screeched to a halt inside Colton. The anger over the money, the indecision with Melanie, even his fatigue flew away. "Is he—"

"No. I don't know any details, and Jake is on the phone with his military contacts, but we know Hawk is alive and survived the crash to be brought home. We just don't know where he is right now," Quinn said.

"I'll be right over." Colton pressed harder on the gas pedal.

"Actually, we're meeting at Mom and Dad's in an hour to figure things out. Meet there." Quinn clicked off.

Colton swallowed. Where was Hawk? Why had life gone to shit? He'd had a plan, and he'd been a cocky bastard, now hadn't he? How was he going to fix everything?

There was only one place to go now.

• • •

After being awakened by the doorbell, Melanie opened her front door to find a disheveled Colton standing in the snow. Hollows accentuated his high cheekbones, and fatigued darkened his eyes. Along with pain. "What?" she whispered.

"Hawk's helicopter went down," Colt said.

Melanie blinked and half shook her head. Panic burst through her, heating her lungs. "No—"

"He lived through the crash and was transported to the States." Colton stepped forward and enveloped her in a hug. "We're trying to find out which hospital he may be in right now."

Relief weakened her knees, and she drew in a deep breath of male. "He didn't die?"

"No, and he was healthy enough to bring home for medical treatment, apparently." Colt stepped back. "We're meeting at the main ranch in an hour to figure things out. Get dressed, and I'll drive."

Melanie scrambled upstairs to throw on clothes. If Hawk was okay, where in the world was he? He had to be okay. Too much was changing—way too fast. They couldn't lose Hawk. She finished dressing and ran downstairs to find Colton on the phone.

He clicked off.

She held her breath until he'd turned around.

"Hawk was transported back to the States and checked himself out of the veterans' hospital in Helena. He should be heading home," Colt said.

Melanie frowned even as the world finally settled. "Why didn't he call?"

"That's exactly what we'll ask him when he gets home," Colton said, grim lines cutting grooves into the side of his generous mouth. "I just left him a message to meet at Mom and Dad's. Let's get there before he does."

Melanie yanked on a coat before following Colton into the storm and his vehicle. She settled against the leather in his truck, turning on the seat warmer. Best invention ever. "How was your trip?" she asked as he started the truck and drove into the blowing wind.

"I got the patents, but we're broke until they pay off." His lip twisted.

She clicked her seat belt into place. "Your family will understand."

"I don't know why they would. I was reckless and stupid." He shook his head as wind hissed against the windows, and marble-sized hail pounded the truck. "My plan didn't exactly fall into position."

Melanie studied his hard profile. Why did his plan always have to be perfect? Everyone made mistakes. "They'll support you."

"They shouldn't."

She didn't have any other words to offer. So, turning to watch the wild storm, she slid her hand under his as it rested on the console between them. He tangled his fingers through hers with a tight grip.

Yeah, it felt right.

Ten minutes later, they'd ensconced themselves at the Freeze main ranch house, and Melanie headed to help Loni in the kitchen. Per orders, Mel sliced potatoes in Loni's gourmet kitchen and jerked when thunder yelled outside. The hail turned to a freezing rain.

Now she sliced while Loni finished stirring her famous breakfast casserole in a Crock-Pot. Tom Freeze stood next to his wife and kept getting his big hand slapped as he tried to steal a taste of the fragrant concoction. Colton stormed into the kitchen, Quinn on his heels. "He should be here by now," Colt said.

Quinn snagged an apple slice from a platter off to the side. "There was a holdup when he checked himself out of the veterans' hospital outside of Helena. Apparently he did so against doctor's orders."

Now that sounded like Hawk. Melanie slid the potatoes onto a plate. "How badly injured is he?"

"Some internal bleeding, a broken arm, a head injury, and a generally pissed-off attitude," Jake said, loping into the kitchen. "Apparently Hawk refused medical help until they transferred him to Montana, and the second he got there, he discharged himself. I finally got ahold of my buddy in Helena, and he gave me the information."

Melanie sighed, her mind whirling. "Can Hawk do that without getting in trouble with the military?"

"Yep." Jake snaked raw potato. "Hawk was honorably discharged three months ago."

"What?" Colt's head jerked up.

Jake nodded. "He went back as an independent

contractor to assist his old unit with something. None of my contacts know what, but well…"

It wasn't a huge secret that Hawk was a sniper. Melanie swallowed. "So he didn't tell us the truth."

"I'll kick his ass." Colton shoved a rough hand through his hair. "After he's healthy."

"That seems fair," Quinn mused.

"Where is he?" Colton growled, punching in numbers on his cell phone again. "He's not picking up."

Quinn rubbed a hand over his eyes. "If I knew what he was driving, or who was driving him, I'd put out a BOLO. But right now, I have no clue."

Juliet wandered into the kitchen, carrying a covered dish. "Sophie is resting in the guest room, and I almost had to tie her down to get her to stay there." Amusement lifted the redhead's lips. "She says she's feeling better."

Melanie's cell phone rang, and she glanced at the screen before excusing herself to the other room. "Hello, Mr. Carmichael," she answered. The elderly man owned the ranch to her east and had been one of her grandfather's best friends.

"Hi, Mel." He coughed for a moment. "I thought I should tell you that several of your Black Angus are wandering around the side of Shilly's Mountain."

Dread slammed through her. "Are you sure?"

"Yep. Used my new binoculars to make out the brand. It's yours." Carmichael coughed again. "Darn allergies, and spring isn't even here yet. So be careful when you head out to fetch the cattle. That mountain ain't safe for them with the coyotes, wolves, and bears."

"True. Thanks, Mr. Carmichael." She ended the call,

her mind spinning. At least five fences had to go down in order for those cows to end up in danger. The spring storms had it out for her.

Colton poked his head out of the kitchen. "What's up?"

She turned. "My western pasture has all downed fences. The Black Angus I had settled there are roaming Shilly's Mountain."

Colton lifted his chin and stepped into the room. "There are at least four fences between the pasture and the mountain."

"Five," she said.

"How many head?" he asked.

"About fifty from that pasture." She took a deep breath. "I have to go."

Colt leaned against the wall and crossed his arms. "What's your plan?"

"I'm contracting with Hawk's crew, so I'll give them a call," she said. Even though he'd been out of town, Hawk's crew remained at work.

Colton nodded. "I assumed you'd call in a crew. What I'm asking is what you're planning on doing."

She frowned. "They're my cattle. I'm heading out to round them up."

"All by yourself?" His voice dropped to a softness that would provide warning to anybody with a brain.

She sighed. "You're miffed I didn't ask you to help?"

"Miffed?" Fire lanced through his eyes, highlighting all the different hues of blue.

She bit back a laugh. "I've asked you for help plenty of times, but I figured you'd be busy finding Hawk, and I didn't want to pull you away from searching. We need to find him and make sure he's okay."

Colton nodded. "I understand. How about you stay here and help find Hawk, and I'll head out and gather your cattle. The storm has messed with visibility big-time."

She gaped. "Listen, Colt—"

He held up a hand. "There's a big storm about to settle right over Shilly's Mountain, and I'd rather you were safe here. There's a chance you're now pregnant with my child, and that's how it's going to be."

Holy crap. Amusement bubbled up so quickly she snorted. "*That's how it's going to be.*" Turning on her heel, she chuckled as she headed toward the front door. As much as a jackass as he was being, it shouldn't have surprised her when he grabbed her arm. "Let go of me, or prepare to be a eunuch," she said quietly.

He turned her around, conflicting emotions chasing across his hard face. "What if I asked nicely?"

What if she kicked him squarely in the balls? Man, this new status with Colton, whatever it was, took work. "There's less than a five percent chance I'm pregnant. Even if I were pregnant, I can work my ranch for several months until I'd need to slow down. Considering we just had sex three nights ago, I think I'm safe riding a horse." She yanked her arm free.

His stubborn jaw set. "Fine." Turning slightly, he raised his voice. "Anybody want to go on a cattle hunt?"

CHAPTER FIFTEEN

Three hours later, Melanie stretched her back atop the stallion, wincing as muscles protested. The sleet had slashed down, cold and merciless, for at least an hour. Then the clouds had given the earth a break from the attack, while covering the sun. The world stood still and cold.

A new set of dark clouds began to roll over the mountain. Visibility sucked. She'd go to her grave before admitting she'd give almost anything to be back in the warm kitchen eating Loni's breakfast delight.

Water dripped from the brim of her hat to her gloves, and she shivered.

Tom gave her the high sign from the other side of the valley entrance, and she nodded. She'd sent Hawk's crew to finish rounding cattle from the nearby roads before heading into the final valley. At least five head had been lost, and she needed that money.

A bellow echoed before the thunder of hooves ricocheted off the mountains. At least twenty head ran out, chased by Colton and his brothers. If any of the animals tried to veer out of the path, she and Tom needed to chase them back in line.

For now, all she could do was stare.

Colton rode full bore, his stallion churning mud, his long coat flapping in the wind. The brim of his dark hat was pulled low, and meager light highlighted slanted features and dark hollows in his face.

His chin remained down, his gaze focused on the

cattle. The coat emphasized broad shoulders that narrowed to a tight waist. As he passed, the muscles in his thighs clenched the horse.

On all that was holy, he was magnificent.

There was nothing sexier than a cowboy riding through a storm, controlling a wild stallion. Sure, he was arousing in his suit with his sharp mind making deals. But here, in nature, with him controlling everything wild around him? This was Colton in full force. The more primitive, baser part of his nature.

He was everything she'd ever wanted.

Lightning cracked across the mountain, and her mount jumped. In daydreaming, she'd let up on the reins. Tightening her legs, she tried to hold on as the horse reared up and then dropped his head. Almost in slow motion, she sailed over his head and held her breath until hitting the earth. Mud splashed around her a second before pain radiated down her arm.

She shook her head, trying to get her bearings.

As if laughing at her, the sky opened up, and rain began pelting down again.

Colton reached her first, jumping from his stallion and sliding in the mud and slush on his knees. "Mel?" He leaned in close, studying her face.

Heat roared through her cheeks. "You have got to be kidding me," she groaned.

He slid his hands down her arms. "Where are you hurt?"

"I'm not." Embarrassed but not hurt. She pushed to stand and winced. "I can't believe I just fell off a horse." Because she'd been daydreaming about Colton. She'd never live this down.

"Is she okay?" Tom yelled from the other side.

Colton nodded and waved him on. Tom clicked his horse into a trot and followed the other two so they could secure the cattle.

Melanie wiped mud off her hands. "I'm sorry."

Colton eyed her, head to toe, leaving tingles in the wake. "Are you sure you're all right?"

"Besides mortification? I'm fine." Her arm hurt, but it was just a bruise.

He tilted his hat up in a dangerously sexy way. "It's stormy, it's dark, and we're all tired. It could've happened to anybody."

Any other man would've given her a *told you so* that she should've stayed back at home when he'd asked. Not Colton. He tried to make her feel better even after she'd made such a rookie mistake. She sniffled.

Alarm lightened his eyes. "Are you crying?"

"No." She sniffed again.

He brushed a kiss across her forehead. "We've all been thrown. It happens. At least you didn't land on your butt and break your tailbone like Jake did. Remember?"

Her grin came naturally. Jake had been showing off for some girls in high school. "Yes, I remember."

"Good." Colton pressed a proprietary hand to her lower back, steering her to his horse. "Looks like we ride double until we fetch your horse. Keep your hands to yourself, Jacoby."

Now that might be tougher than he thought. After seeing him in full action, she wanted nothing more than to get her hands on him.

His cell phone buzzed, and he yanked it from his back pocket. "What?" Then he stiffened. "Okay.

Thanks." Ending the call, he glanced at Melanie. "They found Hawk passed out in the driver's seat of a rented SUV on I-90. He's at Maverick County Hospital right now."

. . .

Colton paced the tiled hallway, his thoughts churning. Every once in a while, he glanced at Melanie as she sat quietly by his mom in the orange waiting chairs of the hospital. Sophie and Juliet took up the other two chairs, while Jake and their dad stood like anchors near the doorway. Quinn had been called to a wreck near the lake but had made Colton promise to call him with news.

Mel was too pale, and she kept favoring her right side.

When she'd been thrown, Colton's life had flown before his eyes. While he'd always thought that was a stupid cliché, it turns out it really happened.

He knew any baby in her hadn't even formed baby parts yet, so there was no way a tumble from a horse could've hurt the forming cells. If there were forming cells. Chances weren't good.

Mel could've broken her neck.

Sure, she'd been thrown before. They all had. But now he wanted to smother her in bubble-wrap to keep safe. This new caring about somebody he was sleeping with wasn't nearly as fun as he'd expected.

The doctor finally came into sight down the long hallway, and Colton met him halfway. "Well?" Colton asked.

"Hawk hasn't regained consciousness," the doctor

said, gray eyes tired. "We've requested his medical records from the VA hospital and should know more as soon as they arrive."

Frustration heated Colt's esophagus. "Why hasn't he regained consciousness?"

"I don't know." The doctor rubbed his neck. "Until I see his records, I don't even know what the underlying injury was. I'd like to do an MRI but need to make sure he doesn't have any metal in his body. Thus, the need for his records to get here first."

"I'll make sure you have them within the hour," Jake said, grabbing his cell phone and heading toward the door.

Loni stood and hurried toward the doctor. "How about Hawk's other injuries?"

The doctor nodded. "Your son said Hawk might have internal injuries, and we haven't seen any evidence of that, so that's good news. The arm is broken and has been properly set in a cast."

Loni slid an arm around Colton's waist. "The head injury is the main concern, then?"

"Yes." The doctor sighed. "As soon as I have an idea of what we're dealing with, we can figure out a plan of action. Whether to transfer him or seek an expert here. For now, all we can do is wait."

Colton nodded. "Great. Also, would you mind checking out my girlfriend's arm? I think she hurt it when she fell from a horse earlier."

All eyes immediately turned his way.

Melanie paled and then stood.

Colton frowned. "What?"

"Did you say *girlfriend*?" Tom asked with a grin.

Had he? Without answering, Colton turned and

followed Melanie from the waiting area, placing a hand on her lower back in support. She stiffened but kept walking.

"You don't need to come with me," she muttered under her breath.

"Sure, I do." He propelled her along, not liking how she continued to favor her right side.

"You don't trust me to tell you what the doctor says?" she asked.

"Nope." Something in him felt guilty for allowing her to get hurt on his watch, which made no sense whatsoever. If Hawk had taken a tumble, Colt wouldn't feel responsible. But things were different with Mel now, and she was his to protect. If he told her that, she'd rightfully punch him in the face.

So he steered her into the examining room, hoping nothing was broken.

She sat on the crinkly paper and gave him a look. "I have to take my shirt off."

He grinned. "Why do you think I came?"

His smart-ass reply had the desired effect of making her smile. "You're such a perv."

"So you already told me," he said.

At his reminder of the afternoon in Seattle, a pretty blush wandered across her face. He watched, fascinated. "You have the prettiest skin, Mel."

She laughed and then winced. "Stop flirting with me. I'm in pain."

He instantly sobered and reached to help with her shirt. "How much pain?"

"Not enough to have a doctor take a look," she said.

Colton took a glance at her arm and stilled. "Whoa."

She looked down. "I told you I was just bruised."

Yes, but the bruise extended from her shoulder and down her entire arm in a range of different purples. He gently pulled her arm away from her body to run his fingers along her ribs. They seemed fine.

The doctor came into the room, and Colton turned around. "She's just bruised, but if she's pregnant, would this injury harm a baby?"

The doctor looked up from a chart to focus on Mel. "How far along?"

She gripped her hands together. "A few days."

The doctor finally cut a smile. "Ah, no. You're safe." He leaned in and examined the bruise, as well as her shoulder and ribs. "The bruise is a doozy, but nothing is broken. I recommend rest, aspirin, and a cold compress." He straightened. "Hawk is still unconscious, but you can take turns sitting with him now."

Colt's gaze met Mel's worried one. Hawk had to wake up.

Mel nodded toward the doorway. "You can go first."

"Thanks." He slipped her shirt back over her head and gingerly slid her arm through the slot. "I'll be back in a minute."

Following the doctor, he forced his face into casual lines in case Hawk had awakened.

He hadn't.

Hawk overwhelmed the hospital bed, all ripped muscle, his eyes closed and his breathing even. Electrodes attached lines from machines to his body, and the beep, beep, beep of the machines continued in a rhythmic cadence.

Mottled bruises covered every exposed area of his

tanned skin. Bruises from fists and what appeared to be a bat.

Fury spiraled through Colton so fast he nearly swayed. The helicopter story was a lie. He knew a good beating when he saw one, and somebody had beaten the absolute shit out of his oldest friend. As soon as Hawk woke up, they'd go seeking justice.

• • •

Melanie studied the soda machine at the hospital's break room, her mind spinning and her arm aching. Colt had called her *his girlfriend* to his family. She had seriously mixed feelings about the statement.

Well, once the thrill of hearing the words had dissipated. Girlfriend. Yeah. That meant they were dating and not just having sex. Girlfriends in Colton's life had expiration dates on their time with him.

From the second she'd realized she was in love with him, caution had kicked in. The guy went through women pretty regularly, and she didn't want any awkwardness with her friends or family when they ended.

Well, if they ended.

What if they didn't end? Her mind could easily spin with daydreams of happily ever after with Colton. He wasn't an easy guy, but if he gave his heart, it'd be once and it'd be completely.

A rustle sounded by the doorway, and Sheriff Quinn Lodge strode inside, after having taken care of the lake accident. His black hat was pulled low over his handsome face, and he still wore the long coat from riding earlier. "What are you doing in here?"

She shrugged and looked at the closest person she had to an older brother. "Trying to figure out how to make Colton fall in love with me."

Quinn lifted both eyebrows. "I'd bet he's already in love with you. Who wouldn't be?"

Melanie grinned. "You're biased."

"Of course I am." Quinn smiled. "Jake said Colton called you his girlfriend out there. Want me to beat him up for making the assumption?"

What a sweet offer. "Nah. If he needs a beating, I'll take care of it." She sighed. "I just don't want everything to change."

"Change is good, Mel." Quinn tossed his hat on a nearby table. "Usually. Any word on Hawk?"

"No," she said.

Quinn frowned, worry lining his face. He had his mama's dark eyes and hair, but his large build must've been from his daddy. "Hawk is tough. He'll be okay."

"I know," she whispered.

Quinn leaned and peered at the machine. "Do you have a dollar I can borrow?"

She snorted and dropped quarters in his hand so he could buy a Pepsi. "Thanks for everything, Quinn."

He headed for the door and turned around to shoot her a quick grin after fetching his wet hat from the table. "I'm just getting started." Then he disappeared from sight.

Melanie grabbed a couple of more quarters and bought a soda. Well, time to do what would piss off the entire family and make the phone call none of them would make. Then, she quickly drew her cell phone from her pocket and pressed speed dial.

"Hello?" a sleepy voice mumbled.

"Dawn? It's Melanie." Mel was pretty sure nobody had thought to call Dawn Freeze at college.

"Mel?" Something rustled, and Dawn's voice gained clarity. "What's wrong?"

Melanie forced herself to remain calm. "Hawk was injured in a helicopter crash, had the military bring him home, and checked himself out of the Helena hospital. Then, somehow, he was found by the side of the road. He's in Maverick at the hospital and hasn't gained consciousness."

Silence beat over the line for several seconds. "Nobody called me," Dawn said.

"I'm calling you. We're at the hospital right now and don't know anything yet." Melanie kept her voice calm, sure the boys wouldn't have called their younger sister until knowing something. But she would've wanted to know, and so did Dawn.

Dawn gasped. "I'll head home right away."

"That's up to you, but please drive carefully," Mel said.

"I will. Thanks for calling me. You're a good friend." Dawn disengaged the call.

"Did you just call my sister?" Colton asked from the doorway.

Melanie gasped and turned around. The man moved silently enough to be military trained. "Yes."

Colton frowned, harsh lines in his face and anger in his eyes. "Why did you do that? Now she'll drive through the storm to get here."

"So? She's an adult, and she can make her own choices." Plus, she was Mel's friend. "If you were injured and in the hospital, I would fully expect Dawn to give me a call. That's all I did."

Irritation swirled across Colt's face. "We don't know anything about Hawk, and Dawn needs to stay at school. I'll keep her informed."

Melanie coughed as her temper sprang to life. She was tired, she was wet, and her arm hurt. She didn't need a lecture from one of Dawn's way overprotective brothers. "You dumb son of a bitch. Dawn has been in love with Hawk since he fished her out of Miller's pond when she was four. She needs to be here."

A flush covered Colton's high cheekbones, and he yanked a cell from his back pocket. "That silly crush was over a long time ago. Thanks for the help, but my family can handle this." Turning on his heel, he exited the room.

CHAPTER SIXTEEN

Colton loosened his hands on the stirrups as he led the way through the forest on the edge of their land, finally opening to a wide field. After leaving the hospital, he'd grabbed a few hours of sleep before lunchtime, and then he and his brothers had been repairing fences downed by the storm. "Hey, I was thinking about moving Lodge-Freeze headquarters to Mineral Lake."

Quinn pulled abreast of him on his vibrating stallion. "Works for me."

Jake pulled up on the other side. "The top floor of the Franks building is for lease."

"I know. I actually called Old Man Franks to see if he'd be interested in selling the entire building. Paying rent doesn't sit well with me." Colton eyed the metal building in the distance.

"How is business, anyway?" Jake asked.

Colton took a deep breath. He'd deliver the bad news later—when he could tell everybody at once. "We can have a meeting tonight to discuss the upcoming year. Considering Dawn is coming home." Yeah, he was putting off the inevitable as long as possible.

Quinn glanced at his watch. "She should be here in a couple of hours. I guess we should've called her first."

"Yes. She's pissed." Colton drew up on the reins. "Though not as pissed as Mel is. I didn't handle that well."

"You are a moron," Jake agreed.

"You don't want Dawn coming home right now any more than I do." Colton rolled his eyes. "She'll camp out at the hospital, and that's not a good thing."

Quinn grimaced. "I thought this whole crush thing she had for Hawk was over."

"It is." Jake squinted at the clouds now rolling across the sky. "They're still old friends."

"What if the crush isn't over?" Colton asked quietly.

His brothers didn't answer him. Hawk was family, and they'd die for him. But the guy definitely had issues after his time in the service, and their baby sister was innocent.

"It's over," Quinn said. "What's up with you and Mel, anyway?"

Colton sighed. He'd been expecting the question. "It's complicated."

"Bullshit." Jake blew out air. "If you're just messing with her, I'm going to mess with you."

Colton nodded. "I figured." If he hurt Mel, he deserved both his brothers trying to kick his ass. Of course, he knew how to fight, too. "I won't hurt her."

Quinn groaned. "I have to ask, and I don't want to sound like a girl, but I have to say the words. How do you feel about Mel?"

Jake snorted. "You sound like a shrink, not a girl."

"Shut up." Quinn steered his stallion toward a ridge. "Answer the question, Colt."

"I don't know." Colton hunched his shoulders. "She's different than anybody I've been with, and I'd cut off my arm before hurting her. The idea of her with somebody else makes me want to hit something, and when she flew over the head of that horse—" He cut himself off. There weren't words.

Jake smiled. "He's in love."

"Of course he's in love with Mel—he has been for eons." Quinn shook his head. "He's finally realizing it. Dumbass."

Jake snorted. "He's always been slow."

"Both of you shut up." Colton dug in his heels. "We haven't been dating long enough to be in love. We'll date and then figure it out."

"Ah. The life plan according to numbnuts." Quinn nodded sagely. "Stick with your life plan, and you're going to lose her."

The thought of really losing Mel, of not having her in his life, compressed Colton's lungs. "I'm done talking about this."

"So am I." Quinn dismounted. "What's everyone's plan for the rest of this fine Saturday?"

"I'm heading home to play with the kids and check on my pregnant wife," Jake said slowly, clapping his gloved hands together to wipe off dust. "How about we have a barbecue and the family board meeting at my house tonight?"

"Sounds good. I have paperwork at the office and then I'm home helping Juliet move paintings around in her gallery." Quinn grinned. "Can't wait for the board meeting."

Colton sighed. "I'm heading to the hospital to yell at Hawk to wake up, and then apparently I'm preparing for a board meeting."

"Will Mel be at the board meeting?" Jake asked with a sly grin.

"Why? She's not family," Colton retorted. Besides,

Mel was so pissed at him right now, she wouldn't even take his calls. Maybe flowers would help.

Quinn shook his head. "You truly are a dumbass," he muttered.

People needed to quit saying that. "I'll call when I get a visual on Dawn," Colton said. He finished with the horses and hurried outside to his truck, taking time to appreciate how nice and clean the town was as he drove through. The storefronts all showed green decorations ranging from clovers to drunken leprechauns.

Flashing back to their third grade parade, he grinned. Melanie's grandpop had hand-sewn her a mermaid costume that was spectacular. He'd been so proud until discovering that his new-found talent put him in immediate demand for all school plays and festivities.

Through the years, the good-natured rancher had sewn plenty of costumes. He'd been a good man. While Melanie put on a strong face, she had to be missing him.

Colton frowned. He'd been way too hard on her about calling Dawn. He plotted the way to get her to forgive him as he drove out of town and across the county to the Maverick hospital. Pulling into a parking spot of the hulking wood building, he glanced around for her car.

Disappointment flooded him that she wasn't there.

Sighing, he hustled out of the car and loped into the hospital, winding through hallways until reaching Hawk's room. Once inside, he stopped short.

Dawn sat in a chair, her small hands wrapped around Hawk's large one. Fear sat in her eyes and along her classic face.

Fuck. His sister was in love. The real kind.

Colton hitched inside, and she turned tear-filled eyes toward him.

He paused again. When had his baby sister turned into such a beautiful woman? Dark blue eyes took prominence in delicate features, while her black hair hung straight to her shoulders in a classic cut.

She stood and hugged him, her grip strong and somehow delicate. The scent of huckleberries surrounded her and reminded him of home. She didn't even reach his chin, and a wave of protectiveness swept him. "How are you?" he asked.

She levered back and smiled. "Fine. You?"

Actually, his life was a bit screwed up right now. "Great. Any news on Hawk?"

She turned back toward their friend. "His medical records came in, and he's scheduled for an MRI in an hour. Vitals are good, but he hasn't awakened."

Colton slipped an arm around her shoulder and tucked her close. "I would've come to get you."

"I can drive, Colt." She elbowed him in the ribs. "Though you should've called me sooner."

Maybe. "How's school?" he asked.

"Good. Finals are in two months, and then I'm done with one more degree. Everyone thinks I'm crazy for wanting to study more finance in Europe. It's only for six months." She shrugged.

He grinned. "You're just wanting to put more letters after your name than I have. In fact, I've been to more of your graduations than my own." He was plenty proud of his baby sister.

She tugged him toward the chairs. "I wish Hawk would wake up."

"Me too." Colton settled in to support his sister and guard his friend. "I need your help getting Melanie to forgive me."

"She said you were a complete ass," Dawn said.

"I was," he admitted.

Dawn grinned. "I figured. So, let's plan, and then I'm supposed to help you with the Paddy's Day float."

• • •

Colton cradled little Nathan, his nephew, as he loped over bouncy castles, stuffed frogs, and a smattering of little socks to answer the doorbell. "I'll get it," he called back to Jake, who was busy barbecuing steaks on the back deck.

He'd put everyone to work creating the wolf-bear-leprechaun-themed float, and it was now ready to go.

Then he grinned at the changes in the house since Nathan had arrived. For so long there were princess and mermaid toys all around for Leila, and now miniature footballs and frogs kept appearing. "I'm glad you're here," he whispered to his nephew, who looked up with huge dark eyes in an already strong face.

Yeah, at fifteen months old, the kid looked just like Jake.

Nathan chortled. "Doggie. Dog. Doggie. Dooooo-giiie."

"I might have to get you a dog, buddy." Colton opened the door and stopped short.

Melanie blinked, her hands full of a huge casserole dish. "I thought you were at the hospital."

"I was, but Quinn picked me up." He shifted Nathan to his other arm as the boy held out chubby hands for Melanie. "Ah, switch." Taking her dish, he smoothly slipped Nathan into her arms.

She grinned and cooed. "He has even more hair than he did last week." With a sigh of pleasure, she nuzzled Nathan's wild mane of black hair.

Colton drew her inside so he could shut the door. "I'm sorry about earlier."

Melanie glanced up, obviously trying to hold on to her mad. But with a happily gurgling toddler in her arms, the battle was a losing one. "I don't want to talk about it right now. Why are you here, anyway?"

"My family likes me," he said easily.

"They have to like you in case they need a kidney someday." She kept her voice soft for Nathan's sake, but spunk still shone in her eyes.

Man, he'd love to meet her challenge head on, and better yet, in the bedroom. He grinned. "I overreacted, and I hurt your feelings by implying you weren't family. For that, I'm truly sorry."

She blinked twice.

He knew Melanie as well as he knew himself, and she never could resist a sincere apology. He really was sorry.

"Fine." She brushed past him.

Playing stubborn, was she? The evening just became a whole lot more interesting. He inhaled the scent of her famous huckleberry cobbler with a sigh of appreciation and followed her into the chaotic kitchen.

His gaze only dropped twice to her round ass in curve-hugging jeans. His own jeans suddenly felt too tight.

Dawn hopped off a stool to hug Melanie, the baby sandwiched between them. "Tell me you brought your cobbler," Dawn said, untangling her hair from Nathan's grabbing hands and wincing as he tried to hold on.

"Of course." Melanie glanced around at the abundance of family. "I didn't know this was a family barbecue."

Dawn shrugged and slid her arm through Mel's. "We're having a quick board meeting before dinner, but it's no big deal."

Melanie faltered. "Who's with Hawk?"

Sophie glanced up from chopping a salad on her new granite countertop. "Mrs. Hudson and Mrs. Wilson are with him now, and then the Lady Elks are taking shifts all night. We're back on duty tomorrow."

Colton wasn't sure Hawk would want so many people watching him sleep, but somebody should be there when he woke up. "Hawk's going to be cranky about this."

Dawn grinned. "I know, right?" Although her smile was genuine, dark worry glimmered in her eyes. "I'd stay at the hospital, but the doctors are adamant that only one person be in with him at a time, and the whole town insists on taking a turn."

"Hawk's tough—he'll be all right," Colton said. Yeah, he hoped that was true. Hawk had to wake up. Soon. "The MRI showed brain swelling, but not enough to do surgery. He'll be fine." If he woke up. The longer he remained unconscious, the greater the chance he'd slip into a coma.

Tom loped in from outside. "Let's do this board meeting so we can eat."

Colton nodded and led the way into his dad's huge study, where he'd left quarterly reports. He served as president of the board, while Jake served as VP, Quinn as secretary, and Dawn as treasurer. Tom was ex-president, so he sat in on the meetings.

Colton cleared his throat. "Are Mom, Sophie, or Juliet joining us?"

"They said to go ahead, that since they're not officers, they don't have to stop having fun," Dawn said with a longing look inside. "They're looking on a website for new baby furniture along with Melanie."

Colton called the meeting to order. His hands sweat, and a knot rolled in his stomach. "I, ah, made a mistake."

His dad sat back, eyebrows raised. "What kind of a mistake?"

Colton couldn't do this. "I got cocky and made a risky investment—we lost money."

"How much?" Jake asked, frowning.

"Too much." Colton cleared his suddenly dry throat. "I hunted down and secured the patents for the green stock I told you all about last year, but they won't pay off for at least a year."

Quinn leaned forward, his hands on the table. "What does that mean?"

Meeting Quinn's gaze was one of the hardest things Colton had ever done. "No dividends for the year— maybe two years."

Dawn gasped, her eyes wide. "None?"

"No." Colton shuffled his feet. "The patents will pay well in a couple of years, I'm sure of it."

Silence echoed around the room for several heartbeats. Colton could almost hear rapid minds kicking facts into place. His ears burned, and a tight knot of regret settled hard in his stomach. Why had he been so sure of his plan?

Finally, Tom sighed. "Then we tighten our belts for a couple of years." He glanced out the window at his sprawling acreage.

Quinn rubbed his chin. "Juliet's just starting to see cash flow at the gallery, but we can make it on my sheriff's salary, even if the ranch takes a hit."

Jake nodded. "I have a couple of good court cases coming up—might even have enough to pay ranch expenses for all of us."

"But you have the baby and medical bills," Dawn murmured. "I can forget about Europe or take out student loans." She pushed her dark hair out of her face, intelligence shining in her eyes. "Working for a year or two before studying overseas wouldn't hurt me any."

Colton swallowed. "I'm so sorry."

Then he steeled himself, prepared for their disappointment.

"We'll be back on track in a couple of years?" Quinn asked, flipping through the report.

"It looks like it," Colton said.

Jake kept reading. "Will this affect any of the land holdings we currently have?"

"No, but it will affect our ability to acquire more land for the next two years. And, nothing can go wrong with the ranches." Yeah, right. Ranching by its very definition included risk. Colton leaned forward, gauging their reactions. Why wasn't anybody yelling at him yet?

"Good enough." His dad flipped closed the report. "We're going to need your plan."

Colton dropped into a chair. "My plan?"

"Yes." Quinn tossed his report on the masculine coffee table. "You're our financial guy. We'll get you reports on what we think is coming in for the next year, you figure out expenses, and then come up with a plan."

Jake rubbed his chin. "You are the planner."

Dawn nodded. "We'll just pool our resources. It isn't like we haven't done that before. I'll get a job."

"No," her dad said. "If you want to get that financial certificate in Europe, that goes in Colton's plan as an expense. Period."

Jake and Quinn nodded.

Colton frowned. "Why aren't you all mad?"

Dawn's eyebrows drew together. "Mad about what?"

"About my crappy business decision that has hindered us." Colton rubbed his chin. "I've screwed up." So much for his grand plan.

"You did go to Seattle, and you fixed it." Quinn tapped his fingers on the wooden table. "Running the entire company is a tough job, and we trust you to do it right. The patents look good, and they'll probably end up making us a lot of money."

Dawn reached over and patted his hand. "Everyone makes mistakes. It's okay, Colton."

Emotion welled through him so quickly he nearly swayed.

"In other words, chill out and give yourself a break," Jake said, leaning back to glance into the kitchen. "Now, could we call the meeting over so I can go prevent my wife from buying out the entire furniture store online?"

Colton swallowed. They trusted him. They believed

in him. "The meeting is adjourned."

As he glanced around at people who'd support him no matter what, he was struck with how lucky he was. He wanted to share that…with Melanie.

CHAPTER SEVENTEEN

Melanie breathed in the chilly night air as she left Jake's house, wondering how she'd been so easily outmaneuvered. "Now wait a minute." She paused by the door of her truck to face Colton. "Why do you need a ride home?"

"I rode in with Quinn and Juliet." Colton yanked the passenger door open and slid inside.

"Why couldn't they give you a ride home?" Melanie grumbled as she climbed into her truck.

"They're all kissy-kissy." Colton shut the door. "You look tired. Want me to drive?"

Melanie ignited the engine and decided to enjoy the ride. "Sorry, control freak. Enjoy the passenger side."

"I am not a control freak. I just like to drive," Colton objected.

"Huh." The guy didn't like the wheel in anybody else's hands. Melanie hit a pothole at the end of Jake's drive.

"You did that on purpose," Colton muttered.

Yeah, she'd nailed that one. "Prove it," she said.

"Did you have fun tonight?" he asked.

"Yes." She felt right at home with the Lodge-Freeze family and had truly enjoyed playing with both Nathan and Leila. God, she wanted kids. So badly. "How did the board meeting go?"

"Fine. They didn't call for my head—yet anyway," he said.

"They are a patient group." For some reason, needling Colton had become a good goal since he'd been so serious all night. "There's plenty of time. It's not like you use your head much."

He chuckled. "Any reason you're tempting me to toss your ass over my knee again?"

Heat zinged through her body to land between her legs. "Threaten me again, and you'll walk home, Freeze." Her voice remained level, and triumph filled her.

They came upon the ridge overlooking Mineral Lake, and Colton pointed to the overhang, which stood to the side and could see over most of the nearest valley. "Pull over for a sec. I can see the Angus from here."

Melanie pulled over.

Colton grinned before twisting the ignition and taking the keys.

"Hey." Silence surrounded them, and Melanie turned toward him. "Give me the keys."

"You ever park here?" Colt asked, his voice soft, his eyes glowing in the moonlight.

The sexy tone licked over her skin. "No. Give me the keys." This time, her voice wavered.

"Come and get them." He slipped them into his front pocket.

Images of what lay just behind that pocket filled her mind and heated her body. "You're a little too old for that game," she breathed.

"Ah, baby. You're never too old for that game." He reached down and unbuckled her belt. "You've been pushing me all night. Why don't you just get it out of your system?"

"Meaning, what?" she asked.

"You're mad at my reaction to your calling Dawn, and I get that. But I apologized, so let's get past it," he said evenly.

She drew in a deep breath. "You think you're so charming that an apology can get you past anything, don't you?" He had a right to think that, considering his charm had always worked. Plus, he usually meant his words, so his apologies were sincere.

"If words aren't enough, what do you want?" He caressed down her arm to her thigh, and her muscle bunched beneath his firm grasp.

She swallowed. "Nothing. Words are fine."

He leaned closer, his hand sliding to her knee, his breath heating her ear. "I don't think so. What else could I possible do to make you forgive me?"

Her entire body shuddered as she tried to retain control and not rip his clothes off. "Seduction is a waste of time." She hoped the words emerged logically.

He chuckled, and the sound vibrated straight to her clit. "We both know you just meant to challenge me."

She had no clue what she'd meant to do, since her mind had pretty much shut down. Her body trembled with a need so great it astounded her. The man had barely touched her. "No challenge intended."

He caressed up her thigh to press against the apex of her legs. "Open for me, baby."

She grabbed the steering wheel with both hands, the stars blurring high in the sky. "We're in the truck."

"I know." He nipped her ear, and she stopped breathing.

Then she slid her knees farther apart.

"Good girl," he breathed, quickly unzipping her

jeans and slipping one finger beneath her panties. "So, about our game."

She blinked again, biting her lip to keep from gyrating against his hand. "G-game?"

"Yeah." He licked along the shell of her ear. "The game is called two minutes—over and under."

She shut her eyes and tried to concentrate while the world narrowed to his talented fingers. "I don't know that game." Her words came out in a breathless rush, and she couldn't help rolling her hips.

"It's easy. When I say *go*, I either make you come within two minutes, or I don't. Feel free to fight it." He tugged on her clit for emphasis. "If I win, I choose where we stay the night, and you forgive me. If you win, you can continue being irritated and spend the night by yourself."

Two minutes? She could make it a measly two minutes. "And...I get Feisty's next colt." Feisty was Colt's favored thoroughbred champion, and she should be foaling within the next year.

Colton chuckled. "Fair enough, but if the stakes are that high, you have to keep your hands on the steering wheel and your legs open. You change either of those, and you lose."

"Fine." Drawing on any dignity and pride she could find, she settled her mind to think about taxes next year.

"Are you ready?" he asked, licking down her neck.

Her skin tingled where he roamed. "Give it your best shot, Freeze." *Taxes. Numbers. Shoes. Bunions. What the heck was a bunion, anyway?*

"*Go*," he whispered. Then he released her and leaned back.

Her eyelids shot open. "What—"

"Keep your hands on the wheel." He pushed a button on his watch, and then expertly slipped open her blouse buttons. "You. Can't. Move."

Desire ran with heated claws through her abdomen. She could do this. Two minutes. Only two minutes.

He flicked open the front clasp of her bra.

Crap. She should've worn a different bra. A sports bra, even. Wetness coated her thigh, and she fought to keep from rubbing her legs together.

His rough hand palmed one breast, and she bit back a harsh moan.

He reached across her and pulled a lever, sliding the seat back about ten inches.

"No, you—"

He smiled and leaned in to enclose one nipple. "Be quiet, Mel, and hold on to the wheel."

Her knuckles ached as she tightened her hold.

He bit down enough to have her crying out. Electrical shocks cascaded from her nipple to her sex. "Colton." Her head fell back on the headrest.

Wet and rough, his tongue bathed her smarting flesh. "I love how you respond," he murmured. "Have you ever been tied up?"

A spiraling started deep in her sex, and she fought to concentrate, to hold back the impending orgasm. "No, and it's not going to happen," she panted.

The heel of his palm pressed down on her clit at the same time as he inched two fingers inside her. "I think it will happen," he said, crisscrossing his fingers and zeroing in on her G-spot.

A rushing sound filled her ears, and her body began to gyrate against her will.

He levered up and kissed her, hard and deep. She lost herself in his mouth, in his determination, in the very maleness that was Colton.

She could do this. Kiss him and not come. Except he had two hands.

Without warning, his tongue swept her mouth just as he pushed down on her clit, his free hand tweaking her nipple.

Hard.

She exploded from the inside out, white flashes zipping behind her eyelids. Waves of intense pleasure ripped through her, breasts to toes, undulating her abdomen, making her cry out into his mouth.

His magical fingers prolonged her orgasm, forcing her to ride the waves until her entire body went lax. She flopped back against the leather as he removed his hands and refastened her bra and shirt.

Finally, panting, she opened one eye. "Time?"

Arrogance, amusement, and an alarming gentleness curved his smile as he glanced at his watch. "Eight-two seconds. I guess you're mine for the entire night."

Her stomach clenched, and her breasts, already at attention, yipped a *yahoo*. How in the world was she going to survive an entire night with Colton Freeze?

• • •

Colton nudged his cabin door open, wondering idly if he should carry Melanie inside. Were his brothers right? Was this actually love? The idea was starting to seem plausible and not so alarming.

Melanie stepped inside and grinned. "Colton Freeze, folks. The most organized, well-planned financial genius in town…and complete slob."

He shut the door and grinned. "I'm not a slob." Then he glanced around at his boots by the door, shirts on the couch, and dry groceries he'd failed to put away still sitting on the table. "Maybe?"

She laughed and began folding clean shirts. "You're not dirty, just messy."

"Oh baby, I can be dirty." He wiggled his eyebrows in a way guaranteed to make her laugh harder.

She wiped her eyes. "I love the sound of the stream out back."

"Me too." He liked living to the west of everyone. The one bedroom cabin had one bathroom and a main living space that consisted of a living room, eating nook, and kitchen. A massive stone fireplace took up one wall, and windows another. The stream outside was a constant flow.

Wind rattled pine needles against the window.

He took the shirts from her and tossed them on a chair. "Have you noticed we haven't made love in a bed yet?"

Pink slid across her face, and he watched, fascinated.

His phone buzzed, and only the need to find out about Hawk could pull Colt's attention from Melanie. "Freeze," he answered.

"Colt? It's Dad. Hawk has slipped into a coma."

CHAPTER EIGHTEEN

Melanie left the hospital and drew her coat closer together as the wind tried to chill her bones. When would spring begin to show up? Worry cascaded even more coldness through her.

How could Hawk be in a coma? She'd spent the morning talking to him and trying to get him to awaken, but he hadn't moved. Colton was working on the ranch but would head to the hospital as soon as possible.

Hawk needed to awaken.

She slipped into her truck and drove back to Mineral Lake, stopping in front of Kurt's Koffees to return her shirt. She'd quit her other two town jobs the other day and didn't miss them a bit.

After giving Kurt a hug, she loped next door to the new deli where Dawn already sat in a booth, sipping a soda.

"Hi." Melanie dropped onto the bench, her entire body aching.

"Hi." Dark circles accentuated the hollows beneath Dawn's bloodshot eyes. She'd pulled her dark hair up in a clip and wore jeans with a sweater. "I ordered turkey sandwiches for us both. How was the hospital?"

"He's the same." Melanie signaled for a soda. "Did you stay at the hospital all night?"

"I read a romance novel to him." Dawn's smile barely lifted her lips. "I figured he'd wake up and protest."

Melanie nodded. "That should've done it."

The bell over the door jingled, and Mrs. Joskly, the current town librarian, bustled inside with a hulking blond giant at her side.

"Oh, good. I thought I saw you come in, Melanie. This is my grandson, George, visiting from Boise." Mrs. Joskly straightened her peacoat.

"Ma'am," George said, his deep voice matching his beefy body. Green eyes sparkled out of his round face, giving him the look of the Jolly Green Giant. He gingerly slipped his arm out of Mrs. Joskly's grasp. "I'll go order sandwiches, Naney."

Mrs. Joskly waited until he'd lumbered toward the counter before speaking. "I was hoping you'd show Georgie around town, Melanie."

Melanie glanced toward George's broad back. "He looks about seventeen, Mrs. Joskly."

"Oh no, dear. Georgie is eighteen and perfectly legal. Come on." Mrs. Joskly winked a cataract-laden eye. "We all like to play the cougar once in a while, now don't we?"

Dawn coughed into her water glass.

Melanie tried to keep from wincing. "How long will Georgie be in town, ma'am?"

"Just until next Tuesday," Mrs. Joskly said cheerfully, clapping her mittens together. "Then you'll have to say good-bye forever."

Dawn cleared her throat. "Is Tuesday the day you have for the town pool, Mrs. Joskly?"

"Of course not." The librarian gave her patented hard stare down her nose. "I have the following week. I certainly don't expect a good girl like Melanie to date George on Tuesday and declare her love on Wednesday for Colton. That should take a least a week."

Melanie leaned back when the waitress delivered their sandwiches. "I appreciate the offer, but I'm busy with work. Plus, I'm sure Georgie would have more fun hanging out with kids his own age."

Mrs. Joskly sighed heavily. "Well, I suppose so. But keep two weeks from Thursday in mind, would you?"

"Of course." Melanie smiled weakly and reached for her sandwich.

Dawn waited until Mrs. Joskly had joined her grandson across the deli. "This bet is getting odd, right?"

"Very. Any idea who the bet taker is?" Melanie asked.

Dawn frowned. "I really don't know, but I've been out of town at school, so that's not surprising." She took a bite of sandwich and chewed thoughtfully for a moment. "Did you ask me to lunch to talk or *to talk*?"

"I asked you to lunch to chat and not about Hawk, not about Colton, and certainly not about love." Melanie sipped her soda.

"Perfect." Dawn sighed, relief crossing her classic features. "I don't have the energy for a real heart-to-heart."

"Me either. Tell me about your classes." Melanie snagged a chip from her plate.

They finished their lunches, and right about as Melanie finished her chips, a twinge from the ride side of her abdomen caught her attention. She sat back and took a deep breath. Another twinge.

"Excuse me," she said to Dawn and then slipped from the booth, heading toward the restroom. A quick glance in the one stall confirmed another shattered dream.

She'd started her period.

Her mind swam, and traitorous tears pricked the back of her eyes. Sure, it was foolish. But she'd believed, deep down, since Colton wanted to get her pregnant, that it'd work.

Hurt washed through her along with the rest of her hope.

A five percent chance was no chance at all, especially since that five percent might now be gone.

Her mind clicked to moments of Colton holding little Nathan, of him taking Leila on a date. The man loved kids and certainly wanted his own. Why wouldn't he? The Freeze genes were pretty good.

Logically, she knew this wasn't her fault. But deep down, in a place she hated to visit, shame lived. She couldn't have kids. She'd never feel the beginning of a life, of being kicked in the tummy, of sharing a body.

That awareness brought physical pain.

She knew Colton as well as she knew herself. He'd stick with her, no matter what, especially if she needed him. What about his dreams? Plus, it wasn't like he'd declared any love.

They had friendship, they had trust. Maybe he did love her. The kind of love that came from childhood, that came from genuine friendship. If it had been the happily-ever-after forever kind, he would've said so.

Sometimes silence hurt worse than the most hateful of words. She took a deep breath and left the restroom, already planning her future alone.

Dawn glanced up. "Are you okay? You're pale."

"I'm fine." Melanie placed bills on the table. "Just a little headache. Let's get back to the hospital and force Hawk to wake up." Then she'd plan her life alone.

...

Colton stood outside Hawk's hospital room, trying to keep from punching the doctor in the face. "What do you mean, his vitals are slowing?"

The doctor sighed. "The brain is a mystery, and the longer he's in a coma, the less likely he'll awaken. We'd like to helicopter him to Seattle."

"When he wakes up, he'll want to be home," Colt said. Reality began to spin away.

The doctor nodded. "I understand and think you should prepare yourself for the possibility that he's not waking up."

"No." Colton pivoted on his heel and went into the room to drop into a chair. The quiet silence was filled with the scents of bleach and plastic.

He stretched back in the plastic hospital chair, his gaze on his buddy. The person he'd always told everything to, the person who had his back no matter what.

Hawk lay in the bed, not moving. Although his skin showed his Native American heritage, he looked pale. Wounded. Hurting.

Colton glanced down at his muddied jeans. Mud, snow, and blood.

Despair hunched his shoulders. Life was out of control, and he hated it. The idea of losing Hawk burned like acid in his gut. He had to fix everything somehow. "I'm not leaving this seat until you wake up," he whispered to his silent friend.

And he wouldn't. A promise was a promise.

A rustle sounded by the door, and his dad slipped inside. He walked toward the bed, examined the beeping machines, and rested a large-boned hand on Hawk's forehead. "How is our boy doing?"

Colton wiped his eyes. "His vitals have slowed, which is bad."

Tom turned to take the next chair. "I made Dawn go home and get some sleep."

"I think only one of us is supposed to be in here." Colt said woodenly.

Tom extended long legs and crossed his boots at the ankles. "I'd like to see them bodily remove us."

Colton studied his dad. Although in his mid-fifties, Tom looked much younger. Broad across the shoulders, tall, and in excellent shape. He had the same blue eyes as Dawn. "Good point," Colton said.

Tom glanced down at the bloody jeans and then up at Colton's face. "Cattle kicked you?"

"Yes. The other day," Colt said.

"At Mel's house?" Tom asked.

"Yes. When I stayed over." Colton had always leveled with his dad, and he wouldn't stop now.

Tom scratched his strong jaw. "I wondered if you two would ever get together."

"Me too. But now I'm not sure we'll ever be friends again, if I screw this up, too."

"So don't screw it up." Tom shot him a look. "Do you want things to go back the way they were?"

"No." The word emerged before Colt even had to think about it. "I don't want to just be her friend. She's pretty much everything." At the thought of losing her, of not having her as a constant in his life, his gut clenched. Even more so, the thought of her loving somebody else made him want to hit the wall.

Tom nodded. "Been there. Your mother was a

friend before we got together. In fact, her husband was my best friend. When he died, we both felt lost."

Colton straightened and glanced at his dad. "I never really thought about that. Must've been tough."

"It was." His dad sighed, stretching out farther. "At first, we just helped each other cope, and I looked out for her two boys. Jake was so confused, and Quinn was so angry, we concentrated on them. Then, one day I turned around, and bam."

Yeah. *Bam.* Colt exhaled.

Tom cleared his throat. "It's nice to see you struggle a little."

"What?" Colton pivoted to face his dad.

Tom flashed a dimple. "You've always had girls and now women flocking toward you." He snorted. "No doubt because you inherited my good looks and charm."

Colton rolled his eyes. "Right."

"Okay. Your mama's good looks and charm." Tom cast a worried glance at Hawk. "Mel knows you, and she knows your bullshit. She also won't put up with it."

Colton frowned. "What's your point?"

"You eased into a relationship with no risk, and I bet you haven't even told her how you really feel." Thoughtful contemplation, not judgment, echoed in Tom's low tone.

Had he? Colton rubbed his chin. "I wanted to get my feet under me first."

Tom shook his head. "There's no getting your feet under you when you love a woman the way we do. Just hope you don't land on your face when you fall." He turned to pin his son with a hard look. "But make sure you mean it, because if you hurt that girl, I'll kick your ass myself."

"Fair enough." Colton glanced down at his demolished jeans. "I should probably clean up first."

"If you two are done with your hen fest, I'd like to get some rest," Hawk rasped from the bed.

Colt and Tom immediately launched themselves toward the bed.

"Hawk?" Colton asked, his voice shaking.

Hawk glared up through bloodshot eyes. "Stop hovering. You two block out the light."

"I'll get a doctor." Tom hustled from the room.

Colton smiled down at his buddy. "You're all right."

• • •

Melanie slipped off her gloves as she hurried down the hallway to Hawk's room, where a small celebration had taken over. The Lodge boys and their wives took up one wall, while Tom and Dawn sat in the chairs. Colton leaned against the wall by the head of the bed, and she studiously ignored him.

"Hey, Mel," Hawk said, his voice hoarse. He was sitting up, propped against a couple of pillows.

Relief swept through her so quickly her knees trembled. "It's about time you stopped napping," she said, striding toward the bed to get a better look and to reassure herself that he was actually awake.

His green eyes were clear, and while bandages covered a good part of him, he looked alert. "I'm fine. Stop frowning."

She schooled her face into calm lines. "How's the head?" Reaching out, she smoothed his dark hair away from his broad face. The purple bruise across his temple had faded to a striated red.

"Fine." He glanced at the clock near the far wall. "I'm leaving in a few minutes, probably."

"No, you're not." Loni Freeze swept into the room with a Crock-Pot in her hands. "I brought you soup."

Dawn laughed. "Mom, they have food here."

"Not as good as mine." Loni set the pot on the counter and tugged a bowl from her massive handbag. Her dark hair had been braided down her back, and she wore a pretty purple blouse with a wool skirt. "Chicken noodle has healing properties." Ignoring the amusement around her, she ladled a healthy portion into the bowl and handed it to Hawk. "Eat."

"Yes, ma'am," he said, accepting the spoon.

Melanie kept her gaze on Hawk, although she could feel Colton's on her. Yeah, he knew her well enough to understand something was on her mind. Maybe he wanted for her to end things so he didn't have to do so.

The guy should take the easy out and run.

The doctor entered the room, his weary gray gaze taking in the entire group. "What happened to the limit on visitors we set?"

Hawk blew on his spoon.

"When can he come home?" Loni asked, looking almost miniature next to Colton.

Hawk paused. "To my house."

"No, sweetie. To ours." Loni bent and tucked Hawk more firmly in. "You shouldn't be on your own for a while. Just until we make sure your brain is working all right."

Colton and his brothers all stiffened in an obvious attempt to prevent jumping at the easy one-liner.

Melanie smirked. None of them were brave enough to tick off Loni.

Hawk blinked twice, raw emotion crossing his face to be quickly vanquished.

Loni ignored his struggle for control and pressed a motherly kiss to his forehead. "You're family, and you're not getting out of my sight until I make sure you're all right."

Now a slight panic lifted Hawk's eyebrow.

"Melanie and I can take care of Hawk at Mel's house," Colton said calmly.

Mel's gaze slashed to meet his, which was full of challenge. He hadn't. He really hadn't.

Loni clasped her hands together. "Well, Mel's is closer to Hawk's spread so he can keep an eye on things. Colton's cabin isn't big enough, and I can visit Mel's house daily. Yes, that's a good plan."

The other men in the room were suddenly busy looking elsewhere. Anywhere but at Mel.

Oh, she knew a good setup when one smacked her over the head. "I'd be thrilled to have you stay with me, Hawk. Loni, you're welcome any time and any day. Colton, you don't live with me."

Hawk glanced from Colton to Melanie. "What did I miss?" he asked slowly.

"Nothing," Melanie answered just as Colton said, "A lot."

Anger slid through her veins like Pop Rocks. How dare he put her on the spot like this? Some privacy would be nice.

The doctor coughed. "It's time for a new MRI for Hawk. I'm going to have to ask you all to leave."

Melanie winked at Hawk. "I'll be back later, and

we'll plan your getaway."

He grinned and handed his bowl back to Loni. "That's a plan."

With a hard look at Colton, Melanie turned and exited the room, her boots echoing on the hard tiles as she hurried down the hallway and out into the sunny day.

Weak but bright, the sun glimmered off the frosty ground and a myriad of vehicles scattered around the parking lot.

She almost made it to her truck before Colton swung her around.

Jerking her arm away, she allowed her temper to blow. "What do you think you're doing?"

He frowned, amusement glinting in his blue eyes. "You don't want to help Hawk?"

Exasperation melded with anger. "Of course I want to help him. But I don't need you offering for me, and I sure don't need you making some sort of announcement that we're living together. We're not." In fact, they were breaking up. "It's over." She took a deep breath and tried to keep her face calm. "We're over, Colton."

"What if you're pregnant?" he asked softly.

The tears ignored her and filled her eyes. "I'm not. I've already started and will very soon end my period." One of the dubious benefits of her condition—very short periods, sometimes only lasting a day or two.

"Oh." He exhaled heavily. "So we'll try again."

"No. This is too much, and it's too complicated. We started because of the urgency, and now it's too late. We're just friends pretending to be more, Colton." At least, he was. Unless he disagreed?

He blinked and shook his head. "Mel—"

Her chin lifted. "Back off, Freeze. Whatever we had, it's over. Deal with it."

The slow smile he gave her tingled awareness along her skin, through her breasts, between her legs. "Ah, Mel." He stepped into her space, and her butt hit her door. "Please tell me you meant that as a challenge."

She kept her gaze steady. "I meant that as a brush-off, you arrogant ass."

"Prove it." He settled both hands on the truck, caging her.

"More games?" She tried for sarcasm, but her voice emerged breathy.

He leaned in, his lips brushing her temple. "Last time we played a game, you screamed my name as you came. Wanna play again?"

Lava flowed down her back. "You're boring me." Okay. She may have meant that one as a challenge.

He lifted away, his gaze hot. "Am I, now? Well, let's test that theory with one kiss. I'll kiss you, and if you don't respond, then I'll walk away and believe you're done with me."

"Colt—"

"Afraid?" he taunted.

Stubborn pride straightened her spine. "No. Kiss away, and when you lose, keep your lips to yourself."

"That would be a true pity considering how much my lips love every dip and crevice in your body," he said.

Those crevices began to ache. "Hurry up."

He leaned back in. "Fine." Without warning, his hand fisted in her hair and tugged. The erotic move shot arousal straight to her core. Her neck elongated, and her chest lifted against his torso. His toned body brushed against her in blatant masculinity.

She swallowed and tried to prevent her eyelids from dropping. Her hands clenched into fists to keep from grabbing him.

He twisted his wrist, angling her face.

Colt had a way of overwhelming her, making her feel feminine. That appealing warmth competed heavily with her sense of self preservation.

His lips hovered an inch from hers.

She breathed out, trying not to move.

He flicked out his tongue, licking the corner of her mouth. She shuddered, her breasts scraping his chest. She felt his smile as his mouth slid against hers.

Gentle, sweet, and firm, he kissed her as if they had all day. Slow and drugging, he took his time, his body heating hers, so much bigger and stronger. An edge lived in Colton Freeze, always had, but this was the first time she'd felt its bite.

He increased his pressure until she opened her mouth. Then he swept inside, staking a claim.

He took her under, he took her over, Colt in full force.

She'd underestimated him.

The hand in her hair tightened, holding her in place. Where he wanted her.

Her eyelids fluttered shut, and she fell into the storm, kissing him back, her tongue mating with his.

He growled deep, his free hand clasping the back of her thigh and lifting. His cock pulsed between her legs, and she struggled to get closer. To feel more.

She protested when he broke the kiss and lifted his head. Then she gasped.

Hunger glittered in his sky-dark eyes, crimson spiraled across his pronounced cheekbones. His nostrils flared much like a stallion's as it hunted a mate. The boy she'd known was gone.

Only a fully grown, dangerous man held her tight.

Need flushed through her. Every nerve she owned screamed for release. Her knees trembled, and her sex ached for him.

He released her hair and leg, tugging her way from the truck so he could open her door. His hands encircled her waist, and he lifted her into the seat. Then he shut the door and turned to walk away.

Without saying a word.

CHAPTER NINETEEN

That night, Colton wanted to kick himself as he strode into the hospital, its bright lights cutting through the dark hour. He'd worked on accounts all day, trying to make up for the shortfall from Mark's deception.

He'd sucked at it all day, because his mind had been elsewhere.

On a pretty brunette who'd pretty much blown his world apart with one little kiss in the parking lot.

He'd almost gotten down on one knee and proposed right then and there—after she'd dumped him. What was wrong with him?

Sure, he cared for her. In fact, he loved her. Love didn't have to throw him into a tailspin like this. She'd been correct when she'd called him a control freak. He'd always liked things just so.

Melanie was blowing his *just so* to hell.

He had to get a grip on himself, and then proceed accordingly. First, they would start dating again without any more crap about breaking up. Then, they'd slowly make sure they were right for each other, which of course they were, and then in a year or two, he'd propose.

If she became pregnant in the meantime, the timeline would adjust.

Now that plan worked.

Feeling much better, he strode into the hospital and stopped short at the barracuda manning the receiving counter. A hodgepodge of wrinkles cascaded around brightly painted red lips formed in a scowl. "Visiting hours are over," she said in a deep voice.

He dawned his most charming smile. "My friend texted me to come down and keep him company. I promise I'll be quiet."

"No." She stood and crossed impressive arms. "Visiting hours begin tomorrow at nine in the morning. Come back then."

He scratched his head. "Could I just poke my head in and tell him I'll be back tomorrow?"

"No. Leave, or I'll call security," the receptionist said.

Wow. "Have a nice day, ma'am." He turned and stalked outside, hiding his grin. Then he loped toward his truck, dialing Hawk's number.

"Where are you?" his friend growled.

"Blocked by a wild one in receiving. I'll come back tomorrow." Colton reached his door.

"I'm leaving tonight. Come by the window." Something crashed in the background.

Colt's head jerked up. "You're not okay to leave."

"Yet, I'm leaving," Hawk said.

Damn it. "Stay in bed. I'll be right there." Colton eyed the building and jogged around the manicured lawn to the north. "Flick your lights."

Instead of flicking, Hawk slid open a window.

Colton scaled an overgrown shrub and two hydrangeas to grab the cold window sill and haul himself inside the room. The scent of bleach and plastic smashed into his senses. All of a sudden, they were wild teenagers again. He grinned at his buddy. "What the hell?"

Hawk stood on the other side of the bed, still in a

hospital gown, his white cast almost glowing. "Tell me you brought clothes."

"No. You haven't been released," Colton said.

Hawk scratched the scruff along his jaw. "I can't stay here another minute."

The guy had just awakened from a coma. "Listen, I know it's tough. But you really should stay here another few days." If Colton had to call his mom, he would.

"No." Hawk padded barefoot for the door. "Let's go."

Colton snorted. "The woman at the front will probably call security to stop you...at least until the doctor shows up and gets all those forms you have to sign if you're leaving against medical orders."

Hawk paused and turned around. "I hadn't thought of that."

Relief had Colton nodding. "So you might as well get back into bed and wait for the doctor to do his rounds tomorrow morning," Colt suggested.

Hawk eyed the window. "I have another idea."

Colton shook his head, trying to reason with his buddy. "No, no, no. That's a bad idea."

Hawk shrugged and lifted a leg over the wooden sill, exposing his ass.

Colton blinked. "Now I have to burn out my eyeballs."

Hawk threw him a hard look. "Are you going to help or not?"

Colton sighed. "Your mind is made up?"

"I'm heading out of here with or without your help." Hawk winced as he tried to scoot across the sill with bare legs.

"Fine." Colton pulled him back. "Take my boots."

"No. Just hurry up." Hawk glanced at the empty doorway.

Colton shook his head. "Let me go first." He nimbly jumped back outside the window. "Okay, come on out." He prepared to catch his oldest friend.

Hawk gingerly slid both legs out, hampered by the broken arm.

The sill cracked.

Their gazes met in alarm a split second before wood splintered, and Hawk went flying.

Colton reached up as Hawk pummeled into him, sending them both sprawling into the nearest hydrangea. Dead, sleet-covered leaves crashed against Colt's back, and Hawk's front.

Hawk yelped and rolled over.

Colton sat up. "Is your skull okay?"

"My brain is the least of my worries," Hawk hissed, yanking a rough branch from his groin.

"My eyes," Colton muttered, wiping a forearm across them. "Stop flashing me."

"Jealous?" Hawk snorted and then winced again.

No, but he was starting to feel like a dumbass. Colton stood and yanked Hawk to his feet. "Let's get out of here before they call security."

Hawk brushed dirt and icy leaves from his hospital gown.

Colton bit down on his lip. Hard.

His best buddy stood, legs bare, hospital gown flapping in the wind. A bunch of leaves twisted in Hawk's hair, and dirt smudged his battered cheek. "What?"

Laughter rolled up inside Colton, and he let it loose.

"Shut up." Hawk finally cracked a smile and then snorted.

Lights flipped on in the room behind them. They both stilled.

"Run," Hawk hissed.

Colton nodded and helped Hawk over the shrubs, laughing and trying not to fall. They hitched along, Hawk's ass flashing, until breaking into a clumsy jog and reaching Colt's truck.

They jumped inside, and Colt ignited the engine. He turned to survey Hawk. "Are you sure you're well enough to leave?"

"Positive. Now *go*." Hawk flipped on the heat and shoved his reddened feet toward the blast of air.

With one more chuckle, Colton threw the truck in drive and escaped the security now pouring out of the front entrance. "Did we just break any laws?"

"Dunno." Hawk exhaled. "But it's good to be alive, right?"

"Damn straight." Colton grinned. "When are you going to tell me who beat the snot of you?"

Hawk stiffened and then lifted a shoulder. "I'm not. It's over, and he looks worse than I do."

"Promise?" Colton asked.

"Yes," Hawk said.

"If you needed help, you'd ask?" Colton kept his gaze on the road.

"You're the only person I'd ask, and I promise I would." Hawk leaned his head back.

Colton nodded. Good enough. His buddy was now on the mend. Time to settle things with Melanie.

• • •

The quiet rapping on the door had Melanie padding in her fuzzy socks and peering out the window. The fire in the hearth crackled happily behind her. What in the world?

Yanking open the door, she could only gape. "Brian?"

Brian Milton stood on her porch wearing board shorts, a tank top, and an opened parka. In chilly March weather, he was wearing shorts? His hair was mussed, and he'd allowed a shadow to darken his jaw. "I'm taking your advice and moving to Maui." He brushed by her into the warm living room. "I know it's late to call on you, but I want you to come with me."

Her mouth opened and closed. She shook her head. "It's only ten at night, and you're always welcome to visit. You want me to go to Maui?"

"Yes." He pushed the door shut behind her. "A friend of mine from school owns a surf shop, and I bought in yesterday. Come with me, Mel. Leave the cold of Montana, and let's live on the beach."

She shoved unruly hair away from her face. "We broke up, Brian."

He showed a charming dimple. "I know. Come as my friend. For now."

"Huh?" she asked.

"I don't know. Perhaps our friendship could turn into more in a different environment. One where we relax and live by the sun." He ran a finger down the side of her face. "A new start for us both."

The touch didn't do a darn thing for her. She stepped back. "I appreciate the offer, but I don't think so."

"Come on." His brown eyes sparkled. "Why stay here, anyway?"

For the first time, the idea of leaving tempted her. Well, depending where she and Colton stood. First, she had to figure a few things out. "How did your mom take the new plan?" Melanie asked.

Brian winced. "Not well. But my brothers supported me, and I'm sure Mother will come around. Now how about you?"

She smiled. "I don't think so, but who knows, maybe I'll visit for a vacation."

Brian sighed. "Okay, but promise if you want to get out of Montana sometime this spring you'll give me a call." He leaned in and captured her in a big hug. "I don't know if I'd be making this move if you hadn't encouraged me." His lips smacked her mouth.

The door shot open, and Colton stood there supporting Hawk's weight.

Sparks lit Colton's eyes. He pushed Hawk against the wall and rushed Brian, jerking him away from Melanie.

"Wait—" Melanie started.

Colton shoved Brian against the wall. "What are you doing?"

"Lighten up, dude." Brian's eyes bugged out.

Anger roared through Melanie. "Let him go, Colton." She dashed toward him and yanked on his arm. Impressive muscles vibrated beneath her palm. "Now."

Colton leaned his face closer to Brian's. "Why was your mouth on hers?"

"Stop being a freakin' jackass." She pulled but wasn't strong enough to budge him. She looked for help from Hawk, but he was leaning against the wall and taking deep breaths.

"Fine." Colt released Brian. "Leave."

"I am." Brian gave her a quick nod. "I'm not leaving for Maui until tomorrow morning. Give me a call if you want to come." He sauntered to the door and let himself out.

Melanie rounded on Colton. "What in the fiery pits of hell is wrong with you?" she yelled.

"With me?" he shouted back. "I get here, and you're kissing Milton? *Milton?*"

"Who I kiss is my business, not yours." If she got any madder, she just might kick him in the face.

"Uh, guys?" Hawk asked.

"Just a second," Colton and Melanie said in unison.

Colton stepped toward her. "You are not going to Maui with that moron."

She lifted her chin, both hands going to her waist. "I'll go anywhere I darn well please, with anybody I want. You can suck it."

"Guys?" Hawk asked.

"Suck what?" Colton said, his face calming. "You name it, I will."

He was such an ass. Melanie rolled her eyes. "Get out of my house."

"Not a chance," Colt said.

She saw red and swung.

He easily stepped back. "I taught you to fight better than that, chickie. Try again."

Fire lanced through her. She faked a punch and kicked him squarely in the gut. The impact ricocheted up her leg. Holy ouch.

He grinned, not seeming the bit fazed. "Much better."

"Guys!" Hawk bellowed.

"What?!?" They both turned toward him as he slid down the wall to land on his butt.

Oh crap. Melanie rushed toward him, colliding with Colton. They went down in a tangle of arms and legs. Her elbow thumped on the floor, zinging pain through her arm. Ouch.

"Wait." Colton settled her on the floor and regained his balance. "Hawk? Are you all right?"

Hawk leaned against the wall, his face pale, his eyes shut. "No."

"Why in the world did you take him from the hospital?" Melanie hissed, grabbing Hawk's good hand and holding tight.

"We thought it a good idea at the time." Colton shoved to his feet and helped Melanie up. "Grab his other arm." Reaching down, he hauled Hawk up. "Do we need to go back to the hospital?"

"No. I just need sleep." Hawk swayed and leaned heavily on Colton. "Bed."

Melanie nodded toward the guest room past the kitchen. "Let's take him in there." They slowly maneuvered their buddy into bed, and Melanie judiciously decided not to inform Hawk she'd seen his butt. Once he was all tucked in, he fell asleep within a minute.

Colton inhaled, his gaze on his wounded friend. "I'll have Doc Mooncaller drop by first thing tomorrow morning to check on him."

"Okay," Melanie whispered, shutting off the light and leaving the room.

Colton quietly shut the door. "Do you want to continue our fight?"

"No." Every bone she owned wanted to sleep.

"How about we put the fight on hold and take turns watching Hawk tonight? He shouldn't be out of the hospital."

Colton's eyes warmed. "It's a deal. Why don't you get some sleep, and I'll take first watch here on the couch."

Melanie rubbed her nose. "Say check on him every half an hour?"

"Yes. Night, Mel."

"Night." She tiptoed up the stairs to her room, although Hawk had fallen into a deep sleep. Once under the covers, she glanced at her moonlit room. Tons of pictures of she, Colt, and Hawk decorated the vanity that matched her antique bedroom set.

They'd been through so much together through the years. She counted sheep for a while, and then she counted imaginary dragons. The sexiest man she'd ever met sat just a floor beneath her.

A man who knew how to kiss. *Really* knew how to kiss.

Warmth heated through her, and she shifted restlessly.

Finally, a couple of hours after going to bed, she threw back the covers. Might as well check on Hawk since she couldn't sleep. She trumped down the stairs and glanced into the living room.

Colton sat on the sofa, legs extended onto the coffee table, the firelight dancing over the hard angles of his face. His eyes were closed.

She tiptoed into Hawk's room, her shoulders relaxing at his rhythmic breathing. Good.

Then she left the room and crossed into the living area to grab a blanket to spread over Colton. Although the fire still crackled, the temperature had fallen along with the night.

Just as she dropped the blanket on him, he reached out and grabbed her arm. She tumbled onto him. His mouth covered hers in a deep kiss. She kissed him back for all of two seconds, beyond tempted to fall into his heat.

Instead, she pushed against his chest with both hands. "We need to talk."

"After." He licked along her lips, and fire slammed right into her blood. "First, let's try to make it to a bed. Just once."

She wanted this night. Life was too crazy. "Then we talk."

"Yeah." He kissed her, lifting her and carrying her up the stairs, his mouth never stopping. Never letting her take a breath or find a thought.

As lava poured through her veins, she gave up thinking.

Later.

For now, all that existed was Colton Freeze and his dangerous mouth.

He set her down on the bed, gently lifted her top and yoga pants off. Sure hands unbuckled his belt, and his clothes joined hers on the floor.

She swallowed, her lids half-dropping. "You have an amazing body." Gingerly, she slid her fingers along his ripped abs.

"So do you." He flattened his hand across her upper chest and pushed her back, covering her with heat and male. "Melanie." His mouth kissed, tasted, and licked her neck, warm breath chasing over her. "You smell so good...all woman."

His scent of wild forest washed over her, through her.

She was practically panting, needed him so much it physically hurt. Her hands wrapped around his shoulders as his knee nudged her legs apart.

She was so ready.

But he took his time, his mouth wandering down her neck, his teeth providing bite. Proof that his gentleness, while seductive, could disappear in a second. He nipped a breast, and she cried out.

"You have no idea how many times I've imagined you, open to me." He laved the other nipple. "How amazing you feel beneath me." His talented fingers found her, pushing deep inside.

Wild shock filled her, and she arched against his hand, her hips tipping.

With a grin, he fucked her with his fingers, his other hand teasing her nipples. Thank goodness her period had ended so quickly, or she wouldn't be so comfortable right now. Shock wandered through her at her own boldness while she rocked her hips into his fingers, but one look at his face filled her with confidence.

Gone was the cool, meticulous man. He was transformed into a hungry, primal being, teeth bared, eyes glinting, the sharp edges of his cheekbones flushed with need.

For her. Only for her. "Now, Colton. Please."

His dark blue gaze captured her. She wanted to look away, to protect herself. But as he pressed the head of his cock against her sex, she was trapped.

She spread her knees wider for his hips. He stretched her.

When he was as deep as he could get, he paused and lowered his forehead to hers. He watched her carefully, and she couldn't hide her emotions. Not this time, and not from him.

He slid out and then back in, capturing her hands and pressing them to the bedspread above her head. Taking control, as only Colton could. Steadily, with determination, he began to pound until the only sound in existence was flesh slapping against flesh.

Lava flowed through her blood. Nerves fired throughout her entire body.

His teeth sank into her earlobe. "Come for me. *Now.*"

She exploded, coming hard and fast, sobbing his name. The waves battered her, taking her over.

Her eyelids flew open in time to see him fall over the edge. The tendons strained in his neck, and his entire body went rigid.

He was beautiful.

Finally, he relaxed against her, his heart beating against her breasts.

She smiled. "Colton—"

A bang from downstairs startled them both. Colton lifted up and then withdrew from her body. She groaned at the erotic sensations.

"Stay here," he said as he yanked on his jeans and padded from the room.

A clamoring came from Hawk's room.

Melanie jumped up, threw on her bathrobe, and ran down the stairs after Colt, stopping short at the doorway, her heart slamming against her ribs.

Hawk had thrown the lamp across the room, and was struggling out of his blankets while standing. His eyes were open but unseeing, and muscles rippled in his arms as he fought the sheet.

She started toward him, only to have Colton grab her out of the way. "He's not awake." Colton blocked her with his body. "Hawk? Wake up, buddy."

Hawk stilled, and reality slowly dawned across his face. He frowned.

"You had a bad dream," Colton said, stepping forward to tug the constricting blanket from around Hawk's torso. "Sit down. It's time to talk."

With a nod, Hawk dropped back the bed.

Melanie looked from one to the other, her mind spinning. Instinct took over, and she paid attention. Hawk needed to talk to Colton right now. The both of them would be too much. "I'll see you guys in the morning," she whispered as she shut the door.

She'd finish *her* talk with Colton in the morning.

CHAPTER TWENTY

Colton left the coffeepot on and slipped out of Melanie's house. He needed a shave but didn't have time. In fact, if this was going to work, he had to get a move on.

Hawk hadn't wanted to talk during the night, and Colton didn't feel like pushing him, so they'd played poker. As of five in the morning, Hawk owed Colton two horses and a head of cattle.

Colton grinned. Sure, Hawk would probably win them back the next time they played. Maybe.

They'd spent the night reminiscing and planning. Planning big. But this plan would work. For so long, Colton had lived according to plans, and look where it had gotten him. Sometimes a guy just had to take a chance.

When it mattered.

Hawk had fallen asleep around six, and after Colton checked in on a sleeping Melanie, he made coffee and headed outside. He loved her. Not in the happy, singing, making-out-in-daisies way, but in a his-heart-would-be-ripped-out-with-sharp-claws-if-she-left-him way.

He was about to take the biggest risk of his life, and he couldn't be happier.

Well, or more nauseated. What if this backfired?

With a shrug, he propelled himself full-bore ahead, as he always had. If he was going to crash and burn, there was going to be a hell of a fire.

He pressed speed dial on his phone. "Jake? I need to talk to Leila. Yes. Now." He waited until his niece came on the phone, and then he asked for the help he needed.

With a happy squeal, Leila agreed to help.

He hung up and frowned. They'd need more than the two of them to make this happen. Well, one of the benefits of belonging to a big family was…lots of hands. So he lowered his head and started to make phone calls.

• • •

Melanie stomped her freezing feet on the hard pavement just as the wind picked up its chill factor for the day. "I told you it would be cold today. Now can we go?" she asked her too-silent companion.

"No." Hawk reached over and yanked her coat zipper up with his healthy hand. "It's almost spring. You love the parade."

"Do not—and spring can't show up soon enough. She hadn't gotten enough sleep, her head hurt, and her heart kind of ached. Colton had left without waking her up and finishing their talk. That meant he didn't want to talk, and that pretty much said it all.

Hawk hunched his shoulders against the breeze. "I gave you two cups of coffee and cooked you scrambled eggs with extra cheese. Stop complaining."

Melanie squinted up at her slightly cranky friend. "You'll make some woman a fine wife someday."

He grinned as the little Bluebird troop of five-year-olds sashayed down Main Street. "Thanks."

Melanie glanced behind herself at the warmth all

but vibrating from Kurt's Koffees. The aroma of freshly baked orange rolls wafted out when a customer exited the coffee shop. "I think I'll go inside for a bit."

"Stay with me. I'm dizzy." Hawk sounded more amused than dizzy.

She shook her head. "You are not." Then she peered closer at his calm face. She should've made him stay in bed, but he was so stubborn and had insisted that they both needed fresh air, and the parade would be perfect. "Are you dizzy?" she asked.

He sighed. "No. But just stay here for a minute, will you? Trust me."

"Fine." She blew on her mitten-covered hands and smiled as the mayor drove by in his vintage 1920 Model T. The Lady Elks were next, then the Boy Scout troops, then the high school cheerleaders, and the high school band.

Candy flew from many hands, and she happily caught a couple of toffees. She unrolled an orange one. "Are you all right? I mean, with the nightmare and everything?"

"I'm fine. My head is better, and I'm sure the nightmares will go away." He craned his neck to look down the parade route.

In other words, no more talking about it. Melanie sighed. "You're a pain, Hawk."

"I know." He nudged her closer to the curb.

She shoved a toffee into her mouth and protested. Then loud music and flashing lights from down the way caught her attention.

A murmuring settled throughout the crowd lining the streets.

Melanie stood up on her tiptoes to get a better

look. A couple of floats, one featuring vampires and the other the Flintstones, moved along the route, blocking her view of the noisemaker.

The wind blew her hair into her face, and she flicked it away, chewing thoughtfully.

She swallowed the candy. The music was loud enough she could feel the beat beneath her boots. She tapped along, staring to hum.

She grinned. "Hey. It's 'You're the One That I Want.'" She laughed, glancing around. "Where's Colton? He should be here so I can bug him singing." Humming, she tried to lean forward to see the float.

All of a sudden, fireworks exploded up into the air. The float came into view with an electric heart and two huge four-leaf clovers spinning above it, and words strung along the outside but not lit up. She squinted to read the words as Colton stepped up in full 1950s greaser leather jacket and jeans…with a microphone.

She stepped back.

Then, microphone in hand, he started to bellow out the song.

Horribly. Truly horribly.

Neon flashed, and the lights along the side lit up with a *Marry Me, Melanie*. She shook her head, reality disappearing. *Marry Me*?

Colton jumped down, walking toward her, singing. Kind of.

Leila, Loni, and Dawn hustled behind him, their choruses kind of saving the song.

Melanie's entire body flushed hot.

"Good Lord, his voice is horrible." Hawk coughed out laughter.

"Ah." Melanie's heart jumped hard. Even so, she

searched for an escape. People beamed at her from all around.

Colton reached her and stopped singing. "I'm making a declaration."

The crowed whooped around them. Melanie, her mind spinning, wondered idly who'd won the bet.

She shook her head. "Colton—"

"I love you, Mel." He brushed a kiss on her nose. "I don't care about my life plan, I don't care about a schedule…I only care about you. Here and now."

Tears pricked the back of her eyes. God, she wanted him. "I can't have kids." Even so, she dug her fingers into the lapels of the jacket. "I know you want kids."

"I knew that was the holdup with you dropping to a knee and proposing." He shook his head.

"Dropping to a knee?" she asked. Was he kidding?

His gaze ran over her face in a warm caress. "I would adore a spunky miniature brunette baby with eyes like chocolate." He sobered. "But it's a *we* situation. Either *we* can have kids, or *we* can't. If not, we'll adopt. But our lives start with a *we*."

She took a deep breath. Everything she ever wanted stood in front of her in a weathered leather jacket and cocky smile. She knew him, and she'd loved him forever. How in the world could she turn away from such happiness? She wanted a life with him. "I love you, too. Marry me?"

He whooped and picked her up, swinging her around. "I thought you'd never ask. Yes." Then he slipped an antique diamond ring on her finger. "It was my grandmother's."

The crowd erupted in cheers.

Colton kissed her deep, emotion in every line of his hard body. Finally, he lifted his head and looked around, keeping a tight hold on Melanie. "Well? Who won?"

Everyone glanced around. Finally, his mom stepped forward, her face turning a very pretty pink. "Ah, Mrs. Hudson and I did. We went in halfsies," Loni admitted.

Mrs. Hudson danced across the street, her wool coat flapping beneath a knitted florescent orange scarf. "Whoo hoo! You were right, Loni. You do know your boy."

Colton's mouth dropped open. "Mom?"

Tom jumped out of the driver's seat of the float. "Loni Eleanor Freeze? You did not bet on this."

Loni laughed. "You're just mad I won and you didn't."

Tom scratched his chin and threw an arm around his wife. "I had tomorrow as my date."

Melanie looked around as Quinn and Jake maneuvered through bodies to reach them. "Well? Who's the bet taker, anyway?"

Hawk cleared his throat. "Well, ah…"

Oh no he hadn't. Melanie laughed. "How in the world are you the bet taker? You've been all over the world lately."

Mrs. Joskly, the librarian, handed Hawk an envelope. "He had help. I mean, since I was here."

"And since I gave ten percent to the library," Hawk said with a grin.

Melanie slipped her arms around Colton's waist. "I'm thinking a June wedding."

He grinned and kissed her again. "You name the date, and I'll be there. In fact, maybe I'll even sing as you walk down the aisle."

The crowd erupted into a series of "Hell no" and groans around them.

Melanie kissed him back. "I love you."

"I love you, too, Mel. Always." He kissed her again.

EPILOGUE

Melanie stood on the raised dais, sucking in her stomach. The wedding dress fit perfectly, but she had to quit eating such large breakfasts if it was still going to fit on her wedding day. Ever since Colton had moved in with her a day after her proposal, she'd been eating whatever he cooked.

Dawn stood on the next dais, her blue bridesmaid gown perfectly matching her stunning eyes. "You have not gained weight."

"Maybe not yet, but I can't keep eating like that. Your brother eats like a horse." Melanie held still as the seamstress tucked pins in along the bodice.

"They all do. Remember them as teenagers? The food was always gone before I could get to the pantry." Dawn gave a mock shrug. "Have you seen the guys in their tuxes yet?" She kept her gaze on her sparkly shoes.

"Not yet, but I bet Hawk looks amazing," Melanie said. The guys were trying on tuxes on the other side of the wall, their boisterous laughter echoing through.

Dawn looked up. "I know, right?"

"Yeah. Did you ask him to your graduation for your master's degree?" Melanie asked.

Dawn shrugged. "Yes, but he didn't confirm. Graduation is in a month, and I know he'll just be getting the gyms started."

"If construction goes as planned." Melanie eyed the snow billowing around outside the window of the Mineral Lake dressmaker. "We just broke ground last week." She couldn't believe she'd been engaged for almost a month. The wedding was planned for the end of June, and she couldn't wait. But she'd wanted everything to be perfect, and perfect took time.

Dawn stepped down. "I'm glad you guys are going to live in your house. I've always loved your place."

"Me too." Melanie's stomach growled. While Colton had planned on building a house on his family's property, he was more than happy to live in hers…while they combined the ranches into an even larger land holding.

Heat climbed up her back, and she breathed deep. "I think the bodice is too tight."

The seamstress tugged on the fabric. "No, I think it's fitting perfectly."

Melanie's head spun. "Um, I don't feel so well."

Dawn glanced up. "Oh, no. The flu is really going around. The elementary school even closed early yesterday, my mom said. Are you hot?"

"Yes." Melanie swayed on the dais. Her knees weakened, and she went down.

"Mel!" Dawn yelled and hustled forward, bending down. "What's going on?"

"I don't know." Melanie rolled over and shoved to her knees. "My head is spinning."

"Melanie?" Colton called from the other section of the store. "Are you all right? Dawn? What's going on?" A rustling echoed, and the door started to open.

"Don't come in," Melanie gasped, shoving down bile.

"He can't see you in the dress," the seamstress hissed.

Melanie's head lolled, and she dropped all the way down.

"Colton?" Dawn called. "Hurry."

Melanie tried to stay conscious, but the world spun. A door banged open, and strong arms cradled her. Colt's strong scent of leather and man surrounded her, offering comfort.

Her stomach lurched. "Oh, God." The room spun as she was lifted and carried into the cold air. "You can't see my dress," she moaned.

"I didn't look." He hurried down the sidewalk.

A door opened, and warmth brushed her cheeks. She shut her eyes and rested against his chest, his heartbeat grounding her. "I think I have the flu."

The lone nurse in the small clinic instructed Colton to take her to a back examination room, where Doc Mooncaller loped in, his hair braided down his back. "Hi, Mel. The flu's going around. Have you vomited?" He reached out and felt her forehead. "You're not hot."

"Yes, she is," Colt quipped.

Doc laughed, his belly shaking. "Funny. Okay, let's check you out, darlin'. Do you want him to leave?"

"No," Colton said.

Melanie shrugged. "I don't care. If I have the flu, he's probably next."

"Hmmm." Doc felt her neck. "Let's see what's up."

During the next hour, he tested her, she peed in a cup, and she finally settled back on the examination table to wait.

"I hate the flu," she moaned, her arm over her eyes.

"Me too." Papers rustled as Colton kept reading through a magazine on fishing. "Your dress is stunning, by the way."

She groaned. Now she'd have to find a different dress. There was no way she was beginning her marriage with bad luck. "Everything is planned and has to be perfect. I'll get another dress."

Doc cleared his throat.

Melanie sat up. She hadn't heard him enter.

He rubbed his chin. "So, about perfect and planning."

She frowned. "Yes?"

"Ah, you're pregnant," the doctor said.

The world screeched to a stop. Her body shuddered. Tears slammed into her eyes. "No, I'm not." She glanced at Colton, whose intense gaze was checking out her abdomen. "I'm not," she said weakly, afraid to believe.

Doc glanced down at the chart in his hands. "Oh, you definitely are with child." He eyed Colton and then her. "Um, is this okay?"

Colton shot to his feet. "Oh, yeah!" He grabbed her and spun her around.

Her stomach revolted, and she slapped a hand against his chest. "Stop."

"Oh." He tucked her close. "Sorry."

She lifted her head, not caring tears slid down her face. "A baby."

Colton nodded, his eyes wet. "Yeah. A baby."

Melanie reached for him, needing his strength. Colton had always been there for her, always loved her. Now he'd love their baby just as strongly.

She looked back and grinned, her heart on fire for him. "I love you."

"I love you more." He kissed her, proving it. Yeah. She'd known Colton Freeze would be able to kiss like that, and now she had the rest of her life to enjoy him. Forever.

∞

ACKNOWLEDGMENTS

ACKNOWLEDGMENTS

There are so many folks who help to make sure a book becomes a final product—many behind the scenes.

Thanks to my husband, Tony, because you're the best! Thanks to Gabe and Karly—I'm so proud of both of you!

Thank you to my wonderful agent, Caitlin Blasdell—as well to the gang at Liza Dawson Associates—you're a wonderful group.

Thank you to my editor, Liz Pelletier, whose edits make me laugh while we make the book stronger. Thanks also to Heather Howland for the awesome covers, and to my entire Entangled team.

Thanks also to my hardworking Facebook Street Team—you're a lot of fun, and you always make me smile. I appreciate the hard work.

Finally, thank you to my constant support system: The Englishes, Smiths, Wests, Zanettis, Chapmans, and Namsons.

Look for **New York Times** *bestselling author Katee Robert's 3-in-1 mass market paperback full of sexy cowboys and the women who tame them.*

WILD
COWBOY
NIGHTS

Enjoy three stories in one with the sizzling hot Foolproof Love series!

FOOLPROOF LOVE

Jules Rodrigez isn't interested in the role of town spinster. Being seen with a hell-raiser like bull rider Adam Meyer is the perfect way to scandalize the residents, make her ex jealous, and prove she's a sexy, desirable woman. And if their plan includes ridiculously hot sex—all the better.

FOOL ME ONCE

Aubry Kaiser's in a bind. She needs a plus-one for a convention, and when annoyingly sexy cowboy Quinn Baldwyn offers to go along in exchange for her being his fake date to a wedding, it looks like the perfect solution. Heck, they already fight like an old married couple. If only their fighting wasn't starting to feel a whole lot like foreplay...

A FOOL FOR YOU

It's been years since Hope Moore left Devil's Falls, land of sexy cowboys and bad memories. Back for the weekend, she has no intention of seeing Daniel Rodrigez, the man she never got over...or the two of them getting down and dirty. It's just a belated goodbye, right? No harm, no foul. Until six weeks later, when her pregnancy test comes back positive.

Hilarity ensues when the wrong brother arrives to play wingman at her sister's wedding.

the
wedding
date
disaster

USA TODAY BESTSELLING AUTHOR
AVERY FLYNN

Hadley Donavan can't believe she has to go home to Nebraska for her sister's wedding. She's gonna need a wingman and a whole lot of vodka for this level of family interaction. At least her bestie agreed he'd man up and help. But then instead of her best friend, his evil twin strolls out of the airport.

If you looked up doesn't-deserve-to-be-that-confident, way-too-hot-for-his-own-good billionaire in the dictionary, you'd find a picture of Will Holt. He's awful. Horrible. The worst—even if his butt looks phenomenal in those jeans.

Ten times worse? Hadley's buffer was supposed to be there to keep her away from the million and one family events. But Satan's spawn just grins and signs them up for every. Single. Thing.

Fine. "Cutthroat" Scrabble? She's in. She can't wait to take this guy down a notch. But somewhere between Pictionary and the teasing glint in his eyes, their bickering starts to feel like more than just a game...